Praise for
Monica Burns

"Burns doesn't disappoint!"
— **RTBOOKreviews**

Monica Burns writes with sensitivity and panache.
— **Sabrina Jeffries, NYT bestselling author**

"powerfully done…the scenes between Tobias and Jane mesmerized me. I loved it."
— **Joey W. Hill**

"No one sets fire to the page like Monica Burns."
— **eCataromance**

"Definitely recommended reading."
— **The Romance Studio**

The

Beastly

Earl

Monica Burns

Kathi B. Scearce DBA Monica Burns - Maroli SP Imprints
P.O. Box 75072
Richmond, VA 23236

Publishing History
Maroli Imprints Print 1.0 edition — 2019
Maroli Imprints Print 1.1 edition — 2021

ISBN 978-1-948505-06-2

Acknowledgements

As always a shout out of gratitude to Viviana Izzo, Enchantress Design and Promo for being a great friend and sounding board. Thank you for giving me cheese to go with my whine.

Affection and gratitude for the ever wonderful Debbie Sansom-Fitts. Thank you for always pointing out the error of my ways when it comes to edits. You are awesome and amazing!

A huge hug and thank you to Laura Polito McEleney. I want to be you when I come back in my next life! Thank you for always listening and offering feedback gently. You know how important honest feedback is to me.

Hugs to Kris Bloom for being an awesome beta reader and a thank you to Debbie Hoopes for catching typos while doing a beta read!

To all my readers. As hard as my journey is sometimes, you make it a wonderful experience! Thank you for all your support!

Author Notes

Gaelic Terms

The Gaelic terms included in this work are derived from different sources, including Outlander Wiki and Dwelly's great Scots Gaelic - English dictionary, as well as mythology resources.

bean nighe - a spirit in Scottish folklore similar to the Irish Banshee
ceilidh - a social event with dancing and drinking
mo leannan - sweetheart
mo ghràdh - my beloved or my love
sidhe - Scottish fairy

Argaty Sahib and Morehouse Sahibah

Language in the middle-East has a complex, fascinating history of evolution. The Sudanese currently speak an Arabic form of the Afroasiatic (Afro-Asiatic) family, which has connections to Ancient Egypt and Persian roots. My limited research showed Arabic being used by the native Sudanese people during the Boer Wars with the Boers speaking Arabic-Afrikaans. On a side note, the Boers were descendants of Dutch immigrants who believed themselves superior to native Sudanese and were slave owners.

While many will associate the word sahib as being of Indian origin. This is because the word has been routinely used in different entertainment mediums as a term of deference and/or a form of polite address by Indians when speaking to other people. However, the word(s) roots are in fact Persian and Arabic, and the word found its way into the Indian language of Hindi during the Ottoman Empire.

The masculine word Sāḥib (also seen as saheb) is an Arabic word of Perso-Arab roots and means friend or companion. Feminine forms of the Arabic word can be seen as sāḥiba /sahibah/sahaba. Sahaba is also used as a girl's first name. Over the centuries, the word(s) came to be used as an honorary form of address, such as Mr., Mrs., or Miss.

I chose to take creative license in the use of sahib and sahibah as it was difficult to find an accurate term of deference and respect that Asadi would use when addressing the man who saved his life and Louisa, a woman of title. I chose a word that seemed logical for the era and culture of the character when it came to his use of language and behavior.

Prosthetics

Prosthetics have been in existence for thousands of years. There have been archeological finds of feet, toes, and legs composed of wood, and the description of Ewan's artificial limb is that of a prosthetic steel hand and arm that was in use starting around 1840.

During my research I found pictures of soldiers learning how to write with a prosthetic hand, and Ewan's artificial limb was in use until 1910 and possibly beyond that. Based on my research, it seemed reasonable to assume that Ewan's appendage would allow him some flexibility when it came to general tasks. However, the various prosthetics I researched did not look comfortable.

As to Ewan's skin being rubbed raw inside the leather cup, I based that description off my own experience. I sit in my recliner at least 15-17 hours a day. My elbow rests constantly on the arm of my recliner where the material, despite its smoothness creates what some refer to as rug burns. An image of the model I used for describing Ewan's arm is at https://monicaburns.net/RRS5-MetalHand

The Black Watch

The Black Watch Regiment saw action in numerous campaigns in the Middle East during the 1880s and 1890s. However, the regiment did not have a role in the 1898 campaign during the Anglo-Egyptian conquest of the Sudan. It was the North Staffordshire Regiment that was with Herbert Kitchener, Sirdar of the Egyptian army in that campaign. Creative license was taken regarding the Black Watch Regiment's participation in the 1898 campaign to accommodate timelines within the Reckless Rockwoods series and Ewan and Louisa's story itself.

Of historical note: For almost 300 years, The Black Watch has been at the heart of major conflicts that have shaped world history. The regiment has a history of service that emphasizes the qualities of honor, gallantry, and devoted service to King, Queen, and country. In the words of a 19th century Black Watch historian, every member of the Highlander Regiment

"...feels that his conduct is the subject of observation and that, independently of his duty, as one member of a systematic whole he has a separate and individual reputation to sustain, which will be reflected on his family and district or glen." **—James Browne, Black Watch historian, 1851**

That statement is summed up by the Black Watch

Regiment's motto *"Nemo me impune lacessit*, translated from Latin means "No One Provokes Me With Impunity." In all their campaigns and battles, including Fontenoy, in the battle of Fallujah in Ticonderoga, Waterloo, Alamein, and two World Wars, the Black Watch regiment has surmounted formidable odds time after time. Their significant contribution to every bloody, crucial campaign they've been a part of has secured their place in history. The regiment's courage and sacrifice exemplify the values described so eloquently in Browne's words. These noble standards explain why those affiliated with The Black Watch take such great pride in the regiment. Honor, duty, and sacrifice are qualities everyone should ascribe to.

The Speerin

The 'Speerin' is an old Scottish tradition where the prospective groom asks a father for his daughter's hand in marriage. If the future-son-in-law completes a series of trials and tasks requested by the woman's father, approval is given. The tests are designed to judge the merit of the man requesting the privilege of marrying the father's daughter.

In Ewan's case, his test wasn't requirement in proposing marriage to Louisa. As a widow, she was in control of own affairs and was the decision-maker regarding marriage proposals.

According to the Dictionary of Scots Language, the term was originally spelled as "speirin." There are, or were, several different usages of the word, including to make or request of a father his daughter's hand in marriage. The word appears to have changed in spelling to Speerin at least as early as 1869. The tradition is still followed today.

Contents

CPrologue

Westbrook Farms
May 1897

The heat from the blaze burned her cheeks as if she'd stayed out in the sun too long. Flames licked the manor's façade and had already begun to dance behind the black clouds of smoke billowing out of the nursery's windows. The sight sent a wave of terror through Louisa unlike anything she'd ever experienced.

"Oh dear God, Charlie. Willie." Her anguished cry echoed loudly in her ears, but the pandemonium surrounding her ensured no one heard her.

Cries went up into the air as someone pointed toward the side of the house that wasn't on fire. She jerked her head toward the sound and saw her nephew, Jamie, quickly walking toward where she, Constance, and Helen stood with the servants who had fled the fire. Following close behind Jamie was Theo and Imogene drew up the rear, carrying a small bundle in her arms. Helen and Constance both cried out with joy and ran toward the children.

Frantically, she looked past the children, searching for more figures hurrying toward them, but there was only the terrifying blackness of the night. For what seemed an eternity, only darkness filled her vision until Nanny emerged from the shadows, carrying Charlie in her arms. A cry of relief flew past her lips as she met the older woman halfway to pull her oldest son into her arms. He was crying wildly and choked her as he flung his small arms around her neck.

Tears flowed down her cheeks as she kissed her son repeatedly and examined him for any burns. Relieved to find him unharmed, the emotion evaporated as she turned back toward the empty shadows. Inside her chest, her heart pounded a fierce beat, not unlike a racehorse's hooves hitting the dirt as it ran. Charlie still in her arms, she saw a shadowy figure moving into the light.

The sight of Aunt Matilda hurrying toward them with Tilly cradled close to her breast made Helen cry out with happiness. Her sister-in-law ran forward with an outstretched arm to pull her daughter into her arms as she kept Theo close to her side.

Another cry filled the air, and Louisa whirled around to see a footman hurrying out of the darkness with Braxton in his arms. The terror and fear gripping her muscles made her tighten her grip on Charlie as the heat of the fire reached out to taunt her, as if it was laughing at her fear.

"Angus!" Helen cried out in relief as another footman emerged from the darkness with her son in his arms.

All the children were sobbing in fear, and the sound scraped across her senses as if someone were slicing into her with a sharp knife. Dear God, where were Willie and Devin? The fear slithering through her closed off her throat until it became difficult to breathe. Tears blurred her vision as she buried her face in Charlie's hair and prayed as she'd never done before in her life. This time it was Aunt Matilda who cried out as two more footmen rounded the house with children in their arms.

"There! Willie. Alma. Saints be praised," Aunt Matilda exclaimed in loud relief.

With a cry of joy, Louisa hurried forward with Charlie still pressed tightly against her chest to pull Willie close with her free arm. Tears of relief streamed down her cheeks as she clutched both of her children close. The boys' tears wet the thin wrap of her night robe, and she tried to soothe them as they clung to her with a desperate terror she was feeling too. Suddenly, a feral scream pierced the night.

The blood-curdling cry sent an invisible, icy hand brushing over her back. She turned with a jerk to stare in horror at the façade of her home burning brightly in the darkness. Another dreadful shriek echoed out into the night. It repeated itself until it became one horrifying, continuous scream filling the air. It was the cry of a wounded animal in agony. Terror swept through her as the scream ended abruptly, and a split-second later, a loud crash filled the air. The violent noise made her jump as flames shattered the nursery windows and shot out of the empty frames to illuminate the dark night. The fire had now reached the main entryway and engulfed one half of the manor.

Another wild scream echoed from the second story, combined with male shouts of panic. The sounds pulled a loud gasp from the small crowd, staring at the burning building. It was a collective breath of horror that died away into silence until the only thing filling the air was the roar of the fire, the soft sound of sobbing children, and the distant clanging of bells from a fire brigade that was already too late.

Indistinguishable male shouts of helpless anger and fear poured out of the burning house. The panic in the male voices sent a sudden stillness through her as she turned her head to account for every child. They were all here. That only left the men and...

"Patience, where is Patience?" she cried out as spun around in a desperate effort to see her sister in the people surrounding her. Constance took up her cry as Aunt Matilda's countenance became ashen.

Without hesitating, Louisa kissed her boys' cheeks and whispered reassurances she would return as she gave each of them into the arms of a maid and footman. Spurred by the fear her aunt appeared ready to collapse, she hurried to Aunt Matilda's side. The woman swayed on her feet, and Louisa quickly wrapped her arm around her aunt to keep her from falling to the ground.

"Constance!" she cried out as she glanced behind her, trying to see her sister. In seconds, her older sister was on the other side of their aunt to help ensure the older woman remained standing. As Louisa touched her aunt's arm, the older woman began to tremble, and it shot a bolt of dread through Louisa.

"Patience," her aunt rasped softly. "She and Caleb stayed behind tae ensure the children were safe."

"Oh, dear God," she whispered as she met the matriarch's horrified gaze and an image of Patience's sunny smile filled her mind.

A barely audible cry of horror escaped the Scotswoman before a violent tremor pulsated out of her. It heightened Louisa's fear as she saw a sudden look of stark grief accentuating her aunt's gray pallor. The older woman's sorrow made Louisa go rigid. The *an dara sealladh*. Aunt Matilda had seen something that had rocked her to the core.

Another image of Patience flashed through her head, followed by Caleb's somber features. It wasn't possible. She refused to believe it. The Rockwoods always rose to a challenge. They never accepted defeat. She couldn't have lost both of her siblings in the space of minutes.

In the next breath, guilt rocked her body with a violent shudder. Her first thought had been for her brother and sister's safety, not Devin's. The memory of the words she'd screamed at her husband mere hours before the fire made bile rise in her throat. They'd been terrible words. Words she wished with all her heart she'd never said. Constance's unexpected, painfully tight grip on the arm Louisa had braced against her aunt's back made her jerked her head toward her older sister. The brilliant light from the fire showed tears wetting her older sister's cheeks as Constance stared at her helplessly. The *an dara sealladh*. The family gift had shown Constance something, too.

"What? What have you seen, Constance?" Her demand went unanswered as a shout filled the air.

Louisa turned her head toward the house and saw a small party of men moving in the shadows. Julian was the first one she recognized. When she saw Patience in his arms, she drew in a breath of relief. Lucien, Percy, and Sebastian followed close behind their brother-in-law. Soot covered their faces, but it didn't hide the dark, grim emotion hardening their faces.

Constance and Helen both released quiet sobs of relief as they ran into the arms of their husbands. Louisa glanced briefly at Julian laying Patience on the grass with Percy kneeling at her side, then turned her attention back to the darkness. The fire was spreading quickly now, and the shadows that had shrouded the side of the house were giving way to the light of the blaze.

A sickening dread made her stomach churn as she frantically looked past Sebastian, waiting for Devin and Caleb to emerge from the darkness. When they didn't stride into view, Aunt Matilda grabbed Louisa's hand.

"It will be all right, my darling lass."

The quiet words of sorrow and consolation wrapped around Louisa's body like a vicious band of metal. Fear and guilt engulfed her with the same strength and power as the fire consuming her and Devin's home. Tugging free of her aunt's hold, she leapt toward her eldest brother and grabbed his arm.

"Where are they? Where's Caleb? Devin?"

Her demands for an answer were met by silence as Sebastian closed his eyes for a moment, then shook his head. She took several quick steps back from her oldest brother as shock pounded its way into every cell of her body. She whirled around to stare at the manor and the fire consuming it. The flames had now begun to spread to the opposite side of the house. The sting of guilt and pain lashed at her as if someone were striking her with a whip. Without thinking, she rushed toward the front door and the flames shooting out into the night. She barely heard the shouts and cries of fear behind her as she raced toward the burning house. The fire roared in her ears like an angry animal as a firm hand yanked her to a halt.

"Stop, Louisa." Sebastian's voice was harsh and commanding.

As she stared up at him, her brother's face became etched with a look she'd never seen before. He looked helpless. It wasn't possible. Sebastian always had a plan. He always knew how to make things right. But now, he looked defeated, and as he stared down at her in deep sorrow, he shook his head. "There's nothing more we can do. Caleb. Devin. They're gone. Both of them."

"You're lying," she screamed as she struck out at her brother. "Let me go. We can't just leave them in there."

She twisted her arm, trying to break her brother's grip on her arm as she looked back at the house and screamed Devin's name again. She heard Sebastian speaking quietly in her ear, but not his words. With the strength of a madwoman, she broke free of her brother's grasp and ran back toward the house. A second later, Sebastian's arms wrapped around her to hold her close against his chest. Still struggling against his embrace, she screamed Devin's name over and over again. Her wild cries shattered the night as guilt slashed into her very soul, then swallowed her whole and everything went black.

Chapter 1

November 1899

Madison said you wanted to see me?"

Louisa smiled at her eldest brother as she closed the door of his study behind her. As she sank down into one of the chairs facing his desk, she frowned at his serious, almost hesitant, manner.

As if aware of his unusual behavior, Sebastian turned away from her to stare out the window. After several moments of silence, it was impossible not to prod him into speaking.

"What's wrong, Sebastian? Has something terrible happened?" Fear rose inside her as she tried to remember where the boys were. A second later, she began to breathe easier as she remembered they were in the nursery doing their lessons. Sebastian cleared his throat, then circled the large mahogany desk to sit in the chair next to hers.

"Louisa, as the head of the family—"

"Clearly you're about to lecture me on some transgression." She smiled at him, despite her sudden sense of unease.

The instant Sebastian grimaced, her heart sank. It was obvious he was uncomfortable with whatever he wanted to discuss with her. It was unlike him. All her life, she'd looked up to Sebastian. Where she was impetuous and prone to fits of anger, her brother had been the exact opposite.

With the exception of when Helen had been kidnapped by the Marquess of Templeton, the oldest Rockwood sibling was always controlled and unflappable. Although in recent years, he wasn't quite as rigid as he'd been before Helen came into his life. To see him hesitate now only increased her tension.

"No, I have no intention of lecturing you." A frown furrowed his brow as he bowed his head to study the floor for a long moment, then looked at her with a familiar unshakeable resolve. "It's time to let go, Louisa."

"Let go of what?" she replied innocently, although she knew precisely what her brother meant.

"Do not pretend to be obtuse, Louisa, it doesn't suit you," Sebastian snapped before he released an oath beneath his breath.

"What is it you really want to say, Sebastian?"

She was now certain she knew what the discussion was about, but she refused to make it easy for him. His status as head of the family didn't grant him *carte blanche* to question her behavior. It was a Rockwood trait to meddle in the affairs of loved ones with the goal of ensuring happiness for their family. But this was different.

Hers wasn't a wound of the heart, it was the guilt that crushed her with every waking moment. Even in sleep, she wasn't completely free from nightmares. As if he knew exactly what she was thinking, he narrowed his eyes at her.

"It's time to start living again. You're far too young to grieve in the same manner as the Queen has done for years. You cannot give up on life when it has so much to offer."

"And *what* does it have to offer?" she said as she heard the bitterness in her voice.

"A great deal if you would simply visit us here in London more often and reenter society."

"I do visit you here. In fact, I've been here for almost

two months," she snapped as she glared at him. Sebastian scowled back.

"And in that time, you've rarely gone out. Other than Helen's and my anniversary party, working at White Willow House, and attending the occasional opera or theater with Percy and Rhea, you're practically a recluse," Sebastian growled in obvious frustration. "You don't receive callers, you don't make social calls, and you don't accept any of the invitations that have been delivered to the house. You've even refused to go for a drive in the park with Helen or Constance."

"Is that all that's troubling you?" Louisa released a soft noise of disgust. "My lack of inclination to attend frivolous events?"

"They didn't used to be so frivolous for you."

She shook her head as she struggled with Sebastian's words. It was true she'd always loved going to parties, but she'd been younger then. Now her shoulders bore the heavy weight of anger, pain, and guilt. When she didn't answer him, Sebastian released a sound of irritation.

"*Damn it to hell, Louisa.* The fire was an accident. A terrible, unfortunate accident. No one is responsible for that damn log knocking over that fire screen and setting the manor on fire." The ferocity of his reply startled her, and she jumped as his words settled in her brain.

"I know that," she said softly as she looked away from him.

"Then end your mourning. It's been more than two years now. It's time to start living again—see old friends."

"Society no longer holds any interest for me. I like my life as it is."

"Of course you do," Sebastian growled. "You hide yourself away in the abbey with only Aunt Matilda and the boys for company. That's not living."

"You know good and well that I have always loved

staying at the abbey. How many times did you threaten to punish me by sending me there, only to realize it wouldn't be a punishment at all?"

"You're no longer a child."

"True. I'm a grown woman who doesn't need her oldest brother dictating to her as to how she should grieve for her dead husband."

"It isn't my intent to dictate how you grieve, Louisa, but there's more to it than that, isn't there."

Sebastian's quiet words made her grow still as a hare sensing danger. She swallowed hard, uncertainty flooding through her as she met her brother's steady gaze. Surely he couldn't know the truth. If he did, she wasn't sure she could bear to see the disappointment in his eyes at the way she'd sent Devin to his death. When she didn't speak, Sebastian shook his head slightly.

"The night of the fire, I was unable to sleep and decided to retrieve a book from the library. It was difficult *not* to hear you and Devin fighting when I passed your door on my way downstairs." Sebastian paused slightly as sorrow darkened his handsome face. "The irony of my timing is not lost on me. If I'd gone downstairs just an hour later, I might have been able to prevent the entire disaster."

"You mustn't say that. You said yourself it was an accident," she exclaimed softly as leaned forward to catch his hand in hers in a gesture of comfort and reassurance.

"And it *was* an accident, but it doesn't mean I don't have regrets, just as I suspect you do."

Louisa dropped her brother's hand as if it were a hot iron. She refused to confess to him, or anyone, the terrible sin she'd committed that horrific night. Refused to share with anyone the words she'd flung at Devin shortly before he perished so terribly. Words she could never take back. Louisa sprang to her feet, then turned and walked toward the door without speaking.

Sebastian had always encouraged her never to shy away from her fears, but to meet them head on. His raising the question of regret was deliberate. It *was* time to heal herself and push aside the pain and guilt rooted deep inside her. She'd come to that realization months ago.

She just didn't know how to live with the pain of Devin's betrayal or the disappointment of knowing he hadn't loved her enough to tell her the truth. Worst of all, she didn't know how to forgive herself for the last words she and Devin had exchanged the night of the fire.

"Devin wouldn't want you to grieve like this, Louisa." At Sebastian's words, a wild, unconstrained anger surged through her. She whirled around to glare at him.

"How do *you* know what he would or wouldn't want me to do?"

"I know because Devin was like a brother to me. He was just as much a part of this family *before* he married into it as he was after he married you." Sorrow swept across her brother's handsome face. "I know Devin would not want you to stop living. He loved you too much for that."

"I don't think you knew Devin half as well as you think," she said with a bitterness that mixed with her anger, pain, and guilt. "My husband had a child with another woman."

"What the devil would make you think such a thing, let alone say it, Louisa?" Sebastian's harsh admonishment and stunned disbelief sent a jolt of irony through her. Clearly, not even her brother had been privy to his best friend's secrets. She laughed mirthlessly.

"Because he admitted it the night of the fire."

"There has to be some other explanation, Louisa," Sebastian protested in a bewildered tone. "Devin loved you. I'm sure of it."

"*Of course he did.*" She didn't bother to hide her humiliation in her scathing reply. "He loved me enough to hide the fact that he had a bastard son. A child he'd provided for since *before* we were married. Provided for the child's mother." She inhaled a deep breath as she remembered the letter from their solicitor she'd mistakenly opened. The same paper she'd thrown at Devin during their argument. The vivid memory stabbed at her heart with the strength of a physical blow that she almost bent over from the pain of it.

"I don't believe it," Sebastian ground out in an obvious struggle to deny the inevitable. "I can't believe Devin would ever betray his vows to you."

"*You* don't know that. *I* don't know that. He says he didn't, but how can I believe that when he kept the truth from me the entire time we were married?" Eyes closed, she shook her head slightly. "He betrayed me by hiding the truth. He made me doubt him—doubt his love for me."

"Devin was my best friend. I'm not surprised he would have kept such a matter to himself. He loved you, Louisa. He would have gone to great lengths to spare you the pain or gossip such news would cause."

"Would you have tried to spare Helen from such news? Do you love her so little as to not trust her with *all* your secrets?" When he hesitated, she glared at him. "*Answer me, Sebastian.* Would you have hidden this sort of truth from Helen?"

"No," he said quietly. "I would have told her everything."

"And yet somehow I'm supposed to believe Devin didn't tell me about his bastard because he loved me? Didn't want to hurt me?"

"Think about it, Louisa. If he'd betrayed you with another woman, the Set would have gone out of their way to ensure you heard about it," Sebastian said fiercely and with conviction. "They thrive on gossip, and most of them are filled with jealousy that all the Rockwoods have happy marriages. A rarity among the Marlborough set."

Louisa winced at the truth in her brother's words. He was right. If Devin had really been keeping the mother of his bastard child as his mistress, the gossips would have gleefully ensured she knew about it. As the logic of her brother's words sank in, she closed her eyes and swallowed hard at the possibility Sebastian was right. Tears welled up behind her eyelids, and she shuddered. The sudden touch of her brother's hands on her shoulders made look up at her brother.

"He *did* love you, Louisa. I firmly believe that."

"But not enough to tell me the truth," she said softly.

Pain, anger, and doubt ate away at her just as the memory of how harshly she'd condemned him that night. Words she'd said in anger. Words that weighed on her every waking moment.

"*Damn it, Louisa.* You need to let all of it go. You'll fade away into someone no one will recognize, not even yourself. If you won't talk with me, then speak with Aunt Matilda, Helen, one of your sisters." Sebastian shook her gently until she jerked away

"I'll keep my own counsel, Sebastian. I've already revealed more than I should have." Louisa waved her hand in a gesture that said she refused to continue with the discussion. "You cannot convince me to change my plans to leave for Callendar Abbey in the morning. I need some time to myself, so I intend to leave the boys here. They enjoy being with their cousins, and Aunt Matilda has agreed to bring them with her when she returns to Scotland."

"Then at least think about what I've said here today."

She'd never heard Sebastian plead before, but that he did so now indicated just how worried he was about her. With a slow nod of her head, she met his concerned gaze steadily.

"Very well, I'll think on everything you've said." At her reply, her brother's expression indicated he believed she was simply appeasing him. Louisa quickly walked forward to kiss his cheek and whispered. "I promise I will, Sebastian. I swear it on the Sword and Blood of Angus Stewart."

The moment the childhood oath softly echoed out of her, her brother's mouth quirked slightly upward. It was an oath she'd always extracted from Sebastian when he'd given his word to her, or when she'd agreed to do whatever her brother demanded of her in some matter. In making her pledge, she knew Sebastian would understand the significance of the promise she'd just made.

Sebastian wrapped her in a warm hug, and relief relaxed his stern expression as he released her. Without another word, she left him alone, suddenly realizing she'd made up her mind more than a week ago that it was time to let go as well. She just wasn't sure how to lift the weight of her guilt. She could only hope going to Callendar Abbey and riding on the moors would give her the answer.

"You lied to me. You lied."

"Sweet Jesus, I'm sorry, Louisa. I love you. I didn't want to hurt you."

"Don't. Don't you dare say that to me! If you'd loved me, you wouldn't have kept them a secret all this time," she shouted angrily as the weight of his betrayal pressed down on her. "If you'd told me when we were first betrothed—married. I would have believed you. I would have admired you for what you were doing."

"Damn it to hell, Louisa. Do you think I didn't want to tell you? I would have, but I didn't want to lose you."

"Lose my dowry, you mean," she sneered. "You didn't have any trouble telling me that your family fortunes were almost nonexistent when you offered for my hand."

"I didn't marry you for your money, and you damn well know it. I married you because I love you." Devin glared at her.

"You don't know the first thing about love! It requires trust, and you didn't trust me enough—love me enough to tell me the truth. And you would have gone on hiding it from me if I hadn't discovered your secret strictly by chance."

"I am telling you the truth, Louisa. All I've done is ensure they've been well cared for—nothing more!" His jaw was hard with anger as he shoved a hand through his hair in frustration.

"And now, after all this time, I'm supposed to believe you provided for them simply out of a sense of responsibility—duty?" she sneered. "Provided for them with my dowry. To think I believed you every time you said you were out late playing cards at the club. To think I let you touch me after you came home. Came home from her bed."

"Christ almighty," Devin roared. "She's not my mistress."

"A man who pays for the upkeep of a woman other than his wife is the very *definition of a man who has a mistress."*

Enraged by his denial, Louisa picked up a container of perfume from her dresser and threw it at him. Devin ducked the missile targeted for his head. Instead, it hit the wall behind him and broke into small pieces while the liquid fragrance darkened the wallpaper. Furious she'd missed him, she grabbed a vase of flowers sitting on a nearby table. Water and flowers flew out of the ornamental jar to hit him in on the side of his head, blinding him to the trajectory of the vase. Triumph sped through her as the glass object hit him on the shoulder before it fell to the floor and shattered. His expression hard with fury, Devin took a step forward, then stopped.

"Enough, Louisa. Enough. We'll discuss this in the morning when you're calm and rational."

"No. We won't. You'll be going back to London to stay at your club. The boys and I will go to Callendar Abbey to stay with Aunt Matilda."

"Don't be ridiculous. You're my wife. I love you. I want you with me." At his quiet rejection of her edict, she drew in a sharp hiss of air and shook her head.

"You are a liar. I wish I'd never married you," she said in a voice devoid of emotion. "I wish you were dead so I wouldn't have to endure

the pain and humiliation of a divorce."

At her icy reply, Devin paled, and he stared at her in stunned disbelief. He took another step toward her, but the moment she jumped back, he flinched. Pain made his mouth tighten in a thin line as he studied her with a cold and unyielding gaze.

"We'll talk in the morning," he said woodenly before he turned and walked through the short corridor that connected their rooms.

With a jerk, Louisa cried out in pain as she sat upright. Disoriented, she looked around her compartment, half-expecting Devin to be kissing her hastily as he told her the house was on fire and ordered her out of the house. The clickety-clack of the train's wheels against the railroad tracks slowly penetrated through the hazy mist of her jumbled thoughts as she realized she was the sole occupant of the compartment. A nightmare. It had only been a nightmare. She closed her eyes as guilt flooded her senses.

It had been almost three years since the fire and more than a year since the last time she'd dreamt about her argument with Devin that horrific night. Louisa slowly reclined back into the seat cushions and exhaled the tension that had held her rigid since she'd awoken. Outside, the bleak, gloomy weather reminded her that in a few days it would be December.

As the train rolled along, she studied the scenery passing by. Scotland's stark beauty had always given her a sense of peace and comfort. The serenity had been especially necessary when she'd retreated to Callendar Abbey shortly after losing Devin, and her brother Caleb, in the fire at Westbrook Farms.

Since the fire, she'd lived at the abbey almost exclusively. It had been her sanctuary from well-meaning friends, intent on easing her sorrow. Her family had been more than willing to let her grieve Devin's death in her own way and time, that is until Sebastian had called her into his study yesterday.

The sudden, jarring sound of the compartment door

opening jerked her out of the past. Startled, she quickly turned her head to see the white-haired conductor standing in the doorway.

"Tis nae far now tae Dunblane, me lady."

The soft burr in the man's voice was a sound that said she was close to the one place she loved more than anywhere else in the world. Not even Westbrook Farms had been so treasured in her heart, even though there had been happy times there until that terrible night. Aware her thoughts had drifted off, and the conductor was patiently awaiting any instructions she had. Louisa winced as she realized she was keeping the man waiting.

"Thank you. If you would, please have one of the porters secure my luggage when we arrive. There are two trunks in the baggage car that need to be unloaded."

"Aye, me lady. I'll see tae it." The conductor nodded, then closed the compartment door to leave her alone again.

The scenery through the window had changed from a barren landscape to one dotted with cottages and farms. Louisa recognized one of the houses that sat on the outskirts of Dunblane as the slowing train rattled past it. In little more than an hour, she'd be at Callendar Abbey with its peaceful, healing atmosphere. For the first time since leaving London, she experienced a serenity she'd not felt for a very long time.

It had been the right decision to leave the boys in London for the next two or three weeks. They would enjoy being with their cousins for a little longer, and she would cherish the quiet in the abbey. As much as she adored her sons, she knew she required the peace to do what she needed to do. It would be far easier to say goodbye to the past in the peaceful tranquility of Callendar Abbey without the rambunctious antics of the boys.

She also didn't want either of them, especially Charlie to see her if they caught any sign of her weeping. Her oldest had taken on more than just his father's title upon Devin's death.

Charlie had become extremely protective of her, and it troubled him deeply if anyone said something to bring her grief to the surface, including himself.

The train lurched to a halt, and Louisa quickly pulled on her black leather gloves then picked up her hat from the seat beside her and set it on top of her head. She was securing it with a hatpin when the door to the compartment slid open. Fergus's tall, lanky frame filled the doorway, and he nodded at her with a cheerful grin.

"Welcome back, me lady. Tis good tae see ye again." Just as the conductor's quiet Scottish brogue had filled her with a sense of homecoming, Fergus's voice had the same effect.

"Thank you, Fergus. I've two bags here." Louisa pointed to the small traveling case and larger portmanteau. "And two trunks in the baggage car."

"Aye. One of the porters has already unloaded yer luggage so I kin load it onto the cart."

"Is Alfred not with you?" Louisa asked in with a small amount of surprise.

"No, me lady. Tis Alfred's arthritis. . His knee locked up so badly last night, he's barely able to walk. Being as it was just ye, I told him I could come by myself."

Fergus picked up her bags and stepped out into the corridor to make his way to the carriage exit. Collecting her purse, she followed him down the narrow hallway. Fergus set down her luggage on the station's wooden platform then offered his hand to assist her down the carriage's metal steps. Satisfied she was safely off the train, Fergus retrieved her luggage and headed around the side of the small station building.

As she followed the long-time servant, Louisa breathed in the cool air. It was a welcome respite from the stuffy train compartment. There was even the faint earthy hint of fall's last remnants of heather. Fresh and sweet, it made her realize how much she loathed the tobacco-like smell of burning coal in London.

The delicious smell of tablets from the town's bakery drifted beneath her nose, and her stomach growled softly. The cold chicken and bread Mrs. Haversham had wrapped in paper for her lunch had been more than filling, but the sweet vanilla scent of the sugary treats made her mouth water.

She drank in another breath of the scent-laden air as she rounded the station to see the abbey's largest wagon sitting in front of the station. With an apologetic look, Fergus grimaced at her surprise as he touched his cap.

"Forgive me, my lady, but Alfred insisted. He says his knee tells him there's a terrible storm coming. He thought it best tae bring the wagon, since a carriage could easily get stuck in the mud."

"That makes perfect sense," Louisa said with a smile as she glanced up at the gray sky. Alfred's uncanny accuracy in his ability to predict foul weather was a trait the family heeded without question. "If it rains, I suspect we'll be warm and cozy inside the abbey before it begins. Besides, I confess that after being on a stuffy train all day the fresh air is preferable."

Fergus's relief was evident in the way his posture relaxed as he continued to load the wagon with Louisa's luggage. In minutes they were pulling away from the station. On their way out of town, they passed the bakery, and she asked Fergus to stop to buy a tablet for the two of them. They washed the sweet pastries down with milk the servant had bought as they headed out of Dunblane along Doune Road.

They were well past Doune Castle when a light rain began to fall. Fergus muttered something under his breath and reached behind him to pull out a wool blanket. He handed it to her with a frown.

"It will help keep ye dry, my lady."

Louisa accepted the blanket and threw it over head. With each passing mile, the rain began to fall harder, which caused Fergus to mutter with growing irritation. He threw up the collar of his jacket as the sky darkened considerably. Thunder boomed over their heads, and Louisa sighed. As much as she loved the highlands, she didn't enjoy being soaked to the skin with winter so close at hand. It made the rain cold as ice.

In her eagerness to reach Callendar Abbey, she'd miscalculated the timing of the storm. Her mouth tightened with self-disgust. As always, the Rockwood trait for casting caution to the wind had made her dismiss Fergus's suggestion they seek shelter at Doune Castle a few miles back.

It made no sense to turn back now. They were closer to the abbey than the castle. She deserved to be wet and cold, although Fergus didn't. Irritated by her reckless decision, she blew out a small puff of air in silent frustration and recrimination. Another shiver rippled through her as daylight slowly gave way to the approaching night. The sprinkle of rain began to fall harder, and she pulled the wool blanket tighter around her shoulders.

As they approached the Cambus Burn, she inhaled a sharp breath at the sight. Unlike the last burn they'd crossed, the stream was swollen to more than three times its normal size. Fergus drew the horses to a stop and stared in dismay at the raging water.

"It was nae like this earlier, me lady. Perhaps we should turn back." The young man's shoulders sagged with . Despite her own trepidation, Louisa patted his arm.

"This is the last burn between us and the abbey. Once we're across, it's only a few miles from home." She smiled and nodded toward the sturdy animals pulling the wagon. "The horses will get across with little trouble. Besides, I'm certain Mrs. Campbell will have a hot stew and fresh bread waiting for us."

"But ye are soaked, my lady."

"It isn't the first time," she said with a twist of her lips. "But the sooner we reach the abbey, the sooner we'll both be dry and warm."

Still troubled, Fergus didn't reply. He simply nodded then slapped the reins against the horses' backsides to urge them forward. One of the animals shook his head in protest, but the other one simply moved forward forcing the other to follow.

The water rose high on the wheels of the wagon, and the stout vehicle shuddered slightly from the strength of the water's flow. Ever so slowly the horses pulled the wagon through the burn and up onto the muddy road. His grin one of relief, Fergus glanced in her direction.

"I'll nae doubt Colman or Tulipan again, me lady."

Fergus praised the animals as he urged them forward. They'd gone only a quarter of a mile from the burn when the wagon hit a pot hole hidden by the dim light. A loud crack filled the air, and the wagon lurched violently to one side. The jolt sent Louisa crashing into Fergus so hard it threw him out of the vehicle. Quickly righting herself, she leaned over the side of the wagon to see the young man sprawled in the mud.

"Fergus, are you all right?"

When he didn't move or speak, Louisa drew in a sharp breath of dismay. Scrambling down from the wagon, she leaned over the unconscious man. Her heart sank at the bloody wound on his temple, and she straightened upright to look around her. There wasn't even a hint of shelter anywhere as she stared out at the moor. Aware she needed to get Fergus out of the rain, Louisa quickly searched the back of the wagon for another blanket, but the only thing available was the canvas that covered her luggage.

It was a struggle to drag the heavy cover off her trunks, but she managed to keep the dry part of the canvas free of water and mud as she spread it out beneath the wagon. She turned back to Fergus and debated how to move him under the wagon. With as much strength as she could muster, she tried to drag the man toward the underbelly of the wagon but barely managed to move him a few inches.

"Damn," she muttered.

The unladylike curse would have earned her a dark frown from Sebastian, and Percy would have simply laughed. Lord how she wished they were here now.

She wiped her eyes free of rain and moved to put the man between her and the wagon. Sinking down onto her heels, Louisa grunted with exertion as she rolled Fergus under the wagon and onto the dry side of the canvas.

The man didn't utter a sound, and Louisa's heart sank again as she struggled to cover Fergus's body with the remaining half of the heavy tarpaulin. Huddled beneath the wagon, Louisa cherished the small reprieve from the icy rain as she contemplated her next move. She wasn't unacquainted with serious injuries, but Fergus's silence as she'd dragged him to shelter worried her deeply.

Louisa glanced down at the man and noted the pallor of his skin. It was obvious she would have to go for help. Alfred was the only other man at the abbey as everyone else had accompanied Aunt Matilda to London. If Alfred's knee made it difficult to walk, her only other option was Doune Castle or Argaty Keep.

The Earl of Argaty's estate had to be nearby, but she had no idea where. Aunt Matilda had made it clear she couldn't tolerate the earl's wife, and she'd never even met the man or his countess. While she had never shown fear when committing herself to any reckless behavior, Louisa knew better than to try and find the earl's home in the dark. That left Doune Castle. Louisa muttered a curse even Percy would have denounced as she scrambled out from under the wagon.

With as much speed as possible, she unhitched Colman and loosely tied the horse to the back of the wagon. Despite the horse being the steadier of the two animals, Colman was much older than Tulipan. It would much harder for the gelding to cross the burns, which were still rising. She found a small knife in a makeshift tool box beneath the wagon seat and used it to cut a reasonable length of rein from Tulipan's tack.

Louisa discarded the unneeded portion of leather straps, then quickly unhitched the horse and led him to the wagon's front seat. Quickly climbing onto the floorboard of the wagon, she tugged Tulipan into place, hitched up her skirts, and climbed onto the animal's back. Until now her legs had been dry, but Tulipan's wet coat immediately remedied that situation. Shivering, she gathered up the makeshift reins and headed back the way they'd come. When they reached the burn they'd crossed earlier, the horse indicated his reluctance to enter the water. Irritated by his fractious behavior, she released a harsh breath of disgust.

"Stop being a ninny you blasted animal. You just crossed this stream a few minutes ago."

Louisa pressed her heels firmly into Tulipan's sides and urged him forward. Slowly the horse made its way into the rushing stream. A finely-edged blade of fear sliced across her senses as she looked down. The water was now almost up to the horse's knees, and she flinched as he stumbled slightly and water splashed up over her foot.

"Come on, Tulipan. Just a few more feet," she muttered. As if understanding her encouragement, the horse took two more steps forward then quickly scrambled up the bank of the burn. A few yards away from the water, she stopped him and leaned forward to pat his neck.

"Good boy. See, that wasn't too hard, was it?" She smiled as the horse bobbed his head then danced sideways at the flash of lightning in the sky, which was followed by a loud crack of thunder directly overhead. Tulipan snorted loudly in fear, and maintaining a tight grip on the makeshift reins, she tried to soothe the animal. "It's all right boy. It's just a little thunder.

Louisa pressed her knees into the animal's side and

urged him into a slow trot. It didn't take long to reach the last burn that stood between them and Doune Castle. Buchany Burn wasn't nearly as wide as the one they'd cross moments before, but the water looked much deeper. She would have to jump.

Barely thinking through the decision, she rode Tulipan a short distance away from the burn before turning him around and prodded him into a gallop. The horse cleared the burn easily, but the landing caused Louisa to slip slightly to one side on the animal's wet back. She'd barely recovered her seat when a bolt of lightning hit the ground several yards away, and the horse reared in terror.

Desperate to remain seated, Louisa grasped the animal's mane and pressed her body into the horse's neck. The animal's feet hit the ground in a hard jolt, and Louisa barely managed to maintain her already precarious seat on the animal's back. Another loud boom of thunder sounded above their heads, and with a wild cry of fear, Tulipan lunged forward.

Another flash of lightning lit the sky followed by booming thunder. It caused the animal to sharply change direction. Unable to maintain her seat on the horse's rain-slicked back, she flew through the air to the ground. Her hip and shoulder hit the soggy moor a split-second before her head hit something hard. With a cry of pain she lost consciousness.

The first thing she felt was the icy sting of the rain on her cheek. For a moment, she laid where she was. Every part of her body ached, and while she'd been soaked before, now it felt as if Tulipan had dumped her into the burn they'd crossed. Even worse was the hammer beating a loud, powerful rhythm in her head.

The storm was still raging around her, and she slowly pushed herself up into a sitting position. The movement caused her stomach to lurch unpleasantly as the pounding in her head sharpened. Eyes closed, she remained still until the pain had eased to a dull throb.

She'd never been so wet and cold in her life. Teeth chattering, she stood trembling and huddled over as the icy rain beat down on her. It was impossible to tell how long she'd been unconscious, but it was completely dark, which meant it had been at least two hours, maybe more, since Tulipan had thrown her.

A small voice in her head told her to look up. When she did so, she saw a light flickering in the darkness. Hope swelled inside her, and she stumbled toward the faint glow. She'd only gone a few feet when she tripped over a rock and fell. Slowly she climbed to her feet and continued toward the light.

The rain-soaked skirt of her dress grew heavier with each passing moment until it felt as if she were dragging a heavy cart behind her. Exhaustion settled in her limbs while the pounding in her head only added to her misery. The sensation of walking on broken glass made her bite her lip as the rest of her body protested against the tiny little needles of pain trying to puncture her skin.

Willing herself not to cry, Louisa plodded her way forward. Suddenly the light disappeared, and a hard wind knocked her off her feet. As she tried to stand up, a wave of hopelessness swept over her. Slowly, she sank back down to her knees. No more. She was in too much pain, too cold, and too weary to take another step.

"Stand up *right now*, Louisa Rockwood Morehouse. A Rockwood does *not* quit." Harsh with anger, Caleb's voice rang out clear and strong above her.

Startled by the sound, she jerked her head up to see her brother standing in front of her, arms folded across his chest as he glared at her.

"Caleb...?" She blinked rapidly as she made out his solid form. Certain she was dreaming she closed her eyes against her brother's image. With a growl of disgust she remembered so well, Caleb squatted in front of her.

"If you're a true Rockwood, little sister, you'll get up onto your feet this minute."

"I...can't...I'm so cold."

"I don't *give a fuck* how cold you are, Louisa. *Get up.*" Outraged by the brutally caustic tone of his voice more than his crude language, she scowled fiercely at him.

"Do...not...talk...to...me...like...that," she said angrily through her chattering teeth. "Sebastian...wouldn't."

"I won't mollycoddle you like our oldest brother would. And Sebastian's not here to tell you what to do," he snarled viciously. "I am. Now for *once* in your goddamn life, do as I say. Act like a Rockwood and *get up on your feet.*"

Anger drove her to stand upright as the Rockwood stubbornness suppressed the throbbing in her head to a dull murmur. Although she swayed unsteadily in place, she was standing, and she scowled at her brother as he smiled with smug satisfaction.

"So—now that I'm dead you decide to listen to me." At the mockery in his voice, she cried out in sorrow.

"*No.*" The anguish in her objection made him grimace.

"It's all right, little sister. Everything will be all right," his voice was soft with affection.

She'd always hated it when Caleb had referred to her as his little sister, but at the moment, it was the sweetest sound she'd ever heard. The sensation of a gentle kiss brushed against her brow even though he didn't move.

"Turn to your right and look, Louisa. Look hard."

Like an obedient child, she did as he commanded and peered into the darkness. In the far distance, a small light flickered. Sanctuary. She took a slow halting step toward the light. It was an excruciating one.

"I know it hurts, Louisa, but you can't stay here. You'll die, and I won't let that happen," Caleb whispered in her ear. "The boys need you. *He* needs you."

She didn't understand what he meant, but the thought of Charlie and Wills made her obey her brother. Every part of her body was stiff with cold. Each of her limbs protested savagely as the icy rain and frigid wind seeped its way deep into her bones. It made every step she took agonizing, but she pushed on knowing her brother was right. If she stayed where she was, she would die. Overhead another flash of lightning lit the sky, and she blinked away the rain and searched for the light again. It was gone. Louisa's heart sank.

"It's there, little one. Keep going. He's coming for you."

"I...don't...under...stand." Her teeth made a loud clacking sound as she spoke, but she continued in the direction she'd been heading. She forced herself to put one foot in front of the other trying to ignore the pounding in her head and how numb her body was.

Unable to see where she was going, she encountered a small drop in the landscape and lost her footing. With a cry she pitched forward to land hard against the ground. She tried to push herself up, but she didn't have the strength to do so. The salt of her tears mixed with the stinging rain drops on her cheeks as she cried out for help. An invisible, tender touch brushed against her cheek.

"He's coming, Louisa. It won't be much longer, little sister." With each whispered word, Caleb's voice grew fainter as she slipped into the abyss.

Chapter 2

The harsh wind outside pelted the window of Ewan's study with a hard rain. A powerful gust shook the double doors that led out to the small balcony overlooking the moors. He turned around in his seat half expecting to see the doors give way and fly open with a resounding crash.

Satisfied the fragile-looking doors would hold under the weight of the storm, he settled back into his seat once more and returned his attention to his book. In his effort to ensure the doors would stand up against the storm, he'd lost the comfortable placement of the book he was reading.

A noise of frustration escaped him as he struggled to adjust the position of the volume so he could see the text with the only eye he possessed. Although it wasn't in as comfortable position as it had been, he could at least see the text. He picked up where he'd left off, and a moment later reached out to turn the page with the hand he no longer possessed.

"*Fuck.*"

In a violent move, he sent the book flying through the air with his only hand until it landed on the table several feet away. The heavy volume hit an oil lamp, which teetered for a moment as if it would remain standing. It lost the battle and careened downward. The instant the lamp's flame hit the sizeable amount of oil spilling out onto the floor, a small fire erupted.

Another oath of fury erupted out of him and Ewan leapt to his feet. He snagged the wool blanket off the back of his chair and threw it over the flames to smother them. With vicious stomps on the blanket, the fire died a quick death. The sound of running feet made him turn toward the study door as Asadi burst into the room at full tilt. The boy jerked to a halt just inside the room.

"You are all right, Argaty sahib?"

"The lamp broke." Ewan shrugged as he jerked his head toward the mess on the floor. "I had to put out the fire."

"It broke, Argaty sahib?" Dark eyes wide in his light brown face, the boy's gaze darted to the charred edges of the blanket before shifting to the table where Ewan's book had taken the place of the lamp. "Perhaps your book did not like the lamp?"

Ewan growled with irritation as he glared at Asadi, who had already begun cleaning up the mess. Wheeling about on the edge of his heel, he returned to his chair, and stared into the fire. The heat of the flames reminded him of the desert. Gunfire and screams suddenly echoed in his head, and he stood up to pace the floor waiting for the cries to fade as they usually did, except in his sleep.

"Shall I bring you dinner, Argaty sahib?" At the boy's question, Ewan directed a scowl of aggravation in his direction.

"Leave me be, Asadi," he snarled.

The boy quietly moved toward the door carrying the remains of the oil lamp and scorched blanket. As Asadi reached the doorway, Ewan blew out a harsh breath of disgust at his abrupt manner with the boy.

"Asadi. You may bring me something to eat."

"As you wish, Argaty sahib," the boy said cheerfully at Ewan's unspoken apology.

Ewan didn't bother to look in the boy's direction as the

door closed behind him. Instead, he continued to pace the carpet. For some reason, he knew tonight would be another restless night. He snorted loudly. When was any night not filled with the screams of injured men having their limbs sawed off? He strode over to the window behind his desk and with his only hand threw up the window to welcome in the cold damp air.

The fire in the hearth his only source of light in the room, it allowed him to see the landscape more easily. Off in the distance he thought he saw a movement, but quickly dismissed it. What madman or animal would be out on a night like this? A tentative knock made him glance over his shoulder as he saw the door slowly opening.

"My lord." McCallum's quiet, yet steady voice was filled with respect. A long-time retainer of the Argaty family, McCallum had known him since he was a boy. The Scotsman was the only member of the household, other than Asadi, he allowed in his quarters.

"Finn just sent word from the stables that a horse has appeared out of the storm."

"What the devil does that have to do with me? Tell Finn to stable the damn thing. We'll find the owner tomorrow."

"Aye, my lord. However, there is a slight complication."

"Then say it McCallum, stop dancing around what you came to say." Ewan frowned as he turned toward the Scotsman who never seemed troubled by Ewan's foul moods.

"The horse appears tae have been unhitched from a carriage."

There was a quiet note in McCallum's voice that said he expected Ewan to respond to the situation. What that response was, he had no idea. Irritated by the retainer's unspoken belief that Ewan was required to do something, he glared at the older man.

"And what the hell makes you think that?"

"The animal has no saddle or tack other than a bridle.

And the reins had been deliberately cut tae a shorter length tae make the horse easy tae ride."

"In this weather?" Ewan snorted his disbelief. "A man would have to be daft to be out in a storm like this."

"Unless a vehicle had come tae some harm, my lord." The Scotsman's words made Ewan scowl at the man with disgusted disbelief before he turned back to the open window.

In the distance, he saw something move against the landscape once more. He narrowed his one eye to focus on the spot. Perhaps McCallum was right. If a carriage had experienced a mishap on Doune Road, it would make sense for someone to try to seek help. At that precise moment lightning flashed in the sky to illuminate the countryside. In the bright light he realized the movement he'd seen was a figure staggering toward the house.

Whoever it was came to a sudden halt and stood swaying in the heavy wind and rain. A fraction of a second later, the figure disappeared like an apparition on the rain soaked moor. For a moment, he continued to stare out at the spot where he'd seen the figure expecting to see whoever was out in the storm to rise to their feet. Ewan released a soft noise of disgusted skepticism at the likelihood he'd actually seen someone.

"I dinnae like tae think we ignored the possibility of leaving someone out on the moor on a night like this, Master Ewan."

McCallum only used his childhood title when gently rebuking Ewan. The man had become a father figure to him after his father had died in a riding accident when he was just a boy, and he allowed the familiarity. He grimaced as he turned toward the man.

It would be a fool's errand to send Finn out onto the moors in the middle of one of the worst storms Ewan had seen in a long time. The lad had not grown up on the moors as Ewan had. Not to mention it would be difficult to find someone in the dark if the lad didn't know where to look, when even he wasn't sure if what he'd seen had been real. With a grunt of displeasure, Ewan slammed the window shut then turned to glare at McCallum.

"Tell Finn to saddle Lachlan, and send Asadi in with that infernal contraption as well as my coat."

"Yes, my lord." Although he remained stoic, McCallum's voice echoed with approval.

As the Scotsman left the study, Ewan acknowledged the older man was proud of him for agreeing to the search, even if it were for naught. Almost as if he'd expected Ewan's request, Asadi appeared moments later with the artificial device a physician in London had given him when he'd returned from the Sudan. Ewan glared at the metal and wood attachment as Asadi adjusted the straps that went over his shoulders and under his arms to secure the device. God how he hated the thing.

Asadi offered Ewan his black glove, but he waved it away. The device was more flexible without the leather covering the metal. Lachlan could be contrary at times, and he could control the animal better with the unnatural fingers free of any glove. He also cared little that the grotesque metal fingers might frighten someone, particularly when he was certain he was on a fool's errand. With a growl of irritation as Asadi tightened the strap, he glanced over his shoulder at the boy.

Regret made the boy flinch, and Ewan looked away. He knew the lad would do anything asked of him, and Ewan didn't like it. He hated how Asadi believed himself beholden to him. Ewan shrugged on the coat the brown-skinned boy held up for him. The metal fingers snagged a piece of thread and pushed back on his thrust. The result was a twinge in his shoulder. A quiet oath of frustration blew past his lips. Asadi immediately darted around him and gently wiggled the coat sleeve free of the metal device.

With a nod, Ewan strode out of his study and downstairs to the front door. McCallum was already there with the door open. Outside the rain had eased slightly, but the wind was bitterly cold. He strode out to where Lachlan stood stomping his front hooves into the ground. A cry behind him, made Ewan turn back to the house.

"Argaty sahib. Argaty sahib. Your hat for deer."

The boy's description of his deerstalker twisted Ewan's lips slightly. He accepted the hat then ruffled Asadi's hair in an affectionate gesture. The boy grinned up at him, and Ewan immediately regretted the move. The gesture would only encourage the boy to do more for him. A quiet sound of irritation flew past his lips as he turned toward Lachlan. Ewan's natural fingers slid through stallion's thick mane as he launched himself up onto the pewter gray animal.

In a smooth movement, he adjusted the horse's reins in his fingers then accepted the small lantern Finn offered him with the paltry excuse of metal that substituted for a hand. Adjusted solidly in the saddle, he turned the stallion in the direction of where he'd last seen the figure on the moors. If there *were* someone out on the moor on a night like this, he should just leave the fool out here.

But something in the darkness of his soul compelled him to begin the search. At a slow trot, Lachlan moved forward into the dark with only the small lantern to light their way. They'd gone almost a mile from the house when he slowed the horse to a walk. Lantern held high over his head, he guided the light across the ground surrounding him.

"You came out here for nothing, Argaty," he muttered with disgust. "It was probably some damn animal you saw from the window."

Ewan urged Lachlan forward once more then paused after a few yards to raise the light again. His eyes had adjusted to the darkness, and as far as he could see there was nothing moving on the moor. Disgusted with his efforts, he started to pull Lachlan around when he heard a faint sound above the rain and wind. Lantern lifted high, he studied the area and saw nothing.

With a grimace, Ewan tugged on the reins to turn Lachlan back toward the house when he heard the sound again. Twisting in the saddle, he raised his lantern high above his head to see the surrounding area with the only eye he possessed. Another pitiful sound echoed through the air, and he jerked his head toward the miserable cry.

Overhead a flash of lightning lit up the area for only a second, but it was enough to glimpse a movement on the ground about fifty yards away. Ewan quickly turned sound and nudged Lachlan forward. Lantern raised high, he slowly moved the light in a sweeping arc.

"Please...help..."

The cry was hoarse and weak, but it was a distinct plea. A small nudge of his heel sent Lachlan forward. It wasn't until the stallion danced to one side and snorted loudly that Ewan saw the figure lying at the feet of the horse.

"*Christ Almighty, man*, what the devil are you doing out on the moor on a night like this?" Ewan exclaimed as he leaned down and dropped the lantern onto the ground.

By some miracle, the light source landed upright to cast an unearthly glow across the surrounding field as he dismounted close to the fallen figure. Ewan gently rolled the man over then grew rigid.

"A woman," he muttered to himself in disbelief.

Dark hair plastered against her forehead and cheeks, she could have been a ghost for how white she was. Alarmed by her condition, he uttered a harsh oath. At the sound, her eyes fluttered open then closed, and she murmured something. Unable to hear her, Ewan bent his head so his ear was close to her mouth.

"Are you real?" The fear in her almost inaudible whisper

made him growl deep in his throat.

"Aye, lass, I'm real."

Without thinking, he used his metal fingers to push hair off her a white cheek. At the touch, she opened her eyes and released a small cry at the sight of his unnatural fingers. Fear made her shrink away from him and the metal device that served as his missing hand.

A fraction of a second later, horror widened her eyes, and he realized he'd failed to wear his eye patch. Without it, she had an up close view of the scarred skin stretched tight across the empty eye socket. The revulsion on her pale countenance was an all too familiar reaction.

"I'm not the devil, lass, although I come close," he bit out between clenched teeth.

When she didn't respond, he realized she'd fainted. A growl of exasperation rumbled out of him as he realized she'd be of little assistance climbing onto Lachlan. Quickly shifting his position, Ewan slid his good arm under her legs and shifted her onto his good shoulder like a sack of flour.

The sodden wool dress she wore quickly soaked his own coat. It clung to her legs almost like a second skin. She'd obviously been out in the storm for quite some time. He rose to his feet and strode toward Lachlan. His mechanical arm and hand sought to hold her steady as Ewan slowly slid her body down over his chest. The moment her feet touched the ground, he gently patted her cheek until her eyes fluttered open in response to the action.

"I need you to stand for a moment, lass."

He barely saw her nod of understanding as he turned her toward Lachlan and allowed the horse to absorb her weight. Almost as if the stallion understood the woman's need for support, Lachlan didn't shy away from her. As she leaned into the animal's wet coat Ewan guided her icy hands up to Lachlan's thick shock of hair running the length of his powerful neck.

"Grab hold of the mane here."

Slowly, her fingers grasped the animal's mane as she used the horse as a means to hold herself upright. He briefly glanced down at the lantern on the ground, knowing it was impossible to carry it and the woman as well. Certain her legs were about to give way beneath her, Ewan vaulted into the saddle then leaned over and dragged the woman up onto the stallion. A soft moan escaped her as he cradled her against his chest. Her body shuddered against his in a constant barrage of small tremors. It was two miles to Doune Road from Argaty Keep. How long had she actually been out in the storm? With a tug on the reins, he turned Lachlan back toward the house.

Lightning flashed above their heads followed by a loud crack of thunder. The sound made Lachlan dance nervously to one side, but Ewan soothed the animal with several words in Gaelic before nudging the horse into a quick trot to the house. The ride to Argaty Keep was accomplished in minutes as opposed to the time he'd spent on his search. As he rode up to the front door, he saw McCallum waiting in the open doorway.

The Scotsman stepped aside to let Finn run out into the rain to meet him. The groom grabbed the horse's halter as McCallum hurried forward to support the woman as Ewan slid her off the horse and dismounted. The moment he was on the ground, Ewan lifted the woman up into his arms. The majority of her weight cradled against in his good arm, he used the metal contraption he wore to hold her steady against his chest. The movement exacerbated the sting where the leather cup encasing his stub of an arm had rubbed ruthlessly at his skin. As he entered the keep, Ewan paused as he debated what room to use for the keep's unwelcomed guest.

"I had Maggie prepare the King's bedroom, my lord," McCallum said quietly.

It shouldn't have surprised him the older man had

thought to prepare a room when there had been no indication Ewan would return with a lost soul. McCallum always seemed to be one step ahead, and it made him think the man had a bit of the sight. The woman hadn't stopped trembling since he'd found her, but her tremors seemed to have become even more pronounced on the way back to the house.

"Send Maggie up to help undress the woman, and make sure she brings night clothes," Ewan said brusquely as started up the main staircase with his unexpected guest in his arms. "Then send for Doctor Munro."

"Doctor Munro, my lord?" McCallum's surprise made Ewan pause at the foot of the steps to look over his shoulder and glare at the older man. The family retainer raised his eyebrows as if Ewan was still a boy. "'Tis unlikely the burns will be safe tae cross for two or three days, my lord."

The Scotsman's observation made Ewan frown with displeasure. The man was right. Even in the daylight it would be difficult to reach the physician without endangering someone's life, even his own. The fact the woman's teeth had begun to chatter and her trembling was worsening with each passing second indicated she would need care through the night.

"Then, I'll have to care for her myself."

"My lord?" McCallum eyed him with stern disapproval.

"Is there someone else in this infernal place who knows how to care for her if she develops pneumonia?" he snarled. "And have Asadi bring me my eye patch. The woman was terrified by the sight of me out on the moor."

Without waiting for a response, Ewan climbed the steps. He glanced down at the woman in his arms. She looked as if she were already at death's door. If? He snorted. Even with the limited training he possessed from his time in the Sudan, he could tell the woman was seriously ill. He was more than halfway up the stairs, when a slender figure in nightwear and a shawl wrapped around her shoulders appeared at the top of the steps.

"What has happened, Ewan? Who is she?" his aunt exclaimed.

"Go back to bed, Aunt Wallis."

"But your mother sent me to see what the fuss was about."

"It's nothing my mother needs to concern herself with, and I've no time to explain."

Ewan reached the top of the stairs and headed down the hall to the room McCallum had had prepared. Wallis ignored his command and followed close on his heels. His aunt was one of the few people he tolerated to have around him, and any other time he would not have spoken so harshly. But the fact his mother had sent his aunt to investigate the disturbance in the house irritated him beyond any patience he normally had.

Close on the heels of the thought, he quickly admitted he would rather have Aunt Wallis asking questions than his mother. The dowager's caustic manner would only aggravate him more than he was already. He entered the King's bedroom and set his charge down in one of the chairs facing the fire. As he struggled to undo the buttons on the front of her dress with his one hand, his aunt gasped loudly.

"You mustn't, Ewan. It's not proper." At her protest, he slowly turned his head toward her.

"Would you have me leave the lass in these wet clothes? Now go report back to the Lady Argaty and then go to bed."

At his angry snarl, his aunt took a quick step back in apprehension. He immediately regretted his sharp words. With a grimace, he shook his head slightly and softened his voice. "The woman is seriously ill, Aunt Wallis. We both know that short of Dr. Munro, I'm the only one capable of caring for her. Send Mrs. Selkirk to assist me."

The older woman hesitated before she nodded her head in understanding and left the room. Ewan's free hand fumbled with the buttons on the woman's dress, and he grimaced at the sight of Maggie in the doorway followed by Asadi. The maid eyed him with trepidation, which caused him to bow his head so she couldn't see the mass of scars crisscrossing his cheek. Where the hell was Mrs. Selkirk?

The boy who'd taken it upon himself to be Ewan's valet, hurried across the room to offer him the black patch he wore routinely along with his glove. In a swift movement, Ewan covered his eye with the leather patch. He looked at Asadi and nodded toward the door. Without questioning the silent command, the boy darted out of the room.

"Help me undo the woman's dress, Maggie."

Out of the corner of his eye, Ewan saw the maid hesitate. In a deliberate move, he turned toward her and held up his artificial arm in silent explanation. The maid still didn't move, and with a slight movement of his shoulder, he made the spindly metal fingers click together in an ominous sound. The maid flinched violently before she jerked her gaze away from the grotesque appendage and hurried forward. In the back of his head, a voice reprimanded him for taunting the girl. He ignored his conscience.

Silently, he watched Maggie undo the woman's dress then moved forward to help the girl remove the sodden wool garment off the woman. In the back of his mind, he noted that the woman's clothing was that of a lady of quality. Black without any trace of color, he suspected she was in mourning. A husband perhaps? She wasn't wearing a ring, so perhaps a relative.

He tossed the woman's dress aside then held her up slightly so Maggie could quickly pulled the wet underskirts off the woman. When the maid undid the laces of the woman's combination, the garment gave way to a wet chemise that clung to her as if she were naked. An odd sensation tensed his muscles as he couldn't help but notice her sweet, lushly full curves. She had the body of Titian's Venus of Urbino.

Rounded in all the places where a woman should be curved, his gaze drifted over her shoulders down to her breasts and the dark pink nipples the thin, linen chemise highlighted so enticingly. The tension in his body made him stiffen as he failed to stop himself from perusing the rest of her lush body down to the apex of her thighs and her full, voluptuous legs. Incensed by his interest in the woman, Ewan looked away as the maid struggled to remove the last of his guest's clothing. The woman's shivers were still hard and fast, and as Maggie reached for the night dress she'd brought with her, Ewan shook his head.

"No. I'm certain the lass has a fever, and it's better she not be restrained with anything but the bedsheets." He saw the maid's look of consternation. "I will not be taking advantage of the woman, girl. Throw a blanket over her then turn down the covers so I can put her in bed."

"Yes, my lord."

The maid bobbed her head at his instructions, and despite his desire to do otherwise, Ewan managed to keep his gaze from skimming the woman's naked body. When Maggie had covered the woman with a light-weight blanket, he carefully lifted his unexpected guest up into his arms and carried her to the bed.

Throughout the entire process, the only sound the woman made was her teeth chattering. Even against his dry clothing her body chilled his through his wool vest and jacket. His brow furrowed with concern, he laid her on the sheets and allowed Maggie to cover her up to her neck. Despite lying beneath the dry covers, the woman's body didn't stop shaking. Ewan pressed the back of his hand against her forehead and grimaced. As he'd expected she was running a fever. It was a high one at that.

"Have Asadi bring me a pitcher of cool water, towels, and have Mrs. Selkirk prepare some peppermint tea and chicken broth." Ewan gave the command as he tightened the covers around the woman. When the maid didn't move, he turned his head toward her.

"*Now*, not tomorrow." His fierce tone made the maid bob her head before she darted out of the room. Left alone with his charge, Ewan sat down on the side of the bed to study her.

A light coating of sweat glistened on her forehead, and he gently wiped it away with his fingers. Her hair was drying quickly, and it reminded him of the soft brown feathers on the heads of the kites that flew over the keep on a regular basis. A soft murmur drifted out of her, and he bent his head in an attempt to hear what she was saying, but her words were impossible to make out.

It was several minutes before Asadi appeared with the water and towels. The boy left them within reach then hurried out of the room to fetch the other items Ewan had demanded. Ewan soaked a cloth in the cool water, wrung it out, and proceeded to gently stroke the sweat from her forehead. As he tended to her, he studied her oval-shaped face.

"Where do you come from, lass, and why were you out in the storm?" he asked softly.

Ewan continued his attempts to remove the perspiration from her forehead. When the woman's shudders caused the pillow beneath her head to move into an awkward position, he gently lifted her head to push the pillow back into place inadvertently disturbing some of the hair near her forehead. He drew in a soft hiss of air at the bruise on the side of her temple.

Despite his efforts to cool her fever, her symptoms continued to worsen with each passing hour. As the woman's fever deepened, she began thrashing beneath the bedcovers and tried to throw them off. Gently, he pulled her arms out from beneath the covers to provide her relief. He did the same for her legs. With the cool, damp clothes, Ewan wiped down her exposed limbs in an attempt to make her more comfortable.

He turned away for a moment to soak a cloth and wring it out before he shifted on the mattress to tend to her again. The moment he moved, he inhaled a sharp breath that he immediately exhaled as he stared at the bare breast exposed to him. The full, plump curve of it made his mouth go dry as the image of Titian's nude filled his head again. The sensation it aroused in him was one he didn't like.

With a growl of disgust at his reaction to her, he quickly drew up the covers over her again. Throughout the night, Ewan continued to remove the beads of sweat from her brow as her fever showed no signs of breaking. It was only when the first gray light of the day tried to push its way through curtains covering the bedroom windows that he realized his efforts might be a hopeless cause.

Although her fever had weakened, she was still hot to the touch, and he heard a soft rattle in her breathing. The mold out on the moor combined with the rain and cold could not have done her any good. But she was young, and she seemed in reasonably good health. He would not allow her to die without making every effort to save her. She stirred slightly as her eyes fluttered open. With the curtains closed, only the fire provided any light. The woman's reaction when he'd found her on the moors had not left him, and he'd purposefully kept the room with as little light as possible.

"Lie still, lass," he said quietly then crossed the room to retrieve some of the chicken broth Mrs. Selkirk had left on the hearth so the fire would keep it from going cold.

Before he filled a bowl with the broth, he pulled the glove from his pocket and pulled it on over the metal spindles that substituted as his hand. The broth was still warm, and he knew it would do the woman good to take some of it. Ewan returned to her bed, and there was a glassy look to the large hazel eyes staring up at him.

"You need to eat some of this broth. It will help to make you feel better."

She didn't answer and she appeared ready to drift back to sleep. Determined to have her take some broth, Ewan sank down on the edge of the bed. He awkwardly raised her up and braced her against his chest with his metal arm, then fed her the warm liquid with his good hand.

His charge tried to avoid the spoon he pressed between her lips, but Ewan refused to let her do so. Once more she looked up at him. He wasn't sure if he saw horror in her gaze or if it was merely the look of someone quite ill. Ewan ignored the thought. Although he only managed to have her take six or seven spoonfuls, he knew it was better than nothing at all. She needed liquids, and the broth served that purpose. When she refused to eat anymore, he laid her back down into the pillows and realized how damp her sheets were.

The idea of changing her sheets meant trying not to look at her sweet curves. The notion that he would succeed in not enjoying one more look of her delightfully lush figure made him release a soft snort of disgust. Ewan sprang to his feet and quickly crossed the room to throw the door open. As he'd expected, Asadi was sleeping on the door's threshold. The boy had still not grown accustom to the idea of an actual bed.

"Asadi," he said quietly. The boy stirred slightly, but when Ewan said his name again, the young man was immediately on his feet.

"Yes, Argaty sahib?"

"The lass needs her sheets changed. Ask Mrs. Selkirk to bring fresh sheets so we can change the woman's bedding," he said softly. The boy started down the corridor, and Ewan quickly clarified his command. "And tell Mrs. Selkirk *she's* tae come. I don't want Maggie. The girl is afraid of her own shadow."

"Yes, Argaty sahib."

Ewan returned to his patient and bent over to feel her forehead. It was still hot, but for the first time in hours it was a great deal cooler. He straightened and studied her for a moment. Even with her hair damp from her feverish sweat, she was lovely. What had driven her out onto the moors at night in the driving rain?

She stirred beneath the sheets, and he quickly bent over her to ensure they were up to her neck to prevent any other erotic displays. He didn't like the effect the sight of her naked curves had on him. The woman was ill, and he was a sick bastard for enjoying the few glimpses he'd seen of her sweetly curved figure. Her eyes fluttered opened as he busied himself adjusting her covers. The moment he turned his head toward her, she shrank back into the mattress. Despite the dim light, he knew his close proximity gave her plenty to see, and she was clearly frightened by the sight of him.

"I'll not harm you, lass," he growled softly as he turned his head away so she could only see his unblemished profile.

Her reaction wasn't unexpected, but he didn't like the way it made him feel. In the past year since his return from the war, he'd grown used to the way people responded to his damaged body. Ewan jerked upright and turned away to hide his deformities. Her reaction to his mangled body troubled him far more than it should have.

A quick glance over his shoulder revealed she'd succumbed to sleep again, and he drew in a deep breath then exhaled slowly. When their guest was out of the woods, Mrs. Selkirk and Aunt Wallis could tend to the woman until she was well enough to leave the keep. It would spare her any further horror when it came to his appearance.

His mother would no doubt vehemently protest the imposition of not having her sister at her beck and call. The idea of irritating the dowager countess sent a rush of vindictive pleasure through him. It would also give his aunt a brief reprieve from his mother's habit of browbeating her sister. His gaze focused on the woman again, and he watched her carefully for a moment until he was certain she was fast asleep.

Ewan crossed the floor to the window and pulled one of the curtains back slightly to look out over the landscape. It was still raining, almost as hard as it had been last night. Despite the gloomy weather, he still saw the beauty of the land he owned for as far as the eye could see. He'd always loved Argaty Keep, but it was difficult to take any pleasure from it given the pain within its walls. He looked back at his ill guest. She was a mystery, but he was certain the secret of who she was would be solved soon enough.

The soft knock on the bedroom door made him drop the curtain back into place so it closed out the daylight. The door opened and Mrs. Selkirk entered followed by Maggie. He grimaced at the sight of the young maid. He'd specifically told Asadi he didn't want the girl in the room with him. The keep's cook and housekeeper shook her head at him with a stern, silent look not to voice any objection. Mrs. Selkirk, like his retainer McCallum, had been at the keep since he was a boy and didn't have any trouble taking him to task or overriding him in certain circumstances. The woman apparently considered this one of those moments.

"I brought Maggie tae help me with the sheets."

"I could have helped you."

"Ye are barely able tae stand, Master Ewan." Mrs. Selkirk snorted with affectionate disgust as she berated him as she had when he was a child. "I want ye tae go tae bed. Ye have been up all night with the woman."

"I should—"

"Get on with ye. We can see to her care well enough for a few hours."

The woman's firm, no-nonsense tone made him jerk his head in silent agreement, and he left the King's Chamber.

Once he reached his rooms, he undressed and slid beneath the covers. He had thought he would find it difficult to sleep, but he was asleep in seconds.

"Argaty sahib." Asadi's voice echoed softly in his ear like a noisy fly. With a grunt he rolled away from the sound. Two scrawny hands rocked his shoulder. "Argaty sahib, it's the woman. She is worse."

Still groggy, Ewan lifted his head to stare at the young man. What woman was the boy talking about? He blinked several times as Asadi's slender frame came into focus.

"You must come now, Argaty sahib. The woman is very ill." Asadi's words finally penetrated the fog of sleep, and Ewan stumbled out of bed to dress. In less than ten minutes he was crossing the floor of the King's Chambers to bend over his patient as if he'd never left the room. He'd been wrong to think her fever had passed.

"I don't like the looks of her fever, my lord." Mrs. Selkirk was standing on the opposite side of the bed with a look of deep concern furrowing her brow.

"How long has she been like this?"

"Not long, Maggie called for me as soon as the woman's fever started again."

"And how was she during the day?"

"She was restless off and on, but not much. She seemed tae have been sleeping peacefully until the fever returned."

Ewan bobbed his head in understanding as he pressed his hand against the woman's forehead. If possible, she seemed hotter than she had last night.

"Did she take any broth or water today?"

"No, my lord. She was unwilling to take even the slightest spoonful." Mrs. Selkirk's answer made him frown.

"Have Asadi bring fresh water and towels. I'll stay with her until her fever breaks again."

"Very well, my lord," the older woman said quietly as she left the room.

When Asadi appeared with fresh towels and water, Ewan renewed his efforts to end the woman's fever. The hours passed slowly as dusk blended into the deepest night. Toward the early hours of morning, her fever broke for the second time. This time there was something about her coloring that made him think she was over the worst of her illness. Although she was still pale, a small bit of natural color had returned to her cheeks.

Wearily, Ewan sank down into the over-stuffed chair he'd pulled closer to the bed. The action made him grimace slightly as he moved his amputated limb in the wrong direction. Before going to bed yesterday morning, he'd removed the mechanical device. He'd not been surprised to find the leather of his artificial arm had rubbed the skin raw where the device was attached to what was left of his arm.

Ewan ignored the pain and studied the woman sleeping quietly in the bed. There was something so peaceful about her that he decided to let her sleep some before he attempted to give her any broth. Head pressed into the back of the chair's cushion, Ewan closed his eye to rest for just a moment. He hadn't meant to fall asleep, but when he did, he slept deeply. A sound pierced his sleep, and he jerked upright in his chair. As he blinked and looked at his patient, he saw a small figure standing beside the woman, holding her hand.

"What are you doing in here, Ross?" The sharpness of his tone made the boy flinch, and Ewan jerk his gaze away from the child.

"She was restless, my lord. She cried out for someone, so I held her hand to let her know she wasn't alone."

It was a quiet, fearless reply that made Ewan respect the boy for his refusal to be intimidated. No matter how much he ignored the child or how harshly he spoke to him, the boy never faltered beneath Ewan's abrasive disapproval. The boy didn't even seem to realize that Ewan wanted nothing to do with him, or if he did know it, the child was determined to ignore it.

Ewan rose to his feet to check on his patient. Her sheets were clean and crisp, and he could only assume Mrs. Selkirk had changed the woman's sheets again while he slept. The clock on the mantle began to chime the hour, and he looked over his shoulder at the to check the time before returning his attention to his patient.

"The woman is fine now. You're not to trouble her again. Now go. Mrs. Selkirk will be waiting on you for breakfast." Ewan didn't look at the boy as he spoke. Instead, he adjusted the covers over the woman. The boy didn't move, and Ewan slowly turned his head toward the child. "Do as your told, lad."

"Yes, Father," Ross said softly. The child's response aroused a fierce anger inside him, and Ewan glared at the boy. Ross grimaced slightly as he laid the woman's hand down on the bed then left the room.

When the boy was gone, Ewan bowed his head with his eye closed. He knew he shouldn't be hard on the boy. The child was innocent. A familiar anger hardened his muscles. The boy might be free of sin, but the mother was not.

His patient stirred and murmured something unintelligible. He checked her forehead again for any sign of fever, but it was cool to the touch. The woman's eyelids fluttered, and he quickly stepped back to hide in the shadows. It was irrational to desperately want to shield her from his deformities. Even worse was his need to avoid her horrified gaze again. Aware she no longer needed him, Ewan strode toward the door.

"Wait. Where am I?" she asked in a soft, unsteady voice. He looked back toward the bed, and saw her looking in his direction with a sleepy-eyed, bewildered look.

"You're at Argaty Keep, lass. You've been sick ever since I found you on the moor." Ewan pulled the door open. "I'll send Mrs. Selkirk in to tend to you."

He didn't wait for her reply. He simply left the room and closed the door behind him, grateful to be done playing nursemaid. A voice in the back of his head cackled like a *bean nighe*.

Chapter 3

L ouisa blinked to clear her vision until she found herself staring up at the unfamiliar ceiling. Her head was throbbing, and she closed her eyes against the pain. Almost immediately she regretted doing so as her nightmares from last night filled her head.

Images of a one-eyed beast hovering over her. Its boney fingers clicking in her ear like knives scraping against each other as they menacingly threatened to cut her into small pieces.

A shudder jarred her body, and Louisa's eyes flew open in an attempt to make the image disappear. The vivid memory slowly faded to be replaced by the memory of a boy. It was impossible to visualize him clearly, but she was certain he'd been real. She touched the back of her hand where she could still feel the warmth of his touch.

The memory of the boy receded, and the image of a man pushed its way forward. Engulfed in the shadows his tall figure had been barely visible. He'd spoken to her, and although she couldn't remember what he'd said the sound of his voice had been kind and soothing. But it was what he didn't say that made her heart weep for him. The man's emotions had been almost tangible, and they'd pressed relentless against her senses.

Only one other time in her life had she sensed such pain, anger, and despair in someone. The stranger's emotions were as deep and profound as the ones Caleb had projected when Georgina had died. As Louisa tried to piece her jumbled thoughts together in some coherent fashion, a crackling pop echoed out of the fireplace.

Where was she? The small fire casting its light on her surroundings made it possible to see most of the room except for its shadowy dark corners. The only other light in the room were the thin lines of soft gray that outlined curtains over a large window. Louisa tried to sit up, but she'd barely raised her head up off the pillows before the room began to spin around her. Instantly, her stomach lurched in the same nauseating way it had when she'd carried Wills.

Closing her eyes, Louisa inhaled several deep breaths for a moment in an effort to make the nausea go away. She looked up at the ceiling once more, then slowly turned her head first to her left and then her right. There was nothing recognizable in the room, which made it obvious she wasn't at Callendar Abbey. She winced as a small throb pulsed in her temple. In bits and pieces, the events of the past day fluttered through her head like puzzle pieces coming together.

"Caleb."

Her quiet cry echoed softly through the room. Aside from her nightmares, the last thing she remembered clearly was Caleb standing in front of her, ordering her to get up off the ground. Louisa squeezed her eyes tightly shut to keep the tears from rolling down her cheeks. The *an dara sealladh* had never been as vivid or clear for her as it had been last night. Her brother had been so real she could have reached out and touched him.

The throbbing in her head made her wince as she touched the side of her head. Her fingers brushed over a small knot on her temple to lightly trace the lump. It was just a little smaller than the size of an egg. She must have hit her head on a rock when Tulipan had thrown her. Louisa blew out a sharp breath of exasperation. She should have known better than to choose the blasted animal over Colman as the best horse to ride to Doune Castle. The wagon.

Oh dear God, Fergus. Had someone found him?

Louisa shot up, then quickly sank back into the mattress as nausea rolled over her. Eyes closed, she shivered as the room's chilly air blew across her skin. She pulled the bedcovers up over her shoulders, and a split second later she drew in a sharp breath. Dear Lord, she wasn't wearing any clothing. Who had undressed her?

The memory of the man in the shadows made her inhale a sharp breath. Surely, *he* hadn't undressed her. Humiliation swept through her at the possibility. Devin was the only man who'd ever seen her naked. As she looked around the dimly lit room for her clothes, she saw nothing that resembled her clothes. If she were to ensure Fergus was safe, she needed to dress, which meant finding her clothes.

The sudden sound of the door opening made her grow rigid. A second later, she relaxed as a smiling, plump woman entered the room. The woman carried a tray while a young girl followed close behind carrying Louisa's dress.

"'Tis good to see ye awake, lass. We were quite worried about ye there for a wee bit." The woman glanced over her shoulder at the younger woman. "Maggie, open those curtains then go back tae the kitchen and see tae it Lord Argaty's breakfast is ready for Asadi tae take it up tae his lordship."

The woman carried the tray to the night stand, and the dishes on the large platter rattled noisily as she set it down. The young maid laid Louisa's clothing on the end of the bed then scurried to the window to open the drapes. Although it was gray and rainy outside, the light gave the room a much more inviting atmosphere.

Louisa caught the warm scent of porridge with a small whiff of honey. It smelled as good as what Mrs. Campbell made every morning at Callendar Abbey. Her stomach growled as the delicious smell of bacon wafted beneath her nose, but she ignored her hunger.

"Where am I? Is this Doune Castle? Has someone found Fergus? Is he all right?"

"You're at Argaty House, lass. But I dinnae ken a Fergus."

"Fergus is my driver. He was injured. I left him at the wagon and went for help."

The woman stared at her in confusion, and Louisa's heart sank. Fergus had been out in the storm all night, and the canvas would provide only so much protection. Horrified, the man was most likely still lying injured on Doune Road, Louisa pointed toward her clothes at the end of the bed.

"I must dress," she said fiercely.

"It's too soon for ye to be out of bed, lass."

"I'm perfectly fine," Louisa said stubbornly. "Now, hand me my clothes."

A frown creasing her brow, the woman's cheery expression faded as she reluctantly retrieved Louisa's garments. As Louisa dressed with the woman's help, the effort took its toll on her weakened state. When the buttons on the back of her dress were done up, she rose to her feet. Instantly, another wave of nausea careened through her. One hand clutching the corner of the night stand, she sank back down onto the mattress.

"Och, now, lassie. Dinna ye fash none. I'll tell McCallum tae be seeing after your driver." The older woman clucked softly in the same fashion Aunt Matilda always did when she was consoling her. "You're too weak to be up and about yet."

"Mrs. Selkirk is quite right." The sharp voice made Louisa lift her head and look toward the door of her room. "You must stay in bed or you'll undo everything my son has done to make you well."

The woman walked toward the bed with a regal bearing,

but it was her cold, unwelcoming expression that made Louisa remain silent.

"I am the Dowager Countess of Argaty. And you are?" The woman arched one eyebrow as she eyed Louisa with dislike.

The sudden image of a young boy filled Louisa's head. She was certain it was the same boy she'd seen in her dreams, but his forlorn look made her heart ache. The child desperately needed love. It was an emotion this woman withheld from all those around her, including the child.

Without thinking twice, Louisa gave the woman her married name, deliberately omitting her title. She had no idea why she'd done so, she'd simply followed her instincts. Almost as if she could tell Louisa wasn't being completely truthful, the dowager countess narrowed her eyes at her. Not even her childhood harridan of a governess, Miss Crimwald, had ever looked so sternly at her.

"Well, Mrs. Morehouse. You've managed to turn this household upside down since your arrival." The woman pinned a look of disapproving appraisal on her, which puzzled Louisa. It wasn't as if she'd planned on coming to Argaty.

"I am sorry, my lady. I can assure you it was not my intent. I was on my way to Callendar Abbey—"

"That's several miles north, why would you have left Doune Road to come here to Argaty?" The cold question immediately set Louisa's teeth on edge.

"Our wagon broke an axle, and my driver was hurt. I decided to ride for help, but lightning made my horse bolt. He threw me and I was knocked unconscious for some time."

"And yet you somehow managed to ride in the direction of Argaty."

Anger bubbled up inside Louisa at the woman's unpleasant manner and insinuation. No wonder her aunt didn't care for the dowager countess. Lady Argaty wasn't just unpleasant, she was malicious as well. Louisa almost bit through her tongue as she struggled to hold temper in check.

"If by *managing*, you mean I failed to control a frightened animal and as a result was knocked unconscious when I landed on the ground then you would be correct," Louisa said through clenched teeth, barely succeeding in keeping her response polite.

She knew Sebastian would commend her restraint, especially when what she really wanted to do was to give the woman a scathing response to her blatant and absurd accusation. The implication that she'd purposefully chosen to ride Tulipan in the direction of Argaty was preposterous, particularly when she'd had no idea where the Keep was.

"You are either very brave or very foolish, Mrs. Morehouse, *if* you really *are* a widow." The woman's contemptuous words made Louisa stare at the woman with indignant astonishment before she slowly rose to her feet.

"I lost my husband in a fire almost three years ago, my lady. That you suggest otherwise is not only rude, but cruel."

Louisa's fierce words were icy with disklike, and her chin tilted upward in defiance, she glared back at the woman. If she'd expected even a small measure of respect for not being intimidated, Louisa was wrong. The woman's open look of contempt only seemed to deepen. Without apologizing for her insult, the dowager countess turned to the woman standing beside Louisa.

"I shall leave Mrs...Morehouse in your capable hands, Mrs. Selkirk." The woman's pause was another deliberate insult, and Louisa drew in a sharp breath of anger.

The only reason she failed to reply with a scornful retort was because she was too amazed at the woman's blatant dislike and disdain. If Sebastian were here, even *he* would have trouble being polite to this woman. Deep inside Louisa wished her eldest brother was here. Although she was quite capable of standing up for herself, Sebastian had the ability to condemn and silence someone with just a look.

Louisa had absolute faith in the Earl of Melton's ability to make the dowager countess wilt beneath his withering gaze. Regrettably, her brother's talent was one she'd never mastered. With the bitter taste of outrage still in her mouth, Louisa watched the dowager countess turn and walk toward the door. The woman had gone only a few steps when she looked over her shoulder at Mrs. Selkirk.

"And see to it she has some suitable nightwear as it appears she'll be with us for at least one more night. I understand from my sister that the woman wore no clothes while my son cared for her."

As the woman walked out of the room, Louisa was unable to offer any form of retort as she stared after the obnoxious woman while a wave of mortification rolled over her. Dear God, the Earl of Argaty had been her nursemaid, and she'd been naked while he cared for her. A tremor shot through her, and the moment she swayed on her feet, Mrs. Selkirk quickly wrapped an arm around her waist. The plump woman gently encouraged Louisa to sink down onto the bed.

"There now, lass. Don't ye be minding the countess and her cruel words. She only has ice where her heart is supposed to be, that one does," Mrs. Selkirk muttered with disgust. "Come now, why don't ye get back into bed. Maggie brought a nightgown for ye."

"No," Louisa said firmly. "I need to know that my driver is all right. Someone needs to go to Doune Road and see to his care. He's been out there all night."

"All night, lass?" Mrs. Selkirk eyes widened. "But his lordship brought ye tae Argaty two nights ago. The burns were too high to cross, and we couldn't fetch the doctor from Dunblane. The earl learned how tae treat fevers while he was in the East fighting the savages. The mon barely slept trying to make ye well."

"Two days?" Louisa gasped as she stared up at the

woman in horror. "Oh dear God. If no one found the wagon or Fergus...he could be dead."

"I doubt that, dearie. A little rain never hurt a Scotsman. I'm sure the mon will be all right." Mrs. Selkirk patted her hand in a comforting gesture. "Here now, eat your porridge, and I'll go find McCallum to send someone out tae look for your driver."

With one last pat of Louisa's hand, the woman hurried from the room. Louisa watched the door close behind the woman then turned toward the breakfast tray. The thought of food made her nausea return, and she slowly stood up to unsteadily make her way toward a nearby chair.

As she sank down into the cushions, she sighed with relief. She probably should have crawled back under the covers, but she was already dressed. Tucked under the covers would only make her restless, even if she were still feeling ill. She had always been a terrible patient. A point all her siblings, and even Devin, had stressed on the rare occasions she'd been unwell.

Eyes closed, she knew how frantic her family must be at the moment. They would be reacting the same way all of them had when Percy had gone missing just a few months after the fire. When she hadn't arrived at Callendar Abbey, she knew either Alfred or Mrs. Campbell would have found a way to begin a search. The family retainers would have sent a telegram to London the moment she couldn't be found.

The entire family would be in a state of panic at her disappearance. The fire had made everyone deeply aware of how short life was. She needed to send a note to the abbey telling everyone where she was and that she was safe. A soft sound made her jerk her head toward a darkened corner of the room.

"Who's there? Show yourself this minute," she snapped more out of frustration than fear.

Louisa was certain there were plenty of dead souls

roaming the earl's home, but she was more than a match for any ghost at the moment given her level of anger at her situation and the dowager's antipathy. At her command, a young boy stepped into the dim light provided by the fire. Louisa drew in a sharp breath. The child from her dreams.

For a moment they simply stared at each other in silence, and she wondered if the boy was a spirit before she saw his chest move as he drew in a breath. He appeared to be the same age as Charlie, but he had a serious air about him that was unnatural for one so young. A shock of dark red hair with brownish undertones highlighted his pale face.

Tall and slenderly built, she could see his blue eyes were bright and steady as he studied her. But it was his solemn manner that troubled her the most. She was so accustomed to her sons' cheerful smiles and the happy sounds of children playing whenever she was at Melton House. This boy appeared to possess none of those qualities.

"I'm sorry, miss. I didn't mean to alarm you." The boy walked forward to lightly touch her hand. "I came to see how you are feeling."

"I'm feeling much better, thank you…" She paused and arched and eyebrow in a silent demand for his name.

"Ross Colquhoun, miss."

"And I'm Mrs. Morehouse," she said with a smile. "Well, Ross Colquhoun, are you aware that it's quite inappropriate to enter a woman's bedroom without permission?"

"Yes, ma'am." An uneasy look crossed his features. "Father would not be happy with me."

The dismay in his voice made Louisa wince at having teased the child. Only a tyrant could make a child fear reprisal. She'd seen it so often whenever a child was brought into White Willow House. The Rockwood-sponsored orphanage saw far too many children terrified of abusive fathers passing through its doors. Louisa immediately caught his hand in hers and squeezed it gently.

"Well, unless you decide to tell him, I'm not sure how he will find out. I would *never* admit to having a man in my bedroom. It would be scandalous." Louisa smiled mischievously at the boy and tilted her head toward him in a conspiratorial manner. The boy rewarded her with a soft laugh.

"I won't tell him, Mrs. Morehouse."

"Good, I have acted quite scandalously far too often in my life, and I'm afraid my family wouldn't be happy with me if I were to create new scuttlebutt." At her reply, the boy chuckled again and Louisa smiled. "That's better. If you scowl so much your face is apt to freeze in that position."

"Does this mean you will stay?"

"Stay?" She frowned as she eyed Ross in puzzlement.

"Aren't you the new governess my father was supposed to send for from London?"

The last few words of the boy's question faded away as the *an dara sealladh* swept over Louisa. The darkness fell down around her, and it pulsated with fear, pain, and secrets that seemed to rip the fabric of the space surrounding her. Stark and savage, the emotions twisted their way around her as if the roots of a tree were grasping at her, pulling her down into the earth.

The atmosphere changed in a split second as the darkness retreated and she found herself in a dimly lit room. Somewhere close by, she sensed a familiar mix of emotions. The man. He was here. Suddenly the one-eyed beast with its hideous, steel fingers materialized in front of her. The instant she recoiled, the beast grew still. Anger charged the air between them, but beneath that anger was a deep anguish.

The beast turned away from her, and his body slowly took on the form of a man. Like a ghost materializing out of the ether, Ross appeared next to the man. The child's deep sadness as he looked up at the beast was heartbreaking. In a hesitant movement, the man reached out to the boy then abruptly dropped his hand and walked away. From out of the darkness another figure took shape.

As the dowager countess appeared, she eyed the child with vicious contempt, and the child shrank away from her. The dark emotions became a crushing weight. They grew in density until the air contained nothing but malevolence. The intensity of it terrified her, and she whirled around trying to escape. Behind her the ominous sound of stone grinding against stone filled the air. Her heart pounded with the intense fear engulfing her. The soft glow of a light broke through the darkness, and Caleb walked toward her. A tender smile curving his mouth, he kissed her cheek.

"Don't walk away from your destiny, Louisa. They need you. *He* needs you."

Caleb began to fade into the darkness, and she reached out to stop him. Silently she pleaded with him not to leave her. Once more she was left alone in the darkness. Another brighter light appeared, and from a distance she heard the frantic voice of a child.

"Mrs. Morehouse. Mrs. Morehouse."

The darkness receded, and her body jerked as if she'd fallen from a great height to the ground. She blinked several times until Ross's face came into focus. The boy was patting her hand rapidly as intense fear furrowed his brow. Slightly dazed, she straightened in her chair and lifted her hand to rub her forehead. The child's fear made Louisa take his hand and squeeze it in a reassuring manner.

"It's all right, Ross," she murmured. "I simply fainted for a moment. I've had spells like this all my life. I've grown accustomed to them."

"You looked just like old Mrs. Dunmore does when the *an dara sealladh* comes over her." Ross's troubled observation startled Louisa for a moment before she remembered how common it was in Scotland for people to accept the *an dara sealladh* for the gift it was.

"Did I?" She forced a smile to her lips. "Well, I'm quite all right now, so there's nothing to be afraid of. And you really must stop looking like a dour old Scotsman."

Ross offered her a slight smile, but remained silent. There was an air of uncertainty, which made Louisa want to pull him to her and hug him tightly. In an effort to divert his attention away for any further inquiry, she remembered how the child had appeared in her room as if he'd been a ghost.

"How did you get into my room?" The question caused the corner of the boy's mouth to quirk upward and for the first time she saw a mischievous look flicker in his solemn gaze.

"There are hidden passageways that go to different rooms in the house. There are some that even lead outdoors."

The boy quickly walked to the spot where he'd first appeared, and pressed a small place in the coat of arms engraved in the paneling. A second later, a hidden door silently swung outward. Ross looked back at her with a smile of excitement.

"Mrs. Selkirk says Robert the Bruce stayed in this room once. It's why we call it the King's Chamber. He used the hidden corridors to avoid capture by the English."

The child's fascination made Louisa think he might enjoy learning history lessons. It was a subject she had excelled at in her own studies.

"That sounds quite exciting."

"Yes," he said with an enthusiastic nod. "I would have liked to have met the Bruce."

"And *that* would have been extremely dangerous." Louisa shook her head as she smiled. "But there are dangers here too."

"Dangers, ma'am?"

"If Mrs. Selkirk comes back and catches you here, you will not be as lucky as the Bruce. You will cause a huge scandal, and my family will never forgive me."

The amusement that had vanished from Ross's face returned as he grinned at her. For some reason, she was certain it wasn't an emotion he revealed to others very often.

"I'd better go then, ma'am."

"Before you do, I need you to help me to the desk over there. I need to write a note to my family. I'm certain Au...Lady Stewart is wondering why I've not presented myself for my position as her companion." At her words, Ross's demeanor crumbled into deep disappointment.

"So you aren't my governess, ma'am." The despondency in his voice made Louisa long to scoop him up in her arms and hug him close. She was certain it was a display of affection he rarely, if ever, received. As much as she wanted to give him hope, Louisa refused to be the cause of greater despair. Instead, she smiled gently at him.

"I'm sure whoever your governess is, she will be quite lovely." She rose from her chair, and braced herself with one hand on Ross's narrow shoulder as she moved to the desk. When she was seated, she smiled at the boy and nodded toward the hidden door that was still open. "Go on now. You know I cannot afford to be compromised."

"Yes, ma'am." Ross returned her smile then turned and moved toward the secret passage.

As he disappeared into the dark, and the door swung softly closed behind him, Louisa sighed at the way her heart ached for the child. The thought of Ross being the pupil of any woman remotely like her own governess, Mrs. Crimwald, horrified her. The child was already in such desperate need of love. How could she abandon him to the possibility of a harsh governess?

She had no idea what Caleb had meant by her destiny, but he was right about Ross. The child needed her. But Charlie and Wills needed her too. Maybe not as much as Ross, but she loved her sons too much not have them with her. Inside her head, scenario after scenario played out endless possibilities. Her biggest obstacle to overcome was creating a reason for staying here and having the boys with her.

A part of her balked at the thought of bringing Willie and Charlie here. Her visions told her Argaty had seen more of its share of darkness, but she was confident the boys would not be in harm's way. No, the danger she'd felt during the *an dara sealladh* would affect her directly, but she wasn't sure what her vision meant. Louisa bit down on her bottom lip as she contemplated how to attain her goal.

The idea when it came to her was so simple, she almost laughed out loud. Now her only obstacles were her family and the earl. While persuading Sebastian would not be easy, Louisa had no doubt she would succeed in her efforts to convince her oldest brother of her agenda.

It was the earl who was the unknown quantity in her plan. Deep inside she heard Caleb laugh. Her brother had always found it amusing at how easily she could convince others to go along with one of her schemes. Intrigues Sebastian, and later Devin, usually deemed reckless. Caleb's laughter echoed again in her head. The sound reassured her that she would succeed in winning the earl over, if only by sheer persistence. A smile curving her lips, Louisa opened the lid of the secretaire to search for paper and pen.

Chapter 4

Sebastian Rockwood, Earl of Melton, grunted as the small unmarked carriage he was in hit a hole in the muddy road. He opened Louisa's letter and read it over again as he'd been doing since he'd received the note late yesterday. The relief it had brought him had been like a wave tossing him up onto a beach leaving him gasping for breath.

The past two days had been filled with fear and worry as he'd mounted a search for his sister. Mrs. Bruce's telegram had arrived late Sunday morning with word that Fergus had been found late the night before, but Louisa was missing. Everyone might not be in a state of panic at the moment if he'd been alone when he received the telegram.

Unfortunately Constance and Aunt Matilda had been with him in his study when the news had arrived. He'd felt the color draining from his face, and his sister and aunt had immediately insisted on knowing what had happened.

Before the fire, he might not have reacted to the telegram the way he had. But that horrific night at Westbrook had changed the entire family. They viewed life and death with different eyes now. The devastating loss they'd experience had made them value each other and their families in a much deeper way than they ever had before the fire.

If something were to happen to Louisa, it would be another terrible blow to the family, but for him the loss would have been even more devastating than Caleb's death. Louisa had been so young when their parents had died, and in many respects, Sebastian had been both mother and father to her as she grew up. If he were to lose Louisa, it would be no different than if he were to lose Tilly or one of his boys.

He had intended to leave for Callendar Abbey on the first available train, but Aunt Matilda had been adamant in her refusal for him to leave without her. As the telegram had arrived on a Sunday, there were fewer trains running north, and their preparations had delayed their departure until the late afternoon train to Stirling.

The coach made a sharp turn on the road that led to Argaty, and he pulled his pocket watch from his vest to check the time. As he tucked the watch back into place, he smiled as he remembered Helen patting his vest pocket to ensure he'd not forgotten the time piece before she'd kissed him goodbye. The caress had been one of reassurance and comfort as Helen was well aware of his strong feelings where his youngest sister was concerned.

An image of his wife filled his head. As always he realized how fortunate they were to have found each other. All of his siblings had been equally lucky with perhaps the exception of Louisa. Aside from Patience, his youngest sister had experienced far more than the rest of the family. For the past two years, she'd been living not only with Devin's death, but betrayal and guilt. He now understood why she'd preferred the quiet of Callendar Abbey over London.

The devastation Devin's death had inflicted on her had been far worse than anyone had realized. His brother-in-law's secret had made Louisa doubt her husband's love for her. But he knew Louisa too well not to realize there was more to her pain than she'd shared. He had no idea what else troubled his sister, but Sebastian was certain it had to do with the couple's argument the night of the fire. Sebastian grimaced as he considered Devin's behavior.

He was certain his friend had loved Louisa, but perhaps

not in the way she'd deserved. The marriage had appeared to be a happy one, but trust was something every marriage required. For his sister it was critical, and he was certain it was why Louisa was questioning the depth of Devin's feelings for her. The knowledge made him wonder if his friend had ever really understood his wife at all.

Sebastian's stared down at his sister's note again. It had clearly been written in haste as Louisa's handwriting was normally far more elegant and sweeping. Her writing was a reflection of the sometimes dramatic nature that hid beneath her impish streak. She was the only one of his siblings who could charm him into getting her way. Whenever Caleb was witness to her cajoling, he would eye Sebastian in open amusement the moment Sebastian succumbed to her persistence.

The youngest of the Rockwoods, his sister was perhaps the most impulsive of all his siblings. Louisa let her heart lead her in everything she did, and he loved her dearly for it. Unfortunately the trait often ended with Louisa in trouble of some sort, and he was thinking this might be one of those times.

Sebastian stared down at her missive and realized he'd given way to her as always by following her instructions. She'd insisted he come to Argaty as soon as possible in an unmarked carriage, and he was to announce himself as Mr. Rockwood to see his sister, Mrs. Morehouse. The cryptic nature of the note only increased his suspicions that his youngest sister was scheming again. Over the years, it had become an art form where Louisa was concerned.

He pushed the note back into his coat pocket and stared out the window. The rain had stopped shortly before he'd arrived at the abbey, and the burns, while still higher than normal had been fairly easy to cross. As the carriage began to slow, he saw Argaty Keep coming into view. Aunt Matilda had been horrified when she learned Louisa was a guest of the earl while recovering from her night out on the moors.

The Scotswoman had uttered a few choice words about the dowager countess before she'd demanded, quite emphatically, that Sebastian was to bring her niece home immediately. He was convinced Louisa would not be heeding the demand of the Rockwood matriarch. He knew his youngest sister too well. She was up to something, and God only knew what. The carriage rolled to a stop, and a stocky-built man in a dark brown work kilt hurried out to greet the vehicle.

"I've come to see..." Sebastian stumbled over his words slightly as he almost referred to Louisa as Lady Westbrook. "Mrs. Morehouse. I'm her brother, Sebastian Rockwood."

"Aye, sir, she's expecting ye. She's still a mite unsteady on her feet so it will take her a moment to come down to meet ye."

"I've brought a small trunk of clothes for her in the event she's not yet able to travel." Sebastian nodded toward the baggage attached to the back of the carriage.

"Aye, sir. I'll see tae it the lady gets it right away." The man hesitated, and Sebastian raised an eyebrow. "Forgive me sir, but I was wondering how the young man who was injured is doing. I know Mrs. Morehouse was quite worried about him."

"The young man was found by Lady Stewart's staff a few hours after the accident." He suddenly frowned as he realized how Louisa's reckless nature had almost killed her. "If my sister had not been so impulsive she would not be imposing on the earl's hospitality."

"Aye, the lass does have a stubborn streak in her, and she will be relieved tae hear the young man is well."

The Scotsman chuckled, and Sebastian's heart sank. His sister had already caused a stir, not to mention she'd obviously charmed the man in front of him. Who else in the household had she managed to put under her spell? The man nodded toward the house.

"If you would, sir."

With a nod, Sebastian followed the Scotsman into the house and was shown into a large room that doubled as a salon and library. He quietly perused the titles on the shelves as he waited for his sister. The earl, or someone else, had an obvious love for writings of ancient Roman generals and other military greats. Sebastian had just found a small volume of Marcus Aurelius's writings when a small cry of happiness made him turn around to see Louisa hurrying toward him.

"Oh, Sebastian. I'm so happy to see you," she exclaimed as she hugged him tight then looked up at him with a worried frown. "How are the boys? Are they behaving? I'm certain the family is terribly worried. I'm so sorry to have made everyone fear something horrible had happened to me."

As always when she was excited, Louisa didn't allow anyone to answer a question without barreling on to the next. Patiently he waited for her to stop speaking and smiled as her questions died away, and she eyed him with a look that demanded his immediate answer.

"I'm delighted *and* relieved to see you as well. And yes, everyone has been quite worried about you," he said as he kissed her forehead. "In fact, I had to put my foot down when the lot of them demanded to come to Callendar Abbey with Aunt Matilda and me. Although I'm certain they began to make preparations to come north, the moment they received my telegram stating you had been found safe, but a bit under the weather."

"Oh no, they mustn't." Louisa's crestfallen expression made Sebastian sighed with resignation. He'd been correct in his initial assumptions.

"What scheme or plot are you hatching now, Louisa?"

"I do *not* hatch plots," she harrumphed then laughed softly as he eyed her with mocking disbelief. He recognized her lively behavior as one he'd known before the fire. This was the mischievous Louisa of old, and it lightened his heart as she chuckled. "All right, sometimes I do, but you know they're always for a worthy cause."

"Sometimes," he murmured ruefully. "Now then, as you can see, I've followed your instructions to the letter, and I'd like to know what this intrigue is all about?"

With a secretive look, Louisa quickly turned and went to the door to ensure it was closed. As she hurried back to his side, Sebastian saw the sparkle in his sister's hazel eyes, and he suppressed a groan of dismay. The Louisa who'd been missing for so long had returned, and he knew without a doubt he would not like whatever she was about to propose. Despite that fact, Sebastian knew he would give way to her simply to ensure Louisa didn't retreat into the shell she'd lived in for more than two years. He wasn't about to lose her a second time.

"Don't look at me like that," Louisa said with exasperation. "I can't possibly leave Ross here without someone who will treat him kindly."

"You're not thinking clearly, Louisa."

Frustration tugged Sebastian's mouth into a hard line of irritation as he rubbed his forehead. They'd been arguing about her plan to remain at Argaty as Ross Colquhoun's governess for the past fifteen minutes. Louisa knew she was pushing her brother's patience as always, but she was determined to have her way in the matter.

"You have two boys of your own to tend to. You cannot leave them in our care indefinitely. No one in the family would ever object to having the boys with them for whatever length of time you asked of us. We love them as much as our own, but they *need* their mother."

"I don't intend to leave them with the family. I'll have them brought here once the earl agrees to take me on as Ross's governess. The child needs playmates. Charlie and Wills are exactly what Ross needs."

"And what makes you think the earl is going to agree to a woman of title serving as a governess to his son?"

"He doesn't know who I am. No one does. I'm simply Mrs. Morehouse, a widow who was injured on my way to Callendar Abbey to be a companion for Lady Stewart. A position, I've now lost."

"How and why would you have lost your position so quickly?"

"Lady Stewart sent for you when I didn't arrive at the abbey. When you mentioned the boys, she immediately dismissed me from my post. "

"And that calls into question why you would take on a companion role to begin with when you have two boys."

"I'll say it was because I was unable find a suitable governess's position and needed to support myself and the boys."

"What about Charles's holdings? They can't go unattended for forever."

"I trust you to manage them for him. You know I've never had a head for numbers, even when Aunt Matilda tried to teach me how to manage the abbey's accounts of her tenants and properties." She shrugged her shoulders, which earned her a glare from her brother.

"I think this has to be the most reckless idea you've ever concocted," Sebastian snapped with frustration.

"No, it's not, Sebastian," she said quietly. "Caleb would not have come to me if this wasn't precisely where I'm supposed to be. Even if the *an dara sealladh* hadn't shown me what I need to do, my heart wouldn't have let me walk away. I simply can't."

At the soft conviction in her voice, Sebastian pinched

the bridge of his nose and sucked in a deep breath. A second later, he slowly exhaled with the same note of resignation he always had when he agreed to give way to her. Elated that she'd won him over, Louisa restrained from gloating. Instead, she remained silent as satisfaction spiraled through her. Now she only had to persuade the earl to take her on as Ross's governess.

Chapter 5

wan pushed aside his dinner plate and took a drink of the claret that had been on the supper tray McCallum had brought him earlier. He glanced at the note lying on the table next to the serving platter.

Asadi had delivered it to him a short time ago. It was the fifth one since yesterday afternoon. With a grunt of discomfort, he massaged his forehead in an effort to ease the headache he'd developed from lack of sleep.

McCallum had delivered the woman's third note this morning just as Ewan had been on his way out of the keep. He'd been relieved he'd made arrangements to meet with one of his tenants and was unavailable to meet with Mrs. Morehouse, as McCallum referred to her. Any other time his excuse would have been a lie. But Duncansone was the only tenant Ewan visited on the estate.

McCallum had managed the estate and its properties while he'd been in the Sudan. Upon his return, Ewan had told McCallum he had no interest in changing the order of things. Duncansone was the only exception. Ewan found the old Scotsman, who was going blind, to be a kindred spirit. A fellow soldier, Duncansone had lost his leg while fighting in Burma. He was the only person who understood Ewan's anger and frustration when it came to his injuries.

When Ewan had returned shortly before lunch, a fourth note had been waiting for him. He'd not even bothered to open it. Instead, he'd sent Asadi to tell the woman he was still out on the estate. The thought of being caught out in a lie made Ewan uncomfortable. To ease his conscience, he'd gone to the stables to saddle Lachlan again and ride out onto the moors. The moors were his refuge. It was the one place where he was free of his mother's vitriol.

But his refusal to grant Mrs. Morehouse an audience hadn't stopped her from writing. If anything, she'd become increasingly insistent on speaking with him. With a growl of irritation, Ewan rose quickly to his feet and shoved his chair away from him. He strode to the window and pulled the curtain aside to stare out at the moors. The only thing he saw was the faint reflection of his own image.

The scars on his cheekbone beneath his eye patch made his reflection an ugly sight. Louisa Morehouse had been horrified when she'd seen the beast in all his glory the other night. Even with him wearing the patch or his metal hand covered by his glove, he was certain she would act no differently than when he'd found her on the moors.

It was why he'd been refusing to meet with his guest. He had no wish to frighten her again. Ewan snorted loudly. He was lying to himself, and he knew it. He was avoiding the woman like the plague for a completely different reason. The memory of soft, voluptuous curves had been haunting him since the moment Maggie had helped him get the woman into bed.

He'd been transfixed by her. The few hours of sleep he managed to catch over the past couple of days had been filled with dreams of Louisa Morehouse's soft naked curves. Dreams that had made him ache with the need to explore every inch of her with his mouth before he buried himself inside her. But it was the hours when he was awake that caused him the most difficulty.

He was taunted constantly by the memory of a full, lush breast with its dark pink nipple. Every time the image filled his head his cock would stiffen. The way his body reacted at the mere thought of her emphasized how dangerous being in the woman's company would be. Ewan grunted with aggravation.

It had been months since he'd visited Alana in Stirling. The brothel madam was used to sharing her bed with men who were missing parts of their body. A small whisper slipped through his thoughts taunting him with the fact he wanted to visit a different bed altogether.

Irritated by his obsession with his guest, he turned away from the window and reached for the woman's note. Her handwriting was as lovely and lush as her body. Ewan muttered an oath at his fanciful thinking. With a sharp tug, he pulled the note from the envelope. As he unfolded the missive, he crossed the floor to stand at the hearth where he tilted the letter so the firelight could shine on the woman's words.

Dear Lord Argaty,

I understand your time is quite valuable, but I have a matter I must discuss with you immediately. I assure you the matter is of great importance as it concerns your son. I hope you will send for me at your earliest convenience.

Regards,

Louisa Morehouse

Louisa. The name suited her. Ewan closed his eyes with self-disgust at the thought. He shouldn't give a damn what her first name was, and what the hell could she possibly have to say about Ross? If the lad had been bothering the woman, he'd give the boy a tongue lashing he wouldn't soon forget.

Yesterday the woman's brother had paid a visit to their invalid while Ewan had been at Duncansone's farm. When Ewan had questioned McCallum as to why their guest was still in residence, the Scotsman had reported her brother's visit had exhausted the woman. It had been obvious to McCallum and Mrs. Selkirk the woman was still recovering and would most likely be here for the next two days.

The news meant he needed to spend as much time away from the house as possible. The fact Mrs. Morehouse had already charmed McCallum and Mrs. Selkirk annoyed him almost as much as the idea of her remaining in the house for a few more days.

Ewan shrugged his shoulder slightly to adjust the leather shoulder straps that held his artificial arm in place and allowed him to manipulate the metal fingers. The movement caused the leather to pinch the stub of his arm despite the layer of soft wool he'd used to protect his skin.

He drew in a sharp hiss of air at the unpleasant sensation and looked down at the unnatural metal hand attached to his body. At least the hideous steel fingers were hidden by a black glove at the moment. It made him understand the repugnance he saw on people's faces when he came into view. Even *he* found the metal contraption revolting to look at.

From the day he'd first woken up in the hospital more than a year ago, he'd found his appearance nothing more than that of a maimed beast. The unnatural appendage attached to his arm along with his missing eye and facial scars were daily reminders of the fact. He'd never consider himself a vain man, but he now doubted that belief simply because he'd had all the mirrors in the East Wing and the downstairs rooms removed. He'd even found it necessary to throw a sheet over the mirror in the King's bedroom while he'd been tending to Louisa Morehouse.

The memory of having done so made him resume making plans to avoid his guest. As he was debating where he could disappear to, he recalled McCallum mentioning the mines. Ewan smiled with relief. The Scotsman had been nagging him to visit the southern properties in Cumbernauld and Shotts for almost a year now. This was the perfect opportunity to do so.

He'd leave after breakfast in the morning. Between the

ride and the time he'd have to spend at each mine, he would not be back until well after dinner. That solved the problem of how to avoid the woman tomorrow. The day after, he'd find something else to occupy his time and take him away from Argaty. A quiet knock on the study's door interrupted his thoughts, and he turned to see Asadi enter the room.

"McCallum sent me for your tray, Argaty sahib." The boy eyed him with a questioning look and Ewan nodded toward the tray.

"I'm done." At his reply, the boy moved toward the table. Asadi glanced down at Ewan's tray then turned to him.

"You have eaten little, Argaty sahib."

"Just take the goddamn tray, Asadi," he snarled.

He glared at the boy who remained unfazed by his anger. With a shrug that mimicked McCallum's general reaction to Ewan's ill-tempered moods, the Sudanese boy placed everything on the tray and headed toward the door. As the Asadi pulled it shut behind him, Ewan heard the distinct sound of a female voice just as the lock mechanism clicked. The soft lilt of it confirmed it wasn't his mother or his aunt.

"*Fuck*, not even the saints were persecuted like this," he muttered.

Certain Asadi would usher the woman out of his East Wing sanctuary, Ewan moved toward the shelves of books in the far corner of the room. He'd just pulled a book off the shelf when he heard the study door open.

"I take it you sent the woman on her way, Asadi."

"Actually, he did not, my lord." The soft, feminine voice did not hide the steely note layered beneath it. "Please don't be angry with the boy. I insisted on speaking with you and refused to take no for an answer."

Ewan stiffened in angry surprise, but didn't turn around. The woman had invaded his private refuge, and he didn't know whether to make her terrified of him or simply ignore her presence. He chose to act as if he were alone in the room.

A womanly noise of frustration traveled through the air to his ear, and Ewan released a harsh sigh.

"Speak, Mrs. Morehouse. As you can see, I'm busy."

"I understand I have you to thank for saving my life, and I wanted to express my gratitude."

"I don't need your gratitude."

"I disagree. Mr. McCallum tells me you rode out into the storm to find me and brought me back to Argaty then served…as my nursemaid. I'm in your debt, my lord."

The small catch in Louisa Morehouse's voice made him realize she was most likely remembering how she'd awakened to find herself without clothes. A small devil in him made his mouth tip upward slightly. No doubt the woman wouldn't be happy to learn how much he'd enjoyed seeing her beautiful, naked curves. Perhaps embarrassing her was the best way to rid himself of the woman. His mouth curved upward a bit more.

"You aren't in my debt. I was paid quite handsomely when I undressed you."

The sound of a sharply inhaled breath made his mouth curve upward even more. Now the woman would surely leave him to his solitude. He silenced the protests in the far reaches of his brain. When he didn't hear her walking out of the room, he closed his eyes in exasperation.

"You've said your piece, Mrs. Morehouse. Now if you don't mind, I trust you can find the door."

The silence stretched out for a long moment as he waited. When he didn't hear the door open and close, his jaw hardened with anger. Louisa Morehouse was quickly becoming one of his least favorite people. Not about to acknowledge she hadn't left the room, Ewan turned the page of the book he held in his artificial hand.

Silently, he perused the text waiting for the woman to leave him alone in his quiet solitude. A soft tapping suddenly penetrated the air, and he cocked his head as he tried to identify the sound. It took only a brief moment to associate the noise with that of a woman's shoe repeatedly abusing the floor in irritation. Other than the tilt of his head, Ewan didn't react to the sound. Instead, he continued to stare down at a page of words that had suddenly become nothing more than an incoherent mix of letters.

"It wasn't just my desire to express my appreciation for you saving my life, my lord," Louisa said in a crisp tone. "I wanted to speak with you about your son as well."

The mention of the boy caused Ewan to frown in puzzlement while he ignored the fact that he'd thought of her as Louisa and not Mrs. Morehouse. The only time he'd been aware Ross had been in the woman's company was when she'd been ill. He'd given the lad strict instructions to not bother her again. The thought that the boy had disobeyed him angered Ewan.

"If Ross has been troubling you, inform McCallum about it, and he'll see to it the boy won't trouble you anymore."

"Your son hasn't been any trouble at all. In fact, I find him far too quiet and withdrawn for a boy his age."

Despite the firm rejection of Ross being a nuisance, he heard the motherly note of concern in her voice. It was a gentle empathy his mother had never expressed when he'd been a boy, and he'd certainly never heard the dowager countess speak of Ross in such a manner. His aunt and Mrs. Selkirk had always been the ones to offer Ewan motherly concern when he'd been a boy, and he was certain the two women did the same for Ross.

Ewan frowned as he mulled over Louisa's description of the child. Now that someone had pointed it out to him, it was an accurate portrayal of the boy. Perhaps he'd been wrong to keep Ross here. The boy might have been better off at school. A sudden flashback to his days at Charterhouse produced a tactile sensation of antipathy. Not even on Ross would he inflict such a punishment.

"The boy is not a concern of yours...Mrs. Morehouse." The muscles around his eye tugged sharply at an empty eye socket as he barely managed to avoid addressing her as Louisa.

"Perhaps not, but I wish to make it my concern since you seem to be oblivious to the fact that the child needs a governess."

Startled by her condemnation, Ewan almost spun around to confront her before he stopped himself. Louisa Morehouse was becoming an irritating thorn in his side. He turned another page in the book ensuring the sound was as audible as possible.

"And what makes you an expert on what the child needs or doesn't need?"

"If you'd spend time with him, you wouldn't have to answer that question," Louisa snapped.

The woman's impertinence made Ewan close his book in a fierce movement. The violence of the act caused a sharp crack of sound to linger in the room. There was a soft intake of air behind him, and he knew he'd startled perhaps even alarmed her. Satisfaction pounded its way through his limbs at the knowledge. He was accustomed to his mother's criticism, but he refused to be chastised by a stranger no matter how lovely she was.

He uttered an inaudible curse word as he slowly turned around. Self-disgust crashed through him the instant he experienced gratitude that the fireplace was the only source of light in the room. That he even cared about the woman's reaction to his physical appearance emphasized the strength of his awareness for Louisa Morehouse. An awareness he didn't want to feel.

Louisa stood close to the hearth, and the firelight accentuated one of the reasons why he'd done his best to avoid her. As he studied her, the memory of a wet chemise clinging to her skin made his mouth go dry. Infuriated by the direction of his thoughts, Ewan narrowed his one eye at her.

"I don't need a Sassenach to tell me how to raise the boy," he said coldly.

"My mother was Scottish, so you'll have to think of another way to insult me." The condescension in her response only added fuel to his growing anger.

"Then I shall rephrase my words by saying, I don't need a woman telling me how to raise Ross."

"That's where you're wrong. In fact, there's a great deal I can tell you—"

"*Enough*," he snarled as he forced himself to remain in the shadows when what he really wanted to do was silence her in a much different way. He shoved the disturbing thought back into a compartment labeled *don't touch*. "You're a guest in my house, Louisa Morehouse, and I'll thank you to remember that."

"The boy needs a governess," she continued as if she'd not heard a word he'd said. In the back of his head, he noted her stubbornness rivaled McCallum's, only she wasn't as subtle as the old retainer was. "And as I understand from McCallum, each of the last two governesses the child had left in less than a month of arriving at Argaty."

Ewan slammed his book down onto the shelf closest to him as he continued to avoid the firelight. The action rewarded him with the sight of her jumping slightly from the harsh sound. Suddenly she straightened to her full height, which wasn't much less than his, and her chin tipped upward at a defiant angle.

It was a clear display of rebellion, and he couldn't help admiring her for not allowing him to intimidate her. Despite the stubborn set of her mouth, it didn't hide the fullness of her lips. Would her mouth taste as fiery and passionate as she looked? A bolt of desire lashed through him and made his muscles harden like the grand oak on the moor that stood not far from where Ewan had found her. He remained frozen in place afraid he might actually try to answer the question.

"You seem to have made quite a few inquiries about my household." Ewan grounded out between his teeth. He wasn't sure if his anger was directed more at her than himself.

"My questions have only been to inquire about Ross's well-being, and *when* I'd be granted permission to meet with the *exalted* Earl of Argaty." She glared in his direction in obvious disdain for him and his title.

"Now that you've bullied your way into my *exalted* presence, you can explain what your interest in the boy has to do with you, other than a reason to disturb my peace."

As if she'd suddenly realized he'd yet to refer to Ross as his son, her eyes narrowed slightly. In the firelight he saw puzzlement knit her brow for a moment before it was replaced by a confident determination.

"I wish you to take me on as your son's governess."

Stunned by her statement, Ewan stared at her in amazement. He wasn't sure why he was so surprised, but he was. The next thought was how she was unlike the past few governesses who'd accepted the position and left soon afterward. Those women had been weak and easily intimidated the few times he'd been in their presence. Despite being a clear and present danger to his senses, Louisa Morehouse might actually be good for Ross. Floored at the direction of his thoughts, he released a loud, disparaging snort.

"What in the name of all the saints makes you qualified for such a position? Your manner is more that of a termagant than a governess. As McCallum tells it, you're supposed to be old Lady Stewart's companion."

Ewan's words caused her lovely mouth to thin with anger before her outrage vanished beneath a stoic expression. It disappointed him to see her fiery spirit vanish. What he wouldn't give to see that fire ignite in his bed. Another wave of self-disgust lashed out at him for allowing himself to be moved by the woman.

"My brother has informed me that Lady Stewart has rescinded her offer to take me on as her companion." Her reply made him frown in surprise and with renewed concern for her welfare.

"Why would the daft woman do such a thing?"

"Because when my brother informed her as to why I'd failed to arrive at the abbey, Lady Stewart learned I have two boys." For the first time he heard a note of hesitation in her voice. "Her ladyship had no wish to take on a companion who had children."

"Am I to understand you didn't tell the woman you had sons?"

"I needed employment, and I thought...I thought it would be best to ask Lady Stewart's forgiveness *after* the fact came to light rather than asking for her permission beforehand."

"And if I were to agree to your proposition, why have you decided to ask permission as opposed to asking *my* forgiveness *after* the fact?"

"Because my boys are Ross's age. Your son needs children his own age to play with, my sons need their mother, you need a governess, and I must have employment." She drew in a deep breath. "We *need* each other."

"*I* don't have need of anyone," he snapped.

"Yes, *you do*. McCallum said you'd not yet inquired as to a replacement for your last governess, and I'm more than capable of fulfilling that role. I've taught my own children and can do the same for your son."

The logic of her proposal wasn't lost on Ewan. It was true Ross would benefit from the presence of other children, and the boy did need a governess. The only real obstacle was the way Louisa Morehouse made him feel. Ewan immediately brushed the thought aside.

McCallum could easily act as a buffer between them. The East Wing would be off limits to her, just as it was to the rest of the household. He would never have to see the woman. He sucked in a quick breath. Christ Almighty. Was he actually making excuses as to why he should agree to her plan? Deep in the back of his head, a shout of laughter made him close his eyes for a moment. It was enough to make Ewan reject the idea with a shake of his head.

"No. I don't think you'd be suitable as a governess."

"Give me one good reason why not?" she demanded imperiously. Unaccustomed to anyone taking exception to his decisions, Ewan's muscles tightened even further at the way she continued to challenge him.

"Do *not* question my decisions in my own house," he snarled as he strode out of the shadows to stand over her.

She immediately retreated from him, her hazel eyes wide with alarm. Her reaction was everything he'd expected, but it was his disappointment at her retreat that bothered him the most. In the far reaches of his mind, her defiance earlier had made him think she might not view him as the beast so many others did. To his surprise, she relaxed slightly before her mouth thinned with anger.

A split-second later, Louisa reversed her retreat and defiantly closed the distance between them. It was as if a caber had landed on his chest. *Christ Jesus*, he'd never seen anyone so fearless when they were on the receiving end of his anger. And he was finding his anger difficult to maintain as he breathed in the sweet scent of her. His gaze slowly slid downward as he remembered the lush curves hidden beneath her dress. The memory increased his longing to explore her mouth, and he ached to for one more look at her sweetly curved body, which was made for a man to indulge himself in.

When he'd finished his leisurely scrutinization, his eyes met hers again. Other than her cheeks were flooded with a rosy pink hue, her stoic manner revealed nothing of her thoughts. The devil in him made him lean forward until he could feel the warm heat of her breath on his skin. The smell of mint filled his nostrils, and it made him ache to taste the cool fire of her mouth.

The instant she wet her lips with the tip of her tongue, Ewan's jaw tightened until the muscles ached. God help him, he was a fool to even think about allowing her to remain at Argaty Keep. Ewan straightened upright and glared at her, determined to squelch the increasingly powerful urge to tug her into his arms and kiss her.

"For a chattering magpie who entered my study uninvited, your tongue seems to have failed you, Louisa Morehouse," he bit out in an icy voice before he turned away from her to stalk toward the bookcase.

Without thinking, Ewan reached for the book he'd left on the shelf with his artificial hand. The weight and size of the book proved too cumbersome for the device. As the tome slipped out of his gloved hand and the device pinched the stump of his arm, he uttered an oath of disgust. Angered by his clumsiness, and that Louisa had been a witness to it, he lunged downward to retrieve the book.

His fingers missed the book as his only eye miscalculated the distance. A second later, a feminine hand grasped the leather-bound volume and handed it to him. With a growl, he snatched the book from her with his good hand.

"It's time you left, madam," he said in a harsh tone as he opened the book to stare down at the page.

"You've still not answered the question I put to you *before* you charged at me like a mad bull." Her fierce words startled him, but he quickly suppressed his surprise.

"A mad bull?" he bit out between clenched teeth as he jerked his head and sent a frosty glare in her direction.

"Yes. An angry mad bull. If this is how you *always* act it

certainly explains why everyone walks around on eggshells in this house." Clearly exasperated, she didn't flinch beneath his scowl. Instead, she planted her hands on her hips and glared at him haughtily. "If you won't give me a reason for saying no to my proposition so quickly, would you at least think about it overnight rather than rejecting it in haste?"

The revulsion he'd expected to see in her eyes wasn't there. Just as startling was her complete lack of horror and fear. Perplexed by her manner, the anger that had consumed him only a short moment ago ebbed back into the darkness of his soul. He closed his eye for a moment. Louisa Morehouse was a force to be reckoned with, and he wasn't sure he had the wherewithal to withstand her persistent drive to get her way.

"Did you drive your man to drink, Mrs. Morehouse?" he said with an annoyed shake of his head.

At his question, the color drained from her cheeks until they were the same ghostly pallor they'd been when he'd found her on the moors. She had the look of a woman haunted not with grief, but with guilt. Regret slammed into Ewan. His words had inflicted far more damage than he'd expected, and he didn't like how the knowledge of that made him feel.

She swayed slightly on her feet, and Ewan instinctively reached out to steady her. Electricity jolted its way through his body as she braced herself against his chest. The subtle scent of roses filled his nostrils, and he savored the smell as he breathed in her fragrance. It had been a long time since he'd enjoyed the smell of a woman.

Head bowed she didn't move for a moment then dragged in a deep breath and raised her head. The fire he'd witnessed in her only seconds before had been extinguished and replaced by an icy façade. He grimaced at how his words had caused such a drastic change her, and regret slammed into him again. Ewan began to stretch out his hand to her before he dropped it feeling awkward and uncertain as to how to apologize.

"I dinnae mean to cause you pain, lass," he said quietly.

"You didn't." Her voice was devoid of emotion as she stepped back from him. "Forgive me for coming here uninvited."

Still pale, she turned away from him and walked toward the door. In the back of his head, he heard a voice shouting at him. Desperately, he tried to ignore the clarion calls to stop her. The demands were as persistent as Louisa Morehouse had been until the moment he'd caused her to remember something painful.

"Louisa."

Ewan watched her stop and look over her shoulder at him. He frowned at how pale she still was. McCallum had been right. She'd not fully recovered from her ordeal. The fact he'd been so harsh with her made his jaw tighten in remorse.

"I shall consider your proposal and give you my answer in the morning," he said quietly.

An odd expression flashed across her features before she nodded and left the study. Alone once more, Ewan violently slammed his book down on the bookshelf. The room echoed with the loud, abrasive crack of leather against wood.

Why was he even thinking about granting Louisa Morehouse the position of governess? It was a bad idea. The woman would be a distraction. Would be? A snort escaped him. She already was. In fact, she was the most distracting creature he'd ever met. The woman had stormed his study like a general leading a charge. And she'd stood up to him in a way few people ever did.

Not even McCallum had ever confronted him so directly. The Scotsman persuaded or suggested actions to take, but nothing more. Louisa Morehouse on the other hand had been fearless. He went rigid as he remembered how he'd called her by her given name to stop her from leaving the room. It was a warning sign he needed to say no to her proposition.

Wearily, Ewan rubbed his forehead at the sudden pounding assaulting his head. The only way to make his headache go away was to sleep. With a quiet exhaled breath of frustration, he strode out of the study and headed toward his room. He'd make his decision in the morning. In the back of his head, a voice taunted him for being a dolt as it laughed and informed him that he'd already decided. Irritated by the mocking laughter filling his head, he ignored the sound and what his decision might cost him.

Chapter 6

Louisa reviewed a math problem Ross had completed as the child stood in front of the desk McCallum had found for her. Finn and Brown had brought it to the schoolroom the day Ewan had sent a note agreeing to employ her as Ross's governess. She lifted her head and smiled at the boy.

"Well done, Ross. This is excellent work." At her comment, the child smiled as if she'd given him the keys to a candy shop.

"Thank you, ma'am."

The sound of a carriage coming up the drive made her rise to her feet and cross the floor to look out the window. Gray clouds filled the sky casting their shadow across the moor that stretched out to the horizon. It was well past three, and she'd been waiting with growing anticipation for the carriage now rolling up in front of the house. A wave of happiness swept through her. The boys had arrived. She turned around to see Ross studying her with uncertainty. With another smile, she moved to where he was standing and stretched out her hand to him.

"Come, I want you to meet Wills and Charlie. I think you'll like them very much." When he hesitated, she bent over until they were eye level. "Tell me what's troubling you, Ross."

"It's nothing, ma'am." As he bowed his head, Louisa

caught sight of his shuttered expression, and she frowned in puzzlement.

"Although we've not known each other very long, Ross, I don't think you're being honest with me."

Her fingers gently forced the child's chin up until she could see the worry darkening his blue eyes. Louisa's maternal instincts made her want to tug the boy into her arms in a gesture of reassurance. She resisted the impulse, and instead, she caught the child's hands in hers.

"Won't you tell me what's wrong?"

"What if they don't like me, ma'am," the child blurted out. For a moment, she stared at him in confusion before she realized he was referring to Wills and Charlie. She gently squeezed his hands and steadily met his gaze.

"Do you believe *I* like you, Ross?

"Yes, Mrs. Morehouse."

"Then if I like you, it stands to reason my boys will like you too." At her reassurance, Ross frowned as he contemplated her words. With a slow nod of his head, he eyed her somberly.

"If they don't like me, does that mean you'll leave?" The question tugged at Louisa's heart, and this time she did pull the child close.

"I have no intention of leaving Argaty Keep any time soon."

When she released him, the child's obvious relief angered her. She wanted to storm the dark shadows of the earl's study to rage at him for the lack of attention he gave his son. For the past several days, as they'd waited for the arrival of Wills and Charlie, she'd spent most of her waking hours with Ross. The child was desperate for affection, and it was reprehensible of the earl not to show at least some interest in the boy, if not love.

Not even his grandmother, the dowager countess, wanted anything to do with the child. When the earl had agreed to let her be Ross's governess, the woman had summoned her to her rooms to express her displeasure that Louisa was staying. The only member of his family who ever had a kind word or display of affection for Ross was the countess's sister, Wallis. Louisa straightened and tousled Ross's hair.

"Come along now. Let me introduce you to my sons."

Hope shining in his blue eyes, Ross smiled up at her as they left the schoolroom hand in hand and went downstairs. McCallum had just opened the front door as Louisa and Ross reached the main foyer. The sound of her sons' excited chatter made her smile as she pulled Ross toward the doorway. A split-second later, Wills and Charlie walked into the hall. At the sight of her, both boys raced toward her with cries of excitement. Arms wrapped around each child, she welcomed them with kisses.

"Did you behave for Uncle Sebastian?"

"Of course we did, Mama," Charlie said as he rolled his eyes.

"Who's that?" Wills poked his head past her skirts and pointed to Ross. With a smile, Louisa gestured for Ross to come forward.

"This is Ross Colquhoun. His father is the Earl of Argaty, and you'll have your lessons with him."

"Hello, I'm Charlie."

Louisa wanted to hug her eldest son as he stepped forward and offered his hand to Ross. The moment the boys shook hands, she saw a hesitant look of happiness lighten Ross's countenance. A movement out of the corner of her eye made Louisa turn to greet her brother with a hug. His hands on her arms, Sebastian's fingers tipped her chin upward and studied her for a brief moment then smiled.

"You look well, much better than the last time I saw you."

"I'm fully recovered," she said with a smile.

"News the rest of the family will be relieved to hear."

"Thank you for bringing the boys. Ross has no children of his own age here, and I know he'll benefit from their company greatly." Louisa looked over her shoulder at her new charge. The only person in the house remotely close to Ross's age was Asadi, and Mrs. Selkirk had said the young man was at least five years older than the child. Careful to keep her voice low, she glanced about them before she met Sebastian's quizzical look. "You remembered to speak with Charlie and Wills?"

"I did. Although I'm not sure about the reliability of your youngest when it comes to secrets as he is not unlike his mother in that regard," Sebastian murmured with amused irony. "Charlie on the other hand seemed completely nonplused about the entire matter. Either Jamie spoke with him or he's inherited more than one of the Rockwood family traits."

Louisa glanced over her shoulder once more to look at her sons chattering away with Ross. She wasn't sure how to take her brother's observation about her oldest. There were moments when Charlie would say something that made her wonder if he possessed the *an dara sealladh* and simply didn't want to discuss it. She looked back at Sebastian and shook her head.

"He's not said anything to me, but I'll speak with both of them when we're unpacking their things." The sight of McCallum and Finn bringing three trunks into the house made her frown.

"I don't remember the boys having so many clothes."

"Two of them are for you. I thought you would need them."

"*Oh no*, you must take at least one of them back," she exclaimed softly. "The earl's aunt commented the other day on the large array of quality gowns you brought me on your first visit." Louisa bit down on her lower lip as she remembered stumbling through a reply to Wallis MacCullaich's curiosity. "I'm supposed to be in need of employment."

Sebastian arched his brow at her as he eyed her with skepticism. Under any other circumstances he would most likely have teased her about the money she spent on clothes. Instead, he grimaced slightly.

"Can we expect you for Christmas?" Sebastian's question didn't surprise her, and with an apologetic sigh, she shook head.

"Ross told me he's never seen a Christmas tree before, and I thought I'd make the day special for him." The moment her brother's brow furrowed with disappointment, Louisa touched his arm in a placating gesture. "I'm doing the right thing Sebastian. Please trust me."

"Patience and Constance *did* warn me you might not be with us for the holiday," Sebastian said wryly as his mouth twisted into a half-smile, half-grimace. "It will not be the same without you and the boys at the—house."

"Would you like me to ask Mrs. Selkirk to make some tea before you go? While it's not my home, I know she won't mind."

"No. I told Helen I would meet her and the children at the train station. The three of them can be a handful when traveling, and I—"

"Traveling from where?"

Wallis MacCullaich's soft voice drifted into the main hall as the woman emerged from the hallway leading to the back of the keep. Startled, Louisa quickly turned toward the woman. Dear heavens, what had Wallis overheard? Her brain frantically reviewed the brief exchange between her and Sebastian. Had they said anything the woman might find suspicious?

"Not so much where, ma'am, but how," Sebastian said with a conciliatory smile. Wallis eyed him with curiosity then looked at Louisa in the silent expectation of an introduction.

"If I may Miss MacCullaich, this is my oldest brother, Sebastian Rockwood."

"Welcome, Mr. Rockwood. I hope your travels aren't too much of a tribulation." There was an inquisitive gleam in the woman's eyes as she studied Sebastian intently.

"My wife and I have three children, Miss MacCullaich." Amusement relaxed her brother's features as his lips quirked upward in a slight smile. "Traveling is always an adventure with our offspring, yet I still find traveling immensely pleasurable where my family is concerned."

"Where are you travelling to, Mr. Rockwood?"

The woman's persistent line of questioning seemed innocent, but Wallis's intense curiosity caused Louisa's muscles to tighten with tension. Despite Wallis's good-hearted nature, Louisa knew the dowager countess would expect a full report from her sister. The two women had an odd relationship despite being sisters.

Ewan's mother treated her sister as coldly as she did everyone else, perhaps even more so. For whatever reason, Wallis never protested, and Louisa wondered if the woman was paying penance for some past transgression. Now as she stared at Wallis in surprise, Sebastian shook his head, his cordial expression not changing even for a split instant.

"My aunt lives close to Edinburgh, and we're to spend the holiday with her. I came north early to bring the boys to Louisa."

The disingenuous reply forced Louisa to bite down on the inside of her cheek to keep from smiling at her brother's artful response. It was at least a two-hour trip from Callendar Abbey to Edinburgh.

"Oh, that sounds lovely." Warmth and something that could only be described as relief brightened Wallis's smile. She turned back to Louisa. "Will you and your children be joining your brother's family?"

"I thought the boys and I would spend the holiday here instead. As I was just telling my brother, Ross told me he's never seen a Christmas tree, and I—"

"Oh dear, we don't celebrate Christmas. Elspeth has never liked the holiday ever since—" Wallis stopped abruptly and paled before continuing. "I'm surprised Ewan hasn't mentioned this to his mother or me."

"Actually, I've not discussed the matter with Lord Argaty yet."

"What hasn't been discussed with me?"

The brusque question made Louisa turn sharply toward the man walking through the front door. The earl was a towering figure beneath the front hall's high ceiling, and Louisa's heart skipped a beat at the sight of him. All the other times she'd been in his company, it had been in the shadows of his study.

He'd been an imposing figure then, but today he exemplified the image of a man born to lead, even in spite of his injuries. She was certain anyone crossing him would regret doing so. A dark brown jacket emphasized the muscular breadth of his shoulders, while below the dark blue and green tartan of his kilt were sleek, well-toned, calves.

In the shadows of his study, his hair had looked like raven's feathers, but in the light of day, she realized it was actually a dark sable color. It fell casually around his face and softened his rugged, battle-scarred features. The black leather gloves he wore hid the mechanical fingers that replaced his missing hand, while his eye patch seemed to make his blue-gray gaze all the more piercing.

He was magnificent.

The thought made her draw in a sharp breath of dismay. Dear lord, what on earth had made such a description pop up in her head. Almost as if he could read her mind, the earl arched his eyebrow at her, and she could feel her cheeks growing hot. Something close to mocking amusement darkened his eye color, and this time her cheeks burned even hotter. Eager to divert his attention away from her, she turned toward Sebastian.

"Sebastian, this is Ewan Colquhoun, the Earl of Argaty. My lord, my brother, Sebastian Rockwood." Her brother glanced downward at the insignia on Ewan's belt, and his expression somber, Sebastian stepped forward with his hand outstretched.

"I'm honored to shake the hand of a member of the Black Watch. It's a fine and noble regiment."

Louisa stiffened slightly at her brother's quiet words. McCallum had told her the earl had served in the middle east for almost ten years, but had never mentioned the Black Watch. The regiment was legendary for its bravery and fighting skills in every battle they'd fought for more than a century. The respect and sincerity in her brother's greeting was in direct contrast to the stony, unreadable mask Ewan had assumed the moment Sebastian had extended his hand. The earl stared at Sebastian's outstretched hand for several seconds before he gripped her brother's hand in a firm handshake.

"Mr. Rockwood." Ewan bobbed his head in a brusque greeting. His hard, angular features still unreadable, he turned toward her. "There's a matter you wish to discuss with—"

"She wants to celebrate Christmas, Ewan," his aunt exclaimed with dismay.

Louisa glanced at the woman for a brief moment then turned toward her employer. Irritation made the earl's mouth thin with disapproval. It sent a small chill of misgiving streaking down her spine. She should have spoken to him about the holiday the other day when she'd had his attention. He didn't look pleased about this new development at all.

"My sister, like most of my siblings, has a habit of asking forgiveness rather than permission, my lord." The laughter in his voice made Louisa frown at Sebastian with annoyance, but he wasn't fazed in the least by her glare. "Now, if you'll forgive me, I must be off."

Startled, Louisa stared at her brother in silent horror. He was actually going to leave her to fend with the earl's displeasure without support. With an unremorseful smile, Sebastian's dark brown eyes held more than a twinkle of amusement. It was obvious her brother believed she was about to regret not asking permission first.

Sebastian gave her a quick hug and kissed her cheek before saying his goodbyes to the boys. In what seemed like the blink of an eye, her brother had disappeared through the front door. A slight tremor rippled through her as she faced the earl's disapproval alone, and his dark frown was a clear indicator the man was unhappy with her. Unwilling to argue with him in front of his aunt, Louisa quickly turned toward the boys in preparation to retreat. At that precise moment, Wills charged forward to stand in front of the earl.

"Are you a pirate?" the boy asked with matter-of-fact curiosity.

Both Louisa and Wallis gasped in horror at the boy's question. Mortified, Louisa took a quick step forward to admonish her son. With a wave of his mechanical hand, Ewan silently ordered her not to move as he focused his attention on Wills. Although his face revealed no emotion, she saw Ewan's mouth twitch slightly. Was the man actual attempting to refrain from smiling?

"No, but I suppose I could be," he said in a voice that held a distinct sound of laughter.

Astonished by the possibility her son's question had amused him, Louisa stared at the earl in bewilderment. Not once had she seen him display such pleasantry and tolerance to his son. The realization sent anger spiraling through her.

What sort of man could be so kind to her son, yet have such a callous disregard for his own child? Ross and Charlie had stepped forward to watch the exchange between the two, and Louisa glanced down at the earl's son. The pain of rejection she saw in Ross's stiff posture only increased her anger.

"Mama wrote to Aunt Patience that you have a mechanical hand." At her son's audacious comment, Ewan's eyebrow quirked upward as he directed a quick, but probing, look in Louisa's direction. Heat warmed her cheeks as she saw an undefinable emotion flash in his blue-gray eye before he looked back at Wills.

"I do have a mechanical hand. I wear a glove to hide it as it frightens people."

"May I see it? I'm not afraid."

"That's *quite* enough, William Wallace Morehouse," Louisa choked out in mortification as she took a step forward. "Apologize to his lordship."

"For what, Mama? I just asked him a question."

"There is no apology needed when it comes to curiosity," Ewan said quietly with a shake of his head. "I'll let you see to settling your boys in their rooms. When you've finished, come to my study."

It was a command that indicated he would come find her if she failed to obey. The man had no worries on that count. She intended to rake him over the coals when it came to the vast difference in his treatment of his own son and Wills. Beneath her glare, an eyebrow quirked upward in a questioning manner before a cynical gleam of humor darkened his eye. She drew in a quick breath as she saw his mouth twitch again. Was the man actually laughing at her? Irritated by thought, Louisa bobbed her head sharply in a silent reply to his command then turned to usher the boys upstairs.

Several hours later, Louisa knocked on the door to the earl's study. She'd delayed as long as she could in order to allow her anger to cool to a reasonable level. Ross's cheerful expression as he helped Wills and Charlie put away their belongings had made it difficult, but she'd succeeded. As she'd watched the children and their friendly banter, her anger had slowly abated.

In its place was the determination not to jeopardize her position. She'd already been subjected to Ewan's anger once before when it came to the boy. If she challenged him too fiercely, she might be dismissed. That was something she couldn't allow to happen if she was to help Ross. The best course of action was to tread lightly.

At the earl's abrupt command to enter, Louisa stiffened her back and entered the room. The afternoon sun had set, and the study was softly lit by two oil lamps and a blazing fire. Asadi was arranging place settings on a table, while the earl stood in front of a tall reading table.

The top of the furniture had a small flat shelf that one of the lamps sat on. The remaining surface was angled downward to serve as a resting place for the open book he was reading. Other than it was structured like a table, it reminded her of a parson's pulpit. The boy looked up and grinned at her as she came to a halt a short distance from the door.

"You should be finished by now, Asadi." Ewan didn't even looked in the boy's direction as he issued his gruff admonishment. Asadi looked in the earl's direction, with an obvious look of hero worship.

"Yes, Argaty sahib."

With a bow of respect to his employer first and then Louisa, the boy made one last adjustment to the table before he was gone, and the study door quietly closed behind him.

Silence filled the room, and when the earl didn't speak, Louisa glanced around her surroundings. It was a male domain not unlike Sebastian's, but where her brother's study was uncluttered, the earl's had stacks of books everywhere. The man clearly loved to read. Louisa returned her attention to where he sat on a tall stool, his head bent as though deeply engrossed in the book.

Instinctively she knew he wasn't really reading. He was deliberately using silence as a means of intimidating her. Throughout her childhood, all her brothers had tried to use silence as a form admonishment and disapproval where she was concerned. They'd eventually learned it was a tactic that garnered them nothing where she was concerned. One Scottish earl was no match for her stubborn refusal to be intimidated or bullied. Just like her brothers had learned, this man would eventually be forced to confront her directly if he had something to say.

The soft rustle of a page turning drifted through the air as she watched the man continue to peruse the book in front of him. He'd removed his jacket from earlier, and she could see his back muscles harden beneath the vest that covered his shoulders and the white shirt underneath. She bit back a smile of complacent satisfaction. Clearly the Earl of Argaty was surprised at her ability to wait patiently while he ignored her. Another page rustled softly in the air as Louisa watched him turn another page.

"You weren't this quiet the first time you entered my study, Louisa Morehouse."

The lilting burr in his voice was a caress against her senses, and she drew in a quick, soft breath at how her body reacted to the sound of her name rolling off his lips. She swallowed hard and chastised herself for feeling anything but irritation where he was concerned.

"Since *you* were the one who summoned me to your study, I presumed *you* would eventually say what you needed to say."

Louisa bit down on her lower lip to keep from smiling

as she saw him jerk slightly. With controlled, deliberate movements he closed the book he'd been reading. Without warning, a thousand butterflies filled her stomach as he turned around. For some unknown reason, she suddenly experienced the urge to flee the room.

In the fire light, he did look like the pirate Wills had suggested he was. There was an air about him that triggered an immediate, tangible reaction inside her. If the man suddenly chose to appear in London society, she was certain almost every woman in the Set would seek his company simply to learn if he was as dangerous as he looked. The thought reminded her of her observation this afternoon.

He was the type of man who expected his orders to be obeyed. Although his appearance might repel some women, it was the sheer magnetism and raw power he exuded that would make him stand out among other men in the Set. Even his burr would create a stir in most women. Mocking laughter filled the back of her head. Most women? She'd already discovered she wasn't immune to the sound of his voice.

Despite the unsettling sensation flooding through her body, she didn't move. Almost as if he knew her senses were in a state of complete disarray, his sensual mouth tipped slightly upward at the corners. It was barely a smile but Louisa was certain he believed she was unsettled by the silence between them and found it amusing. She was most definitely feeling uneasy at the moment, but not by his silence. She ignored the significance of the thought.

"I believe there was a matter you wished to discuss with me." Arrogance and a whisper of mockery filled his voice. Irritated by her reaction to him and his amusement, she glared at him.

"I would like to put up a Christmas tree in the main hall."

"You want to do what?" His bewildered look of surprise made it obvious his aunt hadn't spoken to him about her plans.

"I would like to have a Christmas tree placed in the parlor for the holiday. You do know what they are, don't you?" A part of her couldn't resist mocking him as he'd done to her seconds ago.

"Of course I know what a Christmas tree is," he muttered in a clipped tone. "We've just never had one at Argaty Keep."

"I know Christmas celebrations in Scotland are quiet affairs, if celebrated at all, but I'm accustomed to celebrating and having a tree. Ross said he'd never seen one, and I thought he would enjoy it."

For a brief moment he looked lost, and Louisa stared at him in puzzlement. It was as if he was remembering something painful in his past. His reaction tugged at her, and she experienced an impulsive with to comfort him in some way. In the next instant, he became aware she was watching him, and the emotion was wiped away by a mask of stoicism. She tipped her head to one side wanted to ask him what he'd been thinking, but chose the better part of valor. The man wasn't about to reveal anything to her.

"Do you have any objection?"

"No," he said in a brusque growl. "I'll have Finn find a fresh pine and bring it into the house."

"Actually, I thought I would let the boys choose a tree together. But I'll gladly accept Finn's assistance in chopping it down."

"Then I'll see to it that he's at your disposal."

"Thank you." Louisa bit down on her lip debating whether or not to express the thought that had just popped into her head. She jumped slightly when he made a quiet sound of exasperation.

"Out with it, Louisa." The fact that he used her first name so easily registered somewhere in the back of her mind.

"I thought perhaps you might join us."

The moment her words flew past her lips, his entire body grew stiff with tension. In a split second, he seemed to grow in stature and presence that made the intimidation she'd experienced earlier nothing compared to now. The icy anger radiating off him now was similar to his reaction the night she'd confronted him about Ross here in his study. It made little sense to her why he would react so harshly when it came to her attempts to create a stronger bond between him and his son.

"Why the devil would I do that?"

"It would be a sign to Ross that you care about him."

"Are you questioning the way I tend to the boy's welfare?" he growled.

"Yes." She glared at him. "Ross needs—"

"Does the boy have a roof over his head? Is he fed well? Does he lack suitable clothing? Does he lack the means of an education now or in the future at a suitable school? Exactly what is it you think the boy lacks?"

"He needs his father. He needs you to take *some* interest in him," she said fiercely as she leaned forward and poked him in the chest.

The dark anger hardening his face made her regret poking him as a sudden wave of trepidation swept through her. The Earl of Argaty was clearly not accustomed to someone taking him to task, but she'd said too much to stop now.

"That's enough." The quiet command went unheeded as Louisa glared at him.

"Didn't you see the way Ross looked this afternoon when you were so kind to my son, but ignored him?"

"I *said* enough."

"What you did this afternoon was cruel and heartless. Are you really so blind that—"

"Enough."

The word was like a thunderclap over her head, and

Louisa swallowed the rest of what she'd been about to say. For a brief instant, guilt and what she thought might be pain was evident in the tightness of his jaw and a tic in his cheek before a cold, stony façade obliterated the emotions. Beneath his icy stare, she remembered her reference to him being blind and flinched.

It had been a tactless remark. She'd overstepped the line in her effort to make Ewan see how much Ross wanted his father's approval. She could have found another way to point out Ewan's lack of consideration where his son was concerned. Apologies weren't always easy for her, but he deserved one. Swallowing her righteous outrage, she clasped her hands in front of her.

"I'm sorry." She wanted to add more, but she was certain anything else she might say would detract from her sincerity.

The soft apology did nothing to thaw the cold anger reflected on his face. Her heart skipped a beat. Not even Sebastian had ever eyed her with such raw fury. Despite the icy finger scraping down her spine, she remained where she was, fully prepared for the man to rain all manner of hellfire and retribution on her head.

"We will *not* speak of this again." The quiet inflection in his voice made the force of his anger all the more threatening. "You are here to *school* the boy—nothing more."

"Yes," she said in a display of meekness she barely recognized as trait she possessed.

"Unless there is something else, *outside* of my personal affairs, you wish to discuss, you may go."

It was the coldest dismissal she'd ever had handed down to her. In fact, she couldn't remember anyone ever rejecting her so scornfully. The knowledge only emphasized how much of the family recklessness she possessed. The Rockwood trait for treading where angels feared to go had been handed down to her in abundance. Louisa nodded slowly and turned to retreat. She'd almost reached the door when a wave of dizziness rolled over her.

Oh God, not now. The last thing she wanted was the *an dara sealladh* taking control of her body before she was out of Ewan's sight. The man would think she was feigning the episode in an effort to soften his attitude toward her. She stretched out her hand hoping to reach the door, but failed before she was pulled into a familiar well of darkness.

A cackle of laughter filled the air before she saw anything. Almost as if someone had abruptly pulled back a curtain, she saw the shadowy figure of a small boy sitting on the floor with his back to her. The child laughed again, and the malevolence in the sound filled the air around her until her skin was as cold as if she'd fallen into an icy burn.

In the next instant, she was staring down over the boy's shoulder at a small brown rabbit bleeding and squirming wildly in an effort to escape the boy's grasp. In the child's other hand was a knife covered in blood. As she watched in abject horror, the boy jabbed the tip of the knife into the rabbit's hind quarters. The small animal squealed in pain, and with a gleeful chuckle, the boy pressed the knife into the animal's chest and opened the rabbit up with a slow downward stroke.

The small animal shrieked with pain before it went limp. It was a horrible sound, but it was the child's laughter that terrified her even more. The suddenness with which the darkness parted and became light was a blessing. But it failed to prevent the powerful surge of nausea cresting over her. Bile rose in her throat, and it forced her to bend at the waist and vomit.

Another rush of bile rose in her throat as her body tried to purge the evil that had touched her. This was the first time the *an dara sealladh* had ever made her physically ill. Although her brother occasionally suffered migraines after a powerful vision, Percy had never mentioned anything such as this.

Despite her physical reaction, she knew the child's laugh and cruelty was a memory she would not forget for a long time, if ever. Directly behind her, Louisa heard Ewan's a quiet oath echo in her ear before he summoned Asadi with a sharp command. The nausea had already begun to fade as Ewan's steel arm awkwardly wrapped around her waist to support her.

The chill of the artificial limb's metal sank through his shirt and the wool of her gown to cool her skin. The sensation was a distinct contrast to the warmth of his hard, muscular body pressing into her side as he guided her to a nearby chair. The loud noise of the study door flying open made her wince as Ewan's man-servant charged into the room.

Still feeling off balance, Louisa barely heard Asadi's quiet words of concern followed by Ewan's reply. Her elbow resting on the arm of the chair, she pressed the heel of her hand against her forehead. Not once since her first experience of the *an dara sealladh* had she ever been made ill or so deeply disturbed by a vision.

She'd always viewed her ability to be a gift and had used it discreetly when helping to solve her family, friends or even her own problems. But what she'd just seen went far beyond anything she'd been shown in the past. A shudder rippled through her at the thought, and she jumped violently as Ewan's gloved hand touched her shoulder.

"Drink this." The glass he handed her contained a generous amount of brandy. She shook her head.

"No, I'll be—"

"*Damn it, Louisa*, do as you're told."

At the sharp, authoritative order, she accepted the brandy snifter. The first swallow washed away the foul taste in her mouth, but she coughed at the fiery sensation it made on its way down her throat. She tried to give the drink back to him, but he didn't take it.

"Drink *all* of it." The command made her wrinkle her

nose with distaste, and as she looked up at him in protest, he scowled at her. "God in heaven, woman, are you always so stubborn?"

The glass halfway to her lips, she started to reply, and his frown darkened with a touch of the anger she'd witnessed earlier. Taking the path of least resistance, she didn't argue and choked down a second gulp. By the third drink, she'd adapted to the taste, and was able to finish the alcohol without coughing.

"Thank you," she murmured as she handed the empty glass to him. He didn't answer as he moved away to set it on the sideboard. Slowly rising to her feet, she heard him utter a harsh oath.

"Sit down, before you faint."

It was a roughly spoken command that dared her to argue with him but contained a note of concern for her as well. Louisa didn't have the strength to challenge his order, and she sank back down into the chair. In all honesty, she was still shaken by her vision and welcomed the respite.

Unlike other instances when she'd pondered the meaning of what she'd been shown, this was one vision she wanted to forget. The memory of the child's laughter suddenly filled her head. It sent an icy shiver down her back as the clarity of the evil sound echoed in her head. She turned her head toward the sideboard then looked up at Ewan.

"Please, may I have another?"

Her whispered request made him hesitate, but he didn't question her. In seconds, he offered her another glass that held far less of the amber liquid than the first one he'd given her. When she'd finished it, Louisa sat staring into the empty crystal snifter.

"So what Ross told McCallum is true." The quiet words made her jerk her head up to see him studying her intently.

"That I've not recovered completely?" she asked softly and bowed her head to avoid showing how shaken she was feeling at the moment. "Yes, it appears I've had a relapse."

"Don't be obtuse, Louisa. You're completely recovered from your illness. I'm referring to your gift of sight." At his matter-of-fact tone, she turned her head toward him in surprise. His eyebrows arched as she studied him with amazement.

"I might have attended Charterhouse and Cambridge, but I'm still a Scotsman. I'm quite familiar with the *an dara sealladh*, but I've only seen it cause someone fatigue."

"It's never made me ill before," she said with bewilderment and another small bout of nausea stirred in the pit of her stomach.

"From your reaction, you must have seen something quite unsettling." There was a question in his voice, but she refused to satisfy his curiosity. Her strength having returned, she rose from her seat.

"If you'll excuse me, I would like to retire for the evening." She turned her head away awaiting his reply.

"As you wish. Allow me to walk you to your room."

"That's unnecessary," she said quietly, but emphatically as she looked at him again.

Other than his mouth thinning with frustration, he didn't protest. He simply nodded. Grateful he had no intention to press her on the matter any further, she walked toward the door. As her hand gripped the door knob, Ewan cleared his throat.

"Louisa. I've seen more than my fair share of horror on the battlefield. Should you have need of someone's ear, I'm happy to listen."

The gentleness in his voice startled her, and she glanced over her shoulder at him. Although it was impossible to tell what he was thinking, she found his offer a comforting gesture. Any other time she might have accepted it, but all she wanted was to forget the horror she'd seen. With a bob of her head, she silently acknowledged his kindness then walked out of the study.

Chapter 7

Ewan tugged his riding glove over his metal hand as he strode across the stable yard. The sound of McCallum's soft brogue made him stop halfway to the barn.

Under the Scotsman's careful eye, Louisa's oldest son and Ross were learning the finer points of riding. For almost a week now, McCallum and the boys had spent an hour or two in the paddock every day on old Treasach's back.

It had been at Louisa's request the boys spend time out in the fresh air, and riding had seemed the logical choice of exercise. She'd not made the request to him directly. Instead, she'd put the question to the family's long-time retainer. In fact, Ewan hadn't seen her since the night she'd chastised him about Ross.

On the one or two occasions he'd caught sight of her, she'd immediately headed in a different direction to avoid him. He was certain her deliberate behavior had nothing to do with fear. The woman had demonstrated more than once how easily she could weather his darkest fury. It was a trait for which she'd earned his admiration. The most likely reason for her avoidance of him was she didn't want to answer any questions he had.

What he'd witnessed almost a week ago in his study had alarmed him. He'd never met anyone with such a strong gift of sight that it made them physically ill. Not even Mrs.

Dunmore's gift of the *an dara sealladh* was so powerful. It hadn't just been Louisa's physical reaction to her vision, it had been the horror he'd seen in her lovely when she'd emerged from her trance.

Whatever she'd seen had terrified her. In the back of his head, a small voice whispered a warning. Argaty Keep had dark secrets, and now he was beginning to question why he'd agreed to let Louisa become Ross's governess. Another voice scoffed at him for being so dim-witted, while in the far reaches of his mind he heard Gilbert's disturbing laugh.

The sound of McCallum slightly raising his voice pulled Ewan's attention back to the paddock. Watching the long-time family retainer calling out commands reminded him of a time he'd learned how to ride in the same small paddock. While Louisa's son had a good seat, it was Ross who displayed the makings of an exceptional horseman.

The boy laughed at something Charlie said, and Ewan froze at the sound. He couldn't remember ever hearing Ross laugh before. Guilt tugged at him before he cast it aside. Any remorse he had was reserved for his own folly at eagerly agreeing to wed the boy's mother to begin with.

Agnes had been his mother's choice. Until that moment, his mother had never shown any interest in him. For the first time in his life, he'd had the opportunity to please his mother, and he'd willingly agreed to marry Agnes. It had been one of the worst mistakes he'd ever made.

On their wedding night, his bride had pleaded her need to know him better before she shared his bed, and Ewan had agreed to give her time. Days later he'd been sent to the Sudan with the Black Watch regiment without ever having touched his wife.

When the dowager had written a few months later that he was to be a father, he'd become numb to everything except the humiliation and fury at being cuckolded. He'd released his rage on the battlefield like a madman fighting invisible demons. His sole comfort had come from the belief no one knew he'd been cuckolded. Even that had been taken from him when he'd returned to the keep at the time of Agnes's death.

Upon hearing Agnes had died in childbirth, he'd chosen to maintain the appearance of a grieving husband by returning home as soon as he received the news. It had taken the dowager less than a day to reveal she'd known about Agnes's pregnancy all along. She had gloated as to how his desire to please her had made it easy to ensure he didn't learn the truth until too late. Her poisonous words had sent him reeling as he'd faced the dowager's venomous amusement in stunned, humiliated silence.

Wallis had been in the room as her sister shared the lurid details of her vicious scheme to humiliate Ewan. When her sister had fainted, the dowager had become even more elated. Ewan had been too furious and shamed by it all to do anything other than catch his aunt as she slid to the floor.

When her sister had recovered from her shock, Lady Argaty had matter-of-factly informed Ewan he was to recognize Ross. Wallis had vehemently protested her sister's demand. It was the first time he'd ever seen his aunt angry. Lady Argaty had dismissed her sister's objections and threatened to tell all and sundry how Ewan had been cuckolded if he didn't accept Ross as his child.

The immoral, sickening treachery of it all had pushed him to the edge of a deep chasm of fury. He'd barely managed to keep his hands away from the dowager's throat. Several hours later, Ewan had left Argaty Keep out of fear he might act on his dark urges. Instead, he'd used that darkness on the battlefield. The carnage he'd left in his wake had made the enemy call him, Savage Infidel.

The sound of McCallum's voice penetrated his dark thoughts, and he glanced around the paddock. For the first time, he realized Louisa's youngest boy, Wills, was nowhere to be seen. Usually the boy was perched on the top rail of the fence surrounding the riding ring watch the older boys. McCallum had chosen to give the younger child lessons without the older two, which gave Wills the opportunity for mischief when his riding lesson for the day was done.

From inside the stable, he heard Louisa calling out to her son. The exasperation in her voice was evident, and he continued across the yard toward the barn. As he walked through the wide entrance of the stable, he saw Louisa with her hands on her hips looking down the corridor that extended the length of the building.

"Wills, where are you?"

"Here, Mama. I'm up here."

The boy's cheerful, disembodied response made Louisa look upward, and she grew pale and swayed as if she were about to faint. Ewan's gaze followed hers, and he grimaced at the sight of Wills sitting complacently on one of the beams that ran from one side of the stable walls to the other.

"William *Wallace* Morehouse, get down from there this instant."

"But Mama, I can see all the horses from up here."

"I don't care if you can see London," she snapped. "Get down from there, *now*."

As Ewan watched the boy get to his feet in a haphazardly fashion, Louisa released a low moan of fear. Ewan muttered an oath beneath his breath. Louisa had every right to be afraid. He'd climbed the same rafters as a boy and had learned the hard way a fall could be quite painful. The boy looked around, clearly debating how best to climb down from the beam. Afraid of startling the boy, Ewan didn't say anything as he strode quickly toward the stall directly beneath Wills.

Louisa's sharp gasp of fear made him look up to see her youngest teeter on the beam. Ewan lengthened his stride and in three more steps he launched himself up onto Balgair's back. The large gelding barely moved as Ewan centered himself on the horse. Directly overhead, he saw the boy regain his balance and continue looking around him for an easy path to safety.

"Mr. Morehouse, I want you to carefully take two steps to the left then hop down here onto Balgair. I'll catch you." At his quiet order, Wills frowned.

"How? You only have one arm." The boy's candid response made his mouth twist slightly with amusement despite his fear that Wills might fall. The child was as blunt and straight-forward as his mother.

"I might only have one good arm, but I had no trouble mounting Balgair. Are you doubting me when I say I'll catch you?"

"No, my lord."

"Then I give you my word that I'm more than capable of catching you."

The boy tipped his head to one side and studied Ewan carefully for a long moment. Then with a cheeky grin he nodded, took two quick steps to the side, and without any warning jumped off the beam. Ewan released a loud grunt as Wills landed hard on his chest. As his body protested the rough action, the boy grinned.

"You were right. You did catch me."

"I'm not in the habit of making promises I can't keep." With his good arm, Ewan lowered Wills to the ground. As he slid off the gelding's back, Wills gave him a small bow.

"Thank you, my lord. I'll be more careful next time."

"There won't *be* a next time, young man," Louisa snapped as she hurried forward to meet Wills as the two of them walked out of Balgair's stall. Her hands gripped her son's shoulders as she bent over him. "If I *ever* catch you doing something so dangerous again, I'll take a switch to you. Do you understand?"

"Yes, Mama." The regret in her youngest son's voice

made Louisa close her eyes as she pulled her child into a tight embrace. The boy immediately squirmed against her. "Please, Mama. Not in front of his lordship."

Ewan eyed the boy with amusement as Louisa released him. Before she could say another word, Wills darted past her and out into the stable yard. The moment her son disappeared from view, Louisa drew in a sharp breath of relief.

"Thank you," she said softly. The fear her son's reckless behavior had caused her still lingered, and she shook her head. "If something had happened to William…"

Silence filled the space between them as her voice trailed to a halt. Ewan couldn't ever remember feeling so awkward with a woman before. As he studied her, Louisa's gaze flitted away from his. With an abrupt movement, she began to walk down the row of horse stalls, and he fell into step beside her.

"He's an adventuresome lad. Quite fearless. A trait I think he inherited from his mother." Ewan didn't look at her, but out of the corner of his only eye, he saw her jerk her head toward him in surprise.

"I'm not sure whether that was an insult or a compliment."

"If you had *thought* it an insult, I've no doubt you would have verbally flayed me without hesitation." Ewan heard a small indignant gurgle of sound come from her, and he bit back a smile.

"I do not flay people verbally," she snapped. Before he had a chance to challenge her, she blew out a puff of air that was a clear sign of exasperation. "Although, I suppose my words the other night might be considered by some to be…mildly vitriolic."

"*Mildly?*" he said with a touch of umbrage mixed with amusement.

When she didn't answer he turned his head to see a look of guilt and sorrow shadowing her suddenly pale features. For reasons he didn't fully understand, he knew he'd triggered a painful memory in her. Ewan didn't like the way it made him feel or the pain it caused him to see her so distraught, and he quickly sought to ease her remorse.

"You *did* apologize."

"Yes, but there are some words that can never be taken back. Words said in anger that can haunt you forever."

From her reply, Ewan knew Louisa wasn't referring to the harsh words she'd directed at him. There was a fragile vulnerability about her, and he was certain she was recalling a painful memory of another time when she'd spoken harshly to someone. An urge to comfort her slammed into him with the force of a blow to his chest.

"There are many things one can regret, but if your words were said to a loved one, I find it hard to believe you weren't forgiven."

"There wasn't time for forgiveness."

The soft reply intensified the painful ache in his chest as he suddenly wished he could take on the burden of her pain. He was accustomed to living with the emotion, it was obvious she wasn't. She came to a halt in front of Morag's stall, and he saw the mare was already saddled. With a gesture for her to stay where she was, he led the horse out of the stall. The horse dipped its head toward Louisa in a display of recognition. A small smile touched her lips at the gentle nudge, and she rubbed the horse's jowl with affection.

"I see you're well-acquainted with Morag."

"Yes, she's a sweet creature," Louisa said with a nod. "She seems to enjoy our afternoon outings despite the chilly weather."

"I believe Lachlan would become quite lazy if I didn't exercise him every day. There are times when I think the animal is too pampered by McCallum and Finn." His annoyance made her laugh, and he was relieved to see her sorrow had disappeared.

"And *you* don't pamper him?" There was a mischievous sparkle in her hazel eyes as he scowled at her.

"I do not."

"Then what is this?"

In a quick move, she tugged on the green foliage attached to a carrot he had in his coat pocket. Louisa dangled the carrot in the air in front of him and smiled at him without even a hint of remorse.

"The animal needs to eat," he growled.

"Of course."

Annoyed by her amusement, Ewan directed his harshest frown at her, and without thinking reached out with his mechanical arm to snatch the vegetable out of her hand. Immediately Ewan's chest tightened at the foolish, spontaneous move. A second later relief streaked though him as his metal fingers tugged Lachlan's favorite treat out of her hand without incident. The last thing he wanted to do was embarrass himself in front of Louisa. The thought pulled his muscles taut with irritation for caring what the woman thought of him..

As her soft laughter filled the air, Ewan scowled at her and turned away to head back to Lachlan's stall, which he'd passed while walking Louisa to Morag. While Louisa Morehouse's brother hadn't mentioned it, Ewan was certain the man had often found himself bedeviled by his sister's teasing.

"Perhaps when Lachlan has had his carrot, his strength will be restored well enough to race Morag." The laughter in her voice made him glance over his shoulder in annoyance. But it was the provocation in her serene smile that made him want to do something unrestrained in response to her challenge. Ewan fought back the urge with a shake of his head.

"Morag is no match for Lachlan."

"Then allow us a head start." She arched her eyebrows

as her laughter became an impish smile that her plump mouth just as sultry as it was enchanting. "That is if you're not afraid of losing."

"Losing?" Ewan snorted as his exasperation slowly changed to amusement at her confidence. There was no doubt in his mind that she would lose, and refrained from smiling smugly at her as he answered her challenge. "Very well. I've yet to saddle Lachlan. Even with that much of a head start, he will still be able to catch Morag without too much difficulty."

"Bold words, my lord. Perhaps you would like to make a wager?"

Fully aware she was goading him into placing a bet, he ignored the warning in the back of his head. Slowly closing the distance between them, he studied her in silence. Surprise caused Louisa's mouth to part slightly, but she didn't retreat. It was one of the things he found delightfully enticing about her. She never showed any bit of fear when confronting him.

But currently, she appeared bemused and somewhat unnerved by his silence. It sent satisfaction barreling through him. For once she wasn't quite as confident as she usually was. The small tremor he saw shake through her confirmed his observation, and it was impossible to ignore how rapidly her breasts rose and fell. It was a remarkable change from the other night.

How unsettled would she be if he kissed her at this exact moment? A rush of desire crashed through him at the thought, and he quickly fought off the impulse to steal a kiss here and now. Pink color stained her cheeks as if she'd read his thoughts, and he allowed a small smile to touch his lips.

"What should we wager?" he murmured as he continued to enjoy her sudden loss of confidence in his presence.

Even if he was wrong about Lachlan catching Morag, he'd already won by watching her reaction to him. Something stirred inside him as she swallowed hard and bent her head to avoid looking at him. It was further evidence of how much he'd rattled her composure, and he took pleasure in how exquisite her bemusement made her. With a sudden inhalation of breath, Louisa lifted her head and tilted it in a silent challenge.

"If I win, you must have supper with me and the children tonight." Startled by her stipulation, he frowned, and she gently scoffed at his hesitation. "I thought you were certain Lachlan could catch Morag."

"Oh, I'm certain of it. Certain enough that when I cross the finish line before you, I will require you call me Ewan from that point forward, and..." He paused as he realized what he'd been about to propose. *Christ Jesus*, he'd almost wagered a kiss in addition to hearing her call him by his given name. Hazel eyes wide with astonishment, the flush of color that had only just faded from her cheeks returned to crest even higher.

"And what?"

The breathless note in her voice made Ewan's muscles tighten with tension. Damnation, but the woman was lovely enough to tempt a saint's desire. The realization indicated the extreme peril he was in at the moment. He swallowed hard and pulled back from her as he quickly substituted another payment.

"You'll dine with me tonight. *Alone*."

He saw an odd flicker of emotion in her eyes that made him think she'd wanted him to ask for something different. Color still high in her cheeks, she nodded.

"I accept."

She turned away from him and led Morag out into the yard. Before she was halfway to the mounting block, Ewan captured her elbow to bring her to a halt. The instant he touched her, an electric bolt zipped through him as if he'd been touched by lightning. His reaction emphasized his poor judgement in helping her mount Morag.

Despite his mistake, anticipation crashed through him at the idea of touching her again, if even for just a few seconds. He almost groaned out loud at the thought. God help him, he was mad. His jaw suddenly painfully tight, he gestured abruptly toward the mare. Ewan bent slightly and formed a makeshift step with his natural hand then braced a substantial portion of his weight against Morag's shoulder.

The moment she touched his shoulder to steady herself, another electrical shock pulsated through his body. It could not have been any more powerful than if he'd been struck by lightning. Ignoring the sensation as best he could, he boosted her up into the saddle. In silence he watched her lift her skirt to reveal her legs covered in black breeches. She placed one leg over the pommel while lodging her other leg under the leaping pad.

Her movements revealed the sweet curve of her thigh and shapely calves, and the memory of seeing her body unencumbered by clothes made his mouth go dry. The sudden urge to run his hand up along her leg to the edge of a softly rounded bottom made him grow hard. *Christ almighty*, what the hell was wrong with him? Louisa Morehouse was proving to be far more dangerous than he'd realized.

He crushed the desire hardening his body and quickly set her foot into the sidesaddle's stirrups then stepped back from Morag with a jerk. At his sharp movement, a flicker of awareness sparked in her hazel eyes. It heightened the tactile tension between them.

Suddenly, a sultry, come hither look softened her features. The sight of it made his body ache as he fought off the urge to pull her off the saddle and kiss her passionately. Muscles tight and rigid with desire he turned toward Morag's head and made a pretense of checking the animal's bridle.

"Do you know where the rock formation is, just across the burn?"

"Yes." The breathless note hadn't left her voice, and it

did things to his insides he didn't like. His brain laughed at him. No. He liked the way she made him feel far too much.

"Whoever reaches the formation first is the winner."

He didn't wait for a reply and headed toward Lachlan's stall. Behind him, he heard Morag's hooves softly pounding the barn's wooden floor as Louisa rode the mare out of the stable. Ewan didn't look back as he entered Lachlan's stall and ran his gloved hand over the stallion's back. God help him. He should never have agreed to a wager, let alone name his prize that she dined alone with him.

For the first time in his life, he was considering throwing a race. Not because he wanted to, but because of what would happen if he won. Ewan grunted with disgust at the predicament he'd created for himself, and he took his time saddling Lachlan. Losing wasn't something he enjoyed, but an intimate meal for two was something to avoid at all costs.

While it wasn't the choice he preferred, it was the best one for his sanity. What he really wanted was far too dangerous to even consider. The memory of seeing Louisa's lush, naked curves the night he'd found her made Ewan's cock stir under his kilt. He quickly crushed the images as he tightened the cinch under Lachlan's belly.

With the stallion saddled, Ewan led the horse out of the stable. He turned his head toward the rock formation that was the finish line. Louisa already had a good head start, which offered him a small measure of satisfaction.

Unless he pushed Lachlan hard, he wouldn't be able to catch her. Having supper with the boys and her was the sane choice, and sanity wasn't something he'd possessed much of since the first time he'd seen Louisa Morehouse. He should never have agreed to let her be Ross's governess in the first place.

The stallion danced to one side, and the action tugged roughly on his artificial arm. Ewan winced with discomfort as the leather cupping the stump of his arm bit into his skin.

Even without the darkness that existed in the walls of Argaty Keep, his own sad state of affairs would be a deterrent toward any type of involvement with the woman. He grimaced at the thought.

Ewan vaulted himself up into the saddle and the shock of the cold leather against his bare skin was a welcome sensation. It meant his body was more likely not to respond to Louisa's presence. In the back of his head he heard a cackling laugh but ignored it. He glanced over at the paddock and saw McCallum watching him. At the Scotsman's sly smile, Ewan release a harsh breath of disgust.

McCallum's wily grin became one of broad amusement on his craggy features, and Ewan glared at the family retainer before his legs applied a firm pressure into Lachlan's sides. As he rode the horse out of the stable yard at a fast trot in Louisa's direction, he heard the old retainer laugh. With a grunt of irritation, Ewan knew better than to look back at the Scotsman. It would only provide the man with fodder for the next time he saw the man who'd been the father figure in his life.

Once on the moor, he pushed the stallion into an easy canter as he gauged the distance between him and Louisa. Satisfied the distance between the two horses made it unlikely the stallion would catch the mare, he pushed Lachlan into a gallop. He wanted to ensure his loss, but avoid the prospect of Louisa realizing he'd deliberately thrown the match. The animal strained at the bit, obviously eager to catch the mare. The action made Ewan want to give Lachlan his head, but he kept the stallion from accelerating to a faster pace.

As Ewan closed the distance between them, he saw Louisa look over her shoulder. That he could clearly see her satisfied expression made him suddenly realize how much ground the stallion had covered in closing the distance between them. As the stone pillar jutting up from the ground grew larger in size, Lachlan strained even harder at the bit.

They were only a few lengths behind Morag, and the stallion clearly wanted to catch the mare. The burn was now clearly in view, and he released a harsh oath. He had no doubt Louisa would try to jump the stream. Normally, he wouldn't have thought anything of her taking Morag over the water.

The burn was usually a small, narrow strip of water, and a relatively easy jump. But all the rain they'd had in the past month had widened the burn to almost twice its size, and Morag wasn't accustomed to jumping.

"*Stop, Louisa,*" he shouted.

Either she didn't hear him or she ignored his command. As the mare leapt up into the air, Ewan dragged in a sharp breath. A second later Morag's front hooves hit the slope of the burn, and her rear legs thrashed in the flooded stream as the small mare struggled to scramble out of the rushing water.

With a tug on Lachlan's reins he forced the stallion to go slower and rode the animal into the stream alongside the mare. Louisa's grim determination was evident in the way her sweet mouth was tight and thin, while a frown of concentration furrowed her brow. It made Ewan hesitate. The woman would not be happy with him, but he could tell from the way Morag was floundering the mare was finding it difficult to gain a solid footing.

Before she could protest, Ewan wrapped his good arm around Louisa's waist then pulled her off Morag and sat her down in front of him. Sputtering with outrage, she jabbed him with her elbow.

"What in the hell do you think you're doing?"

Any other time, her colorful language might have made him laugh, but he was too relieved she was safe to do anything more than grimace. Lachlan carried them up onto solid ground and safety as a soft gasp echoed in his ear. Ewan looked down to see Louisa had gone pale, and she was staring at something behind him.

Ewan glanced over his shoulder and saw Morag lurch

wildly then stagger to one side before she regained her footing and climbed up the embankment. He knew without saying a word Louisa had suddenly realized the high probability she would have been unseated or the mare would have been injured in the animal's effort not to throw Louisa. A stricken expression crossed her face before she turned her head away from him.

"I was certain Morag could make it up the embankment," she whispered with remorse.

"Normally she could, but the burn was too wide for her with all the rain we've had."

"I should have known better."

"You wanted to win," he murmured in response to her self-recrimination.

She muttered something unintelligible as she sank deeper into his chest. With incredible speed, his body reacted to her warmth. Something primitive rose inside him as he watched the rapid flutter on the side of her neck that was her heartbeat.

Desperately he struggled with the growing need to caress the spot with his mouth. At that moment, she turned her head to look at him. Color filled her cheeks, and her soft mouth parted slightly as if she'd gasped. He wanted to groan at the way his body was reacting to her.

"It appears you've won, Ewan."

The soft sound of his name drifting past her lips was the sweetest thing he'd ever heard. He didn't realize his arm had tightened around her until it was too late. For a split-second, she stiffened against him before her body relaxed against him once more. Never in his life had he experienced such a sensation of sheer, agonizing temptation.

Eager to put distance between them, he unceremoniously forced her to slide off Lachlan's back onto the ground. She stared up at him in surprise and with what he thought might be disappointment.

"If anyone won, it was you," he grounded out as he dismounted Lachlan knowing she would need assistance mounting the mare. "In better weather, Morag would have sailed across the burn without any problem at all. I'll not hold you to our wager."

"Very well, but I will, since you've conceded the race in my favor. I expect you to dine with me and the children at six this evening."

"I did not concede the race in your favor, I called the race a tie."

"No, you said 'if anyone won, it was you,' which means you're required to honor your commitment this evening." The triumph threading its way beneath her reply made him grimace.

"Remind me never to enter into another wager with you again."

"Only if I think I might lose." The mischievous reply made him laugh. It was an unexpected sound that surprised him. He couldn't remember the last time he'd actually laughed.

"You should laugh more often," Louisa said with a smile. "It makes you look younger and far less forbidding."

Ewan ignored her gentle barb and walked past her with a shake of his head to where Morag stood several feet away. He quickly checked the mare's girth cinch to determine how secure it was against the mare's belly. Satisfied the cinch was still snug despite the animal's struggle to cross the burn, he grabbed Morag's reins and led the mare back to Louisa. He gestured for Louisa to mount, and this time he steeled himself for his body's reaction to her. Relief relaxed his tight muscles as seconds later he was able to step back from the mare.

"There's a bridge about a mile down the burn. We can cross the stream there."

For a moment it appeared as if she wanted to argue, but she simply accepted his decree with a bob of her head. The moment she was seated in the saddle, he quickly ensured her feet were in the stirrups then mounted Lachlan.

Ewan turned the stallion in the direction of the bridge and rode off without waiting for Louisa. Behind him, he thought he heard a gasp, but he didn't turn his head to look at her. They rode in tandem for a few minutes before she suddenly appeared beside him.

"I understand now, why the *few* servants you have call you the beastly earl." Startled by her disgruntled remark, he eyed her with surprise.

"They call me what?"

"Ewan Colquhoun, the Beastly Earl of Argaty."

He mulled her scornful words over for a long minute. It didn't really surprise him that people had labeled him a beast. In many ways, it was a well-earned title, if only because of his disfigurements.

"A title I'm more than worthy of, no doubt," he murmured with a touch of irony.

"I don't think you're beastly, but you can most definitely be an ass."

The reply was barely audible, and he had to look at her to be certain she'd actually said something. The moment she realized he was watching her, she flushed with embarrassment, but remained silent. She had the look of a schoolgirl when she blushed as she was doing now.

She didn't apologize, but he'd not expected her to do so. Louisa was too forthright to ask forgiveness for speaking plainly. A few moments passed before he made any effort to alleviate the tension between them.

"I assume McCallum has provided you with everything you need for the schoolroom."

"Yes, he's been exceedingly helpful. He had Finn and Brown carry up a large desk for my use as well as table and chairs for the boys."

The mention of Brown made his muscles tighten before

he relaxed. He'd hired the tall, burly Scot shortly after his return from the Sudan. As a deaf mute, he'd been the perfect choice for the responsibility Ewan had assigned to him. The Scot also assisted with the occasional odd task about the keep when necessity demanded it.

When she said nothing else, he remained silent as well. They continued along the burn for a few more minutes until the bridge came into view. Ewan was beginning to feel the weight of the awkward silence between them, and he cleared his throat.

"So you still intend to remain here for Christmas?" He tried to convince himself he was simply making small talk, but he heard a snort of laughter in the back of his head.

"Yes, McCallum has made arrangements for Finn to accompany us on Saturday to find a tree."

"I find it surprising you want to remain here for the holiday," he murmured as he reflected on the manner in which Louisa had said goodbye to her brother a few days ago.

"Why?" The bewilderment in her voice made him glance in her direction.

"It was apparent the other day that you and your brother are quite close." Ewan eyed her with curiosity.

"I'm close with all my siblings. My parents died when I was extremely young. As the oldest, Sebastian took over as head of the family. I've always turned to him the most."

"And that makes it all the more puzzling as to why you would choose to remain here for the holiday." At his observation, Louisa pulled Morag to a halt, and eyed him with a cold disdain as he stopped Lachlan as well.

"At the risk of arousing your anger again, let me be blunt." The sharp words were emphasized by the stubborn set of her full, pink lips and the defiant tile of her chin. "Ross is desperate for attention—love. It's unnatural for a child his age to be so quiet and reserved. And if *you*, or *anyone* in this house, think I'm about to leave him alone on a day that should be filled with laughter and merriment then you're sadly mistaken."

Ewan frowned at the accusatory note in her voice. The woman didn't understand why he was incapable of loving the boy, and he had no intention of discussing the matter with her. Angered by her condemnation, he remained silent and simply nudged Lachlan into a fast trot. A few seconds later, Louisa was riding beside him again. This time the silence wasn't awkward, it reverberated with angry tension. Once more he reminded himself that he'd known it was dangerous to let Louisa stay. He was a victim to his own ineptitude.

"I'm sorry." At her apology, he glanced in her direction. Louisa was studying him with clear remorse, and he released a breath of exasperation.

"I find *that* difficult to believe when you continue to challenge me on how I raise the boy."

"It's a family trait, although I think I have more of it than the rest of my siblings."

"Then I'm glad the rest of your family aren't here," he growled.

She didn't respond, and he found himself grateful for it. He nudged Lachlan into a slow canter eager to distance himself from Louisa and the effect she had on him. The woman had him in knots until he didn't know which way he was going. Louisa made Morag match Lachlan's pace until they rode into the stable yard.

As the horses came to a halt, she waited for him to dismount and help her off the mare. In silence, he wrapped his good arm around her waist to lift her off her horse while stabilizing her descent with his mechanical limb. Her hands pressed down into his shoulders causing the leather contraption he wore to bite into his skin. The instant he drew in a sharp breath of discomfort, she jerked her hands off his shoulders.

To prevent her from collapsing at his feet, he tightened

his grip on her waist and used his chest and legs to ease her off of Morag. Soft womanly curves pressed into him as she slid down the length of his body. The scent of roses filled his nostrils as her hair brushed against his scarred cheek. It took him several seconds after her feet touched the ground to release his hold on her. Confusion made her cheeks rosier than their ride had, and Louisa quickly turned her head away from him.

"I'm sorry if I hurt you," she murmured with remorse.

"It was nothing."

The reply was only partially true. He was hurting a great deal more in other parts of his body. Ewan turned and grabbed the reins of both horses intending to take them into the stable. This was the last time he intended on riding with Louisa Morehouse. In fact, he was going to do his very best to stay away from her. He'd taken only a couple of steps toward the barn when she pressed her hand into his arm.

"I would like to go into the village tomorrow to do some shopping."

"Take McCallum with you then." If she expected him to accompany her, she'd lost her mind. He took another step forward only to have her stop him again.

"Actually, I wanted to ask if I might have a small advance on my salary."

"Tell McCallum what you need, and he'll see to it." With a sharp nod, he led the horses into the stable. Right now, he wanted to put as much distance between him and Louisa Morehouse as he could and as fast as possible.

Chapter 8

The sound of children's voices outside his study door pulled Ewan's attention away from the account log he'd been reviewing. A second later, there was a knock on the door, and before he could call out a command to enter, the door swung open.

Without even glancing in his direction, Louisa stormed his study without so much of a by-your-leave or other explanation. Following in her wake were all three boys carrying cutlery, plates, and cups.

Completely blind-sided, he watched in stunned disbelief as his private sanctuary erupted into a place of chaos. Pointing toward the table where he took his meals, Louisa issued orders much in the same way he had while leading the soldiers of the Black Watch regiment in the Sudan. Just like the men under his command, the children obeyed her orders without question.

"Wills, you and Charlie may set the table. Asadi and McCallum will be here in a moment with supper." Louisa set a tray of cutlery and mugs down on the table and glanced over her shoulder. "Careful with the milk, please, Ross."

Ewan turned his head slightly to see the boy carefully walking toward the table with a large pitcher in hand. As Ross set the pitcher on the table, Ewan recovered his wits and scowled at Louisa as she turned to him.

"What the devil do you think you're doing," he snarled.

"As I recall, you agreed to have supper with me and the children if you lost our wager this afternoon, which you did. Since you refused to come to the nursery for supper, I've decided to collect my winnings here instead."

"I said it was a tie," Ewan muttered with displeasure.

"And I disagreed," she said with a smile that made his chest tighten as the air in his lungs disappeared.

Before he could drag more air into his lungs and order her out of the room, Asadi and McCallum arrived with two trays filled with food. With a smile, Louisa directed the Scotsman and Ewan's self-proclaimed servant where to set the food on the table. On their way out the door, Asadi beamed a wide grin in his direction, but it was McCallum's amusement that made Ewan's lip curl slightly in a silent snarl of irritation. As the door closed between two men, Louisa directed the boys where to sit, and began preparing plates for them.

"Come have supper, Ewan. You don't want it to grow cold." She looked over her shoulder at him, an irreverent smile on her sweet mouth. "It's mutton pie. Mrs. Selkirk said it's one of your favorites."

Ewan grunted as he considered whether to ignore her dictates and go back to his desk. At this point, surrender seemed the better part of reason. If he tried to return to his accounts, the woman would hound him until he joined her and the boys. As he sat down at the table, the satisfaction that flitted across her oval-shaped features made him glare at her profile.

She added a helping of neeps and tatties next to his pie then carried the plate to where he sat at the head of the table. The moment she set the plate down in front of him, he caught her by the wrist and forced her to bend downward until their faces were mere inches apart. Electricity shot up his arm as he touched her.

He'd expected the shock, but not the strength of it. The scent of roses filled his nostrils as she turned her head to look at him. Laughter danced in her hazel eyes, and her smile twisted his insides into knots. As they stared at each other, he saw awareness softening her face, and her tongue flicked out to wet her mouth that was parted in a sultry invitation.

It ignited a fire inside him that could easily spiral out of control if he allowed it to. God help him. He wanted her in his bed looking at him just as she did now. If the boys hadn't been in the room, he would have pulled her down into his lap and taken his time exploring her. A wave of pink color flooded her cheeks, at the same moment her eyes darkened with an emotion that held him captive. Was this what she would look like as he thrust his body into hers? The thought made his mouth tighten as he struggled to curb the desire hardening every one of his muscles.

"You have a habit of storming into my private sanctuary much in the way a mistress of the house might, Louisa," he murmured as he heard his voice thicken with desire. Deliberately, he rubbed the inside of her wrist with his thumb. "If you persist, I'll assume there is another room you intend to invade as well."

A slight tremor shook her body and vibrated against the palm of his hand. It sent another jolt of electricity crashing through him, and Ewan immediately released his hold on her. Although she was free of his restraint, the tension in the air held her frozen at his side. Heat filled the space between them, and the awareness he saw flashing in her eyes was a familiar one. It was a sensation he'd already come to accept as natural whenever he was near her.

In the next instant, her mouth thinned with irritation. Louisa straightened upright with a small jerk and glared down at him before walking away to grab a mug off a dinner tray. She walked back to his side, and with a restrained, yet vicious, gesture set it down hard in front of him.

Beer sloshed out onto the table, and her lips curved upwards in a disdainful smile before she stalked away from him. Unable to help himself, Ewan released a loud laugh, which earned him a blistering glare from her as she moved toward her seat. Louisa Morehouse was apparently accustomed to having her own way, and he'd turned the tables on her. Louisa seated herself opposite him and continued to glare at him.

"Are you all right, Mama?" Wills asked with a frown. "You look angry."

"I am angry, my darling, but not with you." Louisa reached out to squeeze her son's hand and offered him a reassuring smile. The moment her gaze fell back on Ewan, her scowl returned.

Although he'd not been happy to see Louisa show up unannounced with the children in tow, the truth was he was beginning to enjoy himself. Louisa's demeanor was enough to thwart conversation, and everyone ate their dinner in quiet. They were halfway through the meal when Louisa's anger began to abate as she broke the silence.

"Are the three of you enjoying your riding lessons?"

At her question, the solemn expressions on the faces of the boys relaxed into cheerful smiles and excited chattering. To his surprise, he actually liked the noise. He glanced in Ross's direction, and the boy's broad grin startled him. Louisa had only been here for a short while, but in that time she'd managed a transformation in Ross that amazed him as much as it shamed him. He should have recognized sooner the child's need for affection and companionship with other children. Ewan grimaced as he realized he'd inflicted his own painful childhood on the boy.

"Charlie and Wills are both excellent riders, Mrs. Morehouse." Although Ross's voice wasn't as loud as the other two boys, it had a happy note to it that sent another blast of shame through Ewan.

"You have the makings of an exceptional horseman as well, Ross," he said gruffly as he skewered the last bite of

Scotch pie on his plate. As he popped the meat pastry into his mouth, he saw Ross's wide-eyed disbelief and pleasure at the compliment. The child looked as if Ewan had just been given the most wonderful present he'd ever received.

"Thank you, Father," the child said with a radiant smile. Ewan winced slightly and reached for his beer.

"I think it's time McCallum finds a more suitable mount for you. A plow horse is not the best choice for refining one's riding skills," he paused slightly as he looked over the rim of his cup at Louisa. "Charlie and Wills will have one too."

The table erupted with excitement, as the boys cried out a chorus of thanks before discussing the possible choices of animal the family retainer would select for them. Opposite him, Louisa's surprise gave way to a warm smile of approval that sent a rush of pleasure through him. The moment the sensation spread its heat through him, Ewan frowned.

Louisa Morehouse was a formidable woman when it came to getting her way. Her brother had been right. Louisa never asked permission, only forgiveness, and he was beginning to realize how well that strategy worked for her— especially where he was concerned. Ewan shoved his plate away from him in a rough gesture and rose to his feet.

"I have work to do. Work that requires quiet." He deliberately focused his eye on Louisa. She frowned at his abruptness, but nodded a silent agreement.

Satisfied his request would be honored, Ewan walked back to his desk. As he sank down into his chair, he opened the ledger he'd been working on before his unexpected guests had arrived. After a few moments, he heard the soft sound of cutlery being collected and the boys leaving the study. A movement at the edge of his large desk made him look up to see Ross standing in front of him.

"What is it, Ross?" he asked quietly as he studied the boy.

"I...might...I would like to buy a Christmas present for Mrs. Morehouse, Charlie, and Wills, my lord," he stammered before his words echoed out in a rush of air. "I know you always give the servants coin on Boxing Day, but I would like to do something special for Mrs. Selkirk and McCallum too."

"I assume you'll need money for these gifts?"

"Yes, Father." The boy's manner of addressing him made Ewan stiffen. He remained silent for a moment as he studied Ross's hesitant expression then nodded his head.

"I'll see to it that McCallum gives you what you need."

"Thank you, Father, and thank you again for the horse. I'll work hard to make you proud."

The boy's words were like a dagger in his heart as he remembered saying something similar to his mother when he'd been about Ross's age and so desperate to please her. He shook his head slowly.

"You're a good lad, Ross. But don't ever do anything in order to seek anyone's approval. Not even mine." He met the child's bewildered gaze with a steady one. "The only approval you should care about is your own. Always ask yourself, are you a living a good, kind, and honorable life because in the end that's all that counts."

Ross continued to stare solemnly at him when Ewan saw Louisa moving toward him and the boy. She came to a halt behind her charge and settled her hands on the boy's shoulders. Her hands squeezed Ross's shoulders in obvious affection, and the gesture heightened his guilt for treating the boy so shamefully. The child was a victim of circumstances brought about by a woman who enjoyed inflicting pain.

"It's time to say goodnight, Ross," Louisa said in a motherly tone.

"Goodnight, Father." The child stepped back from the desk and bowed in his direction before heading toward the door.

When Louisa didn't move, he arched his eyebrow at her in a questioning manner. The flush cresting in her cheeks made her look like a debutante fresh out of the school room, while her full bosom and womanly curves said otherwise. He drew in a sharp breath at the thought. Christ Jesus, he desperately needed Alanna's services more than he realized.

The cackling laugh in the back of his head called him a liar. There was only one remedy for what ailed him, and it involved more than one dose. The thought made his chest tighten at how easily this woman twisted him into knots. He'd already taken things to far at the supper table when he'd suggested she might enter his bed.

"I wanted to express my thanks for your generous gesture where the boys are concerned."

"You've said them. Now leave. I've work to do."

He deliberately focused his attention on the ledger in front of him and dismissed her with a sharp wave of his hand. Ewan expected her to turn away, but when she didn't, he released a harsh sound of aggravation that was born more out of desperation than actual ire. Determined to make himself as disagreeable as possible, he lifted his head.

"What do you want of me now, Louisa?"

Color flushed her cheeks again before she straightened to her full height and squared her shoulders as if she were headed into battle. Ewan steeled himself for what was to come.

"I wanted to say I was sorry. I was wrong about you."

"Wrong?" Startled, Ewan jerked backward in his seat. His body hardened with tension as he watched her cheeks darken to a deep shade of pink.

"I was wrong to say you were a cruel and heartless man, and I'm sorry."

"And what brought about this change of heart?" he murmured sardonically as he relaxed further into the depths of his chair. She flinched beneath his mockery, but didn't look away. In the back of his head, he acknowledged admiration for her unceasing ability not to be intimidated by him. It also served as a warning where this woman and his reactions to her were concerned.

"Your kindness to Ross at the supper table, and again, just now."

The approval in her voice made him recall the words he'd just spoken to Ross. A good man only did things for the right reason, never to please others. It sent another harsh wave of guilt and shame crashing down on him.

"I was no more kind to the boy than I was to your own children," he said as his scars tightened painfully from the strain of his taut cheek muscles.

"It's not just that you were kind to Ross, it's the fact that you acknowledged his presence by commenting on his riding skills."

Ewan knew she was right, but she didn't understand that shame had been the reason he'd shown interest in the boy. Shame, and a deep regret, that it had taken him so long to realize the injustice he'd done to Ross. Publicly acknowledging another man's son as his own had been a conscious choice. Even though he'd made his decision under duress and as one of self-interest, he'd openly accepted Ross as his son.

Privately, from the first moment he'd seen the lad, he had wanted nothing to do with the boy. What he'd failed to realize was that he didn't have to love Ross, but the boy deserved nothing less than kindness from him. Perhaps the most shameful of all was that he understood what it was like not to be loved by a parent. That he'd inflicted a similar punishment on the boy shamed him the most. He shook his head.

"Didn't you see his face, Ewan?" Palms pressed into the desktop, Louisa leaned over the desk toward him. "Didn't you see how much your words meant to him?"

"Damn it, Louisa, I'll not be chastised about the boy or anything else in my own house." His chair crashed backwards to the floor as he stood up and leaned toward her until he could breathe in the warm fragrance of her. Oblivious to his anger, she didn't retreat, she simply glared at him with righteous indignation.

"Well someone needs to say something, because until now, I don't think anyone's had the wherewithal to call you out on the topic."

"A topic that isn't your concern," he said through clenched teeth.

"As his governess, it is my concern." Louisa's voice held a defiant note as she glared at him. "All he wants is to be loved, Ewan. He wants to be loved so desperately."

"You clearly don't understand what a boundary is, Louisa," he snarled.

With an angry noise of frustration, he lost his head and did the only thing he could think of to silence her. Her eyes widened in surprise as his hand curled around the nape of her neck and tugged her forward so his mouth could taste the heat of hers.

A small sound of shock vibrated against his lips as he kissed her hard. In the back of his head, he heard shouts of warnings, but ignored them as he experienced the first hot taste of her. Sweet and succulent as a summer strawberry, her lips singed his in a way that cautioned him to release her.

The warning went unheeded as he plundered her mouth as a man who'd just found a forbidden treasure. Beneath his kilt, his cock hardened and jutted outward in a silent demand for satisfaction. The soft murmur whispering out of her gave him the opportunity to slip his tongue into her mouth until it mated with hers. The sugary confection they'd had for dessert still lingered in her mouth, and he couldn't remember a tablet tasting any sweeter than it did at this precise moment.

The scent of roses filled his nostrils with every breath he took. It was an aroma he knew he would recognize even in the dark. Until now, she'd been passive against the assault of her mouth, but with a quiet mewl of pleasure, her tongue hesitantly twirled around his. With each passing second, her response grew until it was an uncontrolled, heated response that fired his blood.

Every stroke of her tongue against his made his cock throb. It was an unfulfilled ache he'd only experienced in the dark when dreaming of her or remembering her beautiful lush curves. He wanted to explore every inch of her with his hands and mouth until he'd committed all of her to memory. Desire pounded against his body as the need to drag her off to his bed surged through him.

The thought pierced the red haze of desire engulfing him, and he abruptly jerked away from her. Her hazel eyes fluttered open, and his heart slammed into his chest at the desire he saw there. Christ Jesus, what the fuck was he thinking to kiss her like that. A knot formed in his throat as he retreated even further from her. Determined to avoid something like this ever happening again, he arched a mocking eyebrow at her.

"As I indicated earlier, if you continue to act as if you were mistress of Argaty House then I'll assume you're willing to perform all the duties that accompany the role."

For a moment, she stared at him with a mixture of mortification and disbelief. The impact her expression had on him was as if someone had landed a hard blow to his stomach. A split-second later, anger tightened her sweet mouth. He wanted to groan at the sight. If he'd thought she would flee the room, he'd been wrong. The woman was hopping mad, and he knew Louisa Morehouse well enough by now to know she wasn't about to let him have the last word.

"You kissed me, you arrogant beast. And I am most certainly not trying to act like the mistress of your house," she snapped. "I've become quite attached to your son, and the least you can—"

Louisa froze in mid-sentence as she stared at the wall behind him. Despite knowing he wouldn't see anything, he instinctively glanced over his shoulder to confirm the fact. When he faced Louisa again, he saw her lovely face crumple beneath a look of pain and guilt, while the color drained from her cheeks. She quickly turned away from Ewan, but not before he saw her struggling to hold back her tears. Certain the *an dara sealladh* had shown her something, he moved quickly around the desk to catch her if she were to faint.

"What is it, lass? What did you see?" he asked quietly as his fingers brushed across the warm skin of her arm. She immediately jumped at the touch while keeping her head averted so he could only see her profile.

"The past. I saw the past." The words were less than a whisper as he saw her fingers brush across the cheek she kept half-hidden from him. "If you'll excuse me, my lord, I'll bid you goodnight."

Before he could stop her, she spun away from him and hurried toward the door. He started to follow, but she was gone before he was halfway across the room. Whatever she'd seen, it had stirred memories of a painful past. The emotions he'd seen tearing her apart just now, were the same as those he'd seen the night he'd asked if she'd driven her man to drink. He returned to his chair and sank down into the smooth wood seat as he continued to stare at the door Louisa had closed behind her.

What in the name of all the saints had he been thinking to kiss her? Ewan hit the arm of his chair with his fist. With a groan of self-disgust, he closed his only eye as he remembered how he'd tried to silence her with a kiss. Even now the sweet, hot taste of her lingered on his lips.

He'd seriously miscalculated the depth of his desire for Louisa. A snort of contemptuous laughter escaped him. It hadn't been an error, it had been nothing short of denial. Every time he was near her, he'd convinced himself to believe his attraction nothing more than the amount of time he'd been without a woman. His refusal to admit the truth had brought him to the brink of insanity.

Christ Jesus, it was far worse than insanity. That kiss had only increased his desire for her. It made him want much more than another taste of her lips. No, he wanted the woman in his bed, and that was madness. He needed to stay as far away from Louisa Morehouse as possible.

Another groan escaped him the instant he admitted that action would likely prove to be a futile effort. Even if he tried to keep his distance, he had no doubt Louisa would make it difficult for him to do so.

Louisa swayed as she closed the door of Ewan's study behind her. Asadi, sitting in his usual place outside the door, was on his feet in a flash of movement to hold her steady.

"You are ill, Morehouse sahibah?" At the concern in the young man's voice Louisa shook her head. She patted the young man's hand on her arm in a reassuring manner.

"I'll be fine, Asadi. I'm simply tired."

"I will walk you to your room."

"There's no need to—"

"I will take you." Asadi assumed a stance that said she wasn't to argue with him.

"I think you've been working for the earl too long. You've acquired his stubbornness," she murmured with irony at the idea anyone could be as obstinate as her.

"Argaty sahib would want me to do this." The determined note in his voice made Louisa acquiesce with a nod.

The sorrow and shame consuming her was making her queasy, and it was impossible not to be grateful for the young man's insistence to walk her back to her room. Caleb's appearance in Ewan's study and subsequent condemnation of her behavior, had shaken her to the core. Eager to put off the inevitable reckoning as to her flaws and self-recrimination, she glanced at the boy beside her.

"How long have you been with the earl, Asadi?"

"I cared for Argaty sahib at hospital. He needed help without his arm."

"That was very kind of you."

"I owe Argaty sahib my life. He gave his arm to save me."

The awed reverence in Asadi's voice, made her flinch. Dear God, how could she have been so blind? She'd misjudged Ewan so terribly. Unwilling to ask for any further details for fear she would cry in front of the child, she simply nodded her head and didn't probe any further.

One hand cupping her elbow, Asadi guided her down the hall as they walked in silence. When they reached her room, Louisa hesitated at the doorway afraid of being alone with only the past to haunt her. Asadi opened the door, and when she didn't move, he gently nudged her forward.

"Selkirk sahibah will make tea for you, and I will bring it."

"No, thank you. I'll be fine."

With a small smile at the boy, Louisa turned away and entered her bedroom. Still feeling wobbly on her feet, she pressed her back into the solid wood door for support as it snapped shut. Eyes closed in regret, she shuddered at her behavior in Ewan's study. Caleb had been right to berate her so harshly when he'd appeared to her. She'd misjudged Ewan terribly. In her self-righteousness, she'd tried, judged, and convicted him without knowing the truth. Her brother's words floated through her head.

"The boy isn't his, Louisa. Do not repeat the past and judge him as quickly as you did Devin."

A tear threatened to escape from beneath a closed eyelid, and she released a soft sob of regret and self-recrimination.

"They were words you needed to hear, little sister."

The affectionate childhood endearment echoed gently in the air around her as her brother's translucent, shadowy outline materialized in front of her.

"I know," she choked out. "I had no right to judge him. I'm the one who should be judged."

"You're the only one judging your words and actions, Louisa."

"How can I not?" She raised her hands in a violent gesture of denial. "I told him I wished he was dead."

"Do you think you're the only one who has ever said things in the heat of anger? Words that can never be taken back?"

"No," she whispered as she admitted the real truth. "It's more than that."

Her sin wasn't just in the words she'd said the night Devin died. It was the realization that her love for Devin had been no deeper than his. She'd failed to love him in the same way she'd always wanted to be loved. They'd been content, even happy, but deep inside she'd always known there had been something missing.

Their marriage had lacked the deep, loving bond she'd wanted so desperately. Throughout her marriage to Devin, she'd dismissed her desire for such a profound connection as nothing more than a foolish woman's romantic notions. The expectation of wanting something more from Devin had always made her feel ungrateful for the contentment they'd shared.

Even now, she still wondered if she were being too selfish to have wanted more from Devin. Although she'd always been overjoyed her siblings had found love in their lives, she'd never admitted until now how envious she'd been of their deep happiness. A happiness that deeper and richer than the one she'd had with her husband. The memory of Sebastian confessing he would never keep a secret from Helen had made her heart weep that she and Devin had not shared the same trust and commitment. The painful realization sent tears streaming down her cheeks.

"He loved you, Louisa. He loved you very much, but even he would admit it wasn't in the way you wanted or deserved to be loved."

Caleb's quiet words made her draw in a sharp breath as she realized her brother had seen deep into her heart. Her chest tightened painfully as an invisible caress brushed over her cheek as if to wipe away the teardrops rolling down her cheeks.

"Sebastian has always been your rock and loved you dearly in spite of your faults, Louisa. Everyone has, but of all of us, you know I'm the one who understood you best, little sister."

At the gentleness in her brother's voice, her tears flowed harder and blurred her vision. Her sobs echoed softly in the room as she struggled to forgive herself for all her faults. An invisible caress brushed across her cheek and ended with a gentle tug on her ear. Startled, Louisa gasped at the touch. It was the same caress Devin had always used when she'd been repentant for something she'd said or done. It had been a loving acceptance of her apology, as well as a gesture of understanding for her impulsive, rash manner.

"Devin?" she whispered.

Louisa's gaze darted around the room in search of her dead husband's shadow, but she was alone. Even her brother's shimmering image had vanished. The only response to her small cry was silence. Overwhelmed with remorse and sorrow, she released a sob and stumbled her way to the bed then sank down into the mattress. A soft creak filled the air, and tears still coursing down her cheeks, Louisa turned her head toward the noise.

Dusk had settled on the moors, and the shadows filling the room seemed to move of their own accord in front of her blurred vision. When Louisa didn't hear the sound again, she fell deeper into her bed and continued to sob. In her grief, she failed see the shadow moving stealthily along the wall and passing through the secret door Robert the Bruce had once fled through.

Chapter 9

Louisa accepted McCallum's hand as she descended from the carriage. Once she was standing on the drive in front of the keep, the Scotsman moved to the back of the carriage to retrieve the purchases made in the village.

As she shook out her skirts, the boys tumbled rambunctiously out of the vehicle behind her. Their boisterous laughter had not stopped the entire time they'd been away from the keep. Ross's behavior was as cheerful as her sons, and she marveled at the difference in him from their first meeting.

While the child could still be quite solemn, he smiled and laughed frequently. McCallum looked in the boys' direction and arched his eyebrow at her as he handed her the packages she'd purchased. The twinkle in the man's eye made her laugh as she accepted her packages and walked into the main hall of the keep followed by the boys. Their trip to the village had been a great success. The boys had managed to find small presents for each other while ensuring they remained a secret. She'd been pleased to find something appropriate for everyone. She'd even purchased a present for the dowager countess, although why she'd done so eluded her.

The woman's vitriol was poisonous, and Louisa took great measure to keep herself and the boys away from the woman. She knew Patience and Constance would chide her for being uncharitable, but her sisters hadn't been subjected to the dowager's cold manner or arrogant dictates.

Since taking on the role of governess to Ross, the woman had summoned Louisa to her chambers almost daily to demand the boys refrain from making so much noise. She'd even suggested Louisa had her eye on her son and his title. With a look of disdain, the countess had informed Louisa that an impoverished widow with two children should refrain from aspiring to marrying an earl.

In her role as Lady Westbrook, she would never have allowed the woman's insult to go unanswered, but as Mrs. Morehouse, she'd known to bite her tongue. It had taken a strength of willpower she never knew she possessed not to inform the woman they were social equals. Instead, Louisa had clenched her teeth as she fought hard to keep from telling the woman what a soulless creature she was.

The dowager countess seemed to know it was a struggle for Louisa to bite her tongue whenever the two of them met. She was certain it was the reason for the malicious smile that always accompanied the woman's insults. The boys skirted her as they ran into Argaty Keep's imposing hall. Their laughter echoed loudly beneath the high ceiling, and memory of the countess's complaints about the boys' boisterous behavior made her wince. Wills was trying to grab a toy horse Charlie held over his head, while Ross was bent over in laughter. She frowned and expelled a breath of exasperation.

"Charlie, stop—"

"Stop this noise, *immediately.*" Lady Argaty's words echoed in the hall with a cold ferocity that made the boys jerk around to stare at the dowager's bitter anger in silent apprehension. "I will not stand for this kind of ruffian behavior in my house. Is that understood?"

All three of the children slowly nodded their heads, but Louisa caught the glint of anger in Charlie's eyes. Alarmed her son might say or do something reckless, she quickly headed off any such possibility.

"Let's go upstairs, boys," she said in a gentle voice. *"Quietly."*

Charlie appeared ready to protest as he frowned and glared at the dowager before looking back at Louisa. With a small shake of her head, she silently warned her son not to speak. Disgust darkened Charlie's features, but he didn't argue with her and followed his brother and Ross up the stairs. Louisa was about to do the same when she saw the dowager countess glaring at her from the doorway of the salon.

"Was there something else?" Louisa was proud as to how polite her voice was when what she really wanted to do was eviscerate the woman with a scathing diatribe.

"You may join me in the parlor, Mrs. Morehouse."

The woman's imperious command made Louisa stiffen with irritation, but she tipped her head at the woman in a sign of acquiescence. The boys had almost reached the top of the stairs but she called Charlie back to her and handed him the parcels in her arms. As she instructed him to place the packages in her room, he glared at the empty salon doorway. Touched by her son's obvious desire to defend her, Louisa brushed his forehead with a loving kiss before gently silently urging him to go back up the stairs.

When all three boys were out of view, Louisa turned toward the parlor with a sigh of resignation. Preparing herself for an unpleasant conversation with Ewan's mother, she walked across the entryway. As she entered the parlor, Louisa saw the dowager had selected a regal, almost throne-like chair to sit in. Louisa tilted her chin upward with a resolute determination not to let the woman make her lose her temper. A voice in the back of her head snorted its skepticism. Louisa crossed the room until there were only a few feet between them.

"My sister tells me you've planned a Christmas

celebration here in the keep."

"A small one. Lord Argaty gave me permission to have a tree, and I've asked Mrs. Selkirk if she could make a few special treats for the day."

"I forbid any such activities to take place in Argaty Keep. We do *not* celebrate Christmas in this household."

"I don't understand, my lady. The earl gave me—"

"I *said* there will be no celebration."

The woman's emphatic statement rang out in the room like a crash of thunder. An even colder look than she normally wore emphasized the dowager's harsh, bitter appearance. It made her look old and pinched. Louisa stared at the woman for a long moment in silence. Although it was impossible to determine what the woman was thinking, Louisa was certain her lack of a response was unsettling for the woman.

"If that will be all, my—"

"I have not dismissed you," the dowager snapped.

The sharp words made Louisa grit her teeth as she fought desperately not to give the woman the dressing down she deserved. It could jeopardize her position. She had no idea how much sway the woman had over her son, and it would be foolish to test this particular boundary. Especially if he insisted on kissing her every time he drew a line in the sand that she didn't hesitate to cross. Louisa quickly shoved the thought of his kiss out of her head.

"Forgive me, Lady Argaty, but your *son* employed me to act as Ross's governess, and I must defer to his instructions."

"I suggest you remember your place, Mrs. Morehouse."

The stress the woman put on her last name only increased Louisa's irritation. The dowager wasn't simply unpleasant, she was offensive in her treatment of everyone around her. An image of Ewan as a child made her wince. His life had most likely been as miserable as Ross's had been, if not more so.

Another image fluttered through her head, and she recognized the onset of the *an dara sealladh*. Intuition warned her not to let the dowager countess know she had the gift of sight, and Louisa swallowed hard.

"Forgive me, my lady, but I am suddenly feeling ill."

Lady Argaty sputtered incoherently for a brief moment before regaining her voice to speak harshly. The woman's vitriol was little more than a buzzing in her ear as Louisa bolted from the room. In the main hall, she struggled to remain standing as she staggered toward the stairs. A tall, shadowy figure appeared in front of her but the *an dara sealladh* blinded her as it took hold of her senses. With an outstretched hand, she whispered her brother's name as the real world receded.

The oppressive darkness gave her the sensation of someone pressing her down to the floor. A baby's cries filled the air behind her, and she turned toward the sound. In front of her, the darkness parted slightly to reveal a much younger dowager countess holding a baby in her arms. The woman was staring down at the child in her arms with horror and revulsion.

Wallis suddenly appeared at her sister's side and tried to gently pull the baby from the dowager's arms. With a violent sweep of her hand, Lady Argaty struck her sister hard. The brutal blow caused Wallis to stumble backward before she regained her footing.

The dowager's virulent hatred was chilling as she fixed her icy gaze on her sister. Even though Louisa couldn't hear Lady Argaty's words, they left Wallis stricken and swaying on her feet. It was painful to see. Cold satisfaction twisted the dowager's mouth into a cruel, malicious smile as she watched her sister stumble away into the dark.

A second later, Louisa heard a woman shriek behind her. Fear latched onto her as she whirled around. There was nothing but a pitch black darkness in front of her as she tried to see in front of her. The bitter cold enveloping her grew in strength to hold her paralyzed where she stood.

Fear pulled a moan up into her throat that she couldn't release as the bloodcurdling screech grew in pitch then was abruptly cut off. The moment the woman's cry ended, a horrible, gleeful laugh filled the air. The cold sank through her pores until it became her blood grew icy and it spread its glacial sensation through her entire body. He'd killed her. The child had killed the woman. She didn't know how or when, but Louisa knew it with so much certainty it made her ill to think of it.

Angry muted voices echoed above her as the real world began to seep its way back into her senses. Sharp as glass, Lady Argaty's voice sliced through the air as if from a great distance. The woman's words hovered on the edge of her senses, but the quiet, yet forceful, sound of Ewan's voice made her feel safe. As the *an dara sealladh* slowly released her from its grip, it was as if someone had opened a door that allowed her to hear the argument between mother and son.

"Why didn't you *tell me* the woman had the sight?"

"I saw nae reason tae." Although his voice was steady and calm, the strength of Ewan's burr indicated he was furious. "What are ye afraid of Mother?"

"I have nothing to fear. I simply don't like the way this woman has disrupted my household." Lady Argaty's words vibrated with contempt, but there was an apprehension beneath the woman's denial that puzzled Louisa.

"*Your* household?" Despite Ewan's quiet question, Louisa heard the icy note of rage in his voice. "You forget your place, Mother. *I'm* the Earl of Argaty, and this is *my* household."

"An earl who buries himself in seclusion leaving me and Wallis to maintain order in the house."

"You dinnae have a single drop of domestic *or maternal*

instinct in you, Mother. The only thing you've ever possessed was a tongue as vicious as a viper."

Louisa's eyes fluttered open, and she realized she was lying on her bed. Mrs. Selkirk's matter-of-fact voice beside the bed made her turn her head toward the housekeeper.

"Well, now, ye decided to come back tae the mortal world, have ye." The woman's weathered features was softened by her cheerful smile as she patted Louisa's arm. The solid warmth of Ewan filled her senses as he bent over her.

"How do you feel?" The note of concern running beneath the words startled her, but she brushed the sensation aside.

"Other than feeling a bit woozy, I'm fine," she murmured. Relief softened his battle-scarred features, and the realization he'd been deeply worried about her warmed Louisa's heart. "How did I find my way to my room? I don't remember climbing the stairs."

"My son had no choice but to carry you up here, Mrs. Morehouse, after the stir you caused downstairs." At Lady Argaty's scathing criticism, Louisa winced with embarrassment, and Ewan jerked upright to pin his mother beneath an ominous, frosty glare.

"Leave."

The single word was a vicious, harsh command even Louisa would have found difficult to disobey. The black eyepatch over Ewan's missing eye combined with his dark anger gave him a menacing look, and the dowager countess stiffened. Although she remained cold and patronizing, it was easy to see the woman was afraid. But Louisa didn't know if it was her son's anger she feared or something else.

With one last baleful glance in Louisa's direction, the dowager countess stalked out of the room. Anger still held him rigid as Ewan cleared his throat. His mouth moved as if he wanted to say something, before a soft noise of fierce frustration escaped him.

"I'll leave Mrs. Morehouse in your care, Mrs. Selkirk." Ewan looked away from the housekeeper back to Louisa and cleared his throat. "I told the boys you were feeling a bit under the weather, and I've arranged for the three of them to have supper with me."

The quiet explanation made Louisa stare at him in amazement. Something between exasperation and embarrassment made his mouth tightened in a grimace as he observed her astonished reaction. Without another word, he strode from the room. As she watched the door close behind him, Mrs. Selkirk clucked softly.

"There goes a mon plagued by a mother who has a heart as cold as a winter's wind on the moor."

"Has she always shown such antipathy for him? Her own son?"

"Aye, the woman is dead inside—has been for a verra long time," the housekeeper said as anger darkened her kind features.

An image of Ewan as a young boy filled her head. She was certain he must have been just as desperate for love as Ross. The thought of it made her heart ache for him, especially when she considered how happy her childhood had been even though she didn't remember her parents.

"You're very fond of him."

"Aye, he always was a good lad with a smile or kind word for others." The housekeeper shook her head with a sigh of sadness. "His time fighting in foreign lands changed him."

"How long did he serve with the Black Watch?" At Louisa's question, the housekeeper frowned in contemplation.

"Let me think, he joined the regiment shortly before he was married. He was called to duty only a week or so after his wedding." Mrs. Selkirk shook her head in sympathy. "He came home shortly after Lady Argaty died in childbirth."

"Is that when he came home with his injuries?"

"Och, no. He was only here for two days after the young countess's death. Several of us overheard Lord Argaty and her ladyship arguing bitterly and hours later he was gone. I think he stayed away because of that woman," Mrs. Selkirk said in a contemptuous voice. A moment later she sighed quietly, and a deep sadness lined her plump features. "The mon dinnae come home for seven years. And I think he would have remained in the Black Watch for much longer if he'd nae been injured so badly."

"With the exception of a few minor difficulties, his injuries don't seem to be an impediment for him."

The memory of his firm fingers wrapped around her neck and tugging her toward him made Louisa's heart skip a beat. Warmth tingled her lips as she remembered the taste of him. Devin had never kissed her with such unrestrained passion. His kisses had always been gentle and tender.

Last night, Ewan's caress had been a fiery heat against her lips. The firm, hard, pressure of his mouth against hers had aroused sensations she'd not experienced since before the fire at Westbrook. The desire he'd stirred in her had left her wanting something more than a kiss. She'd been left aching for the pleasure and intimacy of Ewan's touch. The sound of Mrs. Selkirk's voice saved her from contemplating just how much she wanted the man's touch.

"Aye, he does nae let anything stop him from doing what he wants." Mrs. Selkirk nodded with a motherly pride Louisa recognized as one she experienced frequently with her boys. The housekeeper's expression dissolved into one of despair. "But it's his spirit that dinnae come back with him. It pains me to see him the way he is now. There's one thing her ladyship said tis true. The mon buries himself away from most of life's little pleasures."

"It takes time to heal from traumatic events," Louisa murmured as she remembered her own struggle with grief and remorse. Mrs. Selkirk nodded her head in agreement then gasped in dismay.

"Och, bless me if I'm nae babbling on about things instead of getting you a hot cup of tea." The housekeeper leaned over Louisa and patted her shoulder in a reassuring gesture before she hurried from the room.

Left alone with her thoughts, Louisa slowly sat up. A small wave of dizziness made her close her eyes, and she waited for the sensation to pass. She found herself wishing Constance or Percy was here to talk to. She knew the *an dara sealladh* had affected both of them physically. But she was certain her sister would understand better than Percy.

With the exception of Aunt Matilda, Constance had shared little with the family about the time she'd spent at the Lyndham family estate before she'd married Lucien. The most any of them really knew was that if not for Lucien, she and Jamie might have died. It had been her nephew, who'd described the aftereffects of his mother's visions after Jamie had witnessed one of Percy's migraines.

Louisa turned to look at the small secretaire near the window. For a brief moment, she contemplated writing her sister then thought better of it. Constance would want to know more about Louisa's vision, and the moment she told her sister what she'd seen, Constance would tell Sebastian. At which point, Sebastian and the entire family would be demanding she be dragged out of Argaty Keep.

She couldn't take that chance. Ross needed her. In the back of her head, she remembered Caleb's words. He needs you. Instantly, an image of Ewan's scarred features filled her head. What if it had been Ewan, not Ross, her brother had been referring to all along? Louisa sucked in a sharp breath before she pushed the thought back in the furthest recesses of her mind. She was here because Ross needed her, nothing more. The sound of her brother's laughter whispered through her head, but she ignored the sound.

Louisa pulled on her gloves as she walked out of the keep into the stable yard. The day was bright with sunshine, although the air was crisp against her skin. The boys were dancing around with excitement as Finn emerged from the stable with an axe for cutting down a tree. The stable hand placed the axe in back of the small wagon then turned toward the boys.

"Come on, laddies, up you go."

As Finn helped the boys into the wagon, the clatter of hooves against the stable floor made Louisa turn her head. The sight of Ewan leading Lachlan and Morag out of the barn made her eyes widen in surprise.

"I seem to recall you inviting me to accompany you and the boys today." His eyebrow arched arrogantly upward.

"Yes...I mean...of course, I'm sure Ross will like that very much."

"We'll need room in the wagon for the tree, so I thought you and I would ride."

Speechless at his decision to join the party, Louisa nodded her agreement, and she saw his mouth twitch slightly. Certain he was laughing at her befuddled state she narrowed her gaze at him. Despite his solemn look, she saw his lips twitch again.

"You seem amused by something, my lord."

"Aye." He chuckled softly as he gestured toward Morag. "Shall we?"

It was obvious he had no intention of sharing what he found so amusing as he quickly tested the mare's cinch then formed a small stirrup with his good hand. The skirt of her riding habit swished angrily as she lifted the short side of her riding habit up and placed her foot in the palm of his hand. Fingers grasping Morag's mane and the saddle's pommel,

Louisa hopped upward.

For not the first time, it was impossible not to be impressed with how Ewan leveraged his good arm in unison with his entire body to assist her into the saddle. It explained how he'd managed to carry her from the main hall to her bedroom the other day. Louisa lifted her skirt higher and wrapped her right leg over the top pommel and braced her left leg beneath the leaping head pommel.

Ewan's hand guided her boot into the stirrup then reached up to assist her in pulling her skirts down over her riding breeches. The light touch of his hand brushing over her calf caused her to draw in a quick breath as heat seeped through her breeches.

Although she knew the contact was completely innocent, her body responded in the same way it had when he'd kissed her. He lifted his head at the sound, and her cheeks burned as he eyed her with curiosity. In an effort to ease the warmth suffusing her body, she busied herself adjusting her habit.

Ewan made a soft noise she couldn't describe before he turned away and mounted Lachlan. The stallion pranced in place as Ewan settled himself in the saddle. He walked his horse over to the wagon and issued a quiet order to Finn who nodded his understanding. With a light slap of the reins, Finn drove the wagon out of the stable yard.

With a gentle nudge into Morag's side, Louisa urged the horse to follow, and Ewan made Lachlan fall into step alongside her. Excited chatter floated back to fill the silence between them, and Louisa smiled as Ross spoke up in vigorous disagreement with Charlie. For not the first time, she marveled at the change in him. Almost as if he could read her mind, Ewan cleared his throat.

"Ross is thriving under your care." The quiet compliment made Louisa jerk her head in his direction. He arched his eyebrow as his mouth twitched slightly with amusement. "You're surprised by the compliment?"

"I...yes," she murmured.

"A forthright, honest answer."

"Would you prefer I'd lied?" she asked with a laugh.

"I don't think you're capable of lying," he said as a wry smile twisted his sensual lips. "At least not successfully. Your face would give you away."

"Guilty as charged. My family knows not to tell me any secrets because when I deny knowing anything, my expression says otherwise."

"Then you have no secrets to share?"

Ewan's voice was filled with amusement, but her heart skipped a beat at the possibility she might betray her growing attraction for him. But admitting she had secrets didn't mean revealing what they were. She smiled at him and shook her head.

"Everyone has secrets." At her reply Ewan frowned slightly then grinned at her. It was a look of wicked amusement, and her heart skipped a beat once again, only this time it wasn't in apprehension.

"Agreed, but there are many ways to extract a confession."

"That sounds as though it could be quite painful." Laughing she shook her head at him.

"I can think of several ways to learn your secrets...some of them quite pleasurable."

Ewan's battle-scarred features tightened with an emotion that made her draw in a sharp breath. The way he was watching her created a tactile sensation on her skin as she remembered their kiss in his study. Fire burned her cheeks at the memory, and a small tremor slipped through her.

His blue-gray eye had suddenly darkened, and she knew he was remembering the blazing heat of their kiss too. Her mouth went dry as she realized she wanted him to kiss her again. The dangerously wicked thought made her jerk her head to look out at the landscape in front of them.

"I think I'll let Morag stretch her legs across the moor," she said breathlessly in an attempt to control the emotions spiraling through her. "It will take a little while for the wagon to reach the forest."

"Perhaps another race?"

If sin were a voice, it would sound like his. It held an invitation she wanted to accept. She trembled at the thought. What would he demand as his prize? The intensity of his gaze told her exactly what it would be, and strength of her desire for him to kiss her again stole the breath from her lungs. With a shake of her head, she focused her sights on the sun-bathed moors in front of her.

"As I recall, you asked me to remind you never to agree to a wager with me again."

"A request I'm deeply regretting at the moment." The dark seduction in his voice made her body tighten in response.

"If I agreed to give you a head start, Louisa, would that make you reconsider?"

"If you gave me a head start, you would lose just as you did the last time."

Although she tried to keep her voice steady, she failed. Ewan maneuvered Lachlan closer and leaned toward her until there were mere inches between them. The heat of him washed over her as she inhaled the fresh scent of evergreen and leather. It was a heady aroma that tightened her body, most notably the spot between her legs that had begun to ache with a need for satisfaction.

"I have no intention of losing especially as I will demand a kiss as my prize," he murmured. Like a piece of soft velvet, his voice caressed her senses, and a tremor of excitement skimmed across her skin. Louisa swallowed the knot that had formed in her throat.

"I…I don't think—"

"For a woman who continually challenges me with regard to Ross, your reluctance to accept a small wager surprises me. Unless, of course, you know you'll lose." The laughter in his voice made her stiffen in the saddle.

"I would *not* lose," she snapped as she turned her head to glare at him.

Satisfaction was evident in the wicked smile curving a mouth that was so close to hers. The air in her lungs disappeared as she saw a fire ignite in him. It was the same fire heating her blood as desire flowed hot and fast through her. She trembled as she realized how much she wanted to be alone with him.

Louisa swallowed hard at the silent promise of passion he offered as he stared at her intently. It was an offer she knew would consume her and send her hurtling into a fiery blaze of blissful pleasure. The realization made her jump as if she'd suddenly awakened from an arousing dream. Ewan drew back from her body cried out its objection.

If they were alone…Louisa's breath hitched as she didn't finish the thought. Dear God, never in her life had her impulsive tongue sent her down such a dangerous, yet intoxicating path. Louisa quickly shook her head as she tried to refuse his challenge, but he'd already looked away to pull a pocket watch from inside the vest beneath his coat.

"We'll race to the tree line. I'll give you a three-minute head start."

"But I didn't…"

"Agree to a wager?" His wicked smile returned to slowly curve his mouth. "Aye, but you did, my bonnie lass. Are you trying to renege on our bet?"

Louisa's heartbeat quickened it's already frantic pace. There were only two choices available to her. The first meant admitting she was afraid of losing. While a Rockwood was a gracious loser, they never walked away from a challenge. The second was following a reckless path to a destination she found far more exciting than she should.

For not the first time in her life, she cursed the trait that had earned her family the infamous reputation for being reckless. A small sound escaped her as she saw the challenge glittering in his eye. Knowing she couldn't possibly back away from the proposed contest, Louisa pressed her leg into Morag's side. Startled by the hard nudge, the mare bolted forward, and Louisa heard Ewan utter an exclamation of surprise.

He'd not yet opened his pocket watch, and the delay would add several seconds to the handicap he'd agreed to give her. She quickly silenced the laughter in the back of her head at the idea Morag could outrun Lachlan even with a generous head start. If she were to make even a respectable showing, she would need every one of those seconds to win.

As she raced past the wagon, she heard the boys shouting as they suddenly realized there was a race happening. The tree line seemed a great distance away, and she leaned forward with her cheek almost pressed against the mare's neck. The wind had picked up, and a sharp gust tugged her hat off her head.

"Blast," she muttered as she urged the mare to go faster.

Beneath her, Morag's hooves pounded the ground as the mare increased the pace. For what seemed like forever, the forest was a stretch of indistinguishable green. Suddenly the tree line began to take shape more clearly. She could now see the evergreen bushes clumped together in various spots along the edge of the forest.

As she drew closer to the large expanse of woods, Morag's ears flicked back just before Louisa heard Lachlan behind her. The stallion's hooves were hitting the ground hard, which meant Ewan was pushing the horse. Louisa urged the mare to go faster, thinking there might still be a chance to win the race. Despite her urging, Morag began to flag, and the moment Lachlan raced past them, Louisa eased up on the mare.

It was pointless to push the horse any further knowing she couldn't win the race. Instead, she slowed Morag to a slow canter then a walk. When she reached the edge of the forest, Ewan had already dismounted and was walking Lachlan in a circle. She gently pulled Morag to a stop, and Ewan arched his eyebrow as a small smile of triumph tilted the corners of his mouth. Excitement swept through her. Perhaps losing might not have been a bad thing after all. Appalled by the audacious thought, she quickly threw her leg over the pommel and started to slide off the horse.

Ewan reached her before she was halfway to the ground. His good arm wrapped around her waist to pull her into his chest before setting her down in front of him. He didn't release her for a moment, and she thought he was about to kiss her. Instead, he glanced back to where the wagon was.

The small smile still curving his mouth didn't fade as he ushered her to the opposite side of Lachlan so they were hidden from view. Overhead, a screech filled the air, and they both looked up at the sound. A red kite soared high above, its wings dipped from back and forth as it rode the wind. Ewan turned his attention back to her to study her intently. Several locks of hair had escaped the knot at the back of her neck, and Ewan wrapped one of them around his forefinger.

"Your hair is the soft brown color of a kite's feathers." His words sent a heat wave up over her cheeks, and the way he was looking at her made her stomach lurch in a pleasant way. "You blush every time I give you a compliment."

"*I do not*," she exclaimed as her cheeks burned even hotter. His soft laugh made her heart race as his finger released the lock of hair and his thumb pressed down on her lower lip. "I believe my prize was a kiss."

His voice was a soft caress against her senses, and she swallowed hard. Unable to speak, she simply nodded. Desire blazed in his eye as his smile faded, and he slowly lowered his head. Breathlessly, she trembled as his lips brushed over first one corner of her mouth and then the other. A moment later his mouth lightly teased hers.

The caress made her heartbeat quicken with anticipation, and she took a small step forward to return his kiss. Hands splayed open against his chest, the low growl rumbling out of him vibrated against her fingertips. Excitement spiraled and slid its way through her body leaving behind a molten heat that warmed her from the inside out.

It had been a long time since a desire of this strength had assaulted her senses, and she reveled in the sensations engulfing her. With Devin there had been warm, loving, and passionate moments. But this was a different kind of passion. It ignited a fire inside her belly that threatened to consume her at any moment. The instant the hard steel of his metal arm pulled her deeper into his embrace she went eagerly.

In a sensual, provocative movement, his tongue slid along the seam of her lips until her mouth parted. Their tongues danced together in an imitation of a carnal act her body had begun to cry out for with a fervency that made her tremble in his embrace. Her arms slid up to encircle his neck so she could slide her fingers through his thick, sable hair.

The crisp Scottish air mingled with his masculine scent, and it teased her nose as she breathed him in. It was an aroma that brought her senses to a fevered pitch. The faint taste of gooseberry jam from breakfast lingered in his mouth as she matched the passion of his kiss. With her hips pressed deep into his, she could feel his hard, thick length against her thigh.

Dear God, she wanted more than just this kiss. It had been so long since she'd been touched intimately, and until now, she hadn't realized how much she'd missed being held tight and caressed. Lost in the heady sensation of his embrace, her hips moved against his erection in a silent invitation she desperately wanted him to accept. A dark groan rumbled in his chest. It pulsated its way into her fingertips and then her blood to increase the fire streaking through her veins. Every inch of her taut with need, she released a soft moan as his mouth continued to tease and tempt hers

Chapter 10

Rosebuds. She smelled like a soft, sweet rosebud just before it opened. His tongue swirled around hers, and her fiery response made his cock stiffen. A soft mewl feathered its way past her lips. It was a sound of passion and need. Immediately his body tightened with a demand that had him on the brink of laying her down in the grass and pleasuring her body with his.

The thought pulled a groan out of him. As if her mind was in sync with his, her thigh shifted against his cock in a silent, feminine sign of acquiescence. He couldn't remember the last time a woman had aroused him to the point of throwing caution to the wind. Her mouth tasted hot and sweet beneath his, and his heart slammed against his chest at the thought of burying himself between her legs.

Desire surged through him at the image, and if possible, his cock stretched and tightened further beneath his kilt. He wanted to explore every soft curve of her body. He was certain her skin would be silky smooth against his hand.

A sudden sense of danger pierced through the desire engulfing him. The excited voices of the children made him lift his head and stare down at her. Hazel eyes fluttered open, and her hazel eyes were bright with a sultry desire that made him drag in a harsh breath. Passion had made her skin glow, while her slumberous look made him curse the fact they weren't alone. The sound of laughter grew louder, and her eyes widened in dismay.

"Those lips of yours have the power to drive a man to madness, *mo leannan.*"

The pink flush cresting over her cheeks made him capture her mouth again in one last, hard kiss before he stepped away from her. In the back of his head he heard the clanging of bells alerting him to a danger far greater than just the approaching children.

It wasn't just her lips he found intoxicating. Everything about Louisa Morehouse made him want to do something he knew would be a mistake. Ewan turned back to Lachlan to retrieve the hat he'd snatch up off the ground. When he turned around and offered it to her, Louisa's stared at it in surprise then frowned in disappointment.

"You stopped to pick it up? That means I didn't even come close to winning." The despondency in her voice made him laugh.

"No, lass, I slowed Lachlan down just enough to reach down and pick it up off the ground. I would not have jeopardized losing my prize for a hat."

Another wave of pink darkened her cheeks as she glanced up at him then looked down at the hat and brushed some invisible dirt off the crown. Her pleasure at having had her hat returned to her reduced the raw, burning skin on the end of his stump to a minor irritant. Seeing her delight made his discomfort worth it.

"Well, thank you for retrieving it. It's my favorite hat. I would have been sad to lose it."

"Mama, Mama." Louisa's youngest boy ducked under Lachlan's head to stand between the two of them. "Did you see the way his lordship rode his horse? He hung down between Lachlan's legs without stopping and picked up your hat."

Louisa's eyes widened as she looked at him in dismay. Before she could speak, Wills tugged on Ewan's sleeve.

"Will you teach me how to ride like that, my lord?" At her son's request, Louisa gasped with alarm.

"You will most certainly *not* be learning how to ride a horse in that fashion."

"I had years of riding experience before I learned how to do that trick, lad," Ewan said with a shake of his head. His gaze met Louisa's whose dismay had become disapproval.

"Why would you risk harming yourself like that?" she chastised him in the same tone of voice he'd heard her use with the children. "It's just a hat."

"A hat you said was your favorite."

"Well yes, but I *don't love it enough* for you to risk life and limb to save it."

Louisa's scolding sent a rush of pleasure surging through him. She was far too forthright to chide his actions without feeling concern for his safety. The glare she leveled at him was fierce, and he choked back a laugh at her attempt to intimidate him. Before she could chastise him again, Ross and Charlie came bounding around the horses.

Both boys stared at him in awe, and he winced. It had been a mistake to retrieve Louisa's hat in the way he had. Although the pain inflicted by his artificial limb had been worth witnessing Louisa's pleasure, he'd failed to consider the reaction of the boys.

"My lord, that was splendid. Would you teach us how to do that?"

"Yes, Father, would you?"

At Ross's question, Ewan's body tightened with tension. His decision to publicly accept the boy as his own was one thing. But his recent decision to treat the boy more kindly didn't make it easier to accept the boy calling him father. Before he could reply to the child, Louisa shook her head.

"Even *if* Lord Argaty agreed to do so, and *he won't*," Louisa said emphatically as she glanced in his direction with a look that said he would regret going against her edict. "I wouldn't allow any of you boys to do something so dangerous."

Their faces dark with disappointment at Louisa's fierce declaration, the boys stood silently in front of her scuffing the ground with their shoes. A frown of helplessness furrowed her brow as she glanced in his direction. Her silent request for support made him clear his throat as Finn joined the group to lead Lachlan and Morag to the wagon and tie off their reins.

"Am I correct in thinking we're here to find a Christmas tree?" His statement made the boys straighten upright, their disappointment forgotten as their heads bobbed with excitement. Ewan turned his head toward Louisa. "I suppose you have an idea as to the size tree you'd like?"

"I think one a bit taller than your height would do nicely. The main hall is capable of holding a much larger one, but I think it might be a bit much," she said with a smile.

"*But Mama*," Charlie exclaimed. "We've *always* had a tall tree at Christmas."

"Your uncles aren't here to help, Charlie."

Tension made Ewan's muscles harden and a hard jolt of disappointment rocked through him. The idea of Louisa taking pity on him for his physical impairments cut deeper than he wanted to admit.

"I think Finn and I could easily manage a larger tree," he said tersely.

At his abrasive tone, Louisa tipped her head slightly to one side to study him for a brief moment before she exhaled a harsh breath of indignation past her lips. With a deliberate, pointed look at his artificial limb, she glared at him in disgust.

"Considering I *hardly* qualify as being slender *or* lightweight, your recent demonstration of strength in carrying me up a flight of stairs is *more* than enough evidence of your ability to handle a large tree, *my lord*," she snapped. Louisa emphasized the polite address treating it like an insult as she stepped forward to poke his chest hard with one finger. "*Apparently*, I'm the *only* one considering the dangers associated with a tall tree. In order to reach a large tree's top boughs, one requires a ladder. That in turn requires one person to hold the ladder while another person stands at the ready to prevent calamity, and these boys are quite sturdy in size. I am not a weakling Lord Argaty, but there *are* limitations to my strength."

Icicles could not have been as cold and sharp as her voice. It was obvious he'd offended her deeply at the unspoken implication that pity had been the reason for the height requirements of the tree. Regret made him grimace at the silent judgement he'd laid on her.

"Mama, please don't be angry with Lord Argaty," Wills said softly as he tugged on Louisa's skirts. He stared up at his mother with a pleading look before swinging his gaze back to Ewan. "His lordship and Ross haven't decorated a tree before, have you my lord?"

"You're right, my darling. I forgot that," Louisa murmured as contrition replaced her anger, and she bent to kiss her son's cheek. When she straightened, she met Ewan's gaze squarely. "My lord…I'm sorry, and I regret losing my temper."

"You were right to take offense. I should not have been so quick to judge."

He clenched his teeth at the way her eyes still sparkled with anger. With each passing second, he was realizing just how badly he'd insulted her. Ewan turned his head toward the boys who were watching the exchange with confusion and more than a bit of concern. Finn had rejoined them carrying an axe in one hand and a two-handed saw in the other.

"Finn, you know what we're looking for. Lead the way."

"Aye, my lord."

The young Scotsman nodded and without any urging,

the boys charged out in front of the stable hand and into the woods. With a light touch of Louisa's elbow, he gestured toward the trees.

"Shall we?" At his quiet words, she nodded without looking at him.

The silence between them was awkward as they followed the boys and Finn into the forest. They'd only gone a short distance when Louisa drew in a quiet breath and released it.

"I truly am sorry I allowed my temper to get the best of me...Ewan." The slight stumble she made before saying his name made him realize again how badly he'd misjudged her.

"I'm the one who should apologize for suggesting your choice of tree size evolved out of pity."

"I would *never* pity you," she exclaimed softly. "If I did, I would not have...I could not...I've never behaved so brazenly with...with any man except, my husband."

Embarrassment echoed in her words as another bout of tense silence filled the space between them. As they continued to move forward, Ewan remembered how passionately she'd kissed him such a short time ago. Even the first time he'd tasted her lips in his study her response had been unrestrained.

Her reaction on both occasions was hardly that of a woman worried about his physical impairments. His jaw tightened at what that might mean. Ewan turned his head to see she was looking straight ahead.

"It appears I must apologize, " he said quietly. She had no doubt expected a chaste kiss. "I took advantage—"

"*No*, you don't understand." Her voice softened and echoed with either guilt or embarrassment. He couldn't tell which. "I liked it—very much. I wanted..."

Her admission took his breath away as he saw the pink color rising in her cheeks. It gave her the appearance of a young debutante before she turned her head toward him. The desire flaring in her eyes was a punch to his gut. Instantly his body cried out for her, but he knew bedding her was the worst thing he could do to her. Even if she didn't care that he lacked an arm or eye, no woman should ever be saddle with a man who was less than whole.

"Louisa, I'm—"

"Oh, *please* don't. You must think me a wanton hussy for acting as I did."

"*No.*" He came to an abrupt halt and stopped her as well. "I don't think that. What I think is that it's been a long time since you've been kissed."

His reply seemed to have struck a nerve with her, and she appeared to be struggling with a dilemma of some sort. Whatever it was, she shook her head as if she had chosen not to pursue it. Not too far away, the boys were shouting jubilantly, and she glanced in the direction of the noise before looking at him again.

"It sounds as if they've found our Christmas tree." A small smile curved her mouth as she lightly touched his arm. "Shall we?"

The moment her lips curved upward, he realized he would find it impossible to resist her smile if she were to use it to her advantage.

Ewan leaned forward with a grunt and pressed his weight against the tall fir tree they'd brought back from the forest. The tree was much larger than Louisa had suggested, but he and the boys had overridden her when she'd pointed out a much smaller tree. At this precise moment he was regretting the fact.

The soft wool cloth protecting his skin against the

leather cup of his artificial limb had shifted and become useless. Retrieving Louisa's hat had been the first offense to the stump of his arm. The workout he'd performed in transporting and raising the tree in the keep had only exacerbated his discomfort.

Vanity was another part of the problem. Unwilling to let Louisa see any sign of weakness on his part, he'd stubbornly refused to seek a quiet place to adjust the damn piece of cloth. Despite the painful burning of leather against raw flesh, it was easy to dismiss the pain when he saw the excitement in the boys.

Ross was showing an exhilaration he'd never seen in the boy before. Earlier when he'd shown the boys how to cut down the tree using the two-handed saw, Ross had worked opposite him with great concentration. When the tree had fallen, the boy's grin had emphasized Ewan's decision to take a greater interest in the child had been the right one. He should have remembered his own miserable childhood much sooner and how much a kind word meant.

"Would you like help, Father?" The quiet words made Ewan look down to see Ross staring up at him with a hopeful expression on his solemn features. With a nod, he shuffled his feet back slightly to form a small arch and jerked his head in a downward motion.

"Slide in here, and reach through the branches until you reach the trunk so you can hold it steady." The boy did as he instructed, while Louisa's children carried in two buckets of rocks Finn had gathered earlier.

On the floor beneath him, McCallum kept his head under the tree, blindly stretching his arm out to accept the buckets. The noisy clatter of stone against stone sailed upward as the Scotsman poured the rock into the small barrel they were using as a stand for the tree.

"I think this is the last one we'll need, laddie," McCallum said as Charlie's pail of rocks disappeared beneath the branches.

Another noisy clatter echoed up through the tree branches, and Ewan heard McCallum release a satisfied sound. A moment later the Scotsman carefully rolled out from under the tree.

"It should be sturdy now, my lord." At the family retainer's words, Ewan nodded and looked down at the boy leaning into the tree.

"Ross, you can let go now."

At his instructions, the boy carefully slid out from between Ewan and the tree. With the child out of the way, Ewan slowly eased his grip on the tree and stepped back to stare at their afternoon's handiwork. It was the first time he'd ever seen a tree in the Keep, and he enjoyed the sight.

"That tree should never have been brought into this house."

The harsh words spilled out into the air behind him. As always a familiar tension tightened his body whenever he heard his mother's voice. In his youth, it had represented fear and painful rejection. As an adult, the dowager's vitriol had evolved into nothing more than irritation. Ewan turned and arched his eyebrow at his mother who was glaring at him with disgust.

"Exactly what troubles you about the tree, Mother?"

"You know full well, celebration of the holiday was outlawed years ago."

"I also know the ban was done away with not too long ago." Ewan eyed her with scorn at her protest. "Pray tell, to what exactly do we owe the honor of your presence?"

"I came to inform you that Bryce is coming for dinner." The startling announcement made Ewan stare at the dowager countess in amazement. It had been a long time since he'd seen his mother's nephew, and while he liked Bryce, he had no desire to entertain anyone, now or in the future.

"When?"

"Tonight." The dowager smiled with pernicious glee the moment he jerked in surprise. "I saw him in the village today. He said you've been a hermit, and I agreed with him. Naturally, I'd be remiss in my duty as your mother not to remedy the situation."

"If only you'd conducted yourself so diligently over the years," he bit out between clenched teeth. "And I'd hardly call myself a hermit, I've been busy with estate business for the past year."

"And here I was thinking McCallum was the one attending to your affairs. You never were very good at running the estate."

The cold, disparaging remark made Ewan wonder why he'd ever come home in the first place. When he'd returned from the Sudan, he'd chosen to avoid the dowager's company as much as possible. As a child his mother's antipathy for him had been painfully obvious.

Although his aunt had attempted to shield him whenever she could, she'd failed on almost every occasion. For whatever reason, Wallis had never been capable of defying her sister. He'd never understood his aunt's submissive behavior or why his mother disliked him so vehemently. Now he no longer cared.

"Since you were the one who decided to invite Bryce for dinner, you will have the honor of hosting him alone this evening. I'll not be present."

"As you wish, but I'll not be alone in welcoming Bryce," she murmured as a smug smile tilted her lips. "I saw Mrs. Morehouse in the hallway a moment ago, and although startled by my invitation, she graciously agreed to join us for dinner."

"Whatever game you're playing, Mother, I'm warning you not to use Lou—Mrs. Morehouse as one of your pawns," he said with suppressed fury.

"You're now on a first name basis with the woman?"

The dowager arched her eyebrows at him in mock surprise. At that moment, Louisa walked into the main hall, her arms overflowing with a basket filled with paper, ribbon, and an assortment of nuts and berries. The moment she came into view, the dowager looked at Louisa then back to him.

"You're blind to what's happening in this household, Ewan. Mrs. Morehouse has done nothing but cause upheaval in Argaty Keep since she arrived." She darted another look in Louisa's direction and lowered her voice. "You know how difficult Gilbert can be when there's too much commotion in the house, and her children have a terrible habit of nosing about where they shouldn't."

"My brother is always difficult, my lady."

Ewan kept his voice low as he glanced over his shoulder at the scene behind him. When he turned back to his mother, a venomous smile curved his mother's mouth.

"You think I don't see the way you look at her?" She raised her voice slightly, and Ewan stiffened. "You're a fool, boy. There's a reason you had all the mirrors in the house removed or covered. You know what everyone thinks when they look at you."

"I don't care what others think."

"Others perhaps, but you care what *she* thinks." His mother directed a condescending nod toward Louisa, and he clenched his jaw with anger.

"I see Gilbert isn't the only one in the household whose faculties are failing, my lady," he snarled.

"I agree. Your delusion as to Mrs. Morehouse seeing you as anything other than a beast would be laughable it if it weren't so pitiful."

"Your taste for trying to draw blood with that sharp tongue of yours hasn't softened with age, mother." Ewan eyed her with contempt as her words drew more blood than he was willing to admit. "I can only imagine what a hellish existence my father led being married to you."

"Don't you *ever* mention your father to me again," she snapped as a mask of hatred and loathing fell over her face. *"Ever."*

Despite his anger, her vicious reaction startled him. Only once or twice over the years had she mentioned his father to him. Those instances had illustrated her dislike for the previous Earl of Argaty. But it was the flash of humiliation Ewan saw now that confused him. It was the first time he could ever remember his mother ever looking ashamed when his father was mentioned. Before he had a chance to respond, she pinned her icy gaze on him.

"Dinner will be at eight if you choose to join us. Although I'm certain Mrs. Morehouse's presence will ease any disappointment Bryce might experience at your absence."

Without waiting for a response, the dowager countess turned and crossed the floor to ascend the stairs. Ewan stared after her with intense bitterness. In the past, he'd always been able to cast his mother's aspersions aside. Today was different. Today she'd dragged Louisa into their vitriolic relationship.

Ewan turned around to see Louisa and the children sitting on the floor in front of the fire where she was helping them create decorations for the tree. It made for a happy scene. Never in his life had he ever thought to see such a pleasant sight in the Keep's main hall. As if aware he was watching them, Louisa raised her head and smiled at him. If she'd overheard anything of his argument with his mother, it wasn't reflected in her demeanor. Ewan crossed the floor and went down on one knee beside her then arched his eyebrow in amusement.

"I believe there's a table in the dining hall," he said with more than a touch of irony.

"Yes, but it wouldn't be as much fun. Besides the tree smells so wonderful."

Her laughter stirred an unexpected sensation inside

Ewan as she leaned forward to help Wills who was struggling with a paper chain. Ross was busy threading a second strand of holly berries with a needle. The first strand the boy had threaded had been used to make a small circular ornament. Ross stopped what he was doing and grinned at him.

"Here Father, sit beside me. I have another needle you can use to thread these currants and gooseberries."

The invitation made Ewan stiffen, but he forced himself to sink down onto the cold stone next to the boy then accept the needle and thread Ross offered him. As he reached for one of the currants, he glanced at Louisa. A smile of satisfaction curved her sweet mouth, and he instinctively knew she was pleased to see him taking an interest in the boy. Still looking at her, Ewan accidentally jabbed his thumb with the needle. His grunt of pain was quickly followed by an oath of disgust at his clumsiness. It earned him a glare of disapproval from Louisa, while the boys shouted with laughter. He grimaced and held up his injured thumb to her.

"The needle is sharp."

"Then perhaps you should watch what you're doing." The laughter in her voice reminded him of a bright sunlight spreading its way across the moor on a warm afternoon.

"'Tis hard tae see a wee object when I'm blinded by the sun, lass." Deliberately allowing his voice to soften to a thick brogue, he grinned as she flushed a bright pink.

"What sun?" Puzzled, Louisa's youngest shook his head as if Ewan were addlebrained then looking in his mother's direction he tilted his head slightly. "Mama, your cheeks are red."

"Wills is right, Mrs. Morehouse. Your cheeks are bright red."

"Are they?" Louisa flushed even deeper as the paper she was holding slipped from her fingers, and her hands flew upward to cup her cheeks. "It must be the heat from the fire."

"You used to look like that when Papa would

compliment you," Charles laughed.

As if the sun had suddenly been hidden by dark clouds, a stricken look darted across Louisa's face. It aroused an acute protective instinct he'd not experienced since the day he'd thrown himself between Asadi and a Mahdist fighter at Omdurman. Without hesitating, he leaned over to block Charles's view and picked up a large paper star the boy had made.

"This is a fine star, lad. Why don't we begin adding these decorations to the tree?"

A chorus of enthusiastic cries of agreement met his suggestion. The boys needed no further prompting, and they scrambled to their feet and carefully carried their decorations to the tree. Ewan stood up and offered his good hand to Louisa. As he pulled her to her feet, the heat of her filled the small space between them. Her color had returned, but the pain of her grief had changed her hazel eyes to dark green.

She was still grieving for her husband. The realization was an invisible punch to his gut followed by the sharp sting of jealousy knowing she might never be willing to marry again. The instant the thought crashed through his head, Ewan dropped her hand as if it was a hot piece of metal. Surprise widen her eyes as she studied him with curiosity. Desperate to conceal any trace of his laughable wish, he cleared his throat.

"We should join the boys." The warmth of her hand penetrated the sleeve of his jacket as she stopped him. It was a heat he ached to be engulfed by and hold forever. He crushed the thought with a vicious, mental blow.

"Thank you for shielding them. They were both so young when Devin died in a fire almost three years ago. Wills doesn't like seeing me sad, but Charlie..." She peered around his shoulder to look at the children behind him before she looked back at him. "It upsets Charlie deeply when he knows one of his innocent remarks has upset me. At least his guilt is short-lived unlike mine."

"The lad's guilt is understandable, but why should you feel guilty for your sorrow?"

"Because I said things to Devin—terrible things. But it's—" A look of dismay made her bite down on her bottom lip as she brought her explanation to an abrupt halt. Without thinking, he cupped her cheek.

"You're quick to anger and stubborn as an ox, Louisa, but you wear your heart on your sleeve. It's a kind and gentle heart. I find it difficult to believe anyone, even your husband, would be unwilling to forgive you for words spoken in anger."

Louisa's eyes closed as her hand covered his, and she turned her head slightly to press her mouth into his palm. The gesture lodged a knot of emotion in his throat as he realized just how much he wanted to be the one she always turned to for comfort. The thought made him pull in a sharp breath as he struggled not to pull her into his arms. At the soft sound, she jerked away from him and flinched.

"I'm sorry, I should not have—"

"Don't, *mo leannan*," he rasped. "Whether it's simply to comfort you or taste the heat of your mouth, my will power is being sorely tested where you're concerned."

"It would be...a lie...if I denied the way you...make me feel when you—"

"Mama, are you and Lord Argaty going to help?" Wills asked from across the room.

"Yes, my darling."

Her voice emphasized she wasn't really listening to her son, and her gaze didn't leave Ewan's, the emotion he saw there sucked the air out of his lungs. Desire flared in her beautiful eyes as her palm pressed into his chest where his heart was pounding like a runaway freight train. For the second time today she'd acknowledged the attraction between them, and his body ached to pull her close.

Louisa took a slow step back from him in an obvious struggle not to move forward instead. Just as she had earlier when she'd admitted to enjoying his kiss, she appeared embarrassed by her boldness. Chagrin made her cheeks flush with color before she tipped her chin upward in a mutinous display of confidence.

Head held high, she skirted him to join the boys at the tree. As she walked away from him, Ewan realized Louisa Morehouse had just declared war on his senses. It was a war he'd easily lose if he didn't find a way to keep the woman out of his bed, and most definitely out of his heart. The question was, did he really want to?

Chapter 11

"It's true, every word."

Bryce Cowan smiled mischievously. Seated on Louisa's right, he leaned forward to look at his cousin seated on Louisa's left at the head of the table.

Ewan's dark scowl only served as an incentive for Bryce to finish his story with a polished flair. It was impossible not to laugh at his description of McCallum holding Ewan upside down threatening to drop him into the burn for a prank.

"Although I've only known McCallum a short time, I have no doubt as to the veracity of your story, Mr. Cowan," Louisa laughed as she turned her head to smile at Ewan.

"Your skill at story-telling has improved since we saw each other last, cousin," Ewan growled irritably.

"And you've become quite ill-tempered." Bryce reached for his wine glass and eyed his cousin with curiosity. "I imagine Ethan and Iain would agree with me."

Louisa looked across the table at the Ethan MacLean and Iain Drummond who had arrived unexpectedly on the doorstep with Ewan's cousin. For whatever reason, Lady Argaty had been blatantly gleeful when her son had walked into the salon before dinner. A dark frown of displeasure had quickly replaced his surprise as he'd greeted the three men. The Countess's scornful delight had only darkened Ewan's scowl that much more.

The open dislike between mother and son had either

gone unnoticed by the dinner guests or they'd politely not acknowledged it. All three men had greeted Ewan with enthusiastic pleasure, but confusion had clouded their features at the abrupt welcome they'd received in return.

"I'd not go so far as to call you sullen, Ewan, but you have become somewhat of a hermit," Ethan said quietly. "This is the first time we've been to the Keep since your return from the Sudan a year ago."

"I was gone a long time. I've been busy with estate matters." At Ewan's response, Lady Argaty sniffed with derisive amusement but remained silent.

"So busy you forgot old friends?" Ethan asked.

At the quiet rebuke, Ewan's hand froze in midair. Slowly, he laid the fork speared with a piece of venison on his plate. Angry tension rolled off of him, as he pinned an icy glare on his childhood friend. Beneath his anger, Louisa sensed a deep pain and despair in him. It made her heart ache.

"People change. If you find fault with my company or the meal, you do not have to stay." Ewan's sharp reply, made Ethan raise his eyebrows in astonishment as he eyed his companions with a perplexed expression. Seated on Ewan's left and directly across from Louisa, Iain released a chuckle of amusement.

"I highly doubt Ethan will leave the table without a piece of Mrs. Selkirk's Dundee cake, Ewan." Iain shook his head. "Don't you remember the time he stole one of Mrs. Selkirk's cakes fresh out of her oven? We ate like kings that day out on the moor."

For a moment, Louisa thought Ewan might not answer his childhood friend, but his dark, forbidding expression slowly ebbed away before he nodded. He relaxed back into his chair as a small smile twisted his mouth.

"I remember," Ewan said gruffly.

When he said nothing else, Iain looked across the table at Louisa. Open admiration on his handsome features, Iain

Drummond smiled at her.

"Tell me, Mrs. Morehouse. How did a woman as lovely as you come to be in the employ of the surly master of Argaty Keep?"

"Ewan found her out on the moor in the middle of a storm. Although how she came to be there is a wild tale, indeed." The dowager's disdain plainly visible, Lady Argaty eyed Louisa with acerbic disapproval.

"Wild tale, Mother?" There was a dark edge to Ewan's words as he eyed the silver-haired woman coldly. The note of steel in his voice seemed to be a veiled warning for the dowager countess to guard her words. It warmed Louisa's heart to think he'd been subtly defending her against his mother's open hostility.

"A broken-down wagon, an injured driver, and a runaway horse? Reckless behavior for a mature woman now employed to care for *your* child."

Malicious amusement filled the woman's voice. The manner in which she emphasized her reference to Ross made Ewan grow rigid in his chair. Fury rolled off of him, and his rage was a tangible sensation racing over Louisa's skin. Despite the strength of his wrath, he looked as if he was dealing with a bothersome bug.

But his blue-gray eye was dark with virulent hostility as he studied his mother seated at the opposite end of the table. The silent exchange between the two made Louisa wince at how dull-witted she'd been not to realize Lady Argaty would know Ross wasn't Ewan's son.

When he didn't reply to her comment, Ewan's mother shifted her attention to Louisa. Venomous glee reflected in her smile, the dowager's disbelief as to Louisa's story was unmistakably obvious.

"Quite the adventure, wouldn't you agree, Mrs. Morehouse?"

"A most unpleasant one, my lady. I'm fortunate Lord

Argaty found me, or I would have died that night," Louisa said through clenched teeth. The only pleasure the woman seemed to find in life was to criticize and humiliate others with her viper tongue.

"The moors at night are no longer safe for man, woman, or beast," Iain said grimly. At his friend's comment, Ewan's forehead creased in a frown as he set his wine glass back on the table.

"What makes you say that?"

"You've not heard what happened to Rhona MacLaren?" Iain arched his eyebrows in surprise before his features became dark and grim. "Her body was discovered on the moor just off the Doune Road yesterday. I'll spare the ladies the lurid details, but her death had to have been an agonizing one."

The instant Iain's words filtered their way into her consciousness, Louisa's stomach lurched in a sickening manner as she remembered the woman's screams from her vision. In the next breath, she knew who was responsible. The boy. The *an dara sealladh* had shown her enough to convince her the boy was responsible for the girl's murder. But how was that possible?

The memory of the child mutilating the rabbit tried to force its way into her head, but she pushed it back into the grave it had risen from. Nothing about her visions made sense. How could a small child murder an adult? The more important question was whether she should tell Ewan what she'd seen. In the next breath she realized there was nothing to tell. If she couldn't make sense of the *an dara sealladh*, it would do little good to share her visions with Ewan. Beside her, Bryce cleared his throat.

"Rhona's death was remarkably similar to the manner in which Maggie Graham was murdered." The troubled note in Bryce's voice emphasized his worried look.

"Wallace Graham's youngest daughter, Maggie?

Murdered?" There was a stunned note of disbelief in Ewan's voice that made Bryce bob his head.

"That's right. I forgot. It happened a month or two before you returned from the Sudan. Graham's oldest son found her body in almost the same spot they found Rhona." Bryce frowned. "Maggie was a sweet girl. They never found the bas—the man who killed her."

"There were no suspects at all?" Ewan's battle-scarred features had become grim and forbidding as he stared down the length of the table to where his mother sat. As her eyes met her son's, the dowager countess grew pale beneath Ewan's narrowed gaze.

"Constable MacPherson couldn't find any evidence leading to a suspect in the village, and he was forced to attribute Rhona's death to a vagrant just like Maggie Graham."

"A vagrant with blood lust." Ewan's dark scowl emphasized his harsh tone as he captured his mother's attention at the opposite end of the table once more.

Beneath her son's steely glare, the woman's eyes widened with fear, and her stoic appearance of concern crumpled slightly. Something unspoken passed between the two, and Louisa's stomach lurched at the possibility they might know something about the murders. Just as quickly as the thought filled her head, she dismissed it. Ewan hadn't even been in Scotland when the first woman had been killed.

There was also the *an dara sealladh* to consider. Her visions had shown her too much to even think Ewan might be involved in the murders. Fingers trembling, Louisa reached for her goblet of wine and drank a deep draught of the alcohol. At the end of the table, the dowager countess's features became tight with displeasure.

"Gentlemen, this topic is quite unsuitable in mixed company. Mrs. Morehouse is looking decidedly ill," Lady Argaty snapped. Immediately, Ewan bent his head toward

Louisa.

"Are you all right?"

The soft question eased the fear spiraling through her. The silent question in his blue-gray eye as he studied her intently asked if she wanted him to take her away from the prying unspoken questions of everyone at the table. The deep understanding she saw reflected in his gaze took her breath away. Devin had always been concerned when the *an dara sealladh* fell on her, but not once had he ever shown the depth of understanding she saw in Ewan.

The moment her hand moved to touch Ewan's arm in a gesture of reassurance she stopped herself. Instead she shook her head to deny she needed to leave the room. At the slight movement of her hand, Ewan's mouth tightened as if he was hurt by her withdrawal. It made her wish she'd not stopped herself from touching him. With a jerk, Ewan pulled away from her and leaned back in his chair.

His sharp retreat and her inability to determine what he was thinking made Louisa wonder if she'd imagined the understanding reflected in his gaze seconds ago. Dismay swept through her, as she tried to silently express her regret. Ewan seemed to be unmoved by her silent apology as he arched his eyebrow at her.

In the next breath, his look softened as he appeared to accept her unspoken apology. Relief made Louisa drag in a sharp breath as she forced a smile to her lips and turned toward Ewan's friends and cousin to acknowledge their concern. Insisting she was fine, her attention shifted toward the countess.

The older woman had regained some of her color, and while her apprehension had vanished Louisa could see the tension beneath the stoic mask she wore. Like her son, the dowager countess's countenance was almost impossible to read. Whatever or whomever the woman feared, Louisa knew the source of her anxiety couldn't be Ewan. Their acrimonious verbal exchanges were evidence of that. Even the day he'd ordered the woman out of Louisa's room the dowager countess had more startled by her son's harsh behavior

"Our deepest apologies, Lady Argaty, Mrs. Morehouse. There are far more interesting topics to discuss." Ethan smiled at Louisa. "Personally, I'd like to hear more about Mrs. Morehouse's adventure."

"Lady Argaty's brief description of the events is accurate. I was on my way to Callendar, when the wagon that had been sent for me hit a hole in the road." Louisa's turned her head toward the dowager's direction. The woman's blatant skepticism was not unexpected, but no less irritating. "The accident resulted in my driver suffering a serious blow to the head and a broken wagon axel. My intentions were to ride to Doune Castle for help, but my horse threw me when lightning made him bolt. Fortunately, Lord Argaty found me several hours later."

"Callendar?"

The curiosity in Iain Drummond's voice made Louisa's heart skip a beat. Although she'd never met the three men until tonight, Aunt Matilda was a familiar name in the counties surrounding Callendar Abby. Anxious to avoid any questions that might reveal her true identity, Louisa smiled flirtatiously at the man.

Beside her, a soft sound escaped Ewan. The sudden tension radiating off of him surprised her, and she glanced in his direction. The muscles in his unblemished cheek were taut with displeasure, but he didn't look in her direction as he took another bite of venison.

"I was on my way to the Abbey for a position, but Lord Argaty convinced me to remain here as his son's governess."

"*I* convinced you?" The mockery in Ewan's voice sent a wave of heat rising in Louisa's cheeks as she looked at him.

Eyebrows arched, he cocked his head slightly to one side

as a soft snort of what might have been amusement escaped him. Cheeks still burning, Louisa quickly looked away. Beside her, Bryce chuckled.

"Well, regardless of who convinced whom that you remain at Argaty Keep, it affords me the pleasure of asking you to ride with me tomorrow."

A barely perceptible growl whispered in her ears at Bryce's invitation. Louisa darted a glance at Ewan whose features had hardened into a façade of granite. Warmed by the thought he disapproved of her riding with his cousin, she shook her head as she declined Bryce's invitation.

"I'm afraid I must refuse," she said with a smile. "My days are quite full."

"Surely, you could take an hour out of your day to go riding." Bryce said with a smile. "My cousin cannot be that harsh of a taskmaster."

"Perhaps she'd enjoy someone else's company, such as mine, Bryce." Iain laughed at the glare his friend gave him. "Come, Mrs. Morehouse, tell us the truth? Which one of us would you rather go riding with?"

"I would like an answer as well." Ethan eyed her with an appreciative grin. "My company is far more pleasant than these two scoundrels."

"I'm flattered by your invitations, but I cannot accept," Louisa said firmly.

"Surely Mrs. Morehouse is entitled to some free time, Ewan." A derisive smile on her lips Lady Argaty eyed her son with mockery. "Hasn't the two of you gone riding together? You shouldn't make her feel as though she should refuse the pleasure of your cousin or friends company."

At his mother's reference to her riding with her son, Louisa saw Ewan's hand clench in obvious anger before he quickly uncurled his fist. Confused by the woman's encouragement of the invitations the three men had extended to her, Louisa frowned in puzzlement. When the dowager had invited her to dine with them earlier, Louisa had been too startled to politely decline. It wasn't simply an unusual request socially, but Lady Argaty had made it quite clear how much she disliked Louisa. The woman's dinner invitation had been bewildering enough, but the dowager's sudden interest in her social life was baffling.

Uncertain as to why the woman seemed so eager for Louisa to accept the invitations to ride from any of the three men she looked down the table at Lady Argaty. The smile of poisonous amusement she directed at her son caused a muscle to twitch in Ewan's cheek despite his display of indifference. Contempt and distaste darkened his eye as he arched an eyebrow at the dowager across the length of the table. The scorn he hid beneath his nonchalant demeanor reinforced Louisa's opinion as to the depth of the discord between the two.

"Lou—Mrs. Morehouse has a horse at her disposal and may ride whenever and with whomever she wishes."

With a sudden look of boredom, Ewan shrugged his shoulders. Louisa flinched at his cavalier manner. The wall of indifference he displayed cut deep. Had she misread the understanding she thought she'd glimpsed moments ago? Had she mistaken his defense of her at his mother's barbed comments for nothing more than a demand that the woman be polite?

Even his quiet growl of displeasure a moment ago could have been nothing more than his belief Louisa might neglect her duties if she were to ride with one of the three men. And his reaction to the dowager's veiled questioning of Louisa's suitability as a governess could have been merely irritation that his mother was challenging his decision.

"The least you could do is tell Mrs. Morehouse we're a harmless bunch, Ewan." There was a challenge in Bryce's voice as he watched Ewan take another bite of venison.

"Harmless?" Ewan choked out of the side of his mouth.

Whether with amusement or irritation she couldn't tell which. "I think that's a matter of debate. However, as I said, Mrs. Morehouse doesn't need my permission to ride."

"There you have it, Mrs. Morehouse," Bryce said with a triumphant grin. "The exalted Lord of Argaty Keep has granted you permission to accept my invitation."

"*Your* invitation?" Iain's eyebrows shot upward in annoyance.

"I do recall asking her first." Bryce's cheerful, yet arrogant response, reminded Louisa of a recent rebellion within the ranks of her younger charges. Louisa raised her hand in protest and released a breath of exasperation.

"*Gentlemen, please.* While your invitations are truly flattering, I am not being coy in my refusal." Louisa eyed each of the men in quick succession. "My days are quite full, and however much I might regret doing so, I am unable to accept."

The look of dejection on their faces reminded Louisa of the look Wills often displayed when she'd refused to let him do something. Still chafing from her efforts to dissuade her would-be suitors, Louisa released a soft breath of aggravation. Ewan was listening to something Iain had said, and she tried to ward off the disappointment his detached manner aroused in her.

Half-heartedly listening to the dinner conversation, she took a bite of the rumbledethumps on her plate. It had become one of her favorite dishes Mrs. Selkirk made, but at the moment, it tasted like sawdust in her mouth. Beside her, Ewan made a barely discernible sound, and she jerked her head in his direction.

The blue-gray gaze meeting hers was filled with a warmth that made her heart skip a beat. She'd not been mistaken after all. Suddenly the warmth changed to a smoldering desire that sent a shiver down her spine. It was the same look he'd had after their race this afternoon when he'd kissed her so passionately. Fire streaked across her skin at the memory, and her heart beat with the same wild rhythm it had earlier.

The small smile touching his sensual mouth made her certain he was remembering the passion that had flared between them. In the next breath, a possessive look darkened his eye, and the air was dragged from her lungs. It convinced her that he was thinking about her audacious admission of desire just before Wills had interrupted their conversation.

It had been obvious her confession had stunned him, but the dangerous, sinful emotion had swept across his rugged, battled-scarred features a split-second later had sent heat spiraling through her. It had made her wish they'd been alone so she could experience his touch without fear of discovery. Cheeks burning, she quickly bowed her head to study her plate.

Her earlier behavior had been one of the most reckless things she'd ever done. To openly declare her wanton feelings for him would have been viewed as shocking in some social circles. It had been an impetuous moment, but everything about Ewan make her feel reckless and free of any constraints. Even the camaraderie between them as they'd decorated the tree in the main hall had been one of comfortable familiarity.

Everything about this afternoon had been so easy between them. There was something natural, even familiar, about the way he made her feel whether he was kissing her, teasing her, or silently conveying how much he enjoyed her company. It made her happier than she'd been in a long time. Her heart stopped briefly before it started to thud again at a much faster pace.

If all it took was one look from the Earl of Argaty to make her happy she was treading deep waters. The man was dangerous to her senses, especially when she was already halfway in love with him. The thought caused a soft, sharp gasp to escape her. She glanced in Ewan's direction, and her heart slammed into her breast as he eyed her with concern.

In the next instant, his gaze narrowed with speculation as if her expression had revealed her thoughts. Alarmed by the possibility, she quickly looked away from him. The water she was in now was deeper than the lake at the Abbey. Although she knew Sebastian would advise her not to do anything reckless, deep inside she knew she was about to go where even angels feared to venture.

Chapter 12

For the third time, Louisa stopped brushing her hair as she tried to remember the number of strokes she was at. Blowing out a breath of disgust at her lack of concentration, she dropped the brush onto the vanity. The day had left her with so many questions. Dread had accompanied most of them, leaving her with an unsettled feeling.

While mentally reviewing the dinner conversation as she'd changed into her nightgown, she'd questioned her certainty that the murdered village girl was the one she'd heard scream in her vision. Despite challenging herself on the matter, her intuition insisted it was the murdered girl she'd heard scream during the *an dara sealladh*. Lady Argaty's reaction to Iain's news about the murdered girl had piqued Louisa's curiosity as well. The woman's pallor had revealed how badly shaken the news had disturbed her.

It was out of character for a woman who cared little for the welfare of others. When Lady Argaty had met her son's questioning gaze, her eyes had revealed a deep fear of discovery, but of what? Even Ewan's tension had been puzzling. Louisa frowned as she stared at her reflection in the mirror. The only question answered this evening was the reassurance she'd not misunderstood Ewan. His look when she'd refused to ride with his friends had made her stomach flip flop with excitement.

A noise behind her made her look in the mirror, and the sight of the secret door ajar caught her by surprise. Trepidation splashed through her veins as her heart began to pound with an unknown fear. She rose from her seat and slowly walked toward the narrow sliver of darkness that existed between the wall and the open door.

"Ross, is that you?"

A soft giggle was the only response to her question. It was a familiar sound that sent ice seeping through her skin until she was shivering from the cold. With a bravado she wasn't feeling, she straightened her spine.

"Whoever you are, show yourself. I don't have time for childish games."

Another chilling giggle echoed out of the dark passageway along with a shuffling noise. Without thinking, Louisa raced forward and slammed the door shut. Hands braced against the wall, her heart pounded with fear as she waited for whoever was in the hidden passageway to push back in an attempt to gain access to her room.

When nothing happened, she frowned. Had she had a waking occurrence of the *an dara sealladh*? Although it rarely happened, she'd had waking dreams before, but afterward she usually felt drained of all energy. Whether it had been real or not, she would feel better if something heavy was blocking the door. One hand still pressed against the wood paneling, she looked around the room until she saw the chest at the foot of her bed.

Without a second thought, she hurried over to the large piece of furniture and slowly dragged it across the room until it was flush against the secret entrance. When it was in place, she sank down on top of the chest to catch her breath. While it was unlikely the bulky trunk would prevent someone from opening the door, it was of sufficient weight to make it difficult to gain entry to her room.

A knock on her bedroom door made her jump, and she

froze in place. Another rap on the door echoed through the room. This time the knock was stronger, more authoritative. Louisa sprang to her feet and hurried across the room and threw the door open.

The sight of Ewan's tall frame filling her doorway made her heart skip a beat. Heat quickly spread its way across her skin as his blue-gray gaze swept over her. The cheek muscle beneath Ewan's eye patch twitched as desire flared to life across his face.

"I came to see if you were all right," he said gruffly. "You seemed troubled at dinner by the talk of the two women."

"It was nothing," she said with a shake of her head.

"So the *an dara sealladh* didn't come to you?" The harsh note in his voice made her flinch, and he rubbed the back of his neck with his hand in a gesture of regret. "Forgive me, Louisa. I have no right to ask that question."

"I don't mind. But if I'd seen something this evening, I would tell you."

As she had earlier, she debated whether to share her confusing visions with him. She discarded the idea almost as soon as it fluttered through her head. The *an dara sealladh* had shown her nothing but puzzle pieces she'd yet to put together. It was doubtful he would be able to make any more sense of it than she'd been able too. Almost as if he could read her thoughts, he scowled at her.

"Do not lie to me, Louisa. I can forgive mistakes, but not lies." The sharp words made her jerk as she looked up at him.

"If the *an dara sealladh* had touched me tonight, I would tell you," she confirmed once more.

It was the truth, but it didn't make her feel any less guilty about other things she'd kept from him, particularly who she really was. Although her reasons had been well-intended, she knew her deception would anger him deeply. He studied her for a long moment before he accepted her assurance with a sharp nod.

A sudden tic appeared in his cheek muscle as his assessment became another emotion entirely. The raw, potent hunger glittering in his blue-gray eye made her draw in a swift breath. Awareness darkened his features at the sound, and he slowly reached out to slide his fingers through her loose hair.

"Your hair is as soft as a piece of silk."

The gruff note in his voice was hypnotic as she tried to speak. Her breathing grew ragged as she stared up at him. As if he was the embodiment of a fine bottle of cognac, she drank in the warm male scent of him and silently begged him to kiss her as he had earlier in the day. The sudden image of him caressing every inch of her with his mouth made her heart skid out of control and set her heartbeat pulsing rapidly through her.

She knew she should simply bid him goodnight, but the memory of how exciting his kisses made her feel stole the air from her lungs. With the impulsiveness her family was known for, Louisa didn't think, she simply closed the small space between them and reached up to lightly run the tips of her fingers over his mouth. A low rumble whispered out of him as he caught her hand and pushed it away from his mouth.

"Do you enjoy playing with fire, lass?"

The harsh rasp of his voice made her heart race faster as she heard the answer to his question in the back of her head. It increased the level of heat coating her skin. Trembling, she took another step forward despite the voice in the back of her that denounced the movement as being nothing short of madness. The danger she was courting paled in comparison to the passion swiftly taking control of her senses.

She no longer cared how rash her behavior. All that mattered was how much she needed his touch against her skin. It was a craving that grew in strength every time he came near her. The physical nature of it was exciting, but it was the way he looked at her that made her heart beat frantically in her breast.

"I've played with fire all my life," she whispered as she went up on her toes to brush her lips over his lightly. "But until you, I never understood how a simple touch could consume me—make me feel alive."

At her husky reply, he stiffened against her. Tension stretched between them like a taut bow string ready to be released. With an abrupt, rough movement of his artificial and natural arms, he pushed her backward into her room. The abrupt movement made her heart sink as humiliation crawled through her.

In the next second, her despair became jubilation as he followed her. Desire tightened his battle-scarred features, and her heartbeat skidded out of control while a delicious exhilaration sped along every single nerve ending in her body. The sensation intensified as the quiet thud of the door closing behind him was accompanied by the soft brush of metal against metal as he turned the key in the lock.

She dragged in a sharp breath of anticipation, and his gaze narrowed at the sound. As she stared up at him, a hard tremor coursed its way through her at the hunger blazing in the blue-gray depths of his eye. Frozen where she stood, a wild, unexpected pleasure edged its way through her. The spot between her legs tightened and throbbed with a stark need, but something else threaded its way through her that alarmed her almost as much as it excited her.

He'd not even touched her yet, but the anticipation of his caress rolled through her with a force that made her feel alive in a way she didn't fully understand. All she knew was how desperately she needed him. In two quick steps, she closed the small distance between them. With reckless daring, her hand wrapped around his neck to tug his head downward to kiss him.

Beneath her palm, the hard, fast beat of his heart pounded its way through his chest into her fingertips. Her impetuous caress caused a dark, dangerous growl to roll out of him before he took control of the kiss. His mouth dominated hers as his tongue slid past her lips to tangle with hers in a masterful display of seduction that made her blood run hot and fast.

The warm touch of his hand sliding upward over her hip and side to cup one breast sent a small shudder of delight through her. White-hot desire streaked across her skin at his caress, and the tips of her breast grew hard and stiff as she ached for him to take her into his mouth. With a quick movement, she pushed herself away from him and took a step backward.

His expression hardened into an unreadable mask at her hasty retreat from his arms. Instinctively she realized he thought she meant to end this wild, unrestrained moment between them. She shook her head in a silent gesture of reassurance as a small smile touched her lips. Slowly, but surely, she untied the ribbon holding her robe closed then slipped out of it to she faced him in only her nightgown.

The moment the robe drifted down to the floor, the stony façade on his features gave way to a look of hunger. It made her heart skip a beat before her pulse quickened. Beneath the desire she saw blazing in his eye the spot between her legs tighten with an acute demand for her body to join with his.

Tension radiated off him, and she swallowed hard as her fingers pulled at one of the nightgown's shoulder ribbons. The moment the wide strip of material drifted off her shoulder, the front of the French silk garment fell forward to reveal her breast. She swallowed hard at her recklessness, and her fingers fumbled slightly as they undid the ribbon on the opposite side of her neck. She should be ashamed of her wanton behavior, but she was past caring as to how outrageously she was behaving. All she wanted was to surrender herself to the fire of his caresses.

The silk nightgown feathered its way downward across her sensitive skin. A low groan echoed out of him as his gaze swept over her bare flesh. The sound caressed her skin as if he'd actually touched her. She took a step backward toward the bed with her hand stretched out in a beckoning gesture.

In a flash of movement, he tugged her into his hard embrace. The scent of pine and leather filled her senses. It emphasized the masculine strength of him as his mouth conquered hers. The soft kid leather covering his artificial hand pressed into her back as his natural hand cupped her breast. The heat of him soaked its way through her pores and spread its way through every cell in her body. He bent his head to brush his lips over the top of her breast.

The light caress made her inhale a gasp of anticipation. She'd barely released the sound of delight when his tongue swirled around the tip of her rigid nipple. Pleasure cascaded over her in a wave at the way he was raising her desire to a fevered pitch. A second later, his teeth lightly abraded the stiff peak then gently nipped at the sensitive flesh. She released a strangled cry of delight as he repeated the action.

Eager to feel his bare skin against hers, her fingers pushed his jacket off his wide shoulders. He froze against her, and she reached up to lightly touch his cheek without flinching beneath his closed off expression. She didn't look away as she slowly undid the buttons of his shirt to slide her hand over his chest. Hard muscles rose and fell at a rapid rate as her fingers glided over the flexible steel that was his chest.

Above her head, his breathing had become harsh and labored. The moment she bent her head to kiss his hot skin, he shuddered beneath her caress. She wanted to taste every inch of him until he lingered on her lips and his hard muscles were etched into her memory. As she continued to move her mouth across his chest, he shrugged his way out of his jacket in jerky movements. The moment he was free of his jacket, she helped him pull his good arm out of his shirt before he froze again. Hesitation and stark despair slashed across his face, and it tore at her heart.

For a brief moment, uncertainty spun through her. The dark torment she saw in his eye made her stomach lurch with fear. What did she have to do to make him understand his injuries were of no consequence where she was concerned? What could she do to convince him how much she craved his touch? Without thinking, she caught his good hand and forced him to touch her in the most intimate way.

He jerked as she encouraged him to satisfy her growing need hoping to reignite the hunger she'd seen moments ago. The moment his thumb rubbed against the small nub of sensitive flesh between her legs, she pressed her hips forward in a silent plea for more. The low rumble in his chest made her shudder as he caressed the heart of her.

The instant he slid two fingers into her, a fierce desire rushed downward to her sex as his strokes created an unrelenting pressure in the pit of her stomach. Her blood was molten heat sliding through her. It was as if she was on fire inside and would burst into flames with each intimate stroke of his fingers.

Every breath she inhaled was filled with his hard, male scent. It was an aroma she'd breathed in every time she'd been near him. His intimate caresses became more insistent, and she moved her hips against his hand as a blinding desire cascaded over her. The pressure building inside her became a relentless throb until with a loud gasp, a hard tremor rocked her body. The powerful reaction his intimate touch unleashed in her threatened to make her legs give way until she fell to the floor. Blinded by a mist of passion, she struggled to remain standing. Shudder after shudder wracked through her as she clung to him in, and he captured her wild sobs of release with his mouth.

As her trembling slowly abated, she threw her head back to stare up at him. Desire held his facial muscles tight and unyielding. Slowly, she reached up to lightly touch the patch that hid the terrible scars where his eye had been. He jerked violently away from her touch, but she simply pressed her body deeper into his.

"Please don't," she whispered. "I want to be with you—all of you."

Rigid with tension, he released a harsh breath, but remained still as she gently removed his eye patch. For the first time since that night on the moor, she saw the extent of his injuries, and her heart twisted painfully in her chest. Tears welled up in her throat as she touched the rough scars over an empty eye socket.

Dear God, how he must have suffered. Not only the physical agony of his injuries, but the emotional ones inflicted by those who recoiled from him. But where others saw hideous scars, all she saw was the strength of a man willing to throw himself in the way of the enemy's sword to save a boy. He was magnificent, and she was determined to make him see himself as she saw him—a lion among warriors.

Chapter 13

Ewan's muscles were knotted and hard as Louisa's rapid breathing slowly returned to normal. He was a fool for having come to her room to ask if she'd experienced the *an dara sealladh* at dinner. The question could have waited until the morning. Despite the warning bells ringing in his head, the instant she'd confessed her desire for him, he'd been lost.

Every rational thought he'd ever possessed had flown out the window as his willpower failed to let him walk away from temptation. And God help him, when her blue silk nightgown had fallen away, every bit of air in his lungs had been sucked out of him. The moment the delicious curves he'd committed to memory were revealed in all their sweet glory, he knew he'd crossed the point of no return.

Watching her come apart in his arms just now had him hard as iron. While his body ached for satisfaction, he allowed himself to revel in the way his touch had made her shudder with abandon in his arms. A soft glow of satiation warmed her lovely features as her eyelids fluttered open and she stared up at him. She didn't look away as she slowly reached up to touch his disfiguring scars. Immediately his head snapped backward.

"Please don't," she whispered as she pressed herself deeper into him. "I want to be with you—all of you."

The soft plea held him frozen in place as a knot lodged

in his throat. It choked him as he fought the urge to thrust her away and struggled to breathe. The moment her fingers touched the eye patch again, his entire body twitched, but he didn't pull away from her. It was best for her to see the beast she'd invited into her room.

Deep inside, he knew it wasn't the real reason he didn't stop her. The moment he saw her reaction he would have no one to blame but himself. Her touch was gentle as she removed the soft, leather patch from his head. Muscles tight with tension, he waited for her revulsion and pity. Instead her eyes began to glisten with unshed tears.

Stunned by her anguish, he didn't move as her fingers lightly traced a path across the scarred tissue where his eye had once been. It was a venerating touch, and he saw her swallow hard as she went up on her toes to kiss him. The sweet tenderness in the way her mouth brushed across his lips left him reeling.

God help him, what was this woman doing to him? In the dark recesses of his soul, her caress stirred a piece of him to life he'd thought long dead and buried. Slowly, her fingers caressed the top of his shoulder to slip the other half of his shirt off the maimed side of his body. There was a sweet tenderness to her light touch as the material fell off his shoulder. A shudder crashed through him as she gently eased his artificial arm out of the shirt sleeve.

The fear holding him rigid made his mouth go dry as he waited for her reaction. The depth of his emotion revealed how much light she'd already brought into the darkness of his life. It signaled how deeply his emotions were tied to her, and it scared the hell out of him. His breathing was ragged as he waited for her reaction—for the look of appalled horror as his metal appendage was revealed.

The moment the shirt fell to the floor, she lifted her head. Once again, he'd misjudged her. The tears still glistening in her eyes said more to him than anything she could say. Until her, pity was all he'd known since the loss of his eye and arm, but he could tell she understood what he'd lost. The sorrow he saw the way she looked at him said she knew how much his injuries still pained him. Her hand cupped his cheek for a brief second before she turned her attention to the leather straps on his shoulder.

As she removed the bane of his existence, the tenderness in her touch chopped another piece of the darkness out of his soul. She turned away to lay the artificial arm on the stand beside her bed. The intensity of the emotion he experienced as he watched her lightly stroke the metal contraption was a solid punch to his gut.

When she faced him again, another vicious blow slammed into him at the emotions flitting across her lovely countenance. The tenderness, acceptance, and growing desire he saw there made his heart slam into his chest. Unshed tears made her eyes sparkle in the soft glow of lamplight that bathed her sensual, intoxicating curves.

She closed the distance between them to take his hand and pull him toward the bed. With a gentle push she forced him to sit down before she knelt at his feet. Silently, she removed the serviceable military shoes he'd chosen to wear rather than the traditional ghillies brogues. The oil lamp's light cast a soft glow over her shoulders and back as she worked, and he reached out to stroke the brown silk of her hair.

At his touch, she looked up at him then lowered her head to kiss the inside of his knee as her hands slid up under his kilt and over his thighs. The caress sent a thunderbolt pounding its way into every inch of his body. It made him ache for her to take him in hand. The harsh breath he sucked into his lungs made her raise her head, and a sultry smile curved her lips. With a slow deliberate motion, her soft fingertips trailed a lazy, torturous path away from his cock.

Denied the feel of her hand wrapped around him,

disappointment tugged a growl from deep within his throat, and her eyes darkened with desire. A renewed hunger for her tightened every muscle in his body, and he stood up in a sharp moment that made her gasp in surprise. With a hard tug of his only hand, he pulled her to her feet then captured her mouth in a hard kiss.

Stark need speared its way into him, and his mouth didn't leave hers as he fumbled to remove the sporran from his waist. As it fell to the floor, he struggled with the buckles and the leather strips holding his kilt in place. Her mouth slid downward across his jaw to his throat, while her hands brushed across his to help him remove the plaid.

Seconds later, the kilt dropped to cover his sporran, and she wrapped her arms tightly around his waist. The hunger crashing its way through him was a palpable sensation hammering its way into his body as they tumbled down onto the mattress. The fragrance of her filled his nostrils as he rolled her onto her back and pinned her beneath him. With his only hand pressing into the mattress, he pushed himself upward to stare down at her for a moment.

Desire made her skin glow, and her beautiful hazel eyes shimmered with the same hunger flooding his body. As she studied him, a gentle hand caressed his chest before it moved downward. Without hesitating, he quickly lowered his body to trap her hand between them. Puzzlement and frustration flitted across her beautiful face as he prevented her from reaching his cock. The small pout of vexation pursing her mouth tugged a smile to his lips.

Slowly, he lowered his head to brush his mouth across her satin-smooth shoulder. In response, she shifted her body in an obvious effort to free her hand. Despite his body's demand to assuage its hunger, he pressed his body even deeper into hers. She was far too accustomed to getting her way. He wanted her to feel the same intense longing he'd experienced every night since he'd carried her off the moors.

He wanted to hear her soft feminine plea for satisfaction as she experienced a blazing need for his body to conquer hers. A small whisper of frustrated desire floated above his head as he nibbled his way downward. The sound announced her growing need for him to make her his in the most intimate way. It signaled she was experiencing the same desire consuming him. Once more she tried to escape his restraint, and he thwarted her efforts by burrowing his body into hers.

Honey could not taste sweeter than the silky warmth of her skin, and he savored her as one would a fine wine. Another sound of protest whispered in his ears. This time, the sound held the increased pitched notes of hunger and need. He ignored it and continued to work his way down to the full, lushness of her breast.

The moment his lips reached the hard tip of her breast she inhaled a sharp breath. Anticipation echoed in the soft gasp, and she arched her body upward in a silent demand for him to take her into his mouth. Ignoring the unspoken plea, he turned his attention to the indentation between her breasts. With her free hand and a whimper of need, she tried to force him to tend to her breast.

He resisted for a brief moment, before allowing her to guide him toward the rigid peak. His tongue flicked out to swirl around the hard tip of her, and she released a sigh of pleasure. A second later, he bit down on the swollen nipple. Her cry of shock filled his ears as she jerked beneath him in obvious surprise.

With a flick of his tongue, he soothed her sensitive flesh then bit down on the hard tip again. This time her cry was one of pleasure as her body writhed beneath him. Soft fingers dug into his shoulders as he soothed her sensitive flesh while quiet feminine pants of excitement filled the air.

"*Oh, please.*" The hunger and passion in her voice tightened his cock as his body responded to the soft plea.

"Please what, *mo leannan*?" he rasped as he raised his

head to look up at her. Passion burned in her gaze as a soft hand cupped his cheek.

"I want you. I want to be a part of you."

The husky words were a plea and sweet invitation that pushed him over the edge. He captured her mouth in a hard kiss and shifted his body against hers. With a powerful thrust he buried himself inside her, smothering her cry of pleasure with his mouth. He didn't move for a long moment as he savored the slick heat of her.

As their tongues tangled and swirled in a fiery dance of passion, he slowly increased the pace of his steady thrusts. Each time he retreated, her muscles contracted around him like a hot vise. It was a sharp pleasure that pounded at his body. With every stroke, her hips rose upward to meet his in perfect unison. Their bodies rocked against each other with a passion that was spiraling out of control, and he lost himself in the essence of her.

The delicious, subtle scent of rose petals filled his nostrils, while the warm silk of her skin against his ignited a fiery need in the depths of his soul. Desire blinded him to everything but the hunger she aroused in him. It was as if he'd breathed her into every cell in his body, and she was a part of him. A moan poured out of her, and her body jerked hard against him while her muscles tightened around his cock.

In a sudden onslaught of pleasure, her spasms gripped and pulled at him until every part of him was demanding a release. Another hard shudder rippled through her as she arched upward into him with a wild cry. Frozen against him for a brief moment, the white-hot fire of her contractions around him drove him to pump his body into hers at a blistering speed. A powerful wave of pleasure crashed over him dragging him under until he was blindly racing toward an abyss unlike anything he'd ever known. With one last thrust he went rigid against her softness, and with a shout, he throbbed hard inside her. The ragged sound of her breathing echoed in his ears as he slowly lowered his body down onto hers. Long eyelashes rested on her flushed cheeks as her eyes remained closed. Slowly, her breathing became quiet, rhythmic breaths, and the tremors vibrating into his body slowly abated.

Ewan's gaze drifted down to her full mouth, and he brushed his lips over hers in a tender kiss. A soft murmur drifted out of her, and as he lifted his head, her eyes fluttered open. The satiated expression on her lovely features took his breath away as a dreamy smile curved her mouth.

"That was wonderful," she whispered.

Something about the way she looked at him made his heart slam into his chest. How would he ever be able to let her go when the time came? The question made a knot form in his throat, and he slowly rolled off of her. It was an inevitable outcome, he had little to offer her.

Silence hung in the air between them for several moments before Louisa curled up into his side, her head settling in the nook between his chest and the stump of his arm. Once again, he was startled by her acceptance of him. It was as if his missing arm were the most natural thing in the world.

As he marveled at how easily she ignored his injuries, the softness of her lips against his chest made him draw in a sharp breath. His reaction resulted in a smothered laugh whispering against his skin like a kitten purring with satisfaction.

"What do you find so amusing, lass?"

"Nothing," she murmured with distinct amusement.

The denial made him shift his upper body so he could stare down at her. Mischief sparkled in her eyes as her lips found their way to his nipple. He watched her pink tongue flick out to swirl around his flesh. The moment she abraded the nipple with her teeth, he released a growl of pleasure. A quiet laugh parted her lips as she settled back down into the mattress at his side.

"I simply like hearing how you react to my touch."

"You, are a minx, *mo leannan.*"

A chuckle rolled out of him as he found it impossible to resist the sleepy smile tilting her lips. Her hand covered her mouth as she yawned then closed her eyes and burrowed her body into his.

"I like it when you call me *mo leannan,*" she murmured as another yawn parted her lips.

The soft words sent a wave of emotion crashing over him. For the first time since he'd awoken without an arm or eye, he felt whole. His heart thundered in his chest at the realization, and he turned his head slightly to look at her. Louisa was only half-awake, and as he reached across his chest to brush a lock of hair off her cheek, she uttered a quiet sigh of contentment. The sound stole all the air from his lungs, and he struggled to breathe as he realized how much he wanted every night to end like this—with Louisa curled up against him like a kitten.

In the silence of the room, her slow steady breathing indicated she'd fallen asleep. For a long time, he stared down at her as his thoughts careened around in his head like the bullets that had whizzed past his head in battle. He'd questioned his sanity the day he'd agreed to let Louisa stay and be Ross's governess. That he'd not followed his instincts to send her away was only the first of many mistakes he'd made where she was concerned.

What was he supposed to do now? Ewan suppressed a groan as he closed his eyes. Until this moment, he hadn't realized he was falling off a cliff where Louisa Morehouse was concerned. The fact that he was hanging onto the edge of that precipice by little more than sheer willpower scared the hell out of him.

Chapter 14

A quiet sound penetrated Ewan's sleep, and he was instantly awake. The mantle clock chimed softly, and he blew out a harsh breath as he recognized the harmless sound. In the Sudan, the prospect of being slaughtered in his sleep had been a constant threat and fear.

Despite the stillness and deceptive peaceful nature of the desert, his survival instincts had jolted him awake at least once a night, sometimes more. The habit had saved his life on several occasions while in the Sudan.

While the only battles he fought now were with his mother, the sights and sounds of the battlefield stalked his dreams every night. There was no reprieve from the blood and death that made him jerk upright in bed with his heart pounding viciously in his chest. The screams of dying men still rang in his ears as he slept. He'd not even been spared the agony of his own suffering at the hand of an enemy's sword.

The doctors in the hospital had said the nightmares would eventually fade, but they'd been wrong. The blood-curdling cries of the enemy still taunted him in his sleep. He would never be free of the hellish dreams. With resignation he closed the only eye he still possessed before his muscles tightened with a violent jerk.

With a sharp twist of his head, he stared down at the woman beside him in stunned in amazement. For the first time since being carried off the battlefield he hadn't been woken up by a nightmare. It had been the quiet sound of a clock, not a horrific dream or the terrible memory of waking up in a medical tent no longer a whole man.

Beside him, Louisa murmured something incoherent before she turned over in her sleep with her body still pressed into his. It was the first time since he'd gone to the Sudan that he'd slept peacefully. If nightmares had haunted his sleep, he couldn't remember them. Still in disbelief, his gaze slid over the soft curve of Louisa's back and bottom pressed snugly against him. In the space of only a few weeks, she'd changed his life in ways he'd never dreamed possible.

He reached over and pulled a lock of silky brown hair off her cheek and traced a light path across her soft skin with his fingers. Another soft murmur drifted out of her as she shifted her position again. The warmth of her lush curves pressing even deeper into his side created a tidal wave of emotion crashing over him. It was a revelation that he immediately and viciously rejected as truth.

Despite his effort, the strength of the emotion became an invisible vise that wrapped its way around his chest and constricted his breathing. Ewan slowly laid back into his pillow to stare up at the ceiling. He would never be able to express his feelings aloud. Louisa deserved better than a man as damaged and broken as he was.

In the back of his head a voice shouted a reminder as to how she'd gently forced him to bare his body and soul to her a short time ago. A wild cackle followed the reminder as another voice jeered at him for refusing to admit the real reason he would never confess his feelings for Louisa to her or anyone else. The taunt made his jaw harden as the word coward echoed in his head.

He wasn't afraid to confront anything. Fear was a companion he'd lived with closely for years. He'd faced the horrors of battle and being maimed. He would survive when

Louisa was gone, just as he'd survived his childhood. The voice mocked him again, but he ignored it. The sound of the clock chiming alerted him to the fact that it was almost time for the household staff to rise.

Even despite the emotional war waging inside him, he was still loathe to leave Louisa's side. She was like an oasis in the desert, but if he delayed any longer, he'd endanger her reputation. It would also give his mother the ability to humiliate Louisa with scathing disapproval. Ewan winced at the thought and carefully slid away from Louisa to search for his clothes. Although low on fuel, the oil lamp's light combined with that of the fire in the hearth made it easy to find his clothes.

He strapped on his mechanical arm first and released a soft grunt of irritation as he struggled into his shirt. As usual, he found the artificial appendage more of a hindrance than help. With his shirt finally in place, he picked his kilt up from the floor and secured it between his metal fingers. It was relatively easy to wrap the garment around his waist, but the leather tabs and buckles that held the plaid in place was a different matter altogether.

If he had the use of both hands, pushing a leather tab through a slit and into its buckle would not be a challenge, but every time the kilt moved in his metal fingers, he had to adjust the material and begin anew. Frustration surged inside him as he fumbled with the kilt fasteners for several minutes before he pushed the last leather tab into its buckle.

The moment the tab was secured, he grunted softly with relief. It took him almost another half hour longer to finish dressing himself, and when he was dressed, he released a harsh breath of satisfaction at the accomplishment. A soft sound whispered through the air, and he jerked his head toward the bed to see Louisa was still sleeping soundly. With a twist of his lips, he dismissed the noise and took a step toward the bedroom door when he heard the hushed sound again.

Ewan jerked his head toward the secret door Robert the Bruce had supposedly escaped through. For a brief moment, he frowned in puzzlement at the bulky chest blocking the door. It hadn't been there when he was caring for Louisa the night he'd found her on the moors. A second later he saw the furniture move slightly as someone in the hidden passageway pushed on the secret door.

Deep inside he knew who was on the other side of the door, but he prayed it was one of the boys. Quickly crossing the floor, his heart slammed into his chest as he saw short, stubby fingers wrapped around the edge of the door as Gilbert tried to leverage his weight against the secret panel.

"Go back to your room, Gilbert," he growled softly as he gave his brother's fingers a vicious slap.

A soft howl of pain and frustration escaped the man on the other side of the panel, but after a few seconds, Ewan heard his brother shuffling away. Worried the incident might have awoken Louisa, he glanced over his shoulder. Relief swept through him at the sight of her curled up beneath the covers he'd tucked around her.

Quietly closing the panel leading into the hidden passageway, he repositioned the chest so it blocked the secret door. Louisa had clearly moved the heavy furniture into place herself. If anyone else had moved it, or even assisted her, McCallum would have mentioned it. As much as he wanted to deny his suspicions, he could think of only one reason Louisa might have for blocking the door. Gilbert had tried to enter her room once before.

He should have told Louisa about his brother, but had deemed it unnecessary as he'd believed Gilbert was well-supervised and restricted from roaming the keep. Although his brother's presence in the Keep wasn't a closely guarded secret, his mother and aunt had kept Gilbert hidden away from prying eyes for so long, people had forgotten about him.

Longtime retainers, such as McCallum knew about Gilbert, but newcomers to the household had only heard tales. Even Ross seemed to be unaware of Gilbert's existence, or at least the boy hadn't mentioned him to anyone. The Scots were a superstitious people, and if any of the staff ran into Gilbert, they would declare his brother a monster or the devil incarnate. Wild tales, not to mention hysterical maidservants, had been incentive enough to continue the practice of keeping his brother in isolation as his mother and aunt had done for years.

He blew out a harsh noise of regret and self-disgust. Louisa was relatively fearless, and for her to block the Bruce's secret door indicated she'd been frightened. The knowledge troubled him deeply. Why the devil hadn't she come to him? He could have explained things and instructed McCallum to seal the Bruce's panel to keep her safe.

While McCallum and Finn had closed off all the entrances to the keep's corridors they could find in Gilbert's suites of rooms, it didn't surprise Ewan that one had been missed. It wasn't unusual for a structure as old and large as the keep to have numerous secret entrances to the dark passages hidden behind its walls. As the structure had been rebuilt and expanded over generations, new entrances and passages would have been built and old ones forgotten.

He needed to be certain they'd not missed an entrance. If all the entrances in Gilbert's room had been sealed off only two other possibilities could explain his brother's presence in the hidden corridors. Either Brown had failed to confine his brother tonight, or Gilbert had found a key to open his door.

Brown had proven a reliable nurse for Gilbert, and he knew the man locked his brother in his room nightly to prevent exactly what had happened a few moments ago. While Brown wasn't infallible, Ewan found it highly unlikely the man had failed in performing the most critical of all his duties. If the man hadn't failed, that meant Gilbert had found another key to open his door. Aside from himself, Brown and his mother were the only ones who had a key to his brother's rooms.

Ewan's mouth tightened with anger. If his brother hadn't stolen his mother's key, Ewan wouldn't put it past the dowager countess to release Gilbert herself. She'd never been happy at his orders to lock Gilbert up at night, and she took pleasure in thwarting his orders whenever possible.

If she *had* been allowing his brother to roam the keep and it's hidden passages at night, it would explain the dead, mutilated mice and rats found in recent weeks. He'd never actually caught Gilbert in the act of torturing an animal, but several months ago, his aunt had summoned him to see the horrific remains results of his brother's handiwork. The memory made his stomach knot as he recalled the terrible sight of two mutilated rats.

In the next instant, ice flowed through his body until his skin was as cold as if he'd spent a winter's night out on the moor. *Christ Jesus*, had Gilbert found a door that opened onto the Keep's grounds as well?

The memory of his mother's pallor when Iain had mentioned the murders at dinner filled his head. At the time, he'd attributed her distraught look as her concern a killer was stalking the moors. His muscles tightened painfully with dread as a new explanation slithered through his mind. Like puzzle pieces falling into place, memories of things his mother had said or done merged with the memory of minor disturbances inside the walls of Argaty Keep over the past year to form a picture that made his blood run cold.

Until this precise moment he'd thought his brother a harmless simpleton who mutilated small animals without any real understanding of what he was doing. But if he'd found a way out of the Keep, was it possible that he'd found a much larger prey to attack? If Gilbert *was* responsible for the deaths of two women, he needed to be locked up permanently. Even if his brother was innocent of murder, his mother had allowed Gilbert to roam the Keep without supervision. The dowager countess had ignored his orders, and a wave of fury fired his blood and warmed his cold skin.

A soft murmur floated through the air, and he turned his head to see Louisa had shifted position in bed with one arm wrapped around one of the bed pillows. God knows what might have happened if Gilbert had gained access to her room. If he'd not been here—he refused to consider what might have happened. The one thing he knew for certain was that his brother needed to be watched around the clock.

Determined to settle the matter with his mother once and for all, he moved quickly toward the door. Tension snaked its way through him as he cautiously ensured the hall was empty before he left Louisa's room. Fury fueled his pace as he strode angrily toward the dowager countess's suite of rooms. Today his mother would discover she'd pushed him one step too far.

When he reached the dowager countess's door, he pounded his fist against the wood. He didn't care if the woman was still in bed, he had no intention of letting Gilbert roam the Keep anymore. The door to his mother's suite squeaked open to reveal his aunt.

It surprised him to find Wallis fully dressed, but in all likelihood, his aunt was up and ready for another day of slavery to his mother. It never ceased to amaze him as to what would make his aunt serve her sister with such devotion. Wallis's face brightened with pleasure as she stared at him before she winced with misgiving.

"Ewan, why are you here. It's barely past dawn."

"Is she awake?" At his question, Wallis flinched in dismay and looked over her shoulder. He didn't give his aunt a chance to reply as he gently moved her out of his way. "I'll take that as a yes."

"Ewan, please," his aunt whispered as she caught his

arm in an effort to stop him. "She won't be happy you're here."

"I don't give a damn about her happiness," he growled with restrained fury. "It's time my mother came to terms with the fact that *I* rule Argaty Keep, not her."

Apprehension darkened his aunt's countenance as he gently tugged free of her fierce grip. Her visible fear made Ewan paused long enough to squeeze her hand in a gesture of reassurance before he crossed the floor to his mother's sitting room. With a vicious twist of the doorknob, he flung the door open, and it hit the wall with a resounding crash. Satisfaction made him smile with cold amusement when he saw his mother jerk her head toward him in surprise, and perhaps even a bit of uneasiness.

Seated in a chair near the fireplace, she quickly composed her features and bent over Gilbert who was sitting at her feet. She murmured something to his brother as she brushed her fingers across Gilbert's cheek in a gentle, motherly caress and kissed his brow. Ewan's jaw clenched at her tender gesture. As much as he'd come to despise his mother, the tenderness she showed Gilbert still sent a jolt of pain slicing through his mid-section. Not once in his entire life had his mother ever demonstrated any affection for him. All she'd ever displayed where he was concerned was her loathing.

"Why did you let him in, Wallis?" Lady Argaty tilted her head slightly to look around Ewan at the woman who had followed him into the room. "You know how much noise upsets Gilbert."

"I…he was…I…" Her sister's stammering made the dowager countess eye Wallis with contempt and his mother silenced her sister with a dismissive wave of her hand.

"What do you want, Ewan?" his mother asked coldly as she focused her attention on his brother once more.

"How many times this week have you ignored my

instructions and released Gilbert from his room when Brown was off duty?"

At his harsh question, Gilbert made a noise of angry frustration similar to the one he'd made when Ewan had ordered him away from Louisa's room. Ewan glanced down and saw Gilbert's fat, stubby fingers squeezing the neck of a doll he held in his lap. It was an ominous sign and renewed the chill he'd experienced earlier.

"I have no idea why you're questioning me." Lady Argaty's gaze glided over Ewan with a look of intense dislike before she bent over to soothe Gilbert again who had begun to grunt with agitation. "Why not ask that silent brute of a guard you hired. The man doesn't let Gilbert out of his sight."

"Because aside from Brown and myself, you have the only other key to Gilbert's room," Ewan snapped with a ferocity that made his mother stiffen in her seat although she continued to soothe his brother's restless mutterings. "Mr. Brown locks Gilbert in his room at night, and yet my brother escaped his confinement this evening."

"How do you know that?" The dowager countess jerked her head up to look at him with speculation and suspicion.

"I *asked* you a question, my lady." Ewan ignored her response as he noted the lack of concern on his mother's features with a growing sense of alarm. "*How many times?*"

"I don't know," the dowager countess said with a cavalier wave of her hand that horrified him. "Four or five."

"And did *one* of those times occur the night of the MacLaren woman's death?"

"What are you implying?" Scorn filled Lady Argaty's voice as she tipped her chin upward at a defiant angle and glared back at him.

"I am not implying. I am accusing you of disobeying my expressed orders as to the restrictions of Gilbert's movement within the keep. You've allowed my brother to roam the Keep without supervision."

"And what if I do allow him to play when you and Brown forbid him to do so during the day?"

"Brown takes him to the garden twice daily," Ewan said between clenched teeth.

"Only during meals when no one will see him." The harsh, indignant accusation made Ewan stiffen at his mother's inability to see the reason for keeping his brother out of sight.

"Your blindness is ironic given you have two eyes compared to my one. Gilbert and I frighten people. Responsibilities make my presence in the keep a necessity. One monster roam the keep is one too many." Ewan looked pointedly in his brother's direction.

Short in stature, his brother's head was abnormal in size. A large, melon-shaped growth jutted out from the side of Gilbert's skull. The weight of it forced his brother's head to fall downward at an unnatural angle until his ear touched his shoulder. Gilbert's other ear laid flat against the side of his head. He had one eye that was crossed, while the other slanted downward until the eye occupied almost half of his brother's cheek.

As Ewan studied his brother, Gilbert lifted his head. The look of cunning on his sibling's face made Ewan draw in a sharp breath. He'd been right to think his brother might be dangerous. Gilbert's reaction indicated he wasn't quite the simpleton Ewan had believed. Ewan dragged his attention away from his brother's crafty expression to look at his mother who had remained silent.

"You did *not* answer my question, my lady," Ewan bit out as he stared at his mother with intense dislike. "Other than tonight, has Gilbert had the opportunity to go outdoors unattended?"

"Are you suggesting Gilbert is responsible for that village girl's death?" For a second time, she deftly sidestepped answering his question. Ewan's jaw clenched tight as he restrained himself from shaking the answer out of her.

"Was he?"

"Of course not," Lady Argaty snapped as she looked away from him, but not before Ewan saw her guilt flash in her eyes.

"You're lying."

"Even if I were, that you would suggest, let alone think Gilbert could kill someone is preposterous. He's a child."

"A child who's demonstrated he's capable of killing animals."

"Animals fascinate him."

"*Fascinate?*" Ewan stared at his mother in disgust. "He tortures them *before* he kills them, my lady. We both know it's more than possible he's responsible for not just that poor girl's death, but the other girl too."

"You *don't* know that," Lady Argaty exclaimed with a note of alarm in her voice.

In spite of the rancor between them, Ewan saw the fear in his mother's eyes as he studied her in silence. He'd never thought his mother capable of love, yet it was the only explanation for her refusal to believe Gilbert might actually be capable of murder. Ewan had thought himself impervious to feeling anything for his mother except anger and dislike, but it was impossible not to feel pity for the woman as she clearly struggled with the idea that Gilbert had killed two people.

"I should never have allowed Gilbert to stay when I came home. He belongs in an asylum."

"*No.*" The dowager countess sprang from her chair as fury twisted her face into an ugly mask. "This is his home. He belongs here with us—me. You have no proof he was involved in anyone's death."

At her strident response, a low noise of what might have been anger echoed out of Gilbert. The sound made Ewan shift his attention back to his brother. Gilbert was studying him with a malevolence that filled him with dread. Until this very moment, somewhere deep inside him, he'd wanted to believe his brother hadn't killed the two women. The venomous glint in his brother's eyes made him realize it had been wrong to hope for such a possibility.

Ewan's heart slammed into his chest as he remembered his brother trying to force his way into Louisa's room. Christ Jesus if something had happened to her—he stopped in mid-thought unable to contemplate the worst.

"Arrangements will be made immediately for him to be sent someplace where he cannot harm anyone else."

"I will *not* let you send him away," Lady Argaty said viciously as she sprang to her feet.

"Gilbert wants pretty lady." The guttural words rolling out of his brother was a vicious punch in Ewan's gut as he and his mother jerked their attention to the man seated on the floor.

"What pretty lady, my darling?" Lady Argaty said gently as she stroked her second son's brow.

"His pretty. He wouldn't let me see her."

"See her?" There was a note of puzzlement in Lady Argaty's voice before she stiffened then slowly straightened upright to pin her gaze on Ewan.

"How did you know Gilbert wasn't in his rooms, my lord?" Scorn twisted his mother's lips as she glared at Ewan. "You were with her, weren't you? That's how you knew."

"How I came to know of Gilbert's whereabouts is not your concern."

"You settled yourself between her legs quickly, Ewan. I'm surprised she even allowed you near her. What will the household think when they discover what's happening between you and that woman?"

"If you do *anything* to soil Louisa's reputation or do her harm, you'll answer to me, mother."

"I am *not* your mother." Abhorrence made her lips twist

at his manner of address. "Gilbert is the only son I have. You are a *bastard*."

"I know full well how much you despise me, mother." It was impossible for Ewan to keep the bitterness out of his voice as he met the glittering hate in the dowager countess's expression.

"Do not *ever*, call me that again. You are *not* my son." The virulent scorn and contempt in his mother's voice made him bite down on the inside of his cheek.

"Elspeth, please." The raw emotion in his aunt's voice made Ewan glance over his shoulder at her to see Wallis staring as her sister in shocked horror. Confused by her reaction, Ewan pushed aside questioning his aunt and turned back to his mother.

"Disavow me all you like, *mother*," he bit out between clenched teeth, deliberately refusing to acknowledge her insane assertion. "Perhaps you're the one who needs to be sent away, not Gilbert."

With the speed of a snake striking its victim, his mother lunged forward and slapped him. The strength of the savage blow made his head snap to one side. His cheek stinging, he eyed his mother with cold resentment. Eager to distance himself from her hate and venom, Ewan turned away only to have his mother tug viciously on his artificial limb to prevent his departure. The device pinched painfully at his skin causing him to draw in a hiss of air between his teeth.

"*No*. I will no longer continue this farce," the dowager countess spat out as she looked at her sister. "Tell him, Wallis. Tell him how you parted your legs for another master of Argaty Keep years ago, just like Mrs. Morehouse."

Guilt, pain, and regret crossed his aunt's face as Ewan looked at her in confusion before shifting his gaze back to his mother. The dowager countess's expression was contorted with a rage that made him believe her capable of killing, just like his brother.

"Do not bring Aunt Wallis into—"

"*You are not my son.*" His mother shouted with a rage that made him jerk in surprise. "He *forced* me to lie to everyone. He wanted a son so badly he was willing to put a bastard in place as his heir."

"What in god's name are you talking about, my lady," Ewan snapped as an uneasy sensation formed in his stomach.

"*Tell him*, Wallis." The dowager countess took a step toward her sister with a look of fury that made Ewan shift his body to keep his mother from reaching his aunt. "Tell him how, just like his pretty Mrs. Morehouse, you parted your legs for another master of Argaty Keep."

"Don't do this, Elspeth. Please."

There was a deep note of pain in his aunt's voice as Ewan jerked his attention toward his aunt. Tears shimmered in Wallis's eyes as her expression silently pleaded with her sister. Ewan found himself looking back and forth between the two women as he struggled to make sense of his mother's words. What master of Argaty Keep was she referring to?

His father had been an only child, and as the eldest, Ewan had become the earl upon his father's death. Confusion engulfed him as he stared at his aunt. Pale and visibly shaken, he saw her shame and guilt before she bowed her head.

"Since *you* refuse to tell him, I will." The dowager's voice held a note of vindictive malice as she looked at Ewan. "My sister is a whore. She entered my husband's bed *after* I became the Countess of Argaty, and she bore my husband a son."

The revelation left him dazed and battered as if he'd been knocked off his feet by a large wave during a terrible storm at sea. In the dark recesses of his mind, he experienced the beginnings of an understanding that rocked the ground beneath him. As he struggled to comprehend his mother's words, his silence made Lady Argaty sneer at him with venomous glee.

"*You* are *not* the Earl of Argaty. Gilbert is." The

poisonous spite in his mother's voice made him stagger backward a step. The dowager countess looked at her sister. "I think he's taking it quite well, Wallis, wouldn't you agree?"

An incoherent note of pain and anger escaped the woman he'd called aunt all his life, and Ewan turned sharply toward Wallis. He knew the answer to his question before he even asked it, but he asked it nonetheless.

"Is it true?" he rasped harshly. Wallis flinched but didn't avoid his gaze as she nodded.

"Yes," she said softly. "But it is far more complicated than your—my sister makes it sound."

"Complicated?" he ground out with anger and pain. "There is nothing complicated about any of this. Either I am your son or I am not."

"You are my son."

The quiet words pounded against his ears as if he were on the battlefield once more with the cannons booming. For more than thirty years, he'd been living a lie without even knowing it. An invisible vise encircled him and squeezed his chest until it became difficult to breathe. It was as if he'd been thrown into a raging river that threatened to drag him beneath the surface.

The past rose up to greet him as he remembered moments as a young boy when he'd tried so hard to please his mother, only to have her scorn him. Close on the heels of those memories was that of Aunt Wallis offering him the comfort and love he wanted so badly from his mother. As if from a great distance he heard his mother laugh. The moment he thought of the dowager as his mother, he was forced to correct himself. Wallis was his mother, not the countess.

"Your Mrs. Morehouse won't want anything to do with you now when she learns you're not really the earl." The sneer in the dowager's voice made Wallis step forward.

"Ewan will remain Earl of Argaty. Dougal saw to that when he convinced you to claim Ewan as your son, and I will see to it you do *nothing* to change that fact."

Wallis's voice was quiet, yet filled with a steely note he'd never heard in her voice before as she met eyed her sister coldly and steadily. When the dowager started to interrupt, Wallis shook her head.

"Even if you try to sow seeds of doubt, Elspeth, too much time has passed. No one will believe you."

"May you and your bastard rot in hell." The dowager countess spat out the words like a viper spitting venom. Sadness darkened Wallis's features, as she studied her sister's expression of hate.

"I pity you, Elspeth."

"Pity me? Whatever for?" Lady Argaty snapped.

"You've allowed hate to eat away at your soul," Wallis said quietly. "I've asked your forgiveness over and over again in both word and deed."

"I will *never* forgive you. You stole everything from me."

"I stole *nothing* from you because you had nothing to steal. You never loved Dougal. You loved his title. I'm the one who held Dougal's heart. That belonged to me from the moment we met," Wallis shook her head, her voice filled with dignity and quiet conviction.

"But *you*, Elspeth, you did something *far worse*. You punished a child for the sins of his parents, and you punished me after Dougal died by threatening to banish me from Argaty Keep knowing full-well I would endure anything simply to watch Ewan grow to manhood. But it's over now. It will be Ewan's choice whether I go or stay, not yours. You no longer hold any power over anyone, Elspeth. You surrendered that the moment you told Ewan the truth."

Rage twisted the dowager's countenance into a horrible visage as she swung her hand toward her sister, but Ewan managed to emerge from his stunned state to grab the dowager's arm and stop Lady Argaty from hitting her target.

"Enough."

In a sharp, abrupt gesture, Ewan released his hold of the woman he'd called mother all his life. Suppressing the shock that had him reeling as to the truth of his birthright, Ewan pinned Lady Argaty beneath his gaze. "You, my lady, will remain in your chambers today, and see to it that my bro— your son, does not go anywhere without you or Brown at his side. Do you understand?"

"What are you going to do?" Despite her visible anger and hatred, there was a thread of fear running through the dowager's question.

"I have already said what I intend to do, unless you would like me to notify the authorities as to the strong probability that Gilbert has killed two women."

"You wouldn't dare," Lady Argaty gasped.

On the floor, Gilbert made an ominous sound. Ewan glanced down at his brother to see the man scowling up at him with a raw fury that only emphasized his ugly appearance. With a shake of his head, Ewan looked back at Lady Argaty.

"Do not test my patience, my lady," he said coldly. "I will see to it that your son is well-cared for and in conditions befitting any human being, but he will *not* remain at Argaty Keep."

Ewan spun around and walked out of the dowager countess's sitting room. He was almost at the door to the dowager's suite, when a hand touched his arm. For a moment, he almost shrugged off the light touch, but something compelled him to halt. Slowly, he turned around to meet Wallis MacCullaich's sorrow-filled gaze.

"Yes, Aunt Wallis?" No sooner had he spoken than he flinched. A small, sad smile tilted the corners of her mouth slightly.

"I do not expect you to call me mother, Ewan," she said softly as she stepped forward and reached up to touch his cheek. When he flinched again, she quickly pulled her hand away. "I will ask nothing of you, but when you are ready, I will tell you everything and answer whatever questions you wish to ask me." As he stared down at her, childhood memories of his aunt's patience and loving manner raced through his head. It all made sense now, but he wasn't sure he could forgive her not telling him the truth. Why hadn't she told him the truth when he had come of age? It was only one of several questions he wanted answered, but he needed time to think. Ewan nodded his head, and without a word walked out of the dowager countess's suite.

Chapter 15

The bedroom door snapped closed behind Ewan with a quiet click. Asadi had been asleep on the threshold, but had stirred the moment Ewan reached his bedroom door.

With a sharp command, he'd ordered the boy to go back to sleep. For a long moment, he remained frozen with his back against the door then crossed the room to stare out the window.

Dawn had surrendered to a new day as sunlight danced across the moors he loved. It was land he'd thought his without challenge until this morning. The thought made his hand clench around the drapes framing the window. He'd been wrong. Argaty Keep, its lands, and title all belonged to Gilbert. A man incapable of functioning in the real world, and in all likelihood a murderer.

The scenery outside the window slowly gave way to mental images of the dowager countess's malevolent features as she'd revealed the truth of his birth. Everything he'd believed as to who he was had been ripped from him as viciously as the blade that had taken his arm. It wasn't just the lie that had him hanging in the wind like a criminal hanging from a gibbet. It was the betrayal. For years his mother and aunt had lied not just to everyone else as to who he really was, but they'd lied to him.

"Damn them to hell."

The words reverberated like a clap of thunder in the room. With a sudden, violent jerk he turned away from the window. For the first time in his life, everything made sense. All the questions he'd asked himself throughout his youth had been answered in a few short minutes. Ewan knew his antipathy for the dowager countess would make it easy to embrace the truth the woman wasn't his mother. Wallis MacCullaich was a different matter altogether.

Tension knotted his muscles as he remembered how often his aunt—no, his real mother—had comforted him as a child. Every time he'd suffered from Lady Argaty's cruel words and humiliation, Wallis MacCullaich had been there to comfort him. Every time he'd scraped a knee or been ill, she'd seen to his care. Even when he'd fallen from the stable rafters and broken his arm, his aunt had cared for him with a tenderness Lady Argaty had withheld from him.

There had even been times when he'd secretly wished Wallis had been his mother. Those moments of secret longings had been quickly followed by guilt for wishing such a thing. He'd grown up thinking *he* was responsible for being a disappointment to his mother, when in actuality he'd been nothing more than a constant reminder to Lady Argaty as to how her sister and husband had betrayed her.

In some ways it was almost a relief to know why the dowager hated him so much. It was an emotion he understood. The woman had introduced him to the emotion when he'd returned home for those two miserable days after Agnes's death. Lady Argaty's deliberate arrangement of his marriage to a woman she knew carried another man's child had obliterated the last vestige of affection he'd had for the woman. The dowager had nearly destroyed him that day and had sentenced Ross to a life as miserable as Ewan's own childhood.

Guilt sped through him at the thought. That wasn't true. He, and he alone, was responsible for Ross being deprived of affection or even kindness. The only blame Ewan could place at the dowager's feet were her actions and words that had served as the catalyst for his treatment of Ross. The pound of flesh he'd been extracting from the boy he'd claimed as his own was all the more reprehensible because he knew what it was like to grow up without the love of a parent. Ewan's treatment of the boy made him no better than Lady Argaty.

Ewan flinched violently at the realization before a violent rage surged through his limbs. Fury pounded its way through his veins as he reached for a ladder-back chair a few feet away from him. Fingers wrapped tightly around the first rung, he imagined the wood was Lady Argaty neck. If she were standing in front of him now, he wouldn't hesitate to squeeze the life out of the woman until her neck snapped. But she wasn't here.

"Fuck."

Pain and humiliation filled his shout of anger, which was followed by the crash of wood splintering against a stone wall. The sound of the door opening made him stiffen.

"Do you need—"

"*Get out, Asadi,*" he roared.

Seconds later he heard the door click shut behind the boy. In the back of his head he registered the fact that it was the first time Asadi hadn't tried to argue with him. He growled a quiet sound of regret at having taken his rage out on the boy. Asadi was no more to blame for the state of Ewan's affairs than Ross was. Both boys simply wanted to please him.

The thought made him bow his head in shame. He understood far too well the desperate desire to please someone. The need for his mother's approval had driven him to marry Agnes. It had gained him nothing except humiliation. Lady Argaty had nearly brought him to his knees when she'd explained how she'd arranged his marriage to a woman carrying another man's child. Until this morning, he'd never thought it possible the dowager could emotionally eviscerate him ever again as when she'd forced him to publicly claim Ross as his son.

Drawing in a deep breath, Ewan moved to the fireplace and used the poker to viciously stoke the red-glowing coals until they erupted into flames. When he'd finished, he sank down into a chair in front of the hearth. An image of Louisa danced in the flames as he remembered waking up beside her this morning.

The peace he'd experience holding her in his arms last night had been ripped from him by Lady Argaty's revelation. Everything had changed, and the future was uncertain. If the dowager were to announce he wasn't her son, he would have no choice but to confirm the fact. No matter what Aunt Wal—his real mother had said, the dowager still held power over him.

Even if he were to convince himself to continue living a lie, the constant threat of Lady Argaty revealing the secret of his birth would be intolerable. It would give her power over him, and that he would never allow. His ignorance of the truth had placed him under her thumb for too long.

The thought of being labeled a bastard was unpleasant, but it wouldn't be any worse than the revulsion he encountered every time he went out in public. The loss of his title, no Gilbert's title, was one he could adjust to. The true pain and humiliation would be the assault on his honor. There would be many who would question whether he'd known the truth of his illegitimacy all along.

As a member of the Black Watch his conduct wouldn't simply be a stain on his character, it would be a reflection on his father, the tenants of the earldom, and the people he cared about in the keep. The damage to his honor would be irreparable.

Worst of all would be the doubt he was certain he'd see on Louisa's face. The idea of her even contemplating the possibility he had been lying about the circumstances of his birth would drive his soul into the darkness without any hope of survival.

The only option left to him was self-banishment from Argaty Keep. Lady Argaty would want to witness his disgrace, and he refused to give her that. A self-imposed exile would deprive the woman of that malevolent pleasure, and he knew the woman well enough by now to know she'd wait patiently until she found a way to make him return home.

Ewan slumped downward in his seat, his head resting on the back of the chair. Drained of energy, he stared at the fire. His entire body ached as if he'd just fought a major battle. Not even when he'd walked off a battlefield had he ever felt so battered and weary of life. As he stared into the fire, his exhaustion became a numbness that pulled him down into a troubled sleep.

A blood-curdling cry made Ewan jerk upright in his chair. Every muscle in his body taut with tension, it took him several seconds to realize he'd been dreaming. He looked up at the clock on the mantle and saw it was after lunch. Leaning forward in his chair, Ewan rubbed the back of his neck. He needed to leave Argaty Keep as soon as possible, but first he would have to resolve the problem of his brother's confinement.

Gilbert was a threat he couldn't ignore. Finding a place for his step-brother to live under constant watch might take weeks. Even a temporary solution could take days. The dowager countess would be a problem as well. She'd made it clear she would fight him if he tried to send Gilbert away.

Then there was her refusal to keep Gilbert under constant supervision How was he supposed to keep everyone safe if he couldn't control the activities of the rightful heir to the Argaty title? The dowager's lack of concern for anyone other than her son made him certain she'd do little to restrain Gilbert's access to the passages in the keep's walls. His stepbrother was a threat to anyone who crossed his path, especially Louisa.

His brother's fascination with Louisa meant she would have to leave immediately. He'd send Ross with her as well. He couldn't risk her safety or that of the children. And of all the obstacles he had to surmount, Louisa would be the most difficult. She wouldn't need the *an dara sealladh* to know something was wrong the moment he asked her to take Ross with her. It would be necessary to make her think it was her idea to do so, although how he would achieve that goal was beyond him at the moment.

The thought sent his heart slamming into his chest as he envisioned the battle to come. Louisa would vehemently protest being sent away. If there was even one certainty in his life at the moment, it was that Louisa cared for him. Her forthright nature would not have allowed her to give herself to him last night if she didn't harbor feelings for him. Hiding the truth from her would be the most difficult thing he had ever done in his life.

Instinct said she would fight his decision with the ferocity of a wildcat and demand an explanation. She would be relentless in her pursuit of why he was sending her away. From the moment she'd convinced him to let her stay as Ross's governess, she'd displayed a skillful expertise for persuading him to cast aside his better judgement on almost a daily basis. This time she wouldn't succeed. It wasn't simply Gilbert's interest in Louisa that made it imperative he send her away.

The ramifications of what had happened between them last night would have been difficult enough even if the ground hadn't disappeared from beneath his feet this morning. The dowager countess's stunning confession had sealed his fate where Louisa was concerned. He'd had little to offer her to before, but now he didn't even have a home to give her. Last night had changed everything for him, and it reinforced the fact she would take his heart with when she left. The thought sent a fierce wave of hopelessness and pain crashing down over him. It was an emotion even more devastating than what the dowager's words had inflicted on him this morning.

The quiet sound of laughter interrupted his thoughts, and Ewan lift his head to look at the study's closed door. When no one knocked, he frowned slightly in puzzlement. The laughter echoed through the study again. Suddenly realizing the sound was coming from behind the wall, Ewan sprang to his feet with a soft oath. He strode across the room to the door hidden in the paneling and heard Charlie Morehouse's embodied voice float out from behind the wall.

"Quiet. We're on an expedition. We don't know what dangers might lie in front of us." The boy's quiet command made Ewan growl with anger.

Unfortunately, the lad didn't realize just how dangerous the hidden corridors were. With a jab of his finger, Ewan pressed the upper corner of the panel in front of him, and the door popped open. With a rough tug on the upper edge of the panel, he swung it was wide open.

Eyes wide with surprise, the three boys stood framed in the small doorway. Covered in dust, they looked like ragamuffins one might see on the streets of Edinburgh. Any other time, he might have chuckled at their appearance, but today wasn't one of those times. They looked as if they'd been exploring parts of the hidden passageways few people knew about. An image of Gilbert sent a chill through him as Ewan eyed the boys sternly.

"Gentlemen."

Ewan jerked his head in a silent command for the three

of them to enter the study. Apprehension clouded Wills's expression, while Ross, who knew not to enter the dark passages, appeared resigned to whatever fate befell him. As the ringleader of the small party stepped into the light of the study, Charlie squared his shoulders and met Ewan's intense look with restrained defiance, but remained silent. The boy's stance was one he'd seen Louisa's take numerous times.

"Ross, an explanation if you please." Ewan turned his head toward the boy he'd claimed as his son. The lad winced with a hint of apprehension, and Ewan bit down on the inside of his cheek. That the child feared him only deepened Ewan's shame and regret.

"It wasn't Ross's idea, my lord. I found the passageways." Startled by Charlie's admission, Ewan frowned as he turned his head until Louisa's oldest boy was in his line of sight.

"How?" he demanded. As the boy bit down on his lip, Ewan arched his eyebrow in a silent command for the boy to answer the question.

"My uncle showed me the entrance." Head tilted defiantly upward, Charlie faced him without any hint of fear of reprisal.

"Your uncle?" Perplexed by the boy's statement, Ewan studied the boy for a moment before his body grew rigid in surprise. "The *an dara sealladh*. You have the gift."

Trepidation flitted across the boy's face as his bravado disappeared. Whether someone had called him a liar in his past or he feared his mother's disapproval, Charlie had suddenly realized he might have erred in divulging his ability to speak with the dead. Despite his faltering courage, Charlie faced him without any remorse.

"Yes, my lord."

"Did your uncle say why he showed you the secret door?" Ewan's question made the boy's stiffen in surprise. The lad had obviously expected a different reaction on

Ewan's part.

"He said I needed to know in case Mama needed my help."

"Needed your—" Ewan didn't finish his sentence as an icy finger slithered down his back.

Clearly the ghost of the boy's uncle feared for Louisa's safety just as much as Ewan did. If he'd not already made up his mind to send her away, the boy's words would have convinced him to do so. At least he could place Ross in her care without reservation. Her affection for the lad was evident. Ewan studied the boys in silence and frowned sternly.

"I will say this only once. You are never to enter the passageways again. Is that understood?" Ewan waited for their nods of acquiescence before he moved to his desk to put his affairs in order. Not bothering to look in their direction, he waved his hand at them. "I suggest the three of you go to your rooms and clean your appearance before Lou—Mrs. Morehouse sees you or there will be hell to pay for your adventures."

Ewan sat down at his desk and heard the soft breath of relief someone expelled. In the next instant, shoes slid across the floor as the boys raced from the room. He reached for a pen as they left, when a quiet sound whispered through the air on his blind side. With a jerk, he snapped his head toward the noise to see Wills studying him with curiosity.

"Yes, Wills?"

"May I ask a question, my lord?" Ewan hesitated for a moment, before swiveling in his chair so he could see the boy.

"What do you wish to ask me?"

"I heard my Uncle Sebastian say you served with the Black Watch."

"Yes."

"Is that how you lost your arm?" The boy's blunt question took Ewan aback for a moment before he smiled slightly. Where Charlie had his mother's courage to stand up to someone, Wills had her blunt manner.

"Yes. I lost it at the Battle of Omdurman in the Sudan."

"May I see it, my lord?"

Ewan jerked at the question as Wills looked at him with a curiosity he'd witnessed in the boy on several occasions. Uncertain as to why he was even considering agreeing to the boy's request, he looked down at the black glove covering the metal, skeleton fingers. Ever since Louisa had acquired the habit of storming his study, he'd worn the glove simply to avoid her pity. Last night had reinforced how indifferent she was to his lack of a limb.

Ewan's heart twisted violently in his chest at the memory of the pleasure and peace he'd found in her arms. He looked back at the child as he considered the request for a long moment. Wills and his avid curiosity would be gone from Argaty Keep by tomorrow. There was little harm in giving way to the child's inquisitive nature. With a decisive nod, Ewan slowly pulled the glove off his artificial hand. Wills stepped forward and peered closely at the metal fingers.

"How do they work?"

Enthralled, the boy reached out and gently touched Ewan's steel hand. Like his mother, the lad accepted Ewan's amputation as something perfectly natural. Since it was unlikely he would ever see the child again, he decided to satisfy the boy's curiosity.

Ewan slipped his good arm out of his jacket then slowly pulled his artificial limb free of the coat as well. Wills took the garment from him solicitously and laid it on the chair close to the desk as Ewan removed his shirt so his artificial arm was fully exposed.

Wills laid the shirt with the jacket then hurried back to examine the fully exposed infernal device attached to the stub of what remained of Ewan's arm. The boy's look of fascination reflected a curiosity and studious contemplation that surprised him. There was a thoroughness about Wills's examination of the artificial limb that encouraged Ewan to indulge the child's inquisitive nature. With a slight movement of his shoulder muscle, Ewan made the metal fingers close. A gasp of excitement escaped the child.

"How did you do that?"

"When I flex my shoulder muscle, it makes the fingers move."

"Where? Here?" Wills quickly circled Evan's chair and moved out of visual range. A small finger pressed into his shoulder, and Ewan jumped slightly. "I'm terribly sorry, my lord."

"No apology. I was surprised nothing more." Ewan shook his head as he turned looked over his shoulder at the boy. The boy's rapt amazement made Ewan smile slightly. "Watch."

Ewan flexed a different muscle in his shoulder and made the fingers relaxed. Wills uttered another gasp of delighted astonishment. A second later, the boy's small hand lightly traced the narrow leather strap down to where it connected with another strap designed to control the fingers.

"I want to be a doctor," Wills said quietly as he studied the artificial limb raptly. "Charlie wants to be a scientist, but Mama says he can't. He has respon...respon—"

"Responsibilities?"

"Yes, that's it. Responsibilities," Wills said with a bob of his head as he continued to examine Ewan's artificial arm. "Mama says now that Papa is gone, Charlie can't be a scientist because he has responsibilities as Viscount Westbrook."

For a moment, Ewan wasn't sure he'd heard the child correctly. Stunned, he froze in his chair and stared down at the top of the boy's head. As Wills continued his intense study of the prosthesis, Ewan took in the information Louisa's son had innocently revealed.

Louisa was a viscountess, not a poor widow in desperate

need of a position. Why the devil had she lied to him? He frowned slightly as he was forced to admit that she'd not lied to him outright, but she'd not clarified her status as a noblewoman. Anger whipped through him with lightning speed at the thought.

Twice in one day he'd learned of a woman's deceit. Jaw clenched, he deliberately flexed his shoulder muscle to keep the child enthralled while he sought to learn more about Louisa, her social standing, and her family.

"And your Uncle Sebastian, is he a viscount too?"

"Oh no, he's the Earl of Melton. But he's not reckless like the rest of my aunts and uncle Percy. It's why they're called the Reckless Rockwoods." Still examining the artificial apparatus, Wills didn't look up at him as he continued to share more about his family. "Everyone says Mama is the most reckless, but I don't think that's true. Mama says Aunt Constance is worse. Great-aunt Matilda isn't a Rockwood though. She's a Stewart. She lives at Callendar Abbey. Mama was on her way there when her wagon wheel broke."

Now stiff with outrage, Ewan gritted his teeth as he allowed the boy to continue examining the metal and leather device that loosely served as his arm and hand. A knock on the door made him turn his head as he ordered the visitor to enter. The instant Louisa stepped into his study, a bolt of lightning zigzagged through him at the sight of her.

Wills's preoccupation with the metal device enabled Ewan to focus his attention on Louisa. Her mouth formed in the shape of an O, her gaze locked with his before it dropped downward to his bare chest. Desire softened her feature as she lifted her head.

Louisa blushed slightly as if suddenly shy, but it didn't keep her mouth from tipping upward in a warm, sultry smile. It disarmed him completely. His anger ebbed like the tide leaving shore, and he allowed himself to bask in her smile if only for a few more precious moments before he did what needed to be done. Did she have any idea how beautiful she was or how much happiness she'd brought into his life and heart.

What would she say if he told her about this morning's events? The answer immediately followed the question. She would be a lioness ready to do battle on his behalf. Although she'd never said it, he knew she cared little for the dowager countess. The thought made him long to go to her and seek solace in her arms.

A split-second later, the anger he'd pushed aside broke free of its restraints. Under different circumstances he knew his anger would have been short live. He had a strong suspicion as to why she'd deceived him, but he needed to cast that aside and use her deception as the means to send her away. It meant he needed to use every bit of his rage from this morning's revelations to bolster his anger for the battle to come.

Tension hardened his muscles, and in the subconscious movement of his shoulder, he made his metal hand flex again. Wills exclaimed with delight at the movement, completely oblivious to the fact his mother was in the room. At the boy's enthused reaction, Louisa jerked head toward her son, and annoyance crossed her lovely features.

"*William Wallace Morehouse.* You were given specific instructions *not* to ask his lordship any more questions about his arm." A glance at the boy revealed Wills had come to a rigid posture of attention.

"The boy was honest in expressing curiosity," he said coldly, then deliberately paused as he narrowed his gaze at Louisa. "Unlike others who are far more deceptive as to their true intentions, Lady Westbrook."

The moment he addressed her by her title, Louisa jerked in surprise then grew pale as apprehension swept across her features.

"I can explain—"

"An explanation I would like to hear right now." Ewan narrowed his eye at her, and she bobbed her head quickly then turned toward her son.

"Wills, go to the schoolroom. I expect your lessons to be completed by dinner."

"But Mama—"

"*Go.*" The curt command made the child wince, but he nodded with obedience, then hurried toward the exit.

"Close the door behind you, Wills," Ewan said quietly. "I wish to have a private word with your mother."

At his instructions, Louisa jumped, but didn't move as the door closed behind her son. For the first time since they'd met, there wasn't an ounce of defiance in her. Uncertainty was the only thing he saw.

"I'm waiting, Lady Westbrook," he grounded out between clenched teeth.

"My brother said Ross needed me."

"Your brother." A loud snort of condescending disbelief escaped him.

"Yes, my brother," she snapped as her defiance returned. "Caleb died in the same fire as my husband. He's visited me several times since I arrived at Argaty Keep. He's the reason you found me that night on the moor. I was ready to give up and die, but he wouldn't let me."

Ewan slowly rose from his chair and closed the distance between them. The apprehension he'd seen a minute ago was gone. In its place was the usual spirited rebelliousness he'd come to expect—even enjoy. That she'd managed to divert his attention from the matter at hand so easily added fuel to his anger.

"What makes your brother think Ross needs you," he sneered.

She drew in a sharp breath as he stopped a foot away from her. Ewan glared down at her as he fought to ignore the sweet scent of roses mixed with orange blossom filling his nostrils.

"It wasn't just Caleb who said Ross needed me. The *an dara sealladh* showed me how unhappy he was."

"The lad was not your concern."

"The *an dara sealladh* and my brother *made* Ross my concern." She leaned forward and returned his glare. "And if you'd take a moment to let that sink into your half-witted brain, you would agree that he's blossomed since I've been here."

"That is *not* the point." Ewan scowled at her unable to deny what she'd said. "You lied to me, Lady Westbrook."

"I did *not* lie to you."

"You presented yourself as a woman on the brink of destitution."

"And would you have agreed to employ me as Ross's governess if you'd known otherwise?" Hands planted on her hips in a defiant stance, she silently dared him to disagree. Unable to deny the point, Ewan remained silent, and Louisa rolled her eyes in disgust. "I didn't think so."

"That doesn't change the fact that you deceived me."

"Well, if you expect me to apologize for doing what I believed was the right thing to do, then you can wait until hell freezes over." The fierce obstinacy in her voice made him grit his teeth.

"What other lies have you told me, Louisa?"

"Nothing."

Guilt darkened her hazel eyes before she tipped her chin up in a mutinous manner. The instant he eyed her with suspicion, she looked away and nibbled at her bottom lip until it grew dark from the abuse. It aroused the temptation to run his thumb across the plump spot to soothe it. Self-disgust snaked through him at the way she could so easily distract and entice him without realizing she was doing so.

"You're lying to me again, Louisa."

"I haven't lied to you about anything." She winced, and

he expelled a harsh breath, and she looked away from him again. "At least not really."

"Not *really*? Then I shall rephrase the question. What is it you've *kept* from me?"

Hesitation furrowed her brow, and he leaned forward in an attempt to intimidate her. The effort failed miserably as he drank in her sweet fragrance, while her full, rosy lips formed a rebellious pout that heightened his need to explore the heat of her mouth as he'd done last night.

He swallowed hard as her stubborn attitude gave way to a sultry desire, and her hazel eyes softened until they were almost green. In seconds, his entire body was shouting with the need to pull her close and never let her go. God almighty, the woman was part witch, part *sidhe*.

"Tell me, Louisa," he snarled as he fought not to act on the primal urges twisting his muscles into knots until he was hard all over.

"I know Ross isn't your son," she snapped.

Ewan took a quick step backward to stare at her in stunned silence. She knew he wasn't Ross's father. The knowledge tightened his body even further as he stood frozen stiff and rigid before her. He wasn't sure why he should be surprised by the fact. Deep inside, he'd always known she knew the truth simply because of the *an dara sealladh*. The powerful strength of her gift of sight was unlike anything he'd ever heard of or seen. It had been irrational to think she wouldn't discover the truth.

Louisa's defiant expression softened and became one of remorse. Her pain and regret plainly visible her emotions emphasized how much it troubled her to have revealed she knew his secret. Intuitively, she'd understood his anger and humiliation at Agnes's betrayal. In a way, he was relieved she knew the truth. Every time she'd witnessed him berating the boy, his shame hadn't been simply at his own lack of fairness to the child. Last night had revealed how much Louisa's opinion of him mattered to him.

"I only know he's not your son, Ewan, nothing more."

Soft and gentle, Louisa's voice wove its spell over him as she took a step forward, and her sweet scent filled his nostrils. The moment her palms pressed into his chest, he was lost. The need to find solace in her arms, if only for a moment, made him shudder violently. In a swift movement, his good arm wrapped around her waist to pull her close. Without protest, she melted into him as he captured her mouth in a hard kiss. It was as if she'd always been a part of him.

Heat barreled through him, as he explore the fiery sweetness of her mouth with an unrestrained hunger he knew would never leave him. His entire body ached with the need to possess her completely just as he had last night. He wanted to be whole again. A man free to love and be loved by her. A soft murmur vibrated out of her as she pressed her body deeper into his.

Every inch of him cried out for her, and even with her held so tightly in his arms as she was now, he knew it would never be enough. He would always feel this need to hold her close, hear her voice, or simply see her walk into a room. It was a futile wish he could never let happen. The thought made him stiffen against her as he realized the hell he was about to descend into. It would make his existence unbearable for the rest of his life. God help him if the *an dara sealladh* showed her anything to use against him.

Louisa gasped softly in surprise as he roughly pushed her away. The moment he did so, she reached out to touch him. With a jerk, Ewan retreated even further from her. The battle about to ensue would test him unlike anything he'd experienced in the Sudan. The more space between them the better. With stiff movements, he retrieved his shirt, and roughly pushed his artificial arm through one sleeve.

"I am sending Ross away to school, so your services will

no longer be required. You will pack your things and leave here tomorrow morning, my lady." Ewan's harsh words were followed by a wounded cry behind him. He ignored the way the sound lashed at his heart.

"My—" She drew in a sharp breath before her anger became a whip lashing across his back. "You intend to punish Ross because I *deceived* you?"

The outrage in Louisa's voice didn't surprise him, but it was the fear and pain running beneath her words that sliced into him like the sword that had taken his arm and eye. Ewan viciously shoved his good arm through his shirt sleeve and fumbled with the buttons.

"I'm not punishing Ross. I am leaving Argaty in a few days and will not be back for some time. The boy will be best served by going to school."

"You're leaving—*why?*" she demanded. He knew better than to hope he could dodge Louisa's real question, but he needed to at least try.

"Why? Because if there's one thing I've learned since your arrival, my lady, it's that the lad deserves better from me than he's received to date. Ross will do better at school than here in this cold, miserable place."

"You know perfectly well that's not what I mean. *Why* are *you* leaving Argaty Keep? Is this about what happened between—"

"Last night has nothing to do with my decision."

"Please credit me with *some* intelligence, Ewan," she exclaimed with the fire and spirit that had endeared her to him from the beginning. "What other reason would you have for making such a hasty decision?"

"Believe what you like, my lady, but last night did not factor into my decision," he said tersely.

"And *you* call *me* a liar." The accusatory note in her voice made him stiffen as he slowly turned around. Hands on her hips, she scowled at him with a passionate anger that said she wasn't about to leave without a fight. "The *least* you could do is to be *honest* with yourself, if not me."

"Have care with your words, lass. Honesty is the last word you should use with me," he snarled as he began to lose his foothold on the slippery slope he stood on. The woman was far more intuitive than he liked.

"Do not threaten me, Lord Argaty. I've battled my own demons for a long time, and if you think I don't recognize someone else struggling with theirs, then you're mistaken."

Ewan's muscles hardened with tension at how easily she could read him. She easily stood her ground against him as if she were a full-blooded Scotswoman. Hands folded across her full breasts, her stance said she was a force to be reckoned with. It was a silent declaration she would not give way to him without a fight.

Even her glare was an unspoken challenge for him to deny her words. She was the most beautiful creature he'd ever seen in his life. He wanted to sweep her up into his arms and accept the strength she would offer him without hesitation if he confessed his heart to her. It was an offer he didn't dare accept.

Even if Gilbert wasn't an immediate threat to her and the children, he would still send her away knowing he no longer had anything to offer her. It would have been difficult enough to burden her with a man less than whole, but at least he would have had a home to offer her. Now there was nothing. When he didn't answer, the pleading look in her beautiful eyes made him want to groan in helplessness.

"I lied to you out of concern for Ross. He needed me, and in hindsight I realized you needed me too."

"*I* needed *you?*" he scoffed with as much scornful skepticism he could muster. If she were to see even a crack in his resolve, the woman would give no quarter.

Louisa took a step toward him, and the instant he breathed in her sweet fragrance he went rigid. He was on the verge of drowning, and he was certain she knew it. He could only pray that God would give him the strength not to yield to her.

Chapter 16

o you think I don't know how you feel about your injuries? How you think others see you?" Louisa's voice softened as she took a step toward Ewan. The instant he stiffened, she didn't move any closer. "*You* might see yourself as the Beast of Argaty, Ewan, but I don't."

"Do nae test my patience, Louisa. This is another boundary ye do nae want tae cross." As always, his brogue thickened whenever emotions were running high inside him.

Louisa stared up at his noble, battle-scarred features that had been made harsh and forbidding by his anger. Any other time she would have thought him furious, but a flash of pain blazed in his eye before it hardened to the color of a shard of ice. But the way he'd just lashed out at her confirmed her belief that she'd touched a part of him he'd been trying desperately not to reveal to her or anyone—perhaps even himself.

"And if I cross that boundary? What will you do?" she asked defiantly. "Kiss me again? I hope you do. I find kissing you to be quite wonderful."

Ewan appeared stunned by her confession as he shook his head in angry disbelief. A brief instant later, he recovered. With the speed of a large predator, he took a giant step forward and bent slightly to press his body into her hips before lifting her up onto his shoulder like a sack of flour. Taken by surprise, Louisa gasped at his unexpected action. It took her several seconds to realize that he intended to carry her out of his study.

"*Put me down, Ewan,*" she said fiercely as she wiggled furiously against him in a futile attempt to escape. "*Blast you, Argaty*, put me down!"

Ewan ignored her demands and continued toward the study door. A moment later she heard his metal fingers clattering against the glass doorknob. From the sound of metal scraping against the round, faceted handle, he was having trouble maintaining a firm grip to open the door.

"*Fuck,*" he snarled beneath his breath, but Louisa still heard the oath.

She gasped at the crude word and the ferocity with which he'd uttered it. The clatter of metal against a hard glass doorknob ended abruptly as she heard the door creak and swing open. Despite her ongoing attempts to wiggle free of his firm grasp, Ewan's fast, furious stride didn't falter as he carried her out of the wing that was his domain.

Her fist slammed into his back with outrage as she continued to command him to set her on her feet. As Ewan strode into the keep's main hall, Louisa heard someone exclaim with surprise. She turned her head toward the sound and saw Mrs. Selkirk staring at them with her mouth gaping. A wave of humiliation swept through her, and Louisa wiggled harder against Ewan's muscular arm holding her in place.

"Put me down this instant, Lord Argaty," she snapped. The moment she spoke, Ewan came to an abrupt halt and set her down in a hard, sharp motion. His expression dark and menacing, he leaned into her to with a cold scowl of anger.

"Pack your things and leave, Mrs. Morehouse. Your services are no longer needed," he said in a soft, but harsh and emphatic voice.

"What about Ross? Are you going to crush his spirit in the way you're trying to destroy mine?" Her heart ached as if a sharp blade had sliced through her chest. "It would be cruel to send him to school and you know it."

"Ross will survive," he said in a glacial voice that belied the brief glimpse of pain flickering in his eye before it blinked out of existence. "Either you leave Argaty Keep by tomorrow morning of your own accord, or I'll carry you out of the keep myself."

Ewan's expression was an unyielding, stony facade as he stared down at her. The mouth that had teased and pleasured her only a few hours ago was now a hard, thin line of anger. A tremor rippled through her as she searched for some memory of the man who'd made love to her last night. He was nowhere to be found, and her heart sank.

Apparently satisfied with her silence, he wheeled around on the heel of his foot and walked away from her without another word. Dazed that she'd failed to break through his defenses, her vision became blurry as she watched him disappear from view. She'd lost. No, she'd given up. She'd failed to live up to the Rockwood family's battle cry of never admitting defeat

A shudder rippled through her. Had last night meant nothing to him? A small cry of pain lodged in her throat as defeat rolled over her in a wave of despair that threatened to send her crumpling to the floor. Louisa swayed unsteadily on her feet as she struggled not to collapse onto the carpet runner beneath her feet.

Suddenly remembering she wasn't alone, her watery gaze took in Mrs. Selkirk staring at her in great dismay. Unable to bear the thought of the woman pitying her, Louisa bent her head to quickly wipe away the tears threatening to spill down her cheeks. She pasted a small smile to her lips and lifted her head in a proud tilt as she looked at the woman as if nothing had happened.

"Mrs. Selkirk, would you please have Maggie and Hilda come to my rooms? His lordship has dismissed me, and I will need assistance packing my things as well as those of my children."

"Oh, lass, I'm sure Lord Argaty will come tae know he's wrong," the housekeeper said gently with a shake of her head. "Ye've performed a miracle with the young master. Surely his lordship will remember that when his anger subsides."

"No. Lord Argaty will not change his mind," Louisa said with quiet despair. "If you would please send Maggie and Hilda to my rooms immediately, I would be grateful. Also, if you would ask McCallum to send word to Callendar Abbey, someone will come to fetch us tomorrow morning."

" Callendar Abbey, Mrs. Morehouse?" The puzzlement in the woman's voice made Louisa stiffen as she remembered Ewan hadn't addressed her by her title a moment ago. Unwilling to try and explain, she nodded.

"Yes, my brother is staying with Lady Stewart," she said quietly. The housekeeper continued to study her with increased confusion but didn't question her further.

"Of course, Mrs. Morehouse," Mrs. Selkirk said with obvious sadness. "I cannot tell you how sad I will be to see you and the children leave. Master Ross will be beside himself."

"Thank you," Louisa barely managed to choke out a response at the woman's mention of Ross.

Certain she was about to burst into tears, she bobbed her head sharply in the housekeeper's direction. The only thing that kept her from sobbing as she hurried toward her rooms was pride. Pity was the last thing she wanted from anyone. She had more than enough of that of her own making.

The moment she was behind the closed door of her bedroom, Louisa allowed the tears to flow steadily down her cheeks. How could she have failed so miserably? Ewan's expression had revealed nothing but cold condemnation as he'd turned and walked away from her. The man she'd given herself to last night had been replaced by a battle-scarred warrior filled with nothing but crushing anger and contempt. The Beast of Argaty Keep had returned even stronger than when she'd first arrived.

There was nothing left of the man who'd made love to her last night with equal amounts of fiery desire and tender, almost worshipful, caresses. She flinched at the memory. Had she simply convinced herself what they'd shared had held as much meaning for him as it had to her? The idea that she might have deceived herself about what had happened between them made Louisa draw in a sharp breath as the real truth seared her soul.

At dinner last night, she'd thought to convince herself she was only halfway in love with the man when in truth her feelings for Ewan ran deeper than she'd ever thought possible. Even when he'd shared her bed, she'd ignored how his every caress had made her heart swell with happiness. When she'd awoken this morning, she'd considered herself reckless as to how blatantly she'd offered herself to Ewan last night.

Now she understood it hadn't been a reckless desire that had made her so bold. Without realizing it, her actions had been those of a woman giving her heart to a man. Now he intended to send her away. If last night had meant nothing more to him than a tumble, she'd lost far more than her self-respect. She'd given her heart freely only to have it flung back at her in the most humiliating manner possible.

The sudden memory of his passionate kiss just before he'd dismissed her and ordered her out of his house filled her head. He'd held her so tightly against him only to shove her away. Surely her deception could not have changed things between them so quickly. No, she couldn't believe that. Every time he touched or kissed her was a silent confession of his feelings. He cared for her. She was certain of it.

Yet only moments ago, the Beast of Argaty had taken control of him once more. She'd accused Ewan of not facing his demons, and with the stubbornness of a hard-headed Scot, he'd denied the charges. The only explanation for the change was that he believed the Beast of Argaty had nothing to offer her, when all she wanted was his heart. Instead of facing the monsters inside him, he'd chosen to solve his problem by sending her away. Almost as cruel was his determination to send Ross away to school.

Louisa closed her eyes as her stomached lurched at the raw emotions assaulting her. What was she going to do? She'd failed to live up to the Rockwood family's battle cry of never admitting defeat. But that failure paled in comparison to her inability to capture the heart of the man she loved.

How could she help Ewan fight his demons if he refused to even acknowledge them? More tears pushed against her eyelids, before a soft knock penetrated her despair. Quickly pushing herself away from the support of the bedroom door, she blinked her tears away.

She refused to display anything but serene dignity until she was alone in her room at Callendar Abbey. There she would have the privacy to cry her heart out for what she had lost. Tears threatening to choke her, she hurried toward the armoire. Fingers wrapped around the doorknobs, she took a brief moment to compose herself then threw open the doors to the wardrobe.

"Come in."

"Good afternoon, Mrs. Morehouse. Mrs. Selkirk said ye needed help packing."

The recognizable sound of Maggie's voice made Louisa look over her shoulder. Standing beside the maid was Hilda, and the two servants were eying her with avid curiosity. Behind them was Finn carrying one of her trunks. Word had spread fast about her departure. As Finn set her trunk down, Louisa thanked him then gave Maggie some brief packing instructions before she led Hilda to Charlie's and William's room.

More than an hour later Louisa was bent over her portmanteau when Wallis MacCullaich walked through the open doorway of her room. With great consternation, Ewan's aunt swiftly closed the distance between them.

"Mrs. Selkirk said you were leaving." The statement was more of a question, and Louisa jerked her head in a sharp nod of confirmation

"Lord Argaty has discovered I'm not quite the woman I presented myself to be when I first came to the keep." She drew in a sharp breath then released it as she remembered Ewan angrily addressing her as Lady Westbrook.

"Then he's learned you're the widow of a viscount," the older woman mused softly almost as if to herself. The remark made Louisa stare at Wallis in amazement.

"How did—"

"Young master William has a tendency to share things he shouldn't when he's distracted." Wallis said with a gentle smile as she waved her hand at Louisa's gasp of horror. "I've known since the second week your children arrived at the keep. Wills was watching me make a poultice for a nasty cut Finn had. The moment he revealed your secret, I swore I would remain silent."

"But why? Why didn't you tell Ew—Lord Argaty or the countess?"

"Because of Ross and the memory of another little boy." Deep sadness made the woman appear older than she was before she eyed Louisa with a look of gratitude. "Ross is the happiest I've ever seen him, and even Ewan has begun to emerge from his tower. All of that is due solely to you. We both know Ewan would never have agreed to offer you the position of governess if he'd known the truth about your social standing. Your obvious affection for the boy convinced me to say nothing. I knew your heart was in the right place when it came to hiding who you really were."

Louisa stared at the woman for a moment as tears

formed in the back of her throat. Unable to speak, she simply shook her head in disagreement and turned away to set her portmanteau with two trunks packed with her things.

"Give him a few hours until his anger has eased, Lady Westbrook. I'm certain we can persuade him to let you stay. My—Ewan received some disturbing news this morning that has unsettled him greatly."

"Is that why he's decided to send Ross away to school?" Louisa choked out as she stared down at the baggage that emphasized the reality of her departure.

"Ewan's sending Ross away?" Wallis gasped loudly, and Louisa turned to see the other woman had grown pale with dismayed horror.

"Ew—Lord Argaty said he's leaving the keep and will not be back for some time."

"He mustn't do that," Wallis exclaimed softly with a look of anguish. "He needs to stay and fight."

"Fight?" Bewildered, Louisa stared at the older woman in confusion. With a dismissive shake of her head, Wallis reached out to squeeze Louisa's hand.

"I will not allow her to drive him away. I cannot. He's suffered enough already." The woman murmured to herself as a look of determination replaced her sadness. "I will speak to him. I will try to persuade him to remain at Argaty Keep and not send Ross, or you, away."

Wallis squeezed Louisa's hand once more and gave her an encouraging look before she hurried out of the room. Confused by her cryptic words, Louisa stared after the woman in bemusement. As Wallis disappeared, a small spark of hope flared inside Louisa. If Ewan's aunt could change his mind about sending Ross away, then he might let her stay, and remaining at Argaty Keep would give her time to fight for Ewan's heart.

The thought of staying made her gasp in dismay. She'd been so wrapped up in her own despair she'd completely forgotten about the boys. Louisa looked at the small watch pinned to her dress. The boys would have finished their riding lessons more than an hour ago, and she was certain that free of any supervision they'd be neck deep in mischief.

With a vicious shake of her head at having been so caught up in her own affairs, Louisa hurried out into the corridor in the direction of the schoolroom. The memory of Wills engrossed in his examination of Ewan's mechanical limb made her wince.

Louisa had repeatedly instructed her youngest not to question Ewan about his prosthesis simply to ensure Ewan wasn't made to feel as if he were a specimen for Wills to poke and prod. Ewan was as sensitive about his handicap as her sister Patience was of the scars she'd received in the fire at Westbrook Farms. He did his best to hide his artificial arm from her or others. His angry reaction at how difficult it was to open his study door emphasized his frustration.

Now she wondered if her efforts to curb her son's curiosity had done more harm than good. Did Ewan think she'd curbed Will's inquisitive nature because she found his injuries repulsive? Louisa dismissed the thought without blinking. No, last night she'd shown him that his injuries were of little consequence to her.

Yet it wasn't simply his handicap that troubled him. There were other demons buried deep inside him. Last night she'd been jerked out of sleep by Ewan crying out in horror while asleep. She'd only been able to imagine the terrible scenes provoking his low cries and mumbling of orders clearly given in battle. For several minutes, she'd gently stroked his head and whispered reassurances to him until he grew quiet. She wanted to help free him from those demons, but in sending her away he was refusing to let her.

As she reached the schoolroom door, she hesitated as she realized how difficult it would be to tell Ross that she and the boys were leaving tomorrow. At least she could break the news to Ross gently. In his current frame of mind, Ewan wouldn't think to take care with his words if he informed the child of his decision. As she entered the schoolroom, she saw the three boys crowded around one of the large maps she used for their geography lessons.

"Have the three of you finished your schoolwork." Immediately the children whirled around at her soft inquiry.

"We finished what you gave us this morning, Mama."

Charlie's cheerful grin swiftly faded when she didn't smile in return. Aware that he was still in disgrace, Wills bowed his head.

"I am terribly sorry, Mama. I didn't mean to tell his lordship about us." The remorse in her son's voice made her wince. It would not take Wills long to believe he was the catalyst for their being sent away because he'd told Ewan he was the son of a viscount. The remorse he felt now would be multiplied many times over even though she knew none of it was his doing.

"Wills, Charlie, you may go straight down to dinner. I will speak with you afterward. Ross, I would like a word with you." The surprise on all their faces made Louisa flinch, but she maintained a serene expression. Slowly walking toward the door, Charlie stopped at Louisa's side.

"Are we leaving, Mama?" The whispered question startled her, and she jumped slightly as she looked down into eyes that were so like Devin's. The child grimaced as she studied him quietly for a moment. It wasn't the first time she'd considered her oldest boy had the *an dara sealladh*. When he didn't expand on his intuitive question, Louisa bent over to kiss his forehead then gently pushed him in the direction of the door.

The minute her sons disappeared through the schoolroom doorway, Louisa turned to Ross. The child was studying her with a small measure of dread, and Louisa's heart twisted painfully in her chest at what her words would do to him. Quickly blinking back tears, she caught his hand in hers, and led him to the window seat that overlooked the moor where Ewan had rescued her weeks ago. The light had faded as dusk settled over the landscape. It had been gloomy all day, and the emotions ravaging her were as bleak as the view from the window.

"Is everything all right, Mrs. Morehouse?" Ross's voice was as calm and composed as his expression, but Louisa saw fear flicker across his pale features.

"I think that depends on how one looks at things," she said softly as she choked back tears and took his hands in hers. "You're about to have a wonderful experience."

"I am?" Ross frowned and grew still as a mouse waiting for the cat to pounce.

"Yes, I've told Lord Argaty about how well you've been doing, and he's decided you would be best served if he sends you off to school."

"School? But you're my teacher. I don't want another teacher."

"There's only so much I can teach you, Ross." Louisa swallowed the knot that had formed in her throat. "I'm certain you'll like school."

With a sharp tug, Ross pulled free of Louisa's grasp. His expression had reverted to the stoic look he'd worn when she first came to Argaty Keep.

"This means you're leaving."

"I'm afraid so," she whispered, uncertain how much longer she could hold her tears in check. "The boys and I are to leave tomorrow."

Devoid of any sign of emotion Ross quickly stood up and gave her a sharp bow. Her heart breaking, Louisa watched how easily the child retreated into the shell he'd been hiding in when she arrived. Damn Ewan for doing this to the boy.

"I'm glad you have been my teacher, Mrs.

Morehouse...even if for only a little while. May I go now?"
The question held no hint of emotion at, and impulsively,
Louisa leaned forward and pulled the boy into her arms.

"Oh Ross, I wish I didn't have to go. I will miss you
terribly. You have been a wonderful pupil." The boy didn't
reply, he just stood rigidly in Louisa's embrace. Tears welling
in her eyes, she slowly released him from her embrace and
turned her head away from him. "Go along now, I'm certain
Mrs. Selkirk is keeping your dinner warm."

Without another word, the boy walked away from her,
and as the schoolroom door closed behind him, Louisa burst
into tears. Did Ewan have any idea what he was doing to the
boy—to her? How could she bear to leave Argaty Keep and
its master? By the time her tears and sobs had subsided, it was
completely dark, and the only light in the schoolroom was
from the fireplace.

She looked around the dimly lit room and remembered
how Ross had blossomed in recent weeks. The child deserved
more than being sent off to school as if he were being
punished. Christmas was next week. Ross's excitement as the
holiday approached had grown with each passing day. The
thought of him being denied the festivities planned made her
heart ache. It wasn't difficult to imagine how alone he would
be with Ewan either locked up in his study or gone from
Argaty. Tears blurred her vision again.

Her mind was chaotic as one thought after another
rolled through her head. The idea when it first announced
itself almost slipped her notice. But it stubbornly took root
until it tugged a small gasp from her. In a quick, sharp
movement, she sat up straight and stared around the
schoolroom. She would take Ross home with her and the
boys. Surely, Ewan wouldn't be so cold-hearted as to refuse
to let the child go with her.

Intent on demanding Ewan let her take Ross with her,
Louisa scrambled to her feet and started to run toward the

schoolroom door before she came to an abrupt halt. Ewan hadn't just thrown her out of his study today, he'd literally carried her out. His expression had warned her not to enter his sanctuary again. She would have to entrust Asadi with a note and pray Ewan would at least read it.

Louisa quickly stoked the fire and lit the oil lamp she occasionally burned on rainy days to brighten the room. Sinking down into her chair, she pulled out paper and pen. For a long moment, she contemplated what she could say that would make Ewan agree to her plan. Whether the boy was really his son or not, the rest of the world believed Ross was heir to the Argaty title.

It was certain to raise eyebrows when people learned she'd brought the child into her own household. Even her own family would question her decision. With a shake of her head, she leaned forward and stared at the blank sheet of parchment. It didn't matter, she'd done the right thing when she'd convinced Ewan to let her be Ross's governess. She was doing the right thing once more in asking to take the child with her.

Ewan,

As you have instructed, I will leave Argaty Keep tomorrow, but in vehement protest. I am a Rockwood, and we never surrender without a fight. Therefore I must do battle with you using only my written words as you refuse to see me in person. I cannot, and will not, simply walk away from you as if nothing has passed between us.

The beauty of what we shared last night made me believe I had touched something deep inside you. I awoke believing you would view our intimacy as something more than a pleasurable interlude. The man I gave myself to last night revealed himself to me completely. He is not the beast you and others see him as. The scars of battle you carry would test the mettle of the bravest warrior, but beneath those scars is a man who is courageous and kind. I could never have given myself to any less of a man.

My deception was undertaken with the best and purest of motives. Ross needed me, and I could not bear to walk away from him anymore than I can bear to walk away from you now. If I cannot convince you to let me remain at Argaty Keep, I must do my best to make you understand that sending Ross away to school is the worst thing you could do to the child.

We both know Ross has blossomed under my care. I would like to ensure my efforts have not been in vain and continue giving Ross the love and care everyone is entitled to. For years, another boy, just like Ross, was denied affection within the walls of Argaty Keep. If the man that boy became will not open his heart to me or let me heal his wounds then I must try to save Ross from a similar fate.

I have no wish to leave you or Argaty Keep, but if you refuse to let me stay, I beseech you to let me take Ross with me. I know my request is unorthodox, but I promise I will provide Ross with the love and care he needs until he reaches an age when he may attend school with Charles.

If you are truly resolved in your decision to send me away from Argaty Keep—from you—then I beseech you not to make me leave Ross behind. Let me secure for Ross the happiness you were denied as a child. Please do not break my heart a second time by forcing me to say goodbye to you as well as Ross.

My heart is in your hands,

Louisa

For a long moment, she stared down at her handwriting and blinked back tears. Although she'd not openly confessed her love for him, there could be no mistaking her feelings where he was concerned. Perhaps it was too much? Before she could convince herself to write another note, she folded the paper and sprang to her feet. She would have to give it to Asadi and wait outside for an answer. If she were to enter

Ewan's study, it would most likely destroy any chance of him even considering her request, let alone agreeing to it.

With a soft sound of trepidation, she left the schoolroom and headed toward Ewan's quarters. As she'd expected, Asadi was sitting in the corridor outside his master's study. The moment he saw her, the boy's sprang to his feet in obvious alarm and blocked` her way.

"Please Morehouse sahibah, you cannot be here. He will not be happy."

"I have no intention of bearding the lion in his den, Asadi," she said quietly. "But I do want you to give him this and tell him I'm waiting out here for his answer."

The boy accepted the note, and his gaze flitted from it to her. With a nod, Asadi turned and entered Ewan's study. Louisa half-expected to hear a thunderous roar echo out of the study, but she heard nothing. After an interminable amount of time, Asadi emerged from Ewan's study. In silence, he stretched out his arm to hand her a small, folded piece of parchment. Trembling, she opened the note and shuddered as she saw Ewan's strong handwriting.

Take the boy with you. I shall make financial arrangements with my solicitor for his material needs and future schooling.

Argaty

The abrupt formality of the reply made her swallow a sob of despair. He'd acknowledged nothing else she'd written. What could have happened this morning to make Ewan revert to the angry beast he'd been when she first arrived at Argaty Keep? A loud crash echoed through the closed door of Ewan's study, and she took a step forward. In an instant, Asadi planted himself between her and the door.

"No, Morehouse sahibah, he is too angry. Argaty sahib will not speak with anyone." For the first time since she'd met Asadi, the young man's cheerful, nonplussed demeanor was absent. In its place was sorrow.

"What about his aunt? Did he speak with her? " she asked softly. The boy shook his head.

"No, sahibah. Not even McCallum sahib can talk to him. He has been like an angry tiger all day."

The sorrow in the boy's voice made Louisa's heart ache as she looked at the closed door of Ewan's study. Every part of her longed to charge through that door as only a Reckless Rockwood could and demand answers. But for the first time in her life, she didn't act on the impulse. Deep down she knew it was pointless. She had her answer in the note Asadi had delivered. The cold, formal reply to her note said everything she needed to know. Ewan wanted nothing to do with her. Louisa slowly turned and walked away from his study. There was nothing more to do except leave her heart in Argaty Keep with its master who believed he had nothing to offer her.

Chapter 17

Laughter bubbled out of Louisa as she ran across the freshly blooming heather. A quick glance over her shoulder showed her lead was dwindling, but she was close to the finish line.

Still laughing, she scrambled up the small hill to reach the crest they'd set as the finish line. A moment later, a strong arm slid around her waist and stole her victory as she was pulled backward into a chest of hard, warm muscle.

"Did you really think I would let you escape me, *mo leannan*?" The husky words were little more than a whisper in her ear, and her heart swelled with happiness.

"I wasn't trying to escape," she said breathlessly as his mouth nibbled at her neck. His chuckle blew across her skin like a warm summer breeze.

"A *wise* decision, *mo ghràdh*. You'll never be able to run fast enough."

"And you'll never be able to resist catching me." Laughing at his disgruntled growl, she twisted around in his arms and screamed.

She was still crying out in panic as she sat up in bed trembling with horror and fear at the memory of the hideous creature that had been holding her, not Ewan. The terror streaking through her created a level of panic she'd experienced only once before, but this time it wasn't the roar of fire in her ears.

The only thing she heard was the quiet echo of a far too familiar, horrifying giggle. The sound layered her skin with ice and sent her heart racing out of control. Her gaze swept around the room looking for any sign of danger. When she saw nothing that posed a threat, her trembling eased slightly. Her relief was short-lived as the sudden noise of something scraping across the wood floor whispered through the air.

Fear engulfed her again, and she jerked her gaze toward the Bruce's secret door. To her horror, she saw a narrow, black gap between the wall and the panel leading into the hidden passages inside the keep's walls. Panic made her tumble out of bed and race across the floor to shove the door shut with a strength she never knew she possessed. Behind the now closed panel, she heard a squeal of anger that sent fear sliding through her.

"Pretty lady. I want."

The sing song nature of the voice made her shudder as she continued to push against the door and nudge the chest back into place with her leg. Behind the wall, she heard another high-pitched sound of outrage as she continued to resist the renewed attempts to push the door open. The disembodied voice muttered several indistinct words behind the panel before she heard a shuffling noise. The sound of shambling footsteps behind the panel became softer until they faded away completely.

Her heart pounding, Louisa didn't move for several minutes, her body poised to push back on the door if someone tried to open it again. When it was apparent, the person was gone, the pulsating energy that had flooded her body moments ago began to dissipate. As her unnatural strength disappeared, it was replaced by violent shudders. Louisa's gaze never left the panel or chest blocking it as she stumbled backwards to her bed and sank down onto the mattress.

With the trembling came icy chills, and she reached

behind her to blindly find the blanket on top of the bed unwilling to let her gaze stray from the hidden panel. Fingers numb from the cold seeping into her pores, it took her several seconds to grasp enough wool cloth to pull the blanket over her shoulders. She didn't make a sound for fear the evil-sounding voice and its owner would hear her and return.

Louisa had no idea how long she remained silent and still. The soft chime of the mantle clock announced the hour of six, and she shuddered. For the first time, her gaze left the secret door, and she bowed her head. In the back of her mind, she vaguely heard the whisper she needed to go to Ewan. No matter how angry he was with her, he would keep her and the children safe.

The boys. With a jerk, she sprang to her feet and hurried to the door. She was certain Caleb would have come to her if they'd been in danger, but she needed to see them simply to ease her fears. As she threw the bedroom door open, she heard a high-pitched scream coming from the dowager countess's wing. The sound bounced off the stone walls magnifying the chilling cry. The nursery wasn't far from Lady Argaty's suite of rooms, and Louisa's heart began to pound violently in her chest as she ran toward the room where she'd tucked the boys into their beds last night.

"Please God, oh please let them be all right."

She'd only run a few feet when she slammed into an invisible force that brought her to a stumbling halt. Caleb's figure slowly materialized in front of her. His ghostly image was lighter and more transparent than she'd ever seen him. It was if he had little energy to spare in appearing in front of her. He shook his head violently.

They are safe. Argaty is not.

The words were little more than a whisper in her head as her brother's transparent form vanished. Uncertainty gripped her. Caleb had never been weak when he'd appeared to her in the past. Was her mind trying to trick her into believing the boys were safe and she needed to go to Ewan? The screams continued to ricochet off the corridor's walls. Other shouts were added to the screams to become a chorus of horror and fear. The wild cries wrapped around her and heightened her own fears for the boys. She ran forward again only to be halted a second time by an unseen wall.

The force vanished so fast, she almost fell. Stumbling to one side, she braced herself with one hand on the corridor's stone wall to keep her from falling. A soft touch brushed across her cheek before she felt a familiar tug on her ear. Louisa gasped in stunned amazement as she looked around her for a shimmering source of light.

"Devin?"

We. Protect. Go.

The words flitted through her mind so softly, she wasn't sure she'd heard anything at all. Uncertainty held her motionless as she looked toward the nursery with a paralyzing fear as the shouts and cries reverberated in her ears.

Now.

The word echoed in her head strongly this time, and something tugged on her ear hard. Louisa cried out softly in surprise before she obeyed the invisible command and whirled around to race toward Ewan's wing. Behind her the panicked shouts and cries still echoed from the dowager countess's wing, and she whispered a soft prayer as she ran toward Ewan's rooms.

If she'd misinterpreted her brother's cryptic message that he, and perhaps Devin as well, were watching over the children she would never forgive herself. The prayer was answered with an almost nonexistent tug on her ear. The reassuring gesture made her sprint even faster toward Ewan. She had no idea what was happening, but she had to trust Caleb. Her brother had never lied to her when he was alive, he would not do so now.

Unanswered questions collided in her head as the

screams from the dowager's wing grew fainter the closer she got to Ewan's suite. Horrifying images streaked through her mind as she remembered the child the *an dara sealladh* had shown her and the vicious way he'd tortured an innocent rabbit. How could someone so evil be in the keep? Had they found their way into the hidden passageways from the outside? But where had the child come from?

She'd never been to Ewan's bedroom, but she knew it had to be around the corner from his study. As Louisa ran around the bend in the corridor, she slid to a halt. The door in front of her was wide open, while Asadi laid crumpled on the floor near the room's threshold. Louisa sucked in a sharp breath of horror as she hurried toward the boy. He had a long gash on his cheek, but was merely unconscious. The sudden sound of Ewan uttering a loud curse then a cry of pain propelled her forward.

As she reached the doorway of Ewan's room, she froze at the scene in front of her. Horror sped through her, and her stomach churned violently at the sight of Ewan chest and arm covered in blood. She'd never been able to handle the sight of someone bleeding, not even her children's minor scrapes. Bile rose in her throat, and she forced herself to swallow the bitter taste as she gripped the doorjamb with both hands to remain standing.

Pinned to the floor beneath a short, stocky man straddling his chest, Ewan's hand blocked the blade intended for his chest. The blade flashed in the low firelight as it came down again and Ewan's attacker giggled insanely. The laugh sent a shudder through Louisa. She knew that laugh. Desperately, she tried to focus her thoughts on how to save Ewan. She had no idea where McCallum was or even Finn.

With Asadi lying unconscious in the hall, Louisa knew she was the only one who could do anything to save Ewan. Frantically, her gaze swept across the room looking for something she could use as a weapon. Almost as if he had a sixth sense, the man jerked his head in her direction. Louisa opened her mouth to scream, but nothing came out as she recognized the hideous, malformed man in her dream. The difference now was he was splattered with blood, and she swayed on her feet at the sight.

"Pretty," he giggled with glee.

As the ugly little man scrambled to his feet, Ewan kicked at his attacker's leg in an effort to make the man fall. It didn't stop the repugnant creature from starting toward her.

"*Run, Louisa.*" Even in pain Ewan's voice was a harsh command, but she knew there was nowhere to run. Her only choice was to fight.

"Want Pretty."

The knife he held in his hand was dark with blood, but she forced herself to block it out of her vision. Her gaze met Ewan's, and she saw his stark anger, fear, and helplessness as he used his elbow in an effort to sit up. Out of the corner of her eye, she saw Ewan's metal prosthesis lying on the floor at his feet and she simply reacted.

Surprise crossed the man's hideous features as Louisa ran forward before he opened his arms and grinned. Closing her mind to everything except reaching the metal arm lying on the floor, she darted past Ewan's attacker. Fingers gaining a tight grip on the leather cup of the prosthesis, she straightened then whirled around and swung Ewan's mechanical arm at the man.

She hit her mark with a force that made Ewan's attacker scream in anger. No longer grinning, the man lunged forward forcing her to jump back. A wave of fear rolled over her as she swung at him again. This time, the metal fingers penetrated the large knot on the side of the man's head, forcing her to tug hard to pull the prosthesis free. The man went down on his knees with a cry of pain as he swiped at her with his knife.

Louisa darted out of the knife's path and lifted the

weapon up over her head then brought the metal arm down as hard as she could onto the man's head. Almost as if he'd not even felt the blow, he swung the knife in her direction again. To evade him, Louisa lost her footing and stumbled backward. The sudden crack of gunfire filled the air causing her to jerk in fear as she managed to remain upright.

As she watched, the man froze upright on his knees before he fell backward. The assailant's eyes were wide with shocked surprise, while a small trickle of blood rolled out of the dark circle just above his nose. Frozen in place she waited for the creature to move, but he didn't.

The low grunt of pain behind Louisa made her spin around. Ewan was leaning against the side of the bed his nightshirt covered in blood and a pistol dangling from his hand. There was a deathly pallor to his skin, and the gun slid from his fingers to the floor as she leaped forward to keep him from sliding downward.

"Fall backward, Ewan," she gasped. "I cannot lift you up into bed."

With an almost imperceptible nod, Ewan's eye fluttered closed as he obeyed her instructions. The instant he plopped heavily backward onto the mattress, a moan of pain drifted past his lips. Dismay streaked through her as she saw only his upper back was on the bed. Afraid he would slide off the bed any second, she swung his legs up onto the bed with all her strength.

Half of his body still hung over on the edge of the bed, and she pushed hard at his hip to roll him onto his side so he was closer to the middle of the mattress. The strength of her effort to move him into a safer position made him flop face down on the bed. Another groan of anguish escaped him, and she choked back a sob. The shoulder of his good arm had at least one gash bleeding through material covering his back, which explained his cry of distress when he'd fallen backward onto the mattress.

Louisa swallowed her tears and scurried around to the opposite side of the bed. Carefully climbing onto the mattress, she ripped the back of Ewan's shirt open at the spot where the knife had sliced through the cloth. The cut didn't appear too deep, but she had to fight her usual response of fainting at the sight of blood. Most likely he'd been attacked while sleeping, and tried to use the prosthesis as a weapon just like she had. It would explain why it had been on the floor.

Fear made her tremble as she leaned over his body to take hold of the thin strip of blanket not covered by his battered body. Any further movement meant even more pain for him, but she had no choice. As gently as she could, she pulled on the blanket and used it as leverage to roll Ewan onto his back. This time he didn't make a sound, and her heart stopped in sheer terror.

Frantically, she scrambled closer to him to see if he was still breathing. Harsh breaths of air rang in her ears, and Louisa offered up a prayer of gratitude that he was still alive. With care she pulled at one of the jagged tears the knife had made to see the wound beneath it. She drew in a sharp hiss of air between her teeth at the bloody wound. Her stomach roiled at the sight, and Louisa covered her mouth in a silent cry of fear as she fought off the lightheadedness that threatened to render her unconscious.

Steeling herself to continue, she pulled Ewan's nightshirt a little further apart. Several of the cuts on his chest were deep, but none of them were near his heart as she'd first feared by the blood soaking his shirt and his ghostly pallor. As she carefully tore open the sleeve of his nightshirt, Louisa gasped as her stomach began to churn harder.

"Oh, dear God."

Louisa's whisper had barely passed her lips before she was forced to choke back the bile rising in her throat as she took in the sight of Ewan's blood oozing from the cuts on his arm. They crisscrossed in several places until they formed a single wound. Ewan had clearly used his arm to deflect most of the blows to his chest. Louisa pressed her fist into the mattress and bowed her head as she battled with her body's reaction to his injuries. A quiet groan rolled out of him as she struggled with her nausea.

"Get out, Louisa." The harsh command brushed angrily across her senses as she looked up at him.

"I am *not* going to leave you," she snapped. Her anger at his order helped relieve the sickening lurch in her stomach as she resumed examining his arm without feeling the urge to faint. "Stubborn Scot."

The moment she muttered the words under her breath, a strong hand caught her by the wrist and jerked at her arm hard. Caught off guard by his action, Louisa found herself falling to the side before she quickly recovered her balance and glared at him. His eye narrowed when she didn't move.

"I *said*, get out."

"Stop being an ass, Argaty," Louisa retorted as she tugged free of his grip to pull at another tear in his shirt. "I didn't save you just to watch you die in your bed."

"My injuries are...not life threatening," he rasped and drew in a sharp hiss of air as she ripped his shirt open in an angry movement. The soft sound of pain emanating from him made her wince with guilt at having exacerbated his suffering. Not bothering to answer him, she gently moved his arm slightly.

"I dismissed you...and told you to leave today," he said with another grunt of pain.

"And you said you'd carry me out if I didn't, but you're in no condition to do that, are you?"

"Leave. Now."

Ewan's command was soft, but she heard the thundering anger in his voice. She lifted her head to look at him, and the blue-gray eye she stared into was hard, cold steel.

Louisa's heart sank at his harsh determination, and how his mouth was a tight, thin line of angry resolution. Even as badly hurt as he was, he refused to have a change of heart where she was concerned. Had she been wrong after all? Was it possible he really didn't have feelings for her?

"Saints preserve us."

The cry of horror made Louisa jerk her head and look over her shoulder to see Mrs. Selkirk standing in the doorway. The older woman countenance was pale and drawn as she stood looking at the dead man on the floor before she lifted her head to stare at the bed and Ewan.

"The sight of blood doesn't agree with me, Mrs. Selkirk, and I don't know how to deal with his wounds."

Although she was still pale, the housekeeper nodded and hurried toward the bed. Dismay echoed in Mrs. Selkirk's soft gasp when she bent over Ewan. Muttering to herself, the housekeeper gently examined the cuts on his chest. At her probing, Ewan's eyes fluttered open, and he drew in a harsh breath.

"Bloody hell, woman, I'm not a pin cushion." The words were little more than a whisper, but they made Mrs. Selkirk smile.

"By the sound of that snarl, I think you'll live, my lord. Although I'm certain ye will be in a great deal of pain for at least a week."

The relief in the housekeeper's voice made Louisa offer up a small prayer of gratitude that he wouldn't die. A small tremor rippled through her as she looked down at Ewan's injuries. No longer alone in her efforts to help him, Louisa's stomach again began to churned viciously.

"Selkirk, Lady Westbrook is about to faint." The words were an icy wind blasting across her skin as the housekeeper pressed the back of her hand to Ewan's forehead.

"Lord love me, ye can't have a fever that fast. Dinnae ye mean Mrs. Morehouse," the housekeeper said with a note of worry as she looked in Louisa's direction. With her heart aching in her breast, Louisa slid across the mattress and off the bed.

"No, he addressed me properly. My full name is Louisa Rockwood Morehouse, Viscountess Westwood."

Her quiet words made Mrs. Selkirk stare at her in astonishment The housekeeper's surprise slowly changed to one of silent disapproval. Louisa flinched beneath the woman's look of disapproval before she turned and walked toward the open doorway. A harsh, indistinguishable whisper echoed from the bed, but Louisa didn't halt her progress.

"Lady Westbrook." At the housekeeper's call, Louisa looked back toward the bed. The woman's hesitancy was obvious as she glanced down at Ewan then back at Louisa. "His lordship thanks you for saving his life and your willingness to take Ross with you when you leave today. Finn and McCallum will see that your belongings are brought down for your departure.

Louisa's heart shattered in her breast as she stared at the woman who was suddenly watching her with great sympathy. Nothing had changed between them. Not even the life and death situation they'd survived together only moments ago had softened his heart or determination to rid himself of her. Unable to speak, she simply jerked her head in a nod. Tears threatening to reduce her to heart-rending sobs, Louisa turned away and hurried toward the door.

She was only a few feet from the room's threshold when Wallis MacCullaich ran into the room with McCallum close behind. The family retainer came to an abrupt halt in the doorway, effectively blocking Louisa's only exit. Wallis uttered a small cry of fear, and barely glanced at the dead man on the floor as she ran past Louisa to her nephew's bed. A look of shocked horror on his craggy features, the Scotsman stared at Mrs. Selkirk tending to Ewan.

"Sweet mither o' laird. Will he live?" the Scotsman

ground out as his gaze focused on the bed."

"Aye, but he will be less than pleasant for a few days." The housekeeper's words made McCallum look a little less grim as he nodded. He cleared his throat.

"Does he know?" At the Scotsman's question, Wallis jerked her head up as Mrs. Selkirk glanced over her shoulder at McCallum and shook her head.

"I dinnae think so," the housekeeper replied as she looked across the bed at Ewan's aunt. Another muffled whisper floated through the air, and Wallis reached out to stroke Ewan's forehead.

"She's dead, Ewan. Mr. Brown tried to stop him, but Gilbert killed her, just as he tried to kill you." Wallis MacCullaich's voice was filled with sorrow. Another whisper floated from the bed, and Wallis shook her head. "Brown will live, although I think he might be worse off than you are.

Shock rippled through Louisa as she stared at Wallis MacCullaich bent over the bed. The dowager had been murdered. Louisa's eyes flitted toward the dead man lying on the floor near the foot of Ewan's bed. The newfound knowledge barely registered in her mind as the faces of the boys filled her head. Another wave of nausea swirled in her stomach, and she swayed on her feet.

"The boys," she whispered to herself. How could she have forgotten the boys? McCallum quickly stepped forward to steady her, and the Scotsman squeezed her arm in a reassuring manner.

"The laddies are quite safe, lass," he said gruffly. "I saw to them myself and left Finn to watch over them."

Despite the Scotsman's attempt to calm her fears she shook her head hard. The memory of the horrible screams echoing through the halls of the dowager's wing sent a tremor through her. The boys had to have heard the cries. She could only imagine how terrified they must still be. Caleb had said they would be safe, but she needed to hold them and reassure them the nightmare was over.

Louisa tugged free of the man's grip with a shake of her head. Quickly, she pushed past him and then Asadi who was stumbling to his feet in the hall. Running as fast as she could, she entered the dowager's wing a minute later. A stark silence had fallen on the hallway that was almost as terrifying as the screams she'd heard earlier.

The moment she entered the nursery, Wills cried out for her and raced across the room. Louisa sank to the floor with her arms outstretched, and the little boy threw himself into her embrace, his small arms wrapping tightly around her neck.

The older boys were only a few steps behind her youngest son, and she opened her arms wider to pull all three of them to her as close as she could. While Wills sobbed against her throat, Charlie and Ross simply hugged her back. Over the tops of their heads, Louisa met Finn's worried gaze.

"Thank you for staying with the boys, Finn. The danger has passed, and I'm sure McCallum will need you in Lord Argaty's rooms." Louisa's quiet words made the young man bob his head before he left her alone with the children.

Charlie was the first to pull away from her embrace and then Ross. A sudden look of terror widened her oldest son's eyes as he stared at her. Alarmed, Louisa stretched out her hand to him.

"What is it Charles?"

"You're bleeding, Mama," her son choked out in fear as he pointed toward her nightgown.

"What?"

Louisa stared at her son in confusion for a second then looked down at the front of her nightwear. It was smeared with Ewan's blood. Her stomach began to churn, and she closed her eyes against the sight. If she'd reached Ewan's room a few moments later he would be dead.

She'd been helpless to save Devin and Caleb, but she'd

saved the life of another man she loved. The queasy sensation in her stomach intensified as she remembered the stab wounds on Ewan's chest and arm. Charlie's hand gripped her shoulder hard as she sank back down to sit on her heels.

"Wills, go find Finn. Ross, help me lay her down."

The strong, firm commands her oldest son issued made her eyes flutter open. The child sounded just like Sebastian when he was putting chaos into order. The thought tugged a small smile to her lips before she realized Wills was almost at the door. Fear made her shake her head fiercely as she brushed off Charlie's hand and scrambled to her feet. Once he'd secured help, Wills's intense curiosity might easily lead him to the dowager countess's room. He would only see death, and if Ewan's attack was similar to what had cost the dowager her life, she wasn't about to let her son see such a horrifying sight.

"*No.* Wills you are not to leave this room until I give you permission to do so, is that clear?"

Louisa directed a stern look over her shoulder at her son. Wills turned to study her with puzzlement and concern, and she did not miss the boy's look of disappointment. She'd been right to think her youngest wouldn't hesitate to investigate what was happening in the keep once he'd found help. She turned her head to see the startled expressions on the older boys' faces.

"That goes for the two of you, as well." Louisa nodded as she gestured at the blood on her nightgown. "This isn't my blood. Lord Argaty had an…accident, and I helped him."

A soft sigh of relief escaped Charlie before he stared at her in confusion. His bewilderment made Louisa wince as guilt swept through her. She'd brought the boys to the keep. She was supposed to protect her children, not put them in harm's way. The memory of Wallis MacCullaich calling Ewan's attacker by name made Louisa's heart skip a beat. The woman had known the murderer. When telling Ewan what had happened, she'd spoken as if Ewan also knew who Gilbert was. Why hadn't Ewan warned her? In the back of her head, a voice asked why she'd not told Ewan about the child she'd seen in her visions? She flinched as she met Charlie's gaze.

"I'm so sorry," she whispered as regret as a tear slid down her cheek. "I should have come to you before helping Lord Argaty."

"Don't be, Mama. We weren't afraid," her son said nonchalantly as he tipped his head slightly to one side then grimaced. "Well, maybe just a little. When we heard the woman screaming, we were scared. But Uncle Caleb told me it was just one of the maids who was upset that Lady Argaty was dead. He told me to tell Wills and Ross not to be afraid because he and Papa would keep us safe."

It was the first time Charlie had openly admitted he possessed the *an dara sealladh*. Even though she'd suspected he had the family gift, she wasn't sure how to react to the news. Jamie and Alma were the only two children in the family who'd admitted to being able to see and talk to the dead.

Constance had always found her son's ability disconcerting, and until now, Louisa had never understood her sister's concern. A worried frown creased Charlie's forehead in a manner that reminded her of Devin. Louisa stretched out her hand to him and offered him a small smile.

"It's all right, dearest. I knew you'd tell me in your own time if you'd been given the gift of the *an dara sealladh*," she said softly.

"Is my father...is he badly hurt, Mrs. Morehouse?" The worry in Ross's voice made her swallow hard as she remembered the cuts on Ewan's chest and arm. The last thing she wanted to do was frighten the child.

"Mrs. Selkirk says he will be in pain for a few days, but he will be fine."

"Uncle Caleb told Charlie you saved Lord Argaty." Wills voice sounded curious as he studied her with a small measure of awe and pride. "Did you, Mama?"

"That's enough questions for now," she said quietly as she kissed the child's forehead. "I sent word yesterday evening to Uncle Sebastian. He should be here soon to take us to Callendar Abbey."

The words made her heart ache as if someone had ripped it from her chest. The thought of leaving Ewan and Argaty Keep made tears form in her throat, but she swallowed them. At her announcement, Ross turned and walked away to stare out the window. His bearing reminded her of the boy she'd met such a short time ago. Even though Ewan's heart hadn't softened where her deception was concerned, at least he'd given her permission to take Ross with her.

"Ross, would you like to come with us?" Louisa asked quietly. At her question, the child turned and frowned at her in puzzlement as she continued. "Lord Argaty said I may take you with us rather than you being sent away to school. Eventually you would go to school with Charles. Would you like that?"

He didn't speak. He simply nodded his agreement as his shoulders sagged with resignation. Wills and Charlie, clearly unaware of their friend's reservations, greeted the news with excitement and rushed to the child's side. Charlie pumped the boy's hand and patted him on the back, while Wills hugged the older boy.

Ross accepted his friends excited response with a small smile, but Louisa saw the pain dulling his blue eyes. With a small sound of self-disgust she chided herself for not realizing sooner that Ross's unhappiness had been magnified by something other than Louisa and the boys leaving. The child believed Ewan was sending him away because he was unwanted.

Quietly, Louisa told Wills and Charlie to get out of their night clothes and dress for their trip to Callendar Abbey. With the resilience of all children, her sons chattered excitedly as they obeyed Louisa's instructions. Ross watched his two friends leave the room, and she moved to stand in front of the boy.

"You think Lord Argaty doesn't want you here?"

"Yes, my lady." Ross's stoic reply made her start slightly. How did he know about her title? He winced at her surprise. "Wills told us what happened in father's study."

"Ah, I see." Louisa nodded as she struggled to find words of reassurance for the boy without telling him an outright lie. "Your father has decided to leave Argaty Keep, and he thought you would be happier at school. I convinced him to let me take you with me."

"Where is he going?"

"I don't know. I'm just happy he agreed to let you could come with the boys and me." Louisa paused for a moment then cupped Ross's face in her hands. "Lord Argaty did what he thinks is best for you, Ross. It means he cares about what happens to you."

As a teardrop rolled down the boy's cheek, Louisa uttered a soft sound of compassion. Quickly pulling him into her arms, she remained silent as the child soaked her shoulder with tears.

Chapter 18

"My sister has been through a terrible ordeal, Constable. I have no intention of allowing you to make her relive this morning's horrifying events until tomorrow," Sebastian said in the authoritative voice he always used when protecting those he loved.

"I understand the concern for Lady Westbrook's emotional state, my lord, but experience has taught me that one's memory of an event is far more accurate immediately after an incident rather than later."

Although the man's voice was polite, the Scot's stubborn persistence was something with which Sebastian was quite familiar. The Rockwoods weren't simply known for their impulsive, sometimes reckless manner, but the tenacious obstinance of his siblings far surpassed any stubbornness the constable might possess.

"A few moments ago, you explained the order of this morning's events, and stated Lady Argaty was murdered by a mentally unstable man who was allegedly her son and the earl's brother. Is that correct?"

"Aye, my lord, but I—"

"And am I *also* correct that you indicated Lady Westbrook, *my sister*, was not involved in Lady Argaty's murder, and is, in fact, responsible for saving the earl's life?"

"Yes, my lord, but I—"

"Constable Duncan, you may call on my sister,

tomorrow at Callendar Abbey. At that time, she will be able to give you a full accounting of her experience related to this morning's events."

The constable appeared ready to argue with him, and Sebastian narrowed his gaze at the man who was almost his same height, but thin as a sapling. As if realizing he was fighting a hopeless battle, the constable jerked his head in acquiescence, and with a small bow he made his way to the parlor doorway. The constable met Constance at the threshold and politely stepped aside to let her pass. Sebastian's sister offered the man an abrupt thank you before moving deeper into the room.

When Louisa had failed to greet Percy, Constance, and him upon their arrival, Sebastian had feared the worst based on what the *an dara sealladh* had shown his brother and sister. When he was much younger, he'd never put much stock in his siblings visions, but over the years, he'd come to trust information any Rockwood family member with the gift of sight provided.

The fact both Constance and Percy had met him in the hall the moment he'd returned from his early morning ride would have been more than enough for him to investigate something. Their visions describing Lady Argaty's death had been terrible enough. But it was their description of Louisa's nightgown smeared with blood that had sent him charging out to the stables to have another horse saddled, while his brother and sister waited for a carriage to be made ready.

He'd arrived at Argaty Keep to find Constable Duncan presiding over the investigation of the dowager countess's murder, and learned the earl had been injured by the murderer. Although the constable had reassured him that Louisa was unharmed, Sebastian surmised the youngest Rockwood would most likely be deeply troubled.

For almost three years, Louisa's life had been difficult, and he was deeply concerned as to how being embroiled in a murder might be her undoing. The old Louisa had only just returned to him a short time ago. He didn't want to lose her again.

His concerns had not been alleviated when the constable had quietly shared how the manner of Lady Argaty's death was remarkably similar to murders of two village women over the past two years. Now Constance's worried look made his heart sink.

"How is she?" he bit out.

"The horror of this morning's events has left her quite shaken, but her demeanor was remarkably serene when I found her in the nursery. I think it was mostly for the benefit of the boys," Constance said quietly. "She sobbed like a baby when we were collecting the last of her things in her room. She said she needed a few minutes to compose herself so as not to worry the children, but would be down shortly."

At his sister's words, Sebastian muttered an oath beneath his breath. He should have known better than to give way to her plan when she first came to Argaty Keep. He should have insisted she return home with him immediately. As usual, where Louisa was concerned hindsight was often one of regret. Helen teased him constantly about how easily Tilly and Louisa could have him dancing to their tune and not his. He released a grunt of disgust at his failure to prevent his sister from twisting him around her little finger once again.

"Is she still frightened?" Sebastian studied Constance intently as her sister ignored him for a minute as if lost in thought.

"Actually, I don't think the morning's events are as disturbing to her as the fact that she's leaving Argaty Keep," Constance mused softly.

"She wants to stay?" Sebastian frowned in amazement. Why would his sister want to remain here at the keep? Constance's gaze swung from Sebastian to Percy.

"I believe she's more heartbroken than anything else."

"Heartbroken?" Sebastian stared at his sister in confused disbelief. "I don't understand."

"*Damnation*. It's as bad as that?" Percy eyed their sister with a pensive frown furrowing his brow. Constance nodded with a sigh.

"More so than we suspected."

His sister's response made Sebastian clasp his hands behind his back as he eyed the two of them in silent frustration. It was maddening as hell when he was forced to wait until someone apprised him of what others intuitively already knew. At times like these, he'd often wished he possessed the *an dara sealladh* himself.

Sebastian grimaced as he backpedaled the thought. No, he was deeply grateful he hadn't inherited the family gift of sight. He'd seen the price his family often paid for seeing something that only made sense after the worst had happened. It was in those moments of pain that he was the one to take charge and make things as easy as possible for his loved ones. Still it was difficult to solve a problem when he didn't know what the problem was.

"Will the two of you tell me what in blue blazes you're talking about?" At his growl of frustration, Constance quickly touched his arm.

"I'm sorry, Sebastian. I know how frustrating it can be when we don't explain what the *an dara sealladh* has shown us. She's in love."

"Louisa is in love?" Dumbfounded, Sebastian tried to take in what Constance had just said.

"Then why is she leaving?" Percy exclaimed as he diverted their sister's attention.

"Apparently Wills unwittingly revealed who he was, and it wasn't too far a leap to realize Louisa was the Viscountess Westbrook. She said the man was furious that she'd deceived him."

"*Who* is she in love with, and *who* is angry with her?"

Sebastian snapped.

"Argaty, you goose. She's in love with the Earl of Argaty." Constance released a whoosh of air as she eyed her oldest brother with exasperated affection. "When he discovered her deception, the man immediately dismissed her and ordered her to leave the keep no later than today."

"If the man's in love with her, why would he do that?" Percy mused as he bent his head to study the carpet.

"How do you know he's in love with her?" Sebastian demanded as he clenched his jaw. He'd have the earl's head if the cad had broken Louisa's heart. She'd suffered enough for ten lifetimes.

"Constance saw it," Percy said then winced as their sister released a noise of disgust and glared at her brother.

"You are like a bull in a china shop, Percy Rockwood," Constance snapped as she turned her head toward Sebastian with a sigh of resignation. "I only saw Argaty staring at our sister as if he were a lovesick Romeo pining away for Juliet."

"Then why send her away?" Sebastian shook his head as he frowned in confusion as he looked at his sister.

"I don't know, but if Lord Argaty is anything like my husband or my eldest brother, then I have my suspicions." Constance scolded with affection. "But there's something else—"

A clattering of boots on stone echoed into the parlor prevented Constance from finishing her sentence. Sebastian turned his head to see his two nephews charge into the parlor, followed by Ross Colquhoun who moved at a much slower pace. Wills launched himself toward Sebastian and with ease, he swung his nephew up into his arms. The boy hugged him then stretched away from him to meet Sebastian's gaze.

"Mama says we're going to the Abbey and Ross is coming with us."

"Is he now," Sebastian said with a smile as he chucked his nephew lightly under his chin then set the boy down.

As he lifted his head, he looked at Constance then frowned as she tipped her head slightly in Ross Colquhoun's direction. His sister's silent warning told him there was more to his nephew's matter-of-fact declaration than had been said. Sebastian's gaze fell on the future Earl of Argaty who stood stoically just inside the doorway as Charlie pulled the boy forward.

"Ross, this is my Aunt Constance, Countess of Lyndham, you met my Uncle Sebastian, Lord Melton when he brought us to the keep, and this is my Uncle Percy."

"Good morning, my lady, my lord, sir, " the boy said with a polite bow.

His nephew had barely finished his introductions when Sebastian saw a movement at the door. The moment he saw Louisa, he clenched his jaw at her wan appearance. Although her eyes were red and swollen, she possessed the same composed demeanor she had for the past two years. His gut twisted viciously at the thought of what she'd endured in the past twenty-four hours. She walked forward and hugged Sebastian then kissed his cheek.

"Thank you for coming for us, Sebastian."

"Did I not once swear by the sword and blood of Angus Stewart that I would always be here when you needed me?" he said so only she could hear.

Sebastian smiled down at her, hoping to hear a soft laugh escape her as he whispered the vow the two of them had used since she was a little girl. It had always been a way for Louisa to extract his promise to do something. On more than one occasion, he'd sworn the oath to end her relentless nagging, simply for a moment's peace. In most instances, regret would follow later when his promise forced him to follow through on whatever she'd wanted him to do.

The gentle reminder of his brotherly and paternal love for her was met with only a small smile. Sorrow tightened his chest. The Louisa of old who'd charged into this same room only a few weeks ago with a bright smile and mischievous sparkle in her hazel eyes had disappeared once more. A bolt of anger crashed through him. The next time he saw the Earl of Argaty he would whittle the man down to size, preferably in public.

"Come. Everyone is waiting for you and the boys at the Abbey. It's Christmas Eve tomorrow, and you know how much Aunt Matilda loves the holiday," he said with a cheerfulness he didn't feel at the moment. "She's already planned several activities for the children, and heaven knows what mayhem I'll need to bring order to."

This time his words tugged a soft laugh from her. Louisa shook her head as she wrinkled her nose at him and smiled.

"You love every minute of it, and you know it," she teased.

For a brief moment, Sebastian saw the sister he remembered before the fire at Westbrook, but she vanished in the next breath. Her features became pensive, as she looked around him at where his nephews and the earl's son were chattering like magpies with Constance and Percy. Apparently satisfied everyone else was oblivious to their conversation, she looked up at him with a small frown then began to nibble at her bottom lip. It was a familiar expression that said she was about to tell him something he wouldn't like.

"I need to tell you about Ross," she said quietly. "Ew— Lord Argaty has given me permission to take him with me."

"Spending the holidays with us, away from all this tragedy will take the boy's mind off of the loss of his grandmother."

"No, you don't understand." Louisa shook her head and winced as she bowed her head. "Ross will be living with me for the foreseeable future."

"Foreseeable future?" Sebastian frowned slightly. He could understand Louisa bringing the boy with them until the new year, but somehow he didn't think that's what she meant.

"He'll be living with us as if he were my own son until he and Charlie go off to school together. Even then he will continue to be a part of my family—the Rockwood family."

"Until—what the devil are you thinking, Louisa?" he bit out softly between clenched teeth. "You cannot just kidnap the child. He's the earl's son."

"It's far too involved to delve into now, I just wanted you to know before we returned to the abbey."

"You mean give me time to stew over the matter until you begin to appease me and override my objections," he growled with irritation.

It was a strategy Louisa used often, knowing it would work with him and anyone else she wanted to persuade to a particular plan. Aware she'd aroused his anger, she squeezed his arm with a strength that made him wince slightly with discomfort. Her hazel eyes met his, and the look of desperation he saw there alarmed him.

"You have always given way to me in this or that scheme I've concocted over the years, Sebastian, but this is different. Ross needs me, and I need him." For a moment it appeared she might cry before the Rockwood obstinance and determination tipped her chin upward. "If ever there were a time I needed you to believe in me, it's now. I promise never to ask anything of you again, if you'll simply accept my decision in this matter without objection."

"He's the future Earl of Argaty, Louisa. You can't simply—" Sebastian drew in a sharp breath as her fingers dug even more painfully into his muscles.

"The Lord Argaty has agreed to the arrangement, and I'll have your word that you'll not try to interfere or change my mind about any of this. I can barely—swear it." The ferocity and pain in his sister's voice alarmed him. What the hell had happened in this place since the last time he'd been here?

"Swear it, Sebastian. *Now.*"

"I swear by the sword and blood of Angus Stewart that I'll offer up no objection to the arrangement."

The moment he softly vowed to follow her wishes, she uttered a small noise of emotion he couldn't decipher. A second later she pressed herself into his chest with a sob that would have been inaudible if it had not reverberated its way into him. It was at that moment he experienced for a second time in his life the rage that had taken hold of him more than ten years ago when Helen had been kidnapped by the Marquess of Templeton.

His muscles became painfully taut as he struggled not to charge up the stairs to finish the job the earl's brother had begun. The only thing that held him back was the knowledge that Louisa would never forgive him if he were to harm the man.

"Damn the bastard to hell," he muttered beneath his breath as he wrapped his arms around the youngest Rockwood and held her close.

Ewan struggled out of bed as he heard the excited chatter of Louisa's boys below his window. Ross's voice was far more subdued. Fire assaulted his arm and chest as he drunkenly walked to the window. Ignoring his body's shouts of protest as it intensified the fire in his upper body, Ewan pressed himself into the window frame to keep from falling to the floor.

It took a moment for his eye to adjust to the sunlight that almost blinded him as he searched the small group of people gathering in front of two carriages. The moment he saw her, Ewan's gut twisted violently with a pain tenfold that surpassed of the physical wounds his half-brother had inflicted on his body. God help him.

The rest of his life would be an agonizingly slow death. Life had been difficult enough before, but how was he going to live in a world without her? It would be an empty existence without the echo of her laughter drifting through the air, the way her smile could light up a room, the mischievous lilt of her voice when she was teasing him. But it was the nights that would throw him into the deepest depths of hell.

It would be agony never again to feel her soft curves beneath his hard, battle-scarred body. Perhaps worst of all would be waking up without the sweet smell of her curled into his side. Even when they'd taken his arm in the hospital field tent, he'd never really wanted to die. But this—this torment was ripping him apart.

Louisa stepped forward to climb into the carriage, and he saw her hesitate as if she was about to turn and run back into the house. The tall figure of her brother, the Earl of Melton bent his head to say something to her, and she shook her head before entering the carriage. As she disappeared from view, he released a soft sound of anguish.

Melton made to follow his sister then paused and looked up at the keep's façade. The deep anger reflected on the earl's face said Melton would kill Ewan if he were in front of the man at that moment. Ewan didn't blame the earl's desire to avenge his sister's pain. Any blows Melton might have landed would be welcome as he was more than willing to succumb to death than live the hellish existence he knew lay ahead of him.

The magnitude of his decision to send her away was a crushing weight on his chest that only strengthened as he watched the carriages roll down the driveway. In one of the vehicles was a woman who'd made him feel whole for the first time in his life. It wasn't simply that she'd accepted his beastly appearance. It was more than that. Louisa had touched something in his soul that had been slowly dying for a long time. Now that it had been resurrected, it was only going to die again.

"For the love of the almighty, mon. Do ye have a death wish?"

At McCallum's exclamation, Ewan's last bit of strength began to give out as the man who'd been a father to him quickly reached his side. The moment their gazes met, the Scotsman shook his head with a snort of anger.

"Do nae even try to answer that, lad. I know it will be a lie."

"Help me back to bed before I wind up sleeping on the floor," Ewan snarled as the pain of watching his life vanish before his eyes slammed into him with renewed force. McCallum didn't bother to be gentle as he wrapped his arm around Ewan's waist and guided him back to the bed. The moment he groaned, McCallum released a harsh sound of disgust.

"Ye are a fool, lad. The woman loves ye, although why I dinnae know."

"She deserves better than me," Ewan rasped as he fell back into the mattress and allowed the older man to swing his legs up onto the bed.

"Aye that she does, but it's her willingness tae put up with ye that is the true miracle."

"Go away, McCallum. Leave me to lick my wounds in peace."

"I have never seen such a hard-headed Scot in all my life."

"I did the right thing. I have nothing...nothing to offer her."

"Sweet mither of God, mon. All the lass wants is your heart. A woman such as that is hard tae find."

"Go away." Ewan waved his hand at the man as he closed his eye. "I want to sleep."

"Aye. That's the way to run away from your problems."

The man uttered a vicious oath of disgust then walked out of the room, slamming the door behind him. It emphasized how frustrated the Scotsman was, but there was something in the retainer's manner that made him think the man was more disappointed in him than anything else. Ewan drew in a hiss of air as he moved slightly only to be punished by his body.

Would his old friend understand his decision better if he knew the last of the Argaty line had died at Ewan's hand? It didn't matter. He knew the truth. He had nothing to give Louisa in return for her love. Offering his heart and maimed body to her wasn't enough to overcome his inability to provide a name or home. He'd done the right thing, even though it was destroying him with every passing second. Slowly, he allowed himself to sink into the darkness swallowing him whole until he drifted into oblivion.

Chapter 19

E wan dropped another book into the satchel he'd set on the flat surface of his desk. It had been almost a week since Louisa had left, and Argaty Keep had never felt so cold, forbidding, or empty.

He constantly found himself listening for the sound of her laughter or a glimpse of her riding across the moor as she loved to do. It was pointless to yearn for her, but it was impossible to stop himself from doing so.

They'd buried the dowager countess two days after her murder, and the inquest yesterday had been a formality as the constable had confirmed Gilbert had killed his mother then attacked Ewan. At the time of the dowager's funeral, his injuries had still been painful, but he'd attended simply for the sake of propriety.

Even though he understood why Lady Argaty had loathed him, it still didn't make it easier to forgive her or his real mother for their deception. Wallis had tried to speak with him several times, but he'd refused to see her and had ordered Asadi not to let her into his study. The whole matter was an open wound that hurt worse than his physical ones, which had healed almost completely thanks to Dr. Munro's skilled work.

He picked up another book to check the title and put it with the growing collection of books he was leaving behind. Traveling light had never been an issue for him, but for once he was allowing himself to carry a little more than he usually would. It had been impractical to take more than a couple of books with him to the Sudan, but he had a little more leeway now. He wanted a few of his favorites with him as companions when he was alone.

"Argaty sahib, you take this?" Asadi appeared at his side and held up a small package wrapped in colored paper and a simple white ribbon.

"What is it?" he asked as he briefly glanced at the item in the boy's hand before picking up another book to determine if it was one he wanted to take with him.

"Morehouse sahibah left it for you."

Ewan froze then turned his head to stare down at the square package in the boy's hand. Slowly, he took the gift from his self-appointed manservant and sank down into his desk chair.

"Leave me," Ewan said harshly with a sharp wave of his metal hand as he stared at the wrapped gift in his good hand.

An image of Louisa formed in his head as he remembered her courage in standing up to his half-brother's insanity. He couldn't recall how he'd retrieved his pistol from his nightstand. The only thing he could remember was his fear that Gilbert would kill her, and that he would give his life to keep that from happening. Suddenly aware that Asadi had not moved, Ewan raised his head to eye the young man with annoyance. The boy didn't flinch beneath Ewan's angry glare.

"Argaty sahib has not said when we leave." Asadi's stubborn expression made Ewan frown with growing irritation.

"I've already said you *will not* be going with me."

"I must go with Argaty sahib. You will need me."

"*No*, I do *not* need you. I explained all this yesterday. You are to remain here where the village schoolmaster will teach you how to do math and read English. McCallum will teach you how to manage the keep and its property."

"Where Argaty sahib goes, Asadi goes." The young man's posture was straight and rigid as he returned Ewan's glare with a defiance he'd never displayed until now.

"You *will not*," Ewan snarled. "You will do as I have instructed. I do not want anyone's company, *do you understand?*"

"*No*, I take care of Argaty sahib."

The boy's rebellious tone took Ewan aback. It was the first time his manservant had ever refused to obey a command or request. He narrowed his gaze at the young man. Something about Asadi's obstinate expression and posture ignited a sudden suspicion in his head. Louisa had put the lad up to this.

"Did Lady Westbrook instruct you not to let me leave without taking you with me, no matter what I ordered?" he bit out as his jaw clenched with tight anger. Asadi didn't answer the question, but his guilty look confirmed Ewan's suspicions. "I see. Tell me, Asadi. Who saved your life? Was it her ladyship?"

The boy paled beneath Ewan's scowl of anger. It was the first time he'd ever implied the boy owed him anything, and the knowledge sickened him. From the first moment he'd awoken to find the young man at the side of his hospital bed in the Khartoum, he'd constantly emphasized Asadi owed Ewan nothing.

"I apologize, Asadi. You were undeserving of that. You owe me *nothing*."

"You are wrong, Argaty sahib." The young Sudanese shook his head vigorously. "It is a debt impossible to repay."

How could he make the boy understand it was Ewan who owed him? The Sudanese boy had cheerfully and without question allowed himself to be Ewan's whipping boy from the first day he refused to leave Ewan's side. Ewan had no idea where he was going, but he knew his resources would be limited most of the time, sometimes not even enough for himself.

He refused to allow Asadi to suffer that fate, especially when the young man could have a good life here at Argaty. Since he no longer had any right to the title his father had held, he would allow McCallum to serve as the trustee of the estate. By leaving Asadi behind, it was his repayment for everything the boy had done for him. It would benefit not only Asadi, but McCallum as well.

Asadi was not the only one Ewan was indebted to. McCallum, who'd been a father figure to him all his life, deserved to spend his remaining years free of any major responsibility when it came to managing the estate. He refused to let anyone challenge his decision as to Asadi's future when he knew it was the best thing for the boy.

He closed his eye and leaned back in his chair. For a long moment he contemplated what to say. He needed to convince the boy that Ewan's decision was the best for all concern. As he looked at Asadi, he knew he needed to choose his words carefully.

"You say your debt is impossible to repay, and I understand that. It's one of the things we have in common. I too have a debt I can never repay, but with your help I must at least try. Do you understand that?"

"Yes, Argaty sahib," the Sudanese said with obvious reluctance and more than a hint of suspicion.

"I lost my father when I was very young, and McCallum took on the responsibility of being the father I was denied." Ewan paused for a brief moment as he steadily held Asadi's attention. "Like me, McCallum would say I owe him nothing, but that's not true. It's now my responsibility to be the son McCallum never had."

"I understand, Argaty sahib. McCallum sahib is a good man."

"Then you will help me try to repay my debt to him?" When the boy nodded, Ewan relaxed back into his chair.

"Then you will remain here as I told you yester—"

"*No*, I—"

"*Damnation, lad, don't you understand?*" he snarled as he sprang to his feet and leaned across the desk to scowl at the boy. "McCallum is no longer young. *You* are the only one I trust to take care of him, Mrs. Selkirk, and everyone else in the keep. *You* are the *only one* who can do this for me. There is *no one else.*"

"There is you, Argaty sahib," the boy replied quietly.

"That's no longer possible for reasons I cannot explain," he ground out bitterly as the dowager countess's malevolent features darkened the thoughts in his head. "Will you do as I ask? Will you stay and do what I cannot?"

The boy remained still as he studied Ewan for a long moment as if looking for any sign deception. Resignation and sorrow darkened the young Sudanese's face as he slowly nodded his agreement to honor Ewan's request. Relief surged through Ewan as the boy capitulated to his demand.

"Thank you," he murmured as he sank back down into his chair drained of energy by the argument. "Now, go."

This time Asadi did as he was told, and Ewan leaned back in his chair and closed his eye. Christ Jesus he was tired. His wounds were healing well despite his body looking like a piece of material a seamstress had used to learn her trade. But it was the sleepless nights that made it difficult to heal faster. Ewan inhaled a deep breath then exhaled it before looking at Louisa's gift on the desktop where he'd dropped it while arguing with Asadi. He studied it for a moment then pulled open the top desk drawer where he'd placed Louisa's note. Ewan unfolded the parchment and stared at her handwriting. His gaze skimmed the words until he reached the one sentence that had made it so difficult to let her go.

My heart is in your hands.

When he'd read her note for the first time, it had taken

every last bit of control he'd possessed not to storm out into the hall and ask to her stay. Deep inside, a roar of anguish ripped through him at the memory.

"So you're simply going to run away." Wallis MacCullaich's voice echoed quietly in his study, and he jerked his head up in surprise. Lost in the hell he'd been condemned to, he'd not heard his mother come into his study.

"I am *not* running away," he said coldly as he rose to his feet. "Why are you here, mother?"

"What do you call it then?" she said

"I no longer have claim to any of this." He flung his hand out in a sweeping gesture the stitches in his arm tugging slightly in protest.

"Says who?" Wallis MacCullaich demanded imperiously. The muscles in Ewan's cheek grew taut with anger.

"As I recall, madam, you confirmed the late Lady Argaty's claim that I was not the heir to the Argaty title or its lands."

"No, I confirmed you were my son, nothing more. But you are the Earl of Argaty. You have been since your father died."

"I am a *bastard*. I am not entitled to my father's title."

"And the only people who know your father and I were not legally married are either dead or in this room."

"In other words, your solution to the situation is for things to continue as they were before I learned the truth," Ewan snarled. "I'll not live a lie, madam."

"It is *not* a lie. You were baptized as the issue of Dougal and Elspeth Colquhoun. My sister claimed you as her own the moment she signed your baptism record. You are the legitimate heir in the eyes of the church and the law."

"None of that changes the fact that you're my mother or that my father never married you. That detail says I'm *not* the legitimate heir."

"So you intend to label me a whore." The quiet

statement made Ewan go rigid at his mother's quiet words. With a slight shake of his head, looked away from her.

"No. I would never do anything to hurt you. But I'm angry that the truth was withheld from me, and it begs the question of why. *Why* would you allow your sister to claim me as her son? *Why would you give me up so easily?*"

The bitterness in his voice made Wallis flinch violently as she grew pale with anguish. Deep inside he recognized there was more than just guilt in her expression. Her sorrow was so deep and agonizing it made him want to offer her solace. A solace he didn't know how to give.

"I *didn't* give you up easily, and I cannot expect you to understand," she said in a voice filled with suffering.

"Then *try* to make me understand why you'd do such a thing," he said with the restrained rage he'd been nursing for days.

It was a fury he'd only just realized wasn't simply because he'd been lied to for years. The majority of his anger was rooted in the knowledge that his mother had cast him aside. Given him away to her sister—a woman who'd spent every moment in his presence making his life a living hell. As much as he didn't want to admit how deeply it pained him, it was a fact he could no longer ignore.

"I know my choices weren't good ones, Ewan, but I cannot undo the decisions I made. All I can do now is tell you everything I couldn't share with you before."

Wallis paused for a moment then crossed the room to sit on the edge of a chair at the fireplace. She didn't look at Ewan, but stared into the small fire burning in the hearth with a faraway look as she began her story.

"I met Dougal two days after the third reading of the banns for him and Elspeth. I had been living with my aunt in London who had promised my father she would find me a husband. She was in despair over my refusing several offers and was more than happy to see the back of me when I was ordered home for the wedding. I met Dougal while riding on the moors the day after I returned. It was love at first sight for both of us. We tried to stay away from each other, but from that first moment it was impossible for us to do so.

"For almost two weeks we tried think of a way for Dougal to break his contract with Elspeth and marry me instead. Your father argued vehemently that he would break the contract, leave for a year then return and marry me. My father was a harsh man, and I knew he would never allow me to marry Dougal when his oldest child had been humiliated.

"Not even an offer of compensation would have appeased my father for such a slight. I also had no desire to humiliate my sister by marrying the man who had refused to marry her. What I didn't understand then was that injuries to one's pride are usually resolved over time, but I was too much of a coward to agree with your father's plan."

She stopped speaking, and Ewan crossed the floor to sit opposite her. He wanted to demand she continue, but he saw the tears she was struggling to hold back. The torment his parents must have endured was something he understood far too well. Clearing his throat, Ewan studied the brick hearth in front of him.

"I think I understand how hard it must have been for both of you." Out of the corner of his eye, he saw his mother's mouth curved in a sad smile.

"Perhaps you do." She returned her gaze to the fire as she became lost in the past once more. "Elspeth was with child almost immediately, and despite my objections, she insisted I come stay with her at the keep. Our mother had been dead for several years, and Elspeth wanted family with her. I tried to find an excuse not to go, but my father was just as insistent as my sister.

"From the moment I arrived, Dougal and I were plunged into an existence that alternated between heaven and hell. We were able to steal the occasional quiet moment of companionship, only to experience days of hell afterward. When Elspeth miscarried the baby, she begged me not to go, and I agreed to remain at Argaty Keep. Whether it was out of sympathy for my sister or my inability to leave Dougal, I've never tried to answer the question.

"Over the next two years, Elspeth suffered several miscarriages. The last one took a grave toll on her health, and the doctor said it was unlikely she would ever be able to have children. Dougal became more desolate as he began to realize Elspeth might never give him the son he wanted so badly. He took to riding for hours out on the moor, and one afternoon we met unexpectedly. In the past, we'd only touched hands or stolen the occasional kiss.

"But that afternoon we were completely free to laugh, hold hands, and kiss without fear of discovery. Before either of us realized what was happening, I surrendered to him. We knew it was wrong, but how can something that feels so right be wrong? It's what we asked ourselves every time we were in each other's arms. To make matters worse, Elspeth insisted Dougal and she try one more time despite the doctor's warnings.

"Dougal told me it had been difficult enough to lie with Elspeth in the past. The idea of doing so again was repugnant to him. He declared he would divorce Elspeth, so we could marry, but once again I refused to let him hurt my sister. Instead, I told him to go to her one last time. He rejected my suggestion outright.

"We argued for days about it, but I was adamant. I never allowed him to see how much the thought of him being with Elspeth was tearing me up inside. If he'd known, he would never have agreed to share my sister's bed again. But I knew how badly he wanted a son, and I was willing to sacrifice anything for him to have what I couldn't give him.

"When Elspeth declared she was with child again, Dougal decided to take her to Italy where the climate would be better for her while carrying the babe. She demanded that I accompany them. I refused, but Elspeth insisted Dougal persuade me to go with them. He was more than happy to oblige her, and as always I surrendered to his wishes.

"We'd only been in Italy a few weeks when I realized I was with child. I didn't know what to do, and it didn't take long for Dougal to know something was wrong. When he finally managed to make me confess my secret, he was as dismayed as I was. But not once did either of us regret what our love had given us.

"I suggested I return home, and he could set me up in my own house in London, where he could visit us under the appearance we were married. The suggestion infuriated him. He said he'd already compromised me, and he had no intention of compounding that mistake by tucking me away as his mistress. He said I would remain in Italy, and we would tell Elspeth the truth. I pleaded with him to send me away, but nothing I said convinced him to change his mind.

"If anything, I think my pleas only made him dig in his heels all the more, and he insisted we tell her the truth. I was terrified to face Elspeth. I loved my sister, and I knew my betrayal was unforgivable. Her anger was terrifying when Dougal told her that I was carrying his child. In her rage, she threatened me, and Dougal took to sleeping in my room for fear my sister would try to harm me and thus you.

"Elspeth was only a few weeks further along than me, and when her time came, she had a difficult labor. The first time Elspeth saw Gilbert, she became hysterical. She insisted someone had replaced her beautiful baby with the hideous little thing she'd given birth to. The doctor said Gilbert's deformities were so bad it was unlikely he would live more than a few weeks. We also knew that even if the babe lived, there was little chance he'd be able to take Dougal's place at Argaty.

"At first, Elspeth refused to nurse Gilbert, but two days

after he was born, she put him to her breast. When my time came, Dougal defied the mid-wife and doctor and remained at my side until you came into the world. You were beautiful. It was then I told Dougal I intended to take you to London. I said I would find a small house and claim I was a widow with a small child to raise.

"Your father refused to listen. He said he intended to divorce Elspeth and marry me. As much as I loved Dougal, I knew we'd injured my sister grievously. Not only had she suffered betrayal and humiliation at our hands, she'd just given birth to a severely deformed son. I couldn't allow him to take everything from her. I told him I would leave Argaty forever, and that I'd never marry him if he divorced Elspeth.

"He raged, pleaded, even begged me not to condemn him to a life bound to my sister. It took all I had not to give way, but I held firm. I think it was then that Dougal began to concoct the elaborate deception I should never have agreed to. It would have been far more preferable to live in London pretending to be a widow and raising you on my own than the devil's bargain I made."

Wallis buried her face in her hands, and Ewan leaned forward to rest his hand on her shoulder. It felt awkward, but he could think of nothing else to do. It was as if a floodgate had opened up inside her the way she'd been telling him her story. A shudder went through her, then she sat up straight and patted his hand in a way that said she had recovered her composure. Wallis leaned back in her chair and darted a glance in his direction. Just as quickly she looked back into the fire and dragged in a deep breath.

"Several days after you were born, Dougal informed Elspeth and me that he'd reached a decision as to you and Gilbert. He informed my sister that everyone at home would be told she'd delivered twins, and that you had been born first. I listened in growing horror as he told my sister that she would accept my child as her own when we returned to

Argaty Keep.

"I loved your father, but at that moment I hated him. Not only was he inflicting a terrible cruelty on Elspeth, but what he proposed meant I would have to give you up. Elspeth would be the one you called mother, not me. Worst of all, Dougal hadn't asked if I was willing to do this, but perhaps I left him with no choice with my threat to leave if he divorced Elspeth. I think he believed everything would be as it was before I was with child, with the exception that he would have an heir.

"As expected, Elspeth refused to agree to what Dougal had proposed. She called the idea of mothering a bastard revolting. Dougal immediately threatened her with divorce unless she agreed to do as he ordered. Divorce meant more humiliation for her, and I'm certain she knew that her shame wouldn't be discovered if she agreed to Dougal's proposal. Only the three of us would know the truth. I think that was the moment she began to plot her revenge.

"It took almost a week before Elspeth agreed to Dougal's proposal, but there were conditions to her acquiescence. From the moment Dougal and Elspeth were married, I had refused to let him petition Elspeth for a divorce saying I didn't want my sister to be hurt. I believe, with all my heart, that was true in the beginning. But the anger and mortification in Elspeth's voice that day as she laid out her demands made me realize a divorce would have been far less painful for her.

"What Dougal was forcing her to do was incredibly cruel. It wasn't simply that she had to claim her sister's bastard as her own, it was that every time she looked at you, it was a reminder she'd been betrayed by her sister and husband. Perhaps worst of all, it emphasized her failure to give Dougal a son capable of being his heir.

"I had no doubt by then that Elspeth hated us. It was only when she outlined her three conditions that I knew how deep her hatred was. The first condition was that you were never to be told the truth. I agreed to the stipulation readily. I cared little for my welfare, but you were the most precious thing in my life. I think perhaps even more than Dougal at that moment.

"Life for you as a bastard meant you would carry the burden of my shame. The thought of you being tormented and shunned by others for my sin was unbearable. I also knew it would ensure your future. The second condition was a double-edged sword.

"I was to remain at Argaty Keep caring for you and acting as Elspeth's lady's maid for as long as she deemed fit. Caring for you would be a joy, but I knew my sister would make me pay dearly for that happiness. She already knew what it was to be a mother. Even as hideous as Gilbert looked, I knew she loved him.

"It was how she knew I would do anything for you, and we both knew the threat of sending me away from you was her way of holding a knife to my throat. But it was a price I was willing to pay. Even if you never knew I was your mother, I would know it. It would also be a penance for my betrayal of Elspeth. A penance I knew deep inside would hold no real meaning as I wickedly, and shamefully, dared to think Dougal and I would still share quiet moments of happiness watching you grow to manhood.

"Little did I know how dearly my sister would make me pay for my original sin or the treacherous sins I contemplated even as she made her demands in ways I couldn't possibly imagine. But Elspeth had thought of everything. She knew Dougal and I would accept her two conditions simply because we would still be able to share our joy."

Wallis paused and looked at Ewan as if waiting for him to ask a question. He simply looked at his real mother with a growing sense of dismay for what she'd endured. She's suffered at the hand of Elspeth Colquhoun, just as he had, and Ewan was quickly coming to realize the true depth of his mother's sacrifice for him.

In all the years he'd looked to the Countess of Argaty for a word of affection, his real mother had offered her love to him in silence. She'd been the one to wipe away his tears, and hold him tight whenever he was afraid or hurt. It had been Wallis MacCullaich who had expressed praise for anything he'd accomplished. It was a painful and humbling truth that shamed him for not seeing it until now.

This time there was no awkwardness in his movement as he reached out to take her hand and kiss her fingertips. His silent gesture of gratitude and respect for her sacrifice made her hand tremble in his. Grey eyes so like his shimmered with tears before she pulled her hand from his and turned her head back toward the fire. Inhaling a deep breath her mouth worked in silent speech for a brief moment before she continued.

"It was her third condition that extracted the ultimate payment for our sins. She condemned us to the hellish existence we had known when I'd first arrived at Argaty Keep. Elspeth said Dougal, and I were never to meet in private again. Even a single, innocent encounter would be enough for her to seek a divorce where she would expose the charade that was being forced on her.

"Dougal reacted with a fury I'd never witnessed in him before. He told Elspeth he would see her in hell first, and that he would divorce her the moment they returned to Argaty Keep. That cold, malicious smile of hers was born that day. She simply replied that even if he succeeded in securing a divorce, it would be Gilbert who would become master of Argaty Keep, not you.

"I was the first to agree to her demands. Even if Gilbert defied the doctor's prediction and lived, it was doubtful he would ever be capable of being master of Argaty. As agonizing as it was to enter such a devilish pact, I convinced

Dougal it was for the best, not just for you, but for him as well.

"Elspeth held true to her word and told the world you were hers reminding us of her threat if we broke any of her conditions. Even though I couldn't speak to Dougal in private, I could see the anger and frustration in his eyes every time Elspeth tormented him with her threats. This went on for several months after our return to Argaty Keep until Dougal eliminated her threat to expose what we'd all agreed to.

"Without mentioning it to anyone, he arranged for you to be baptized. He knew Elspeth would not be able to avoid adding her name to the birth registry. It was a legal and public declaration that you were her son. My sister was livid, but she knew her leverage over Dougal was gone. She could divorce him, but she wouldn't be able to say you weren't her son.

"At this point, Dougal hated Elspeth as much as she loathed him. It wasn't a secret among the staff, and no one questioned our riding out onto the moors with you sitting in front of Dougal. I refused to give myself to him again, and he eventually accepted my decision. But those hours we spent out on the moors with you were happy ones.

"Then the accident happened. You had been sick, and we decided to go riding without you. We were racing each other when the girth on Dougal's saddle broke and he was thrown from his horse. He died in my arms.

Wallis drew in a sharp breath, and her anguish was something he understood too well. It was the same depth of pain he'd been dealing with since the moment Louisa climbed into her brother's carriage. Before he could interrupt her, his mother continued sharing her story.

"Elspeth gloated in private over Dougal's death. It was then I began to suspect she was responsible for his death. Although the girth didn't appear to have been deliberately cut, Elspeth had hired the stable hand who'd saddled

Dougal's horse only the week before the accident. She and Dougal had argued about her interference with the stable, but after a few harsh words the matter was dropped. When the groom gave his notice, a few days later I confronted Elspeth about it. She simply laughed saying even if my suspicions were true, I could never prove it.

"It was only a few days later that Elspeth began her true plan of revenge. I found her bullying you over some small infraction, and I chastised her for her behavior. She immediately threatened to send me away from Argaty Keep if I challenged her authority to discipline her son. I knew then I had nothing to fight her with. Her name was on the baptism registry, which would have made it impossible for me to establish any claim I was your mother as your father was the only one who could confirm the truth of what had happened."

Wallis stopped speaking, and a glance in his mother's direction confirmed his suspicion she was struggling to maintain her composure. As if aware of his scrutiny, she clasped her hands in front of her and stared down at her lap. Silence hung in the air between them, and Ewan swallowed hard as his mother turned her head toward him.

"You were too young to hear the truth when your father died. It wasn't simply the legal fight I knew I would lose trying to take you away from the keep. I'd just lost your father, and the thought of losing you as well was unbearable. So I convinced myself that by remaining silent I could stay at Argaty Keep and shield you from Elspeth's cruelty. Even in that respect I failed you."

"You shielded me on numerous occasions," Ewan said quietly as he remembered all the times she'd wiped the tears from his cheeks while tenderly soothing him with quiet words of love.

"But it wasn't enough. I'll always bear the weight of knowing how different your childhood would have been if

I'd allowed Dougal to divorce Elspeth as he'd wanted from the beginning rather than the devil's bargain I entered into."

It was obvious his mother was struggling to speak while holding back her tears, but she didn't reach out to him. Her hands remained clasped tightly in her lap before she raised her head to look at him.

"I'm not asking you to forgive me, nor do I expect it of you. But you deserved to know the whole truth."

Her last sentence was little more than a whisper. It emphasized the pain she'd lived with for so many years, not just from her own choices, but at the hand of her sister's malicious manipulation and hatred as well. Ewan wanted to reach out to take her hand, but he was suddenly feeling awkward again.

Over the past few days, he'd come to accept the reality of his parentage. With that acceptance had come the realization of just how deep his affection was for Wallis MacCullaich. Although his fury at being lied to had begun to dissipate over the past few days, it had been eased even more by his mother's explanation as to the events that led them to where they were now.

It was difficult not to feel empathy for his parents' forbidden love and their eventual betrayal of Elspeth. He wasn't certain he could have done any differently if he'd been placed in the same situation where Louisa was concerned. His mother had sacrificed a great deal—not just for his father, but for him as well.

It also answered every question he'd ever had as to why she'd willingly subjected herself to the cruelty her sister had inflicted on her. Over the years, Wallis MacCullaich had paid her penance more than once for betraying her sister. She leaned forward and tipped her head to more easily meet his gaze.

"You are Dougal Colquhoun's son, Ewan. He wanted to ensure your birthright in the only way he knew how. What he did wasn't simply because you were the heir he wanted. It was because you were the embodiment of our love for each other," Wallis said with a fervency that emphasized her belief in what she was saying. "He loved you before you were born, Ewan. We both did. If either of us had realized how dearly you'd pay for our mistakes, we would have charted a different course. Please believe that."

"I cannot judge you or my father for making choices you thought were in my best interest," Ewan said softly. At his reply, Wallis paled slightly as her hand grabbed his and squeezed it tight with her fingers.

"*Then don't let her win, Ewan.* Don't let Elspeth take Argaty Keep from you as she did your childhood, and God knows she made you pay a high price."

Ewan shoved his hand through his hair at the urgency in his mother's heartfelt plea to do as she asked. Rising from his chair, he walked across the room to stare out the window. The light was beginning to fade, and the moors were beginning to take on the purple shroud of darkness. It was hauntingly beautiful, and if he listened to his mother, he didn't have to give it up.

But could he live a lie? The irony of the question wasn't lost on him. For years he'd been doing just that. His newfound knowledge of the truth didn't change how others saw him. To everyone outside of this room, he was the Earl of Argaty. Other than his word and that of Wallis MacCullaich, there was no evidence to prove the life he led was based on a falsehood.

Elspeth's signature on his baptism record was a legal confirmation impossible to repudiate. The law and the church would never see him as anyone other than the son of Dougal and Elspeth Colquhoun. Any claims he might make regarding his illegitimacy would be met with disbelief. People would ask why Elspeth had claimed a child that wasn't hers.

The answer to that question would open his mother to

public condemnation or denouncement. That he couldn't allow. Unconsciously, that very thought had been in the back of his mind as he'd made his plans to leave Argaty Keep. He'd instinctively known any public declaration of his illegitimacy meant revealing Wallis MacCullaich was his real mother. The silence in the room ended as Wallis released a sigh.

"Have you considered what will happen to Ross? Do you intend to tell the boy the truth about your lineage as well as his own? Do you intend to destroy his childhood in a manner similar to the way Elspeth destroyed yours?"

The question made him jerk his head up in anger. He had no intention of hurting Ross. That his mother might even suggest it offended him, and Ewan directed a scowl at her over his shoulder. His silent reply made her wince slightly, but he saw her understanding as well. Ewan turned away again as he tried to contemplate how all of this would affect the boy. He'd thought nothing about the child's future other than to ensure the rest of his childhood was the happy one he knew Louisa could give him. An instant later, he jumped as his mother touched his arm.

"Ewan, it is one thing to deny yourself happiness, but do you care so little for her that you're willing to sacrifice her happiness too?"

"What do you mean?" Ewan's voice was harsh as every muscle in his body became as taut as a bow ready to launch a volley of arrows.

"Elspeth was not the only one who noticed the way you looked at Lady Westbrook," his mother said softly as she gazed out the window at a memory he couldn't see. "I remember times when I'd look up to see your father staring at me the way you do, Lady Westbrook. You're in love with her, and I'm certain she loves you as well."

"I have nothing to offer her. Not even the keep is really mine to give."

"You have more to offer than you realize because

there's only one thing she wants." The conviction in her voice made Ewan jerk his head toward her. A knowing smile touched her lips. "She wants your heart. If you give her that, you give her everything."

"She deserves better than a man who's less than whole," he said in a hoarse voice as he looked out the window again. "a man who isn't what others believe him to be."

"Don't you think that should be her decision to make?" Wallis squeezed his arm slightly. "You have a chance for the happiness your father and I only had fleeting glimpses of. Don't let anything stand in the way of that. Life is far too short and precious, Ewan."

With another squeeze of his arm, Wallis left him standing at the window. Ewan turned his head and watched her walk out of his study. *Don't let anything stand in the way...* his mother had said. An image of Louisa's filled his head. Everything she'd ever said or done had made it clear she saw past his war-ravaged body. He glanced over his shoulder at the parchment lying on his desk. She'd bared her soul to him, and offered him her heart in that passionate letter. The question now was whether he had the courage to do that and more.

Chapter 20

S ebastian closed the note in his hand, and with a vicious
flick of his fingers threw it onto the desk. The Earl of
Argaty's note had arrived a few moments ago, and
Sebastian's initial reaction was to send a curt refusal to the
man's request.

Glaring at the folded piece of paper, he debated how
best to handle the problem of the earl. A soft squeak of sound
made him lift his head to see the study door opening.

The sight of Helen entering the room sent a familiar
emotion crashing through him. It would always be this way
for him. No matter how old they grew, everything else would
fade from view every time he saw his wife. That he'd won her
love was something he gave thanks for on a daily basis.

"I've come to rescue you," she said with a mischievous
smile.

"Rescue me?" Sebastian's mood lightened as he moved
around the desk to meet his wife halfway. "I wasn't aware
that I was in need of such extraordinary measures."

"Perhaps I should have said, *I'm* in need of rescuing,"
she laughed as she stepped into his embrace and kissed him
lightly. "The children have been pestering me for the last
hour to come see when you'll be done with those diplomatic
pouches. They're all under the impression that a certain Lord
Melton promised to take them riding when he finished his
correspondence, *including* our youngest who doesn't even

possess a riding habit yet."

Helen eyed him with exasperated amusement, and Sebastian looked heavenward as if he hadn't any idea what she was talking about. When his wife made a small noise of aggravation, he bent his head to kiss her deeply. A long moment later, he lifted his head and drank in a deep breath at the way his heart pounded in his chest.

As always, his deep love for her made him ache to demonstrate how much she meant to him. He wanted nothing more at the moment, but to carry her up the stairs to their bedroom and spend the rest of the day worshipping her body with his. It was a wish that would go unfulfilled with the children waiting on him. Instead he looked down at her and smiled with satisfaction at the languorous desire reflected in her gaze.

"That, my love, is how you should always look." As she arched her eyebrow in a silent demand for an explanation, he grinned. "As if you'd been thoroughly kissed by a husband who adores you."

"Why do I think this is your way of avoiding a discussion about Tilly going riding with you and the boys?"

"She needs to learn how to ride at some point, and she loves spending time in the stables."

"She's only five, Sebastian."

"And she has her heart set on riding, but if you don't want her—"

"You know as well as I do the child will convince Fergus that you instructed her to have him saddle *heaven knows* what animal and ride him out of the stable without batting an eye. She is a Rockwood through and through." Helen shook her head in exasperation, but Sebastian saw his wife struggle to hide her fear for their daughter's safety. "At least I know she'll be safe riding in front of you."

"And you know I'll guard her and the boys with my life," Sebastian quietly reassured his wife with a light kiss.

"I have no doubt you will, it's simply that you're almost as bad as Lucien when it comes to encouraging our daughter to be a tomboy." A small frown of disapproval furrowed Helen's brow. "Constance continuously expresses her frustration with Lucien's habit of using Jamie's nickname for Imogene."

"We're about to enter a new century, my love. I think the next generation of Rockwood women will find their world completely different from what you and my sisters have experienced. Lucien and I are of the same mind when it comes to giving the girls the same experiences as the boys whenever possible."

"Surely it won't be that different."

Helen's frown deepened with concern as she smoothed the lapels on his jacket. Uncertainty had always been an unsettling sensation for him, and his mouth twisted with a deep foreboding he'd been unable to shake for weeks now. He preferred order as opposed to chaos, but recent political events had made him become uneasy on almost a monthly basis. He knew better than to try and hide his concern from his wife.

It would be a pointless exercise when she read his moods with such ease. Even after more than ten years of marriage they only had to look at each other across a room to instantly know what the other was thinking. It was the one piece of order in his life that had remained constant from the moment Helen had said she loved him after her ordeal at the hands of the Marquess of Templeton. He shook his head slightly.

"I think the next ten to fifteen years will bring a turmoil and upheaval unlike anything the world has ever seen."

"Do you mean more war?"

Helen drew in a quick breath of alarm. They'd had several acquaintances who'd recently lost loved ones in the Boer War, and the thought of a larger conflict was one he'd been unable to dismiss in recent months. He cupped her lovely face in his hands and kissed her gently. When he pulled back, he shook his head.

"I don't know. I simply want the next generation of Rockwoods to be ready for whatever trials might lie ahead for all of us."

"Is that why you were scowling so darkly when I came in here?" The reference to his mood when she'd first entered the study made his mouth tighten with irritation.

"No. I received a note from Argaty. He's asked me to come to Argaty Keep later this afternoon." His words didn't appear to surprise her at all, and the troubled expression on Helen's sweet features became one of somber acceptance. Instantly, his muscles tensed with wary expectation. "Someone's seen something."

"Actually, Tilly said something as I was putting her to bed last night that tells me our youngest is the latest Rockwood to display signs of the *an dara sealladh*."

"*Good God,*" Sebastian breathed in a sharp breath.

Resignation and fear crashed through him. He had been hoping his children wouldn't inherit the most volatile of all the Rockwood family traits. But the idea of Tilly possessing the *an dara sealladh* alarmed him in a way he rarely experienced. All three of his children possessed daring and courage to spare when it came to challenges, but Tilly gave new meaning to the words 'Reckless Rockwoods.'

The child was quickly overtaking Louisa's title as the most reckless of the family. Tilly also possessed her aunt's ability to charm and cajole others to fall in line with whatever scheme she concocted. Her brothers were always the first to succumb to her charm, no matter how outrageous the idea or plan.

It wasn't the first time his well-ordered existence had been rocked with a harsh reminder there were things in life he was powerless to control. The *an dara sealladh* always enhanced the impulsive nature of the Rockwood who possessed the gift of sight. Perhaps worst of all was that by exhibiting the family gift at such a young age, Tilly's command of the *an dara sealladh* might easily rival Jamie's ability.

The difference was his nephew possessed a maturity that belied his years. While the boy was impulsive at times, he had a good head on his shoulders. But the *an dara sealladh* when combined with Tilly's adventurous nature had the potential to create utter mayhem. As always when confronted with the unexpected, Sebastian struggled to control his concern. Helen touched his cheek in a gesture of reassurance.

"I know you had hoped the children wouldn't inherit the *an dara sealladh*, but there are some things neither one of us can control, my darling."

"What did Tilly say to you?" he rasped.

"She'd said it was the old earl who was a beast not the new earl. She said the new earl was very nice and would teach her riding tricks."

"I can see now why you were alarmed at her riding with me and the boys this afternoon," Sebastian said with more than a hint of relief. "As for her references to Argaty, it's obvious she's heard the boys or one of us discussing the man. Not to mention we both know she has an active imagination."

"Does she? I'm no longer certain of that, particularly when she was adamant that the bad earl and his mother were dead," Helen frowned slightly.

"And we all know the earl was forced to shoot his brother to save himself and Louisa." Sebastian's mouth tightened at the memory of the details the authorities had shared with him about the events that had happened at Argaty Keep only days ago.

"Any other time I would agree, but Tilly insisted the bad earl was dead, and the new earl was coming to Callendar

Abbey on Hogmanay to get her Aunt Louisa."

"I *still* think it's our daughter's imagination running amok," Sebastian said quietly as he watched Helen's green eyes darken with concern.

"No, it's more than that. You didn't see how distraught she was when I didn't believe her, Sebastian." Helen shook her head as he eyed her with skepticism. "Yes, she's prone to crying like any other child, but this was different. She was sobbing, Sebastian. She was sobbing as hard as she did last year when Percy couldn't save her puppy after it was hit by a carriage. Tilly said I was mean not to believe her, and that I'd have to say I was sorry when the earl came for Louisa."

"Something that will *not* happen if I have anything to do with it. The man's hurt Louisa enough," Sebastian said with harsh resolve.

"She's a grown woman, Sebastian, I know you want to protect her, but she's in love with him. Nothing you say or do will change that."

"Perhaps not, but I'll do my damnedest not to give Argaty the chance to break her heart a second time." Sebastian closed his eyes for a moment as hopelessness scored his insides. "I saw the Louisa we knew before the fire that day I first went to Argaty Keep. Now, she's acting no differently than she did after the fire, and the blame rests squarely on Argaty's shoulders."

"Then what do you plan to do?" Helen asked as she tucked her arm through his and gently pulled him toward the door.

"Well, I'm definitely *not* going to mention to Louisa that the man asked me to come to Argaty Keep this afternoon. As for Argaty, I have no intention of passing up the opportunity to thrash the man."

"Something tells me that won't happen. I have it on good authority the Earl of Melton is renowned for his self-control," Helen said impishly as her mouth tipped upwards.

He grunted with irritation before he smiled down at her.

"I can think of several times when Melton has lost control of his senses, and last night was no exception." His teasing sent pink color flooding his wife's cheeks, and he grinned broadly. She buried her head in his shoulder for a brief instant before looking up at him.

"You are a scoundrel, Lord Melton." With mock severity, Helen playfully squeezed his arm in a half-hearted reprimand. But it was the love he saw sparkling in in his wife's eyes that made his heart crash into the wall of his chest. Basking in the warmth of her love, Sebastian kissed Helen's brow and pushed all thought of the Earl of Argaty out of his head as they went in search of their children.

Hours later Sebastian recalled his wife's prophetic words as he faced the Earl of Argaty in stunned amazement.

"You want what?"

"I thought I was quite clear when I asked my question the first time," the earl growled. "I would like your permission to ask Louisa to be my wife."

"Permission to—*what in God's name* made you think I'd be willing to do that?" He glared at the earl with extreme dislike. "And *what* makes you think Louisa would *even consider* such a proposal?"

"There are a number of reasons she might not." Despair flitted across Argaty's battle-scarred features before his expression became hard as stone except for a tic on his unmarred cheek. "But I will ask her with or without your permission, my lord."

"You're fortunate I value my wife's good opinion of me, Argaty, or I'd drop you where you stand," Sebastian snarled viciously. "If you intend to speak with my sister regardless of what I say, why bother to ask my permission?"

"I know you believe I wronged your sister, and I wish to explain my behavior."

"Then by all means, explain." Sebastian didn't hide his sarcasm or anger as he glared at the man with contempt. The earl's face darkened with an emotion Sebastian recognized as humiliation, and Sebastian frowned in puzzlement.

"What I am about to share with you is known only to my mother and myself. I know from Louisa that you are an honorable man, and I believe you will keep my confidence." Argaty drew in a deep breath and straightened his posture as if bracing himself for a terrible storm headed in his direction. "I am a bastard and as such, not the true heir to the Argaty title."

For a second time since he'd entered Argaty Keep, Sebastian experienced a moment of stunned amazement as he jerked his head back in disbelief. What the devil was the man about making such a preposterous statement? Quickly recovering his senses, Sebastian arched his eyebrows in contempt. Did the man take him for a fool?

"Is this an attempt at humor, Lord Argaty?" his voice harsh with sarcasm he suppressed the urge to lunge forward and pound the man into the ground for hurting Louisa.

At his scornful reaction, the man's humiliation was painfully obvious. For the first time since being shown into the earl's study, Sebastian's outrage cooled to a slow-burning anger. There was something about the man's appearance and the way he held himself rigid that said Argaty was struggling with a great burden. Perhaps he'd been wrong about the man. Sebastian immediately released an imperceptible snort of disgust at the thought.

"A jest?" the earl said with a mirthless laugh. "Yes, I suppose it could be viewed in that manner, but the joke is on me, and it is far from amusing or pleasant."

Shame swept across the earl's face once more, and his

throat bobbed as if swallowing something unpleasant. With a jerk, he turned away from Sebastian and crossed the floor to study the view outside one of the room's tall windows.

"The day before Lady Argaty was murdered by my brother, she informed me that I was a bastard, and that she wasn't my real mother. The revelation was confirmed by the countess's sister."

The silence in the room was thick with tension as Sebastian stared at Argaty's back with a growing sense of bewilderment. The man was as mad as his dead brother. The earl cleared his throat, but didn't turn away from the window.

"It is a story not even the Bard himself could write, but I speak the truth, my lord. My mother is Wallis MacCullaich. She was my father's mistress after he married her sister, Elspeth MacCullaich."

"Good God," Sebastian breathed softly as he slowly began to accept the other man was speaking the truth. If the earl heard him, he didn't acknowledge Sebastian's soft exclamation.

"While the behavior of my parents was disreputable, the reasons for their actions are those I understand, and I cannot condemn them for it. My father convinced Lady Argaty to publicly claim me as her son." Argaty turned back to Sebastian who remained silent not because of his steely self-control, but because he was speechless—a rare occurrence for him.

"Even if I were to share the truth of my birth outside of this room, my words would be met with disbelief as it is Elspeth Colquhoun's signature on my baptism record not that of my real mother."

Sebastian studied the earl's battle-scarred features closely. The veracity of Argaty's confession was emphasized by the humiliation darkening the man's one eye. Even the tight, thin line of his mouth declared the depth of Argaty's shame and embarrassment. As Sebastian struggled to find something to say in response to the man's confession, the earl cleared his throat.

"Even before I knew the truth of my birth, I believed I had little to offer Louisa. But knowing I was no longer the legitimate earl meant I had nothing at all. When I decided to relinquish what was no longer mine, I ordered Louisa to leave."

"And what has changed?" Sebastian mused softly as he challenged the earl to explain in further detail. The man's gaze did not waver from Sebastian's.

"Despite being Dougal Colquhoun's bastard, the fact that Elspeth Colquhoun's signature is on my birth record means that for all intents and purposes I am my father's legitimate heir. There are no other heirs to the title, and my mother reminded me that there are a great number of people who might be adversely affected if I left Argaty Keep."

Argaty bowed his head to study the floor, and Sebastian pondered the man's decision. Uncertain as to what to say to the earl regarding his confession, Sebastian frowned slightly as he realized how difficult it must have been for Argaty to explain himself.

"For the most part, I have always believed myself to be an honorable man, my lord." Argaty lifted his head and winced at his statement. He paused for a brief moment before he shook his head with a firm resolve that said the man had given his decision a great deal of consideration. "If I walk away from those whose livelihood depends on Argaty Keep, I am condemning them to a life they don't deserve. I also have Ross to consider."

Sebastian grimaced slightly at the mention of Ross. The boy clearly missed his father, and Louisa had been surprisingly tight-lipped about what had happened at Argaty Keep. She'd shared that the earl was going away, and she'd asked the man to let her take responsibility for the boy's upbringing rather than sending him away to school. A small noise escaped Argaty as the earl arched an eyebrow in surprise.

"Has she explained why she took Ross with her?" The resignation in his voice made Sebastian study Argaty with assessment. Louisa assuming responsibility for the boy's care was puzzling, and she'd yet to fully expand on her reasons for doing so.

"For a change, my sister has shown great restraint when it comes to discussing the boy or anything about her time here in the keep." Sebastian scowled at the floor for a moment before he looked up to see a flash of relief lighten Argaty's features as a small smile twisted the man's lips.

"That is surprising given your sister's tendency to speak her mind." The earl murmured with more than a hint of amusement, and Sebastian chuckled.

"Indeed."

Silence drifted between them again for a moment before their gazes locked once more. Argaty's mouth tightened again until the corners of his mouth were white and a stoic look crossed his battle-scarred features.

"My decision to share the circumstances of my birth wasn't simply to explain why I sent Louisa away, my lord." The earl's gaze did not falter or veer away from Sebastian's. "I believed you deserved to know the truth so you would know the measure of the man who wishes to marry your sister. Retaining my title might not be the honorable thing to do, but I am doing what I believe best for the people who count on me."

Sebastian nodded as his mind sifted through the events of the past few minutes. It had taken great courage on Argaty's part to confess to a situation that was completely out of his hands. While the earl might see his actions as dishonorable, Sebastian knew the man had made the right decision in choosing to remain. If he'd been in a similar situation, he would most likely have made the same choice.

"Actually, I find your decision an honorable one, simply because you're willing to sacrifice your principles for the sake of others," Sebastian said quietly. Argaty jerked in surprise at his remarks and Sebastian smiled. "That is the measure of a man I would gladly welcome as a brother-in-law."

"I shall do my best to make her happy, if she'll have me," Argaty said firmly. "If I'm to have the approval of the rest of the Rockwood clan, I will require a task for the Speerin."

"The Spee—" Sebastian objected with a firm shake of his head. "I don't think that's really necessary."

"As far as I'm concerned it is, and it should be done in public." Determination hardened the earl's expression, and Sebastian bit back a chuckle. Louisa might delight in winning battles with this man, but she would most definitely lose the war.

"I should warn you the privilege of asking my sister to marry you may come at a much higher price than you think. There will be no quarter, no mercy given by my siblings when it comes to their selection of the Speerin task." Sebastian arched his eyebrows at the man as he glanced at the earl's missing arm. "However, I will see to it that they—"

"No. I am not to be afforded any measure of restraint. I expect to be treated as you would any other man seeking your sister's hand in marriage."

Argaty's reply was harsh and uncompromising. It illustrated his strong objection to any accommodation the Rockwoods might give him. It made Sebastian admire the man all the more, and he nodded his understanding. The earl relaxed slightly at Sebastian's silent reassurance, and the man drew in a breath of what Sebastian determined was relief.

"Will you and your clan be attending the Hogmanay celebration in the Callendar village tomorrow evening?" Argaty asked as an uncomfortable hesitation hardened his features.

"Yes, the entire family will be there." Sebastian grimaced

as he contemplated his sister's current state of listlessness. "Louisa might be reluctant to join us, but I will see to it she's there."

"Thank you. Asking for Louisa's hand in an open forum will emphasize how much she means to me," Argaty said with an uneasy frown. "She knows I do not enjoy public events."

"Very well, I will send you a note with the Speerin task by tomorrow morning." Sebastian extended his hand to the earl. As they shook hands, he smiled at Argaty's uneasy look. "If it helps, I understand what you're experiencing at this moment. I'm certain my brother-in-laws' Lucien and Julian would also commiserate with you. But I know my sister, and I'm confident she'll not refuse you."

Argaty's only reply was a twist of his lips that declared the depth of his uncertainty in a way words could not. Biting back a smile, Sebastian said goodbye and walked out of the study. As he moved through the front door of Argaty Keep, Sebastian remembered his conversation with Helen earlier. Tilly had been correct in her prediction as to the old and new earl.

Sebastian groaned as he threw himself into his carriage. Life was about to become chaotic in a way he'd never dreamed. He closed his eyes for a moment as he remembered Tilly's decision this past summer to go swimming without supervision in the small lake at Melton Park. She'd frightened Helen to the point of tears, and even he had been shaken by the incident. Now that his daughter possessed the *an dara sealladh*, all manner of hell would ensue. A grimace of resignation twisted his mouth before he grinned. It was a journey he wouldn't trade for the world.

Chapter 21

"I should send you to bed instead of letting you go to the celebration this evening, young man." Louisa released a small noise of exasperation as she leaned over Wills and brushed cobwebs off the back of his jacket.

"But, Mama, I had to rescue Roscoe."

"The dog would have found his way out of that rundown farmhouse without your help," she scolded. The last of the white gossamer she could find removed from his coat, Louisa straightened and eyed her youngest son sternly. "You are *not* to go to the Banks croft again, do you understand?"

"Yes, Mama." Wills nodded his head contritely, and Louisa sighed.

"Did you at least find Roscoe?" Her question made the child grin with satisfaction.

"Yes, Mama, I left him with Fergus in the stables."

"Left who in the stables?" A deep male voice asked.

Louisa turned to see Sebastian standing in the salon doorway a twinkle in his dark eyes as he looked down at his nephew. With his scolding complete, a cheerful expression lightened Wills's small features.

"Roscoe. I rescued him from old crofter Banks's farmhouse, uncle Sebastian. But it was filled with spider webs."

"Which explains this," her brother said with a grin as he

pulled a piece of cobweb off of the child's jacket that Louisa had missed. Sebastian held it up for inspection as he chuckled softly. "Off with you, scamp. Your brother and the other children are waiting for you at the wagon."

Without hesitating the boy rushed past his uncle, his shoes tapping against the wood floor of the main hall. As her son disappeared from the room, Louisa shook her head as she pressed one hand against her stomach.

"Dear heaven, he's almost as bad as Tilly when it comes to adventures."

"He comes by it naturally." The teasing note in Sebastian's voice made her scowl at her brother before she laughed.

"Yes, I suppose he does." Louisa rolled her eyes then turned away to find the book she'd set down when Wills had appeared covered in spider webs.

"Come, with the exception of Rhea and Constance, who is always late, the rest of the family is waiting outside." Sebastian stretched out as his arm, and his fingers flicked in a commanding gesture for her to join him.

"I am *not* always late, brother dear," Constance declared with mock severity before her gaze skimmed over Louisa. "Why aren't you wearing that new coat you bought from Madame Sabine? You practically swooned over it when you saw it the day we visited Ophelia."

"Ach, why are ye nae ready, lass?" Matilda Stewart bustled into the salon and circled her niece and nephew to study Louisa with dismay. "The wee bairns are all tucked snugly in the wagon and demanding to know when we're leaving."

"Actually, I thought I would stay home this evening and read The Black Corsair," Louisa murmured as she moved toward the end table where she'd set her copy of the book. "I thought it might be one the boys would enjoy, but I wanted to be sure it's suitable for them to read."

"You will absolutely *not* stay here," Constance said firmly. "I refuse to let you remain here wallowing in misery over the man."

"I am not wallowing," Louisa snapped as she glared at her older sister.

It was a lie, but she wasn't willing to admit it. For the past week she'd spent every night sobbing into her pillows. Her family knew she was unhappy, but she'd done her best to keep them from realizing just how miserable she was. Her heart had been ripped out of her the day she'd ridden away from Argaty Keep. She'd left it behind her, and knew she would never be whole again.

The first two or three days after she returned to the abbey, she had hoped Ewan would defeat his demons and come for her. But the hope she'd dared to harbor inside had shriveled up and died with each passing day. All she wanted to do now was block out the darkness that had settled on her shoulders for the second time in her life. But this was a weight that she knew she would never defeat.

Without Ewan, there was little joy in her life. If it weren't for the boys, she wasn't sure how she'd managed to hide the majority of her sorrow from her family. But for Wills, Charlie, and Ross, she had no other choice than to move forward no matter how difficult or painful it was to do so.

"*Tilly. Stop this instant.*" Irritation threaded Helen's voice from out in the hall, and everyone turned toward the sound. "*Lady Matilda Rockwood*, don't you run away from me, young lady."

"But I must see Aunt Louisa, Mama."

Tilly's response echoed through the salon as the five-year-old dashed into the room and bolted straight for Louisa. As the little girl flung herself against Louisa's skirts, the room erupted into a soft buzz of exclamations as to the child's behavior. Louisa sank down until she was at eye-level with her niece.

"Whatever is the matter, sweetheart," Louisa gasped as she saw tears forming in Tilly's eyes.

"Uncle Caleb says you aren't going to the *ceilidh* with us, and I want you to. You promised you would let me dance that highlander dance with you."

The child's words elicited a quiet groan from Sebastian, and Louisa looked up to see her brother rubbing the back of his neck as resignation twisted his mouth into a small grimace. She knew her brother had been hoping the *an dara sealladh* would bypass his children, and his look of defeat made her shake her head at him. She returned her attention to Sebastian's youngest and gently wiped the tears from the girl's eyes.

"I do seem to recall telling you I would dance the Gay Gordon with you, and since it's usually the first dance of the evening, we should hurry." At Louisa's reply, her niece's tears vanished as she nodded vigorously. Still looking somewhat dazed, Sebastian picked up his daughter and sighed.

"You are far too impulsive, Tilly."

"I know Papa, but Uncle Caleb insisted I remind Aunt Louisa to keep her promise."

"Did he now," Sebastian murmured as he frowned with resignation before he turned toward Louisa. "It appears the *entire* family is determined to see you attend the celebration whether you want to or not."

"Oh, that much I've gathered." Louisa's mouth curved in a wry smile of surrender as she looked up at her brother.

"Then get that coat Constance mentioned. The one that came with that quite sizeable bill."

"That was paid for out of my own account," Louisa sniffed with affectionate exasperation.

"An account that at this rate will be non-existent in five years."

She rolled her eyes at Sebastian's chiding as Constance appeared in the doorway with the item being discussed.

Louisa allowed her sister to help her put on the ankle-length garment and usher her out of the abbey and into the cold night air.

"Enough. *Three* is my limit, dearest."

Louisa tugged her protesting niece off the makeshift dance floor that had been erected in the center of the village. When it was obvious, her aunt wouldn't give into her demands, Tilly released a noise of exaggerated suffering. A moment later she pulled free of her aunt's grip and charged toward Ross who was being playfully shoved around by her oldest.

"*Lord Westbrook*, act like a gentleman, please." At her reprimand, Charlie grimaced and bowed slightly in her direction.

"Yes, my lady." As always when he was being scolded, there was a distinct note of rebellion in his voice. She opened her mouth to chastise his manner, when Percy appeared at her side and gently squeezed her forearm.

"Don't you dare," he said with a grin. "You were the same way when you were younger, and you haven't changed one bit."

"*I was not.*" Louisa tilted her head toward him and glared at him in sisterly disgust. The minute he arched his eyebrows, she released a sigh of concession. "All right, maybe just a little. But I wasn't anywhere near the challenge for Sebastian that Tilly is."

She bobbed her head toward her niece, who was holding Ross's hand as he bent down to say something to her and pointed out toward the dance floor. It had taken only a day for the child to become attached to Ross. Whenever Tilly saw the boy, she followed him around just like a puppy. Ross didn't seem to mind, and like the rest of the Rockwoods he succumbed to her charms on a regular basis.

"I think it will take all the Rockwoods to ensure Sebastian's youngest doesn't do something rash. I think she has the ability to exceed even the most reckless of your escapades."

"At least I'll no longer be the subject of exasperated gasps and reprimands by my siblings."

Percy mocked her as he clutched at his heart as if mortally wounded. Louisa laughed at his dramatic display of injury. Her brother grinned as his knuckles gently jabbed her below the tip of her chin. Before she could tease him on his lack of acting skills, she looked over Percy's shoulder to see Aunt Matilda's eyes open wide as she gasped with astonishment.

As her aunt turned toward Helen and Patience, the Scotswoman bobbed her head with excitement at something her sister-in-law said. Behind her, Louisa heard loud cheers, laughter, and whistles filling the air on the other side of the village square where it narrowed down into one of the side streets. Percy nodded over her shoulder as a complacent grin curved his mouth.

"It appears someone is performing the Speerin for the privilege of asking for his sweetheart's hand." Percy's words made her heart wrench at the thought of watching a happy couple become engaged at the *ceilidh*, and before he could stop her, she slipped away from him and turned to push her way through the crowds.

"Fear, Lady Westwood? You've never shown a reluctance to face the beast in the past."

The arrogant taunt rang out loud and clear above the frolicking laughter and whistles. Louisa came to an abrupt halt wanting to turn around, but terrified to do so. It was wishful thinking on her part to believe it had been Ewan's voice ringing out in the winter night's air. Ewan hated being out in public. Certain she was experiencing a delusion born out of wishes she had buried in her heart, she moved forward again only to come up against a hard chest.

She looked up to see Lucien smiling down at her. Quickly stepping to one side in an effort to move past her brother-in-law, another hard body blocked her way. This time it was Julian preventing her retreat. She drew in a sharp breath as Sebastian appeared at her side.

"A Rockwood never runs from a challenge, Louisa," Sebastian said quietly.

Her heart beating frantically in her breast, she didn't move as she stared up at her oldest brother. He bobbed his head in the direction of the square behind her. Still terrified she was having a waking vision, Louisa slowly turned around. The sight of Ewan standing on the edge of the dance floor with a caber on each shoulder made her suck in a sharp breath of disbelief.

He was here. The beastly earl was here in the middle of the village square surrounded by a multitude of people. The image made her throat close as she tried to believe what she was seeing was real. Ewan's good hand balanced the caber on his good shoulder with ease. The second heavy log wobbled as his artificial hand tried to hold the unwieldy weight steady.

Rooted in place, Louisa saw how the heavy logs had forced him to hunch over slightly in order to shift some of the weight onto his upper back. Louisa shook her head slightly as she struggled to grasp the notion that Ewan was standing in the village square, surrounded by dozens of people, and carrying two cabers on his shoulders.

"*Bloody hell, Percy!* Lucien and I told you two cabers was asking too much of the man," Sebastian growled directly behind her.

Her heart skipped a beat as she saw Ewan's mouth twist into a visible grimace of pain. She took one step forward before her brother's words suddenly sank into her brain. The

Speerin. Her family had given Ewan a task to perform in exchange for his right to ask for her hand. Annoyance swept through her the instant she realized he'd gone to her brother instead of her. If the man had come to her in the first place, he wouldn't be carrying two cabers at this very moment.

"*Damn it, Louisa,*" he grunted. "These cabers are heavy, lass."

"I'm sure they are," she said sharply as she scowled at him. "Especially when you were so dull-witted as to ask my brother and not me about an offer of marriage. I wouldn't have asked you to perform any Speerin task."

"Your brother didn't ask me to, I insisted," Ewan growled. At his reply, Louisa's mouth sagged open slightly as she stared at him in amazement until her annoyance returned with a vengeance.

"Then I should let you stand there a little while longer for not using the good sense God gave you, you stubborn Scot," she snapped.

Gasps and sharp inhalations from her family echoed behind her, but she ignored them as she met the glittering frustration in the eyes of the man in front of her. A hand on her shoulder made her jerk her head to meet Percy's worried gaze.

"For the love of God, Louisa. The man has a body full of sutures."

"And you knew that, *didn't you?*" she bit out between clenched teeth. A flush of color and shame crossed her brother's handsome features. "Oh, you're not alone in your feebleminded foolishness, brother mine. He's just as thick-skulled as you are. Isn't that right, my lord?"

"*Damnation, Louisa.* I love you more than my own life, and I'm asking you to please put this beast out of his misery," Ewan roared.

"*What did you say?*" Louisa gasped as she stared at him in stunned disbelief.

"I said, I love you," he snarled like a caged animal.

Had the man actually said he loved her in the middle of the village square? In front of the entire village? The glare he pinned on her was just as fierce as ones she'd seen before, but there was something different about his expression now. There was a desperation about him that had nothing to do with the weight he was slowly bowing beneath. It frightened her.

Did he think she'd refuse such a courageous public display of devotion? Was it possible he didn't realize how well she knew him? She knew the price he'd paid for declaring his love for her in the middle of the village square. With a small cry, she ran forward determined to reassure him that her heart was his until her last breath.

Her brothers were close behind as they removed the cabers from Ewan's shoulders. The instant the weight was off him, Ewan pulled her tight against him and captured her mouth in a hard kiss. Louisa clung to him oblivious to the shouts of laughter and cheers echoing around them. As he lifted his head, he pressed his forehead against hers.

"You have a wicked temper, *mo ghràdh*."

"It's no more than your stubborn nature, my lord, but I am sorry for allowing my pettiness to cause you more pain," she whispered as her hand caressed his scarred cheek.

"It's a price I was willing to pay to prove how much I love you. I'll go to the depths of hell for you, *mo leannan*."

"I love you, Ewan," she said huskily as he kissed her again. As he lifted his head, the desperation she'd seen a few seconds ago had returned as he inhaled and exhaled a sharp breath.

"And I hope you will say that again after we speak in private, *mo ghràdh*."

Startled by the bewildering remark, Louisa drew in a sharp breath of alarm. Before she could question him, three boys surrounded them whooping and cheering. Laughing at their excitement, Louisa kissed the three of them and out of the corner of her eye, she saw Ewan ruffle Ross's hair. Seconds later the rest of the Rockwood clan encircled them.

The hours that followed were a blur, except for one thing—her hand caught snugly in Ewan's strong grip. At different intervals their hands were pulled apart, but Ewan always found hers a moment later. Despite his obvious determination to keep her hand locked in his, it was impossible not to sense the underlying tension running just beneath the surface.

It surprised her that he'd followed the tradition of the Speerin task, but had not given her a Luckenbooth brooch, another centuries old tradition. Just as the Speerin task declared the intention of a marriage proposal, the brooch was a token signifying the marriage offer had been accepted. His wonderful and heroic declaration of his love was more than enough for her, but his failure to offer the jewelry still puzzled her.

While it was quite possible he wanted to present her with a brooch in private, as the new year rapidly approached, she began to realize Ewan hadn't mentioned marriage at all. It was also becoming painfully obvious that he was avoiding the matter at all. Whenever someone mentioned the subject, he found a way to dodge the question or redirected the conversation.

Then there was the air of desperation she'd sensed in him when he'd faced her with two cabers on his shoulders. It hadn't disappeared. He'd simply hidden it from her. Whenever she suddenly turned her head and caught him watching her, the brief glimpse of anguish on his beautiful warrior features frightened her. The bleakness would vanish as if it never existed, but she knew it was there beneath the surface.

It became a worrisome dread that nibbled at her in small bits. But every time he smiled or refused to let her hand leave his, the sense of calamity swirling the fringes of her happiness retreated. As the midnight hour drew near, the excitement of the crowd grew. The moment the church bells rang out into the cold, crisp night, Ewan's hard body pressed into hers from behind.

The warmth of him melted into her, and she reveled in the joy and happiness of the moment. Ross and Charlie stood in front of them, and as her hands came to rest on their shoulders, the two boys look up and grinned. Wills had pushed his way into Ewan's side and gently pulled Ewan's artificial arm over his small shoulders. As he grinned up at them, Louisa's heart swelled with happiness. Sebastian had been right, the new century was upon them, and her future was brighter than she'd ever dreamed.

Ewan dragged in a deep breath as he continued to stare into the fire waiting for Louisa to say something now that the truth was out in the open. The silence that greeted him gnawed at him like an angry beast feeding on its young.

When everyone had returned to the abbey after the Hogmanay *ceilidh*, Louisa's family had quickly ensured their privacy. Her sisters had ushered the children upstairs, while the men had clapped him on the back as they'd directed him into the salon where Louisa had taken a seat at the fire.

The look of trepidation on her beautiful face as she'd looked up at him had made his gut twist viciously. Somehow he managed to gather his courage for the second time that night and began telling her the squalid story of his birth. The entire time he spoke, she'd sat quietly. There had been no rustle of skirts or gasps of surprise. It was a devastating quiet that had made it impossible to look at her.

Instead, he'd kept his back to her the entire time he

spoke. Yesterday it had been humiliating to tell Louisa's brother about his situation, but this was a trial by fire. It didn't matter whether Melton believed he was doing the right thing or not by keeping a title that wasn't really his. It was what Louisa thought that mattered.

The silence deepened as he waited for her to say something. When she didn't speak, Ewan experienced a painful gnawing at his insides. Every tick of the mantle clock in front of him emphasized one more step toward the reality that he had lost her. He was about to turn and confront her when he heard the rustle of her skirts as she stood up.

Troubled by her silence, Ewan turned and watched her walk to the sideboard to pour more than two fingers of whiskey into a glass, which she downed in one gulp. Uncertainty barreled through him. This wasn't the reaction he'd expected. Actually, he'd not known what to expect, but if he had, it would certainly not be the sight of Louisa tossing liquor down her throat.

Ewan wasn't surprised when she coughed violently after swallowing the liquor. It was the reaction of someone unaccustomed to the drink. She kept her back to him, her head bent as if studying the bottles on the sideboard. Tension held her rigid, but he thought he saw a tremor shudder through her as continued to keep her back to him.

"And that's," she choked out as she coughed again. "And that's why you sent me away from Argaty Keep? From you? You used my deception to send me away because you learned you were a bastard?"

Every one of Ewan's muscles were pulled taut until he ached as if someone had sewn him up for a second time in little more than a week. The restrained anger in her voice offered up an explanation for her downing a glass full of whiskey. He could only assume the drink had been an effort to calm herself before speaking.

"Yes," he said tersely. "It was hard enough to believe I

had anything to offer you *before* I knew I wasn't the true Earl of Argaty. After I learned the truth, even that was gone."

In a sharp gesture, she slammed the empty glass down on top of the sideboard. It rent the air with a loud, vicious crack as she whirled around. Anger had sent color flaring high in her cheeks, while her hazel eyes flashed with outrage. Ewan dragged in a harsh breath at how beautiful she was in the firelight.

She didn't move for a moment, she simply glared at him from across the room. Hands pressed deep into her sweetly curved, full hips, Louisa began to close the distance between them in slow, measured steps.

"*You* are the most *annoying, insufferable, beastly* man I have ever met," she sputtered with a fiery anger that accentuated her Scottish heritage. "Do you think so little of me that you believed I would *actually care* who your parents are?"

"*Damn it*, Louisa, I didn't—"

"*I am not finished*," she snapped as she stepped forward and jabbed her finger into his chest. "I didn't fall in love with a title, *Lord* Argaty. I fell in love with a man who thinks no one can see past his physical wounds. But, *I did*. I saw beneath your scars, pain, and ill-tempered manner.

"I saw you for the strong, brave, honorable, caring man you are. A man who, *despite* his best efforts to be as curmudgeonly as possible, has the heart of a lion. *That's* the man I fell in love with, Ewan Colquhoun. I don't want any other man except him, and if you think telling me you're a bastard and not the true Earl of Argaty makes me think—"

With a quiet noise of frustration, Ewan caught her by the arm and tugged her into his chest. The moment his mouth captured hers, a sigh of surrender escaped her as she parted her lips beneath his. Soft and pliable against his hard, angular body, the warmth of her pressed its way through him and heated his blood.

Sweet as honey, he plundered her mouth as if in doing

so he could possess every inch of her. The fervor of her response tugged a groan from him, and his cock hardened with a demand for satisfaction he knew would go unanswered for a little while longer. Before he lost control of his senses completely, he lifted his head. An incoherent protest passed her lips, and she leaned into him to nibble at the side of his neck.

"*Christ Jesus, Louisa*," he choked out as her mouth worked its way to the base of his throat.

She ignored his protest and slid her hand down the front of him to just above his erection. With a deep groan of regret, Ewan winced as he used his artificial hand with his good one to pin her arms behind her back. Louisa frowned up at him in frustration, and he bent his head to press his forehead against hers.

"God help me, *mo leannan*, ye have no idea how difficult it is nae tae take ye here and now," he rasped, hearing his voice thicken with his brogue. "But I want more than a few seconds of pleasure. I want tae be able tae worship your body in every way possible, and take my time doing it. Something I cannae do here in your aunt's salon."

"Then I'll come to you," she whispered. "I know someone has asked Mrs. MacGregor to prepare a room for you."

"Absolutely not," he growled.

"The abbey has its own hidden corridors, and I won't be seen." Her mischievous look dissolved into one of tenderness as she gently pulled free of his grasp and cupped his cheeks with her hands. "I've missed you. I want to be with you."

"And I want tae make sure your brothers dinnae tar and feather me or worse, prevent ye from marrying me," he bit out. His words made her draw in a sharp breath as her beautiful hazel eyes grew luminous with tears. Fear lunged through him. "Do ye nae want to marry me, *mo ghràdh*?"

"Of course I do, you daft man," she exclaimed and threw her arms around his neck and feathered his face with soft kisses. "But it's the first time you've actually mentioned it."

"Is your memory so short you've forgotten me carrying two cabers on my shoulders into the village square this evening and shouting out I love you in front of the entire county?" He glared down at her. "A far from easy task I might add."

"I know that my love," she whispered as she kissed him again. "I know what it cost you to walk across that square. But when you'd not said anything…"

"I wanted you to know the complete truth before I asked you to be my wife. After all, you'll be contributing to a fraud by marrying me." At his reply, she pushed herself away from him to fold her arms across her full, lush breasts and glare at him.

"You truly *are* an exasperating and beastly man." Her irritation caused him to swallow a chuckle.

"Does that mean you intend to refuse the beast of Argaty Keep?" he asked softly.

Ewan reached into his pocket and pulled out the Luckenbooth brooch his mother had given him earlier in the day. It had been made for her by his father, despite knowing they would never be together.

The brooch was made of two hearts intertwined around a stag and doe with a thistle nestled inside each heart, while a delicate crown rested on top of the two hearts. Despite the absence of jewels, the simplicity of the brooch made it all the more beautiful. Louisa released a small gasp of pleasure as he opened his palm and offered her the Luckenbooth token.

Slowly taking the brooch from him, Louisa stared at it for a moment then quickly pinned it to her dress. With a soft, gentle caress of the silver hearts, her gaze met his again, and the love he saw shining there drew the air from his lungs.

"No, I'll not refuse the beast of Argaty Keep," she whispered. "I'll not refuse *my* beastly earl."

Epilogue

Christmas Day 1913

The soft light of dawn had begun to push its way through the curtains of Ewan's and Louisa's room at Callendar Abbey as Ewan awakened. Beside him, Louisa murmured something in her sleep.

As was his habit most mornings, he turned over onto his side to study his wife's lovely face. The night he'd found her on the moor had changed his life in ways he'd never dreamed possible.

She was an angel with a fiery passion for life and a lioness when it came to protecting those she loved. Ewan gently brushed a strand of hair off her cheek, and in her sleep, she batted his hand away as if a fly was buzzing around her head. A smile curved his lips, and he swallowed a laugh as his forefinger brushed its way down across her cheek. She slapped at his hand and opened her eyes to glare at him.

"You had better have an excellent reason for waking your wife in the middle of the night, my beastly Lord Argaty." Her prickly tone was filled with affectionate irritation.

"It's actually dawn, *mo ghràdh*," he murmured. Clearly still annoyed at having been awakened, she lifted her head to look over his shoulder. She glared at the gentle light growing brighter by the minute then with a loud sigh of resignation flopped back into her pillows. "I shouldn't have allowed

Percy to goad me into playing that last game of cribbage."

"I seem to recall urging you to come to bed with me, *mo leannan*. And from your contrary mood, I'm assuming you lost." His obvious amusement made her scowl at him as she closed her eyes again.

"You enjoy depriving me of sleep, don't you?" she grumbled.

"In instances such as these I do," he said with a chuckle.

"One of these days, *I'm* going to be the one who interrupts *your* sleep."

The peevish note in her voice made him snort with laughter. She immediately responded to his amusement by calling him an unflattering name beneath her breath, and he laughed again. Eyes still closed, her lovely mouth twisted in a line of annoyance.

"It's far too early in the morning to be up and about."

"Did I say anything about leaving our bed?" he teased as he leaned forward to nibble at her shoulder. The corners of her mouth tipped upward slightly as her bristly tone became soft and tender.

"Are you trying to seduce me, Lord Argaty?"

"I'm the one who's been seduced, *mo leannan*," he whispered against her silky skin. "I was lost the moment you stormed into my study that first time."

"I did not storm into your study," she huffed.

"Aye, but you did, lass." Ewan abraded the skin of her shoulder with his teeth. "You weren't intimidated by me in the least, and I remember wanting to kiss you to see if you tasted as fiery and passionate as you sounded."

"And was your curiosity ever satisfied?" she murmured as she slowly opened her eyes and reached up to caress his scarred cheek.

"Every day since you agreed to marry the beast of Argaty."

"And should I help satisfy your curiosity once more?"

An alluring smile curved her beautiful mouth as her hand glided across his chest in a leisurely fashion. The sultry look in her hazel eyes made Ewan's heart slam into his chest. God, how he loved this woman. Her hand slid up around his neck as she pulled him downward to brush her mouth over his in a sweet, tender kiss that held the same promise of love she'd pledged to him the day they were married.

She moved against him until the warmth of her burrowed its way into his body. With an eagerness that betrayed her growing passion, lushly curved legs tangled with his as he rolled her onto her back and pressed her deep into the mattress. His mouth trailed a lazy path down her throat to her breast. The moment his tongue swirled around a stiff peak, she inhaled a sharp breath. The sound made him smile slightly as he nipped at the rigid tip then lifted his head to look at her. His smile broadened at the frustration tightening her lips into a small pout. One eye opened to glare at him, she frowned at him.

"*First* you wake me at an ungodly hour, *then* in the middle of seducing me you stop," she said with exasperation. "Are you deliberately trying to irritate your wife this morning, my beastly earl?"

"I can assure you, Lady Argaty, I have no intention of ending this seduction," he said with a smile as he shifted his body slightly to illustrate his arousal. His heart swelled with emotion as he shook his head. "No, *mo ghràdh*, I simply wanted to say how much I love you."

Louisa's scowl vanished at his words as she caressed his cheek. Hazel eyes shining with love, her lips moved in a silent reply as he lowered his head to kiss her deeply. When he lifted his head, she uttered a sigh of what he knew was the same profound level of happiness he felt. She stared up at him for a moment, before her hips shifted beneath his suggestively, and she slid her hand between them to caress his cock. He inhaled a sharp breath, and a familiar smile curved her mouth.

It was filled with the mischief he loved so dearly about her and yet despaired of whenever she did something impulsive.

"Stop teasing your wife, my beastly Lord Argaty," she whispered with a smile. "She loves you far more than she can ever say, but there *are* limits to her patience when it comes to satisfying your curiosity."

The heat of her hand warmed his skin as she ran her fingertip along the hard length of him. It was an intoxicating caress that tugged a quiet groan from him as she opened herself up to him. The familiar fragrance of roses wafted up off her skin to mix with the subtle scent of desire. It sent his heart slamming into his chest as her fingers pressed deep in his hips with a silent demand for his possession.

Not about to deny her any longer, he sank into her with a hard thrust. She gasped his name then met him stroke for stroke as their passion grew in strength until it was spent in a powerful completion. As he throbbed inside her, Ewan buried his face in the side of her neck his harsh, ragged breaths equaling hers.

Neither of them moved for several moments as they reveled in the afterglow of their lovemaking. Silence had never truly been silence between them. Whether with a small touch or a glance, they always knew what the other was thinking. When he pulled away from her to lie on his back, she curled up into his side with one leg draped over his.

It was one of the things he loved to wake up to in the middle of the night. The sensation of her body pressing into his was as much of a comfort as it was arousing. Fingers lightly caressing his chest until her palm came to rest over his heart, Louisa stretched upward to kiss his scarred cheek.

"Was your curiosity slaked to your satisfaction, Lord Argaty," she teased.

"It was, my lady," he said with a chuckle as he pressed his lips to her forehead.

"I thought it might be." The affectionate, smug note in

her voice made him reach across his body to playfully slap her pleasingly plump bottom. She simply laughed at his loving punishment. Soft lips brushed across his chest as she yawned, then snuggled even deeper into his side.

"I love you, Ewan." It was a mere whisper, but he heard it echoing in his ears as if it was shout.

"And I you, *mo ghràdh*." His hand stroked her cheek before he cleared his throat. "I know our anniversary isn't for another two weeks, but the children have pointed out that my present will be a difficult surprise to keep from you. They suggested I give it to you today instead of waiting."

"*A present,*" she exclaimed with a look of pleased excitement as she sat up in bed.

The sight of her bared to him reminded him of the night he'd carried her off the moor. Her body had filled out slightly over the years, but it made her even more lush, beautiful, and exquisite. When he remained silent, Louisa leaned over him and shook him gently.

"Stop teasing, you beast. *Where* is my present?"

The exasperation on her face made him laugh. He kissed her quickly before he rolled out of bed. He grabbed his robe and struggled to pull it on. Gentle hands caressed his as she helped him into the robe then caressed the back of his neck with her mouth. Ewan glanced over his shoulder and grinned at the impatience on his wife's face. With a deliberate, unhurried stride, he crossed the room to a large chifforobe. Behind him, Louisa uttered a small imprecation, and he looked over his shoulder again to grin broadly at the scowl on her face. The door of the large chifforobe squeaked as he opened the furniture's door and stuck his hand into the dark area behind his suits where he'd told Asadi to hide it. The moment his fingers touched the box, he realized it was too wide for him to grip with one hand.

"Fuck," he mumbled beneath his breath. Louisa released a sound of disapproval, and he turned to see her scrambled out of bed and hurry to his side. "Forgive me, *mo leannan.*"

"I don't mind you saying it in bed as it's quite naughty and exciting. But you need to avoid saying it within ear shot of the children." Louisa gently pushed him aside as she reached inside the large wardrobe to pull out the box. "I heard Fiona say it the other week when she was having trouble putting Masie's bridle on."

"The hell she did," he muttered in surprise. Louisa pulled the box out of the chifforobe and looked up at him in silent rebuke. He shrugged slightly.

"I cannot give up all of my curses, *mo ghràdh*, but I promise to guard my tongue when the children are nearby." At his reply she gave him an absentminded nod as she stared down at the box with the craftsman's name on the lid.

"*This* was supposed to have been your Christmas present. Since the children convinced me to alter my plans, I wanted to be alone with you when you opened it."

Ewan saw the small chill bumps covering her arms and quickly retrieved her robe. She'd moved to stand in front of the fireplace, and as he offered her the garment, Louisa set the box on the table to push her arms through the sleeves then tie the belt at her waist.

"I should have put that infernal arm on before doing any of this."

"I wouldn't have let you make me wait that long," she said as she kissed him then turned toward the small, bulky box on the table.

As she started to lift the lid, Ewan experienced a small twinge of misgiving. It was not a gift most men would give their wives, but he'd wanted something unique, and with a hidden message no one else would see. Louisa set the box lid aside and gently pulled apart the crumpled paper cushioning the gift. She inhaled a sharp breath of delight and darted a glance in his direction before gently pulling the mantel clock out of the box.

"Oh, Ewan, it's beautiful," she exclaimed softly.

The pleasure on her face released the tension holding him rigid, grateful she wasn't disappointed. Her hands glided over the wood carving before her fingers brushed over the front of the timepiece. In the center of the clock face, beneath the hands, was a flat silver ring of entwined thistles. Four small amethysts stones representing the plant's flower had been placed inside the delicate circle at each quarter hour.

"It has a special key," Ewan said gruffly.

He reached out to pull the key from the box, which the clockmaker had made to Ewan's specifications. Ewan held it up so she could see the top of the key was a dainty circle of thistles that matched the medallion on the face of the clock. On the opposite end was a heart with only two teeth on it.

"This is the only key that will open the clock face," he said softly as he handed it to her. "Wherever the clock is, the key must be with it, and like the clock, wherever you are is where my heart is."

Her head bowed slightly, Louisa stared at the key she held in her hand. When she raised her head, a single tear slid down her cheek before she threw herself against him to hold him close. His one arm wrapped around her waist, he used his forehead to push her head up so he could look at her. Hazel eyes shimmering in the morning light, she shook her head in a display of emotion that made Ewan's heart soar. He'd chosen wisely after all.

The main salon was a cacophony of laughter and cries of excitement as the Rockwood clan opened their presents from each other. The windows had been opened slightly to let in cool air to offset the heat in the room.

Over the past week, the next generation of the Rockwood clan had been busy decorating Callendar Abbey for Christmas. The scent of freshly cut pine permeated the air from the numerous pine wreaths and garlands adorning almost every room in the abbey. Purple ribbons and bows gaily decorated the intertwined garlands of tree branches with nuts and pine cones as accents. There was even a mistletoe ball hanging in the center of the salon doorway from a purple ribbon.

Estate business at Melton Park had forced Percy to send Rhea and the children to Callendar Abbey ahead of him. When he'd arrived two days ago, he'd brought the plant with him as an apology. Upon Percy's arrival, her sister-in-law had laughingly succumbed when her husband had held the plant over his head demanding she forgive him with a kiss.

The large fir tree however had been the work of the entire family, with the exception of Aunt Matilda and Uncle Roderick. The matriarch of the Rockwood clan had refused to traipse through the woods. She'd stated she would remain at the abbey to ensure hot chocolate and wassail was ready for their return along with hot venison stew.

Her decision had made Uncle Roderick also refuse to go as he'd insisted someone needed to remain and supervise his wife. Although Aunt Matilda had feigned annoyance, Louisa had seen her aunt beam a happy smile at her husband when she thought no one was looking.

The tree had been erected in the main salon later that same evening, and everyone had decorated it with paper cornucopias of sweets, fruits, bows, garlands of nuts, cranberries, and popcorn as well as the careful placement of candles. Years ago, Sebastian, ever conscious of the tragic fire at Westbury had suggested they forego the tree candles to prevent a fire. She and Patience had rejected his suggestion saying precautions could be taken, which their brother had reluctantly agreed too.

Louisa's gaze searched for Sebastian's tall figure and saw him opening a gift Helen had handed him. With a wide smile, he carefully pulled out a fly-fishing lure from its box. He gave his wife a quick kiss before continuing to admire the gift. Theo laughed at Sebastian's obvious delight, and her brother arched an eyebrow at his son in mock disapproval. Theo simply laughed harder as he said something to his father.

Sebastian shook his head in amusement then looked in Louisa's direction. He held the lure up for her to see, and despite the silver edges along his temple, his expression was one of boyish delight. Louisa laughed at her brother's excitement before her attention was diverted by Constance nudging her elbow.

"I didn't think there was anyone who was immune to our niece's charms, but Ross appears to be the exception."

Her oldest sister bobbed her head in the direction of the Christmas tree, and Louisa's gaze followed the direction of her sister's nod. Tilly, her hand pressing into Ross's arm appeared to be fervently pleading with him. The stepson she'd loved as dearly as the children she'd given birth to shook his head. Amusement crossed Ross's features as her niece's expression dissolved into one of frustration. Tilly had clearly failed in her attempt to persuade Ross to do whatever it was she wanted.

With an abrupt toss of her head, her niece flounced away from him with her nose tilted upward in a demonstration of disdain. Louisa saw her stepson smile with amusement as Tilly stalked away. A second later, his amusement disappeared as pain darkened his handsome face. Louisa's heart skipped a beat at his expression. The emotions vanished almost instantly as if he was aware someone might see his distress.

From across the room, Fiona gestured excitedly to him, and with a grin, he obeyed his sister's demand for his attention. Louisa turned her head searching for Ewan's tall figure. When she found him, he was standing close to the Christmas tree with his mother. Wallis laughed at something he said, then nodded toward Ross.

The frown on Ewan's forehead said everything as he watched the boy he'd claimed as his own cross the room to where Fiona waited impatiently at the fireplace. Ewan turned his head toward her, and Louisa arched her eyebrow in a silent triumph that she'd been correct about their son. Resignation twisted his mouth as he crossed the room to her side.

"All right, I concede you were correct about Ross," he whispered as his mouth brushed across her ear. "What do you propose we do?"

"Nothing," she exclaimed softly. "At least not for the moment."

From across the room, her brother's namesake whooped loudly in excitement and they both turned to look at Caleb. Holding a pair of ice skates high in the air, their youngest son was taunting his oldest brother with the threat of losing a race on the ice. Ross grinned and taunted Caleb in return. Louisa touched Ewan's arm.

"Clearly Caleb loves his present."

"Does this mean you intend to admit you were wrong?"

"*Never,*" she exclaimed in mock alarm before smiling and squeezing his arm. "You were correct, my love. I should have known better than to question your opinion when it comes to selecting an appropriate gift. You demonstrated your capabilities wonderfully with mine this morning."

The look of pleasure that crossed Ewan's battle-worn features made her rest her head on his shoulder, and the gentle kiss he pressed against her temple made her sigh happily. While the youngest members of the Rockwood family continued to display their exuberance with each gift they opened, their older cousins were not without their own exclamations of delight.

It was more than an hour before the younger members of the family had completed opening their gifts. As the clan had grown in size, Louisa and her siblings had started a tradition years ago not to exchange gifts. Instead, they drew names and were tasked with finding small, funny trinkets to wrap and set alongside a sibling's cracker at the dinner table.

To Louisa's delight, she'd drawn Sebastian's name this year. The ornament of an old man surrounded by excited children would be greeted by a great deal of laughter from the rest of the family. Louisa was certain her oldest brother would find himself the target of a great deal of teasing, and she bit back a smile.

The image of the ornament filled her head, and she stole a glance at the man who'd been father and mother to her when she was a child. The true significance of her gift would not be lost on Sebastian. It was an expression of love for a brother who was always the quiet center of a storm bringing order to chaos.

As the excitement died down somewhat, Louisa quietly asked Fiona to fetch the cuff links Louisa had bought for Ewan. When she handed him the small box, he grinned at her and started to shift the box into his artificial hand.

"*Wait*," Wills exclaimed as he saw Ewan adjusting his artificial hand to hold her present. At his cry, Charlie and Ross hurried toward them while Wills pulled one of the few remaining presents out from under the tree.

With his devilish smile and penchant for daring escapades, Wills was living up to the Reckless Rockwood title with more spirit than Louisa liked. Whenever she expressed her concern, Ewan and the rest of her family would arch their eyebrows with assurances she'd been much worse. Both Wills and Charles, with their dashing dark looks, continuously caused a stir whenever they attended a society function.

Of the two boys, Charles was the one who bore the most striking resemblance to Devin. He took his responsibilities as Viscount Westbury with great gravity without taking himself too seriously. Wills had followed his curious nature and was close to finishing medical school.

They'd lost their father at such a young age, and Ewan had become the father figure they needed as they grew up. Ewan had taken to fatherhood with a zeal Louisa knew was born of his desire to give the children what he'd never had as a child. But it was his relationship with Ross that haunted Ewan the most.

The two had developed a tight bond, and Ewan had become increasingly worried about what would happen to their close relationship when he told Ross the truth about who he was. It concerned her as well as the *an dara sealladh* had shown Louisa a glimpse of what might be to come. But she'd remained silent, refusing to add to Ewan's concern about their son. The irony of her decision was not lost on her as she knew her choice would astonish her family given her impulsive nature.

Now as she watched Wills and Charles facing Ewan with looks of excited anticipation, she knew Devin would be proud of them. Along with Ross, they'd grown up to be strong, honorable men. Smiling broadly, Wills handed a box to Ewan.

"This is from the three of us, Father. It was Ross's idea," Wills said, but Ross immediately shook his head.

"I just suggested it. Wills did all the work. Charlie and I just found what he needed to make it."

Louisa reached over to hold the box as Ewan used his good hand to untie the ribbon. As he lifted the lid, Louisa inhaled a sharp breath and jerked her gaze toward the three young men in front of them. A hesitant look crossed their faces as they heard her gasp. Tears welled in her eyes as she watched Ewan picked up the prosthetic hand encased in a black glove with its joints visible only if it was turned palm up.

"Wills said it's easy to switch this one out with the one you already have, Father," Charles said as he beamed at his youngest brother. "He gave it an extra joint too, right between the knuckle and fingertip. And he designed a new locking mechanism to hold its position."

Louisa looked up at her husband and saw him struggling with emotion as he stared down at the gift. His jaw was rigid with tension, and a muscle in his cheek twitched violently. When he said nothing, Wills glanced at his brothers who returned his gaze with expressions of confusion and obvious concern that they might have erred in thinking it would be a well-received gift. Ewan clear his throat.

"Thank you," he choked out a quiet voice. "It is...it is a wonderful gift."

Ewan didn't move for a second before he reached out to hug each of his boys in succession. Louisa wiped a teardrop from the corner of her eye. She couldn't remember a time when she'd been happier or more proud. As Ewan struggled to regain control of his emotions, Fiona called out from where she stood at the Christmas tree.

"Papa, Papa, you haven't given Mama her Christmas present yet." At their daughter's scolding, Ewan laughed, clearly grateful for a chance to regain control of his emotions.

"Then bring it here, my bonnie lass," Ewan said with a grin as he bobbed his head in a command to do as he ordered. To her surprise, the entire family moved forward to gather around her in a large circle. As she stared around at the smiles of anticipation on everyone's faces, she directed an arched look at her husband.

"Why do I think this is a secret everyone has been in on except me? Is this a real present or am I going to be the subject of amusement?"

"You will like it, Mama, I know you will," Caleb stated emphatically.

"Yes, Mama. Open it quickly."

Her daughter bounced on her toes with obvious excitement, while her youngest son met her gaze with unswerving confidence. With a smile, Louisa opened the gift. Parting the layers of paper inside, she arched her eyebrows as she saw the bridle nestled in the paper. With a rising sense of excitement, she lifted her head to look at Ewan.

"A bridle?"

"I thought you might put it to good use racing against me and Napoleon."

"You did, did you?" she said with a laugh. "Does this mean you bought that horse I wanted at Tattersall's two weeks ago?"

"Perhaps," Ewan said with a grin. Louisa threw her arms around her husband's neck and kissed him.

"You spoil me, but I love it."

"The bridle is the real present, Mother. It's not an ordinary one, it's special," Ross said quietly as he met her gaze with deep affection. "And if you don't pull it out of the box, Fiona and Caleb are poised to do it for you."

Confused by Ross's words, Louisa pulled the bridle out of the papers, to look at it more closely. The nose band had been widened to allow for several small medallions. As her gaze fell on each one, her throat closed up as she tried not to burst into tears. In the center of the noseband was a medallion made of the Rockwood and Argaty crests joined by a small bouquet of thistles. On either side of the crests were the children's names etched in small circles of silver. As she stared at the gift, Ewan pressed his mouth against her ear.

"You gave me a family, mo ghràdh. You gave me four sons, and a daughter who is as beautiful, reckless, and headstrong as her mother. You rescued the beast from his lonely tower."

Tears clogging her throat, Louisa stared up into his blue-gray eye. The love in his gaze and on his battle-scarred features made her heart swell with happiness.

"I love you, Ewan. You are my beastly earl, now and forever."

Thank you for reading The Beastly Earl! I hope you enjoyed it. If you did, please help other people find this book by writing a review on BookBub and Amazon.

Be sure to read all the other books in the Reckless Rockwoods series. The series always has one or more members of the family involved in their sibling's happily ever after.

And, when you're done with those books, enjoy more of the Rockwood siblings as they meddle in the love affairs of their friend in The Reckless Rockwoods Novels.

Special Preview of

The Rogue's Offer
The Reluctant Rogues

Chapter 1

London, 1899

Ophelia Fullerton, Viscountess Havenstock, studied the tall man on the opposite side of the Melton House ballroom and wrinkled her brow in puzzlement. He was much younger than she expected, and he looked nothing like the debauched brute she'd imagined.

Where was the monster her father had described? The reply in the back of her head wasn't one she wanted to hear. Attempting to cool her skin in the stifling heat of the room, she waved the peacock-feathered fan she held in front of her to create a gentle breeze. She'd bought the fan less than a week ago. It was the type of luxury that would no longer be affordable unless she was able to secure the return of Marymont. Ophelia tipped her head in her sister's direction.

"Lizzie, are you certain this is the man? He looks nothing like the disreputable scoundrel Father described." The dubious note in her voice prompted Ophelia's sister to bristle like a hen ruffling her feathers.

"Of course, I'm certain. Everyone knows who the Earl of Thornbury is."

"And exactly *when* were you introduced to the earl?"

Ophelia arched an eyebrow at her much younger sister, Lizzie, who had made her debut last year under Ophelia's watchful eye. The one thing Ophelia was meticulous about when it came to her sister was ensuring Lizzie never received an introduction to men of the earl's ilk.

Lizzie was good-hearted, but far too trusting when it came to people. She always thought the best of everyone, with the exception of individuals Lizzie thought had harmed her family. Then Lizzie became a tigress, intent on protecting her cubs.

Ever since Lizzie's debut, Ophelia had hoped her sister would find a nice young man to marry and enjoy the happiness denied Ophelia. That hope had become even more fervent than ever before, given their current change in finances.

"Well...we've not actually been introduced." Elizabeth Sheffield tilted her head haughtily, clearly affronted that her identification of the earl had been called into question. "Lady Alice pointed him out to me the other day during our walk near the Serpentine. But he's definitely the man who stole Marymont from Papa, and if we don't do something soon, we'll have nowhere to go."

There was the touch of the dramatic in her sister's words. It was a trait she'd inherited from their father, who had a flair for exaggeration. Unfortunately, this was one instance where her sister's woeful tone was more than appropriate. They were definitely in dire straits thanks to their father's love of wine and cards. A familiar bitterness rolled through her.

"Naturally, Father is completely blameless in this entire debacle," Ophelia bit out as she sent her sister a scathing look. "Perhaps you've forgotten he's the one who wagered our home and lost."

"No, I've not forgotten, but you know Papa is far too polite to refuse someone's offer of hospitality. Papa said the earl kept plying him with wine. It's obvious the man took advantage of him."

"Oh, of course, Father would *never* turn down a drink." Her caustic remark emphasized her belief that the baron's lack of judgement carried the largest burden of guilt. Even if she were wrong in her assumption as to their father's behavior, the baron still held some responsibility for their current situation.

"You are too hard on him, Ophelia. He's been desolate since Mama's death." The note of sorrow in her sister's voice tugged at her heart. Almost eight years younger than her, Lizzie had been happily planning her debut with their mother when the baroness had become ill, never to recover.

"It has been three years since her death, Lizzie. We miss her as much as Father does, but look where his folly has taken us," Ophelia said quietly. "Where Mama always found a way to keep him from indulging in his vices, I have failed."

"You've done your best, Ophelia. We both have." Lizzie's voice held a forlorn note, and Ophelia quickly squeezed her sister's hand.

"We shall find a way out of this quandary, dearest. I promise you that. At least we have the annual stipend George left me. It might not be much, but we will not starve."

Despite Ophelia's lack of confidence in her statement, Lizzie's dejection vanished, and she nodded her belief in her older sister's ability to save them from destitution. A polite cough made her turn around to see Paul Nickens standing behind them. Tall and dark-haired, the young man was of modest means but was good-natured and had a promising future as a solicitor.

Ophelia had liked him from the moment she and Lizzie had been introduced to him. Deep inside, she hoped the young man would offer for her sister and that Lizzie would accept. Under the current circumstances, she was all the more eager to encourage the man's attentions to Lizzie.

"Good evening, Mr. Nickens," she said with a welcoming smile.

"Lady Havenstock. Miss Sheffield." Paul Nickens bowed his greeting with a smile at both of them before he quickly fixated his attention on Lizzie. "I was hoping I might persuade you to let me claim several dances on your card, Miss Sheffield."

"I would be honored for you to do so, sir," her sister said in a breathless voice as her cheek grew pink with pleasure. She handed the young man a stiff rectangular dance card, and he proceeded to draw a line down more than half of Lizzie's card and dashed off his name in bold fashion.

"There, now. I believe this will ensure that several of my rivals will find themselves suitably disappointed this evening," Mr. Nickens said with a grin. "Perhaps you will allow me to claim my first dance now."

"I would find that most enjoyable." Lizzie flashed a brilliant smile at the young man, then accepted his outstretched hand and allowed him to lead her out onto the dance floor.

Satisfied her sister was in good company, Ophelia resumed her assessment of the earl. Despite the loathing she felt for him, the man's appearance underscored one of the reasons he'd earned his reputation as a master of seduction. He was a picture of masculine strength and beauty. It was impossible not to think of the powerful tigers she'd seen pacing in their cages at the Regents Zoo. The earl displayed the same relaxed, yet powerful, sinewy strength in his movements. It epitomized an image of raw power.

The dark hair falling casually over his brow gave him a sinfully wicked look. Everything about the man's appearance was a far cry from the decadent libertine her father had labeled him. Clean-shaven, the earl had chosen to eschew the large mutton chops she'd found so distasteful on her husband. His profile was sharply defined, and his jaw was square and strong-looking. It surprised her that she found him so fascinating when she was incapable of passion. A fact her husband had repeated every time he'd left her bedchamber in the short time they'd been married.

Less than two years after their wedding, George's death had been a relief from the constant bombardment of his criticism. But their brief marriage had convinced her of one thing. She'd failed in her duties as a wife, and she would never possess the ability to seduce a man or find pleasure in the bedroom. It was a conviction that was at distinct odds with her reaction to the earl, and it confused her.

Despite his reputation, there was an almost angelic look about him, which masked the dangerous predator she knew lay beneath the surface. The woman at his side said something that made him laugh, and he bowed slightly as she departed. Enthralled, Ophelia watched the earl take a glass of champagne off the tray one of the footmen carried. Before she could turn her head away, the man looked directly at her and lifted the flute of sparkling liquid in her direction. She couldn't discern the color of his eyes, but the sensual curve of his lips made her mouth go dry.

Dear God, how long had he been aware she was watching him. The air in Ophelia's lungs disappeared, and her chest tightened until she could barely breathe. Frozen in place, she remained pinned beneath his gaze as a small frisson skimmed its way across her skin. Mesmerized, she watched him drink from the crystal glass. As he lowered the flute, a small tipped one corner of his mouth. Long fingers stroked the fragile neck of the glass, invoking the powerful image of his hand trailing down the side of her throat. A raw sensation spiraled through her. It was unlike anything she'd experienced before. Butterflies swirled in her stomach as his tongue flicked out to erase a droplet of wine from his lips. She had no doubt it was a deliberate act on his part, and it sent a shiver skimming down the back of her spine.

In a split second, her nipples grew stiff beneath her corset until they pressed against her chemise. The soft linen roughened the hard peaks until a pleasure that was almost painful in its intensity assaulted her senses. It aroused something unfamiliar inside her that was as startling as it was unexpected.

Another tiny shudder sped through her. It traveled downward to settle between her legs and made her sex ache. It created a need for his hand to caress her as intimately as he did his glass. Disoriented by the sensations flowing through her, Ophelia jerked her gaze away. What in heaven's name was wrong with her? As she fought to regain her faculties, a light touch on her arm made her jump.

"*Ophelia*, how lovely to see you this evening."

The quiet greeting was a welcome distraction, and she quickly turned to see the youngest member of the Rockwood family standing in front of her. Dressed in a dark mauve-colored gown, the only other color Viscountess Westbrook wore was the Stewart plaid in a sash over her breast.

Despite Louisa's somewhat austere appearance, Ophelia thought her friend was even more beautiful than when they'd both been girls riding across the fields of Melton Park. It had been almost a year since they'd last seen each other, and she greeted her friend with an affectionate kiss on the cheek.

"Louisa, oh, it's wonderful to see you. Our paths never seem to cross anymore."

"The season holds little interest for me anymore, and I seldom come to London. Aunt Matilda and I brought the children from Scotland last month for Sebastian's and Helen's tenth-anniversary celebration. Everyone pressed me to stay for a bit longer, although I confess I'm eager to return to the solitude of the countryside." A sorrowful look darkened her friend's hazel eyes as her mouth curved in a small smile. "I find Callendar Abbey suits me far better. The boys do well in the fresh air, and Aunt Matilda loves having company."

"How is your aunt?"

"She's quite well, and she has a suitor. Although, I don't think she's willing to admit it. She grumbles about his arrogance."

The laugh that parted Louisa's lips reminded Ophelia of a time when her friend had been happy and carefree. The death of her husband and her brother in a tragic fire more than two years ago had changed her friend. The tragedy had changed all the Rockwoods. Their impulsive natures were enhanced by their clear determination to live life to its fullest. Even Sebastian, who as the eldest had always been the least impulsive of the Rockwoods, had become less rigid in manner. Ophelia was certain his marriage to the countess was the primary reason many in the Marlborough Set saw him as less staid.

"And the boys?"

"They're sprouting up like weeds. Charles is six now and has become enamored with botany. I wouldn't mind so much if he didn't bring half the earth with him wherever he goes." Louisa smiled with motherly exasperation, yet more than a hint of pride. "And Willie is becoming increasingly precocious. Just last week, he demanded we begin addressing him as Wills since he is no longer a baby. He has taken an intense dislike to being called Willie."

"It sounds as though he's a great deal like his mother." Ophelia smiled as eyed her friend with an arched look. "I remember a time when you were equally determined to be taken seriously. As I recall, Sebastian's look was one of abject horror."

"Good heavens," Louisa gasped with surprised amusement. "Are you referring to the time I told Sebastian I would unscrew the wires in his piano if he didn't stop calling me Weezie?"

"Yes." Ophelia nodded with a laugh. "I have never forgotten how horror stricken he looked."

"My threat worked, though. He never called me Weezie again," Louisa sighed softly. "We were so young back then."

"I'm sorry life has been so terribly difficult for you, Louisa. I truly am," Ophelia said as she touched her friend's arm. A haunted look flitted across Louisa's features before her mouth curved in a smile reminiscent of earlier days, and she patted Ophelia's hand.

"Thank you, Ophelia. It's kind of you—" Louisa suddenly gripped Ophelia's hand tightly. "You're in trouble."

"What?" she choked out in a soft gasp, staring at her friend in surprise.

"Do not deny it, Ophelia. The *an dara sealladh* doesn't come to me as often as the rest of my siblings, but I *do* possess the family gift," Louisa said in a stern voice as she squeezed Ophelia's hand and shut her eyes. "There's a man. He has something that belongs to you. Letters? No, there's only one, but it's very important to you. You know him, but..."

As her friend's words trailed off into silence, a chill skimmed over Ophelia's skin. Although the Marlborough Set knew of the Rockwoods' gift of sight, it was always discussed with great discretion. As children, she'd been accustomed to Louisa's ability to know things others didn't. But this was the first time her friend had seen something about her. Louisa's eyes flew open, and she stared at Ophelia with a worried frown furrowing her brow.

"You must tell me what's wrong, Ophelia. I trust the *an dara sealladh*, even when the images are confusing and make little sense."

"There's nothing wrong," she prevaricated with as much aplomb as she could muster. "Father lost an important paper the other day, and we've been trying to find it. Perhaps that's what you're seeing."

"No, I don't think so," Louisa murmured as she studied Ophelia closely. "I couldn't see the man's face, but he was much younger than your father."

"Then perhaps you're seeing someone I've yet to meet." Her lips curved in a placating smile, Ophelia struggled to hide how close to the truth Louisa's words were.

"Perhaps..." Louisa said with a look of concentration before a smile of pleasure suddenly curved her lips. "*Mathias*, you came. Percy said you might be here tonight. Why haven't you joined us for dinner recently? I know he's invited you to several occasions, but you keep avoiding us."

"I would never willingly avoid dinner with the Rockwoods," a deep voice filtered its way past her shoulder as a tall figure stopped at Ophelia's side and bent to kiss Louisa's hand. "I've simply been extremely busy."

As she turned her head, Ophelia immediately recognized the owner of the hypnotic voice, and her heart stopped beating for a full second before it resumed again at a faster pace. The most intense jade-colored eyes she'd ever seen locked with hers, and the way he was looking at her made her feel as if he could see the darkest secrets she possessed.

"Ophelia, are you acquainted with—"

"Viscountess Havenstock," the earl said in a voice that was as silky and sinful as one of the rich chocolate truffles she indulged in far too frequently. "I had hoped you would be here this evening."

Speechless that he knew her name, she trembled and slowly extended her hand in a silent greeting. She'd forgone wearing gloves this evening, and his mouth singed her skin in a way that sent a shock wave through her. Dear Lord, what was wrong with her? She'd never experienced this type of reaction to a man before, and it left her feeling completely out of control. The earl raised his head, his gaze never leaving hers.

"Louisa, I hope you don't mind, but Lady Havenstock promised me a dance, and I am here to collect."

"But of course, Mathias," Louisa said with a surprised smile as she looked at Ophelia with avid curiosity.

Still unable to utter a word, Ophelia found her hand clasped in the earl's firm hand as he guided her out onto the dance floor. Her brain sluggish, she didn't even have the wherewithal to protest as he swung her into her arms. The soft, subtle scent of spice and pine swept across her senses, causing her heart to pound a fierce rhythm in her ears. It was a reaction that set her on edge.

She and Lizzie rarely moved in the same exalted circles as the Earl of Thornbury, but tonight had proven an exception. The moment Ophelia had learned the earl might be in attendance, she'd braced herself to do whatever was necessary to capture the man's attention. But her determination had not prepared her for the earl's magnetic presence or the way it affected her equilibrium.

A pulse of panic threaded its way through her. Now that she'd managed to capture the man's attention, every plea she'd rehearsed had fled her brain. Ophelia looked away and remained silent as the earl danced her around the floor.

A low laugh whispered its way past her ear. She immediately glanced up to see green eyes flickering with amusement, and the wicked smile twisting his lips caused her to stumble slightly. The powerful strength she'd noted earlier allowed him to pull her tight against him. Heat suffused her skin the instant her body pressed even more intimately into his chest, and he skillfully whirled her around the dance floor as if she'd not faltered at all.

"Shall I confess something, my lady?" The deep melodious sound of his voice held her spellbound.

"Confess?" she replied breathlessly. Ophelia swallowed hard as she stared up at him. Amusement mixed with something far more dangerous glittered in his gaze.

"You intrigue me."

"Intrigue you?"

"Yes," he said with another soft laugh. "I think I surprised you when I asked you to dance with me."

"Asked me?" she snapped as she remembered her inability to speak one word to the man. "You didn't give me the opportunity to say no."

"You object?" Curiosity echoed in his voice as he arrogantly arched his eyebrows. "From our silent exchange earlier, I was under the impression you wouldn't reject my offer of attention."

"I did not...I was..." Ophelia's voice trailed off at the abrupt tension filling the air between them. Her disdain irritated him, which jeopardized the possibility of Marymont being returned. "Objecting isn't an option for me where you're concerned."

"Once again, I'm intrigued," he said as he whirled her around several quick turns to dodge another couple, and Ophelia experienced a pleasant yet slightly dizzy sensation. "Explain."

"I'm uncertain how to broach the subject."

"Intrigued is becoming an overused word where you're concerned, my lady. Fascinated seems far more appropriate."

The scintillating flash of humor that crossed his face unnerved her. She hadn't expected to find the man devastating to her senses. But then she'd not anticipated feeling anything at all. All she'd ever experienced where men were concerned was either antipathy or friendship. A knot formed in her throat. Perhaps the bargain she'd thought to strike with this man was a foolish one.

It unnerved her to think he might actually be able to awaken something inside her, contrary to established fact. Ophelia quickly dismissed the thought. She was incapable of passion or stirring a similar sensation in a man. George had taught her that. The question was how far she was willing to go to save her childhood home. She'd never been able to bear George touching her. Suddenly, she wasn't sure if she was capable of bartering herself. In the back of her head, a small voice taunted her with the fact that she'd chosen her path the moment she'd looked at the earl from across the ballroom floor. She drew in a shallow breath.

"You have something that belongs to me, or rather my family, Lord Thornbury."

"Indeed," he murmured with an odd look. "What might that be?

"My home."

"*Your home*," he exclaimed softly and his brow wrinkled in puzzlement.

"Marymont. My father lost it in a wager to you several nights ago," she said, as her voice dropped slightly. "I would like it back, and I am willing...I think I have something to offer in exchange."

"And the currency you're referring to?" A glitter of cold calculation darkened the jade eyes narrowing on her.

"Me."

"Ahh, a proposition of the intimate kind." Boredom tugged at his sensual mouth, but his eyes had hardened with something approaching contempt or pity. She was unable to discern which, and it heightened her sense of desperation.

"I do not offer myself up lightly, my lord," she choked out with great effort. "But I believe I am unique enough that I would be unlike other...other women with whom you enter liaisons."

"And tell me, what is this unique quality you possess that makes you think I would be willing to trade a valuable piece of property for it," he murmured with what she was certain was a sneer.

"I...I am incapable of passion," she finished her stumbling statement in a rush.

This time it was the earl's chance to stumble slightly. The awkwardness of the moment was highlighted by his amazement. As the dance music ended with a resounding flourish, he quickly guided her off the dance floor. His sensual mouth was a hard, thin line as he firmly, yet discreetly, maneuvered her through the crowd out into a long hallway that ran the length of the ballroom itself.

Although the corridor wasn't empty, it was significantly less crowded. To anyone else in the hall, his grip on her elbow no doubt appeared solicitous, but his firm grasp indicated he had no intention of letting her escape. He seemed completely certain where he was going, and for the second time in the space of minutes, she was too startled by his behavior to protest. The earl stopped at a door and opened it at the same time he glanced back at a couple who had passed them seconds before.

Satisfied the pair had not turned their heads, he none too gently pulled Ophelia into a darkened room. Firelight created soft shadows against the walls, and as he closed the door behind them, she heard the key turn in the lock. Trepidation spiraled through her, and she quickly put several feet between them. As he turned away from the door, he held up the key.

"To ensure we're not interrupted," he said tersely.

For some reason, she had expected him to be surprised, but he actually appeared angry. Arms folded over his chest, his eyebrows arched upward arrogantly.

"A moment ago I stated I was intrigued and then fascinated, Lady Havenstock. However, I am now attempting to determine precisely what you expect to achieve with your confession." The contempt in his voice sent a chill sliding through her, and Ophelia shook her head.

"It was not a confession, my lord," she bit out in a crisp tone as she stared at him without looking away. "It is a fact. I am incapable of inciting passion in a man or feeling it myself."

"I see," he said in a voice devoid of emotion. "Do you seriously expect me to believe not one of your lovers since Havenstock has failed to arouse you?"

"I've not shared a bed with any man other than my husband."

"None?" The earl snorted with disbelief. "Forgive me, Lady Havenstock, but I find it difficult to believe you've not had at least one lover since you became a widow."

"I am not a liar." Ophelia tilted her chin upward. She resented the insinuation that she was lying. If either of them was deserving of contempt, his disreputable behavior had earned him that distinction.

"Very well, let us put aside the question of your experience," he said as he studied her as a collector might when assessing the value of an antique. "Explain why you believe yourself incapable of arousing a man to passion or experiencing pleasure."

"Because my husband repeatedly stated I was cold and unfeeling in the performance of my wifely duties," she said in a tight voice, remembering George's angry denouncements of her inability to arouse a man.

It had been horrible enough knowing her father had insisted she marry George simply because the viscount had agreed to cover her father's outstanding debts. But knowing she was incapable of inspiring passion in her husband had made her avoid any liaisons in the ten years since George's death.

"Good god," the earl muttered beneath his breath, a frown creasing his forehead as he studied her. Ophelia looked down to fiddle with the ostrich feathers of her fan.

"I realize my proposition is unusual, but your reputation is such that I thought you might...might find me a challenge," she choked out as humiliation swept through her. "I have nothing else with which to barter for the return of my home."

"Havenstock was clearly a fool," the earl bit out as he slowly closed the distance between them.

The way earl was studying made her skin grow hot as he took his time observing her from top to bottom It was as if he were disrobing her in his mind, and the effect it had on her made her senses reel. Her heart racing, she forced herself not to look away from him as he approached her. With each step he took toward her, Ophelia experienced the urge to take two back, but she held her ground.

The man was doing things to her senses that didn't just alarm her—they made her long to possess the ability to entice and seduce him. The moment the thought flitted through her head, she struggled not to race toward the door. Dear Lord, what was she thinking? The earl halted inches away from her, then tipped her chin upward with his finger and forced her to look at him.

"Let me be the first to assure you, Ophelia, that you are more than capable of enchanting a man." His voice was a soft caress across her senses. Even the way her name rolled off his lips it was an invitation to join him in sin. "I've been captivated from the first moment I saw you this evening."

The silky note of seduction in his voice made Ophelia's heart slam into her breast as he lowered his head and brushed his mouth against hers. Fire singed her lips at the light caress, and the air left her lungs. A slight tremor skimmed over skin at the unfamiliar sensation assaulting her senses he lifted his head to study her intently. Gold flecks glittered in his green eyes as the firelight cast half of his profile in relief, while shadows darkened the other half. The earlier angelic impression she'd had of him returned, but this time it was a dark angel she saw. Ophelia swallowed hard as she looked at him.

"Am I to understand that you have decided to accept my proposition, my lord?"

"Perhaps," he murmured. "I wonder if you've considered the ramifications of your decision."

"If you're suggesting I mean to trick you into returning Marymont to me, I have only my word that I shall honor our bargain."

"It's not a question as to whether you'll honor any agreement between us. The question is how quickly you learn."

"I don't understand," she said as she eyed him warily. "It sounds as though you are proposing an extended arrangement."

"Do you think one night is sufficient payment for what must be a valuable piece of property given your willingness to offer yourself up to me so blatantly?"

The harsh note in his voice made Ophelia drag in a sharp breath. It was precisely what she'd thought. She shook her head as trepidation slid through her, followed by a throb of excitement that made her blood race.

"I did not consider the details of any arrangement we might make."

"Then I suggest we come to an agreement on terms that are agreeable to both of us."

His voice echoed with a hint of satisfaction that set off an alarm in Ophelia's mind. The man was clever, and she would need to be equally so if she was to emerge from this bargain with Marymont in her possession.

"Name your terms," she said quietly as he narrowed his eyes at her.

"In exchange for your home, you will give me one month," he said as he folded his arms over his chest. "At end of our month together, your home will be returned to you."

"And how do I know you'll return Marymont to me after I surrender myself to your instruction?" At her question, he grew rigid.

"Are you suggesting I won't honor our agreement, my lady?"

The sharp note in his voice indicated she'd angered him by implying he might fail to respect the bargain they were negotiating. Whether she did or didn't believe he'd honor any agreement they committed to, it was of no consequence. If she wanted Marymont returned to her, she had little choice but to trust he would uphold his end of the bargain. With a sharp nod, she agreed to his terms.

"One month." The moment she replied, the earl's mouth curled in a wicked smile.

"Then let us begin," the earl said smoothly.

"Here? Now?" she gasped as the distance between them became almost non-existent.

"I think you will find the threat of discovery heightens the senses *and* the pleasure."

"You cannot possibly be serious." With a vehement shake of her head, Ophelia took a quick step backward to open up space between them. He closed it just as quickly.

"Pleasure always involves the senses, my lady, but there are many forms of pleasure." He laughed softly. It was a warm whisper across her mouth as he leaned into her. "Anticipation itself can be quite pleasurable."

"I don't understand," she choked out as his head dipped toward her. Her heart skipped a beat as his mouth bypassed her lips to brush across her cheek.

"Tonight, when you're alone in your bedroom, Ophelia, you're to undress slowly," he murmured as his teeth lightly nipped at her ear lobe. "I want you to imagine I'm there watching you. When you're wearing only your chemise, I want you to touch your nipples."

"Oh dear lord," she choked out, unable to look away from him. In a lazy stroke, his finger traced a path along the edge of her bodice. The light touch made Ophelia tremble, and a small smile curved his mouth.

"When you touch your nipples, I want you to imagine I'm there sucking on them. My tongue swirling on your stiff, rigid peaks." Barely able to breathe, it was impossible to look away from him. His smile became even more wicked.

"Please...this is..."

"You're experiencing pleasure right now, aren't you, Ophelia?" The laughter in his voice was mixed with something sinful and tantalizing, and she flicked her tongue out to lick her dry lips.

"Yes." She barely breathed the word.

"Yes, Mathias."

"Yes...Mathias."

"Good," he said softly as his mouth lightly touched hers, lingering for a brief second. "I want you to experience the ache, the need, the desire for my touch. I want you to imagine my mouth on your skin, licking and sucking on you until you shatter in my arms."

"Oh, God." It was little more than a breath of sound as fire spread its way through her body. She swayed slightly, and his hands gripped her waist to steady her.

"I think you are more than capable of passion, Ophelia," he murmured in a slightly thick voice.

There was a fire burning in his eyes that warmed her from the inside out as he stepped back from her. A shiver of excitement streaked down her back as his gaze remained locked with hers. She should have been appalled she'd even suggested their bargain to him. But it was the fact he excited her that alarmed her the most.

Chapter 2

Lust unlike anything he'd ever felt before, slammed into Mathias's chest as he struggled not to pull Ophelia into his arms. Brown eyes, large and wide, shimmered with gold flecks in the firelight. Desire had softened her countenance, and her full mouth was parted slightly. The tip of her tongue flicked out to wet her lips, and Mathias swallowed the dark groan rumbling up in his throat.

The woman had no idea how tempting she looked at this precise moment. A small shudder rippled through her as he gripped her waist to steady her. He would enjoy making Ophelia see herself as the sensual creature she was. A vivid image of her lying beneath him with her lustrous chestnut hair spilling across her bare shoulders made his cock stir in his trousers.

In a split instant, Mathias's lust vanished as if he'd been doused in icy water. He stiffened and took a quick step back from her. What the hell was wrong with him? He'd just said he wasn't a liar, and yet here he was pretending to be Charles. Worse, he'd even gone so far as to negotiate terms for her audacious proposition without divulging who he really was.

Self-loathing twisted his gut into a vicious knot. What in God's name had he been thinking to let the interlude progress this far? The immediate answer that came to mind was a perfunctory one. He was doing what he'd done for years. He was protecting his brother from scandal. Mathias almost snorted with disgust. As the Earl of Thornbury, his brother was a family scoundrel when it came to his dalliances. But even Charles would have arched his eyebrows in disapproval at Mathias's behavior.

He cleared his throat, his body hardening as he Ophelia's sultry look of desire. Christ Jesus, he wanted to explore every inch of her right here and now. The images flying through his head made his muscles grow taut with a need he'd not experienced in a long time. It was a tension and desire that would be unfulfilled because the minute he told her the truth, she'd flee.

It wasn't the first time he'd been mistaken for his brother. Despite the small gap in their ages, they'd both inherited the same dark hair and features of their father. The only difference was the color of their eyes. The fact they were easily mistaken for one another had proven helpful in his efforts to save Charles from female entrapment and a hellish marriage. But for the first time in his life, he found himself wishing he really was the Earl of Thornbury. Mathias took two quick steps back from Ophelia.

"I'm afraid, my lady, we've both made a grievous error." Mathias deliberately kept his voice devoid of emotion as he watched her. Confusion made her brows furrow as if she were lost trying to find her way out of a maze. His jaw tightened painfully with regret.

"An error?" She shook her head slightly.

"Regrettably, I am *not* the Earl of Thornbury." The words hung in the air for a long moment as she stared at him in bewilderment.

"I don't understand."

"My brother holds the Thornbury title," he said quietly. Mathias's gut twisted into a hard knot at her dazed look. He was truly a bastard for having toyed with the woman. It wasn't a pleasant sensation.

"You're not…but you said—"

"No. You *assumed* I was the earl," he grounded out between clenched teeth. Furious with himself for allowing things to become out of hand, his tone was harsher than he meant it to be.

Slowly, Ophelia's confusion became one of mortified shock and horror. The fact he was responsible for her humiliation made his muscles knot with tension. His regret only underscored what a bastard he was. He'd known Ophelia had mistaken him for Charles when she'd addressed him so formally on the dance floor, but he'd deliberately chosen not to correct her.

Over the years, he'd perfected his role of protecting his brother from women seeking nothing more than a title and access to Charles's vast holdings. Unlike other titled peers whose fortunes had been decimated over many decades of excessive spending and poor investments, the Thornbury fortune was still intact. Through the decades, the Gilchrist family members had used their innate financial skills to keep their coffers from being drained. Mathias and Charles were no different when it came to their financial acumen. Between the two of them, the Thornbury finances were sound for many years to come.

It was one of the many reasons women vied for the Countess of Thornbury title. An image of Miriam flitted through his head. When the memory of her betrayal tried to secure a place in his thoughts, he discarded it. Instead, a new image was being seared into his memory as he saw the color drain from Ophelia's cheeks. Humiliation and shame caused her mouth to work slowly as she tried to speak. Her efforts deepened his self-loathing.

Even when Ophelia had made her outrageous proposal, he'd failed to have the decency to reveal his true identity. The idea he'd been looking out for Charles's best interests didn't excuse his demeaning the woman. Disgusted by his behavior, he tried to form a coherent and sincere apology in his head.

The problem was he was failing to come up with anything sufficient to make amends for his behavior. Perhaps the situation could be salvaged by returning Ophelia's home to her without any ties. That might go a long way toward atoning for his sins. Silence stretched out between them as he considered how best to extend his broken olive branch. When she didn't speak, he cleared his throat.

"Naturally, I have no expectations of you choosing to move forward with our agreement, but I—"

"Not move—*you bastard.*" The sharp, brittle words made Mathias tense as he prepared himself for the outrage about to be inflicted on him. Her fury was slowly taking shape, and it was easy to see it would be scathing in its intensity. even in her anger, she was lovely. "You *allowed* me to humiliate myself—offer my body in exchange for something you cannot give."

"No, I didn't promise something I couldn't give," he bit out between clenched teeth. "As my brother's business and estate manager. I have complete autonomy in managing his affairs and properties."

"Do you *honestly* expect me to believe you would have returned Marymont to me?"

"I do not expect you to do so, but it is the truth."

"The *truth*?" she exclaimed with bitterness. "The truth is that your brother displayed no moral compass when he stole Marymont from a drunken, old fool. But *you,* sir, are worse. You are beyond contempt."

Mathias went rigid. Despite knowing his original intent had been to protect his brother, he deserved Ophelia's brutal condemnation. He was more than worthy of her insult, but his brother was not. While Charles had many flaws, his brother was a good man at heart.

It was one of the reasons Mathias quietly investigated every new paramour his brother became involved with. But somewhere in the middle of his efforts to protect his brother, he'd lost sight of everything except Ophelia. Angered by the realization and his responsibility in fortifying Ophelia's poor opinion of Charles, his jaw clenched painfully.

"I will not quarrel with your judgement of me, even though it wasn't my intent to humiliate you." A voice in his head, snorted with disgust. No, he'd simply chosen to ignore how difficult it had been for her to offer herself in exchange for her home. "That said, I'm the wall that stands between my brother and any woman who seeks to become the next Countess of Thornbury through less than honorable means."

Ophelia's head jerked backward as if he'd slapped her. Guilt crashed through him. *Christ Jesus*, this wasn't how to apologize to the woman. He'd simply added insult to injury. Intense dislike darkened her eyes as she stared at him with such loathing that if she'd been holding a weapon, she would have mortally wounded him.

"I have *never* had any designs on your brother *or* his title," she bit out in an acerbic tone. "I have no intention of tying myself to any man ever again."

"Perhaps not, but my brother is not always discreet in his liaisons. It's my responsibility to ensure the women he indulges himself with are not in pursuit of a title." Bloody hell, what was the matter with him, trying to defend his actions. He might be telling her the truth, but it was clearly only making things worse.

"I want nothing more from your brother than for him to return my childhood home to me. And I was willing to pay in the only currency I possess. Unfortunately, I underestimated the depths of your family's depravity."

Pale with humiliation and outrage, Ophelia's brown eyes flashed with gold sparks of anger as she quickly stepped around him and headed for the door. He matched her pace and held up the key he'd pulled from his pocket.

"I will escort you back to the ballroom, my lady."

"*No*. You will *not*," Ophelia snapped as she tugged the key from his grasp and unlocked the door.

With a sharp movement, she jerked open the door and allowed it to fly open. Caught off guard by her action, Mathias didn't move fast enough to avoid the door hitting him. An oath escaped him as he released a low cry of pain. Preoccupied with his injury, Mathias failed to halt Ophelia's flight from the room. One hand pressed to his nose, he felt a warm trickle of blood touch his lips.

Other Titles by Monica Burns

THE RECKLESS ROCKWOODS SERIES

Obsession #1
Dangerous #2
The Highlander's Woman #3
Redemption #4
The Beastly Earl #5

THE RECKLESS ROCKWOODS NOVELS

The Rogue's Offer
The Rogue's Countess

SELF-MADE MEN SERIES

His To Command #1 (Novella)
His Mistress #2

STAND ALONE TITLES

Forever Mine
Kismet
Mirage
Pleasure Me
A Bluestocking Christmas
Love's Portrait
Love's Revenge

THE ORDER OF THE SICARI SERIES

Assassin's Honor #1
Assassin's Heart #2
Inferno's Kiss #3

About the Author

Monica Burns is a bestselling author of spicy historical and paranormal romance. She penned her first romance at the age of nine when she selected the pseudonym she uses today. Her historical book awards include the 2011 RT BookReviews Reviewers Choice Award and the 2012 Gayle Wilson Heart of Excellence Award for Pleasure Me.

She is also the recipient of the prestigious paranormal romance award, the 2011 PRISM Best of the Best award for Assassin's Heart. From the days when she hid her stories from her sisters to her first completed full-length manuscript, she always believed in her dream despite rejections and setbacks. A workaholic wife and mother, Monica is a survivor who believes every hero and heroine deserves a HEA (Happily Ever After), especially if she's writing the story.

Find all the ways you can connect with Monica on the next page.

Connect With Monica

Follow For New Release Alerts

BOOKBUB
www.bookbub.com/authors/monica-burns

AMAZON
www.amazon.com/Monica-Burns/e/B002BM7C5Q

Social Media

FACEBOOK
Monicaburns.net/readergroup

PINTEREST
www.pinterest.com/monicaburns

NEWSLETTER -COMPLIMENTARY DIGITAL BOOK
www.monicaburns.net/newsletter

WEBSITE
www.monicaburns.com

EMAIL
monicaburns@monicaburns.com

Lightning Source UK Ltd.
Milton Keynes UK
UKHW020503230822
407650UK00011B/2690